THE SECRET LIVES
OF DENTISTS

THE SECRET LIVES OF DENTISTS

a novel

W. A. WINTER

SEVENTH
STREET
BOOKS®

Inquiries should be addressed to
Start Science Fiction
221 River Street
9th Floor
Hoboken, New Jersey 07030
PHONE: 212-431-5455
WWW.SEVENTHSTREETBOOKS.COM

10 9 8 7 6 5 4 3 2 1

978-1-64506-031-4 (paperback)
978-1-64505-024-6 (ebook)

For my pal Dick Coffey

Who are these people, and what do they want? And why don't we like them better than we do?

—David Owen,
"The Secret Lives of Dentists," *Harper's*, March 1982

All human beings have three lives: public, private, and secret.

—Gabriel García Márquez

CHAPTER 1

The skinny blonde isn't working tonight.

The driver doesn't know her name and doesn't think it would be smart to ask her whereabouts, but he picks it up in the chatter between the Greek and his gimpy son. That's what the driver does—watches and listens. The Greek, whose name is Anatoli Zevos, and Tony, the son, who has a hip full of Jap shrapnel and three kids of his own, presumably by the surly, heavyset woman who sits like a bad meal at the far end of the counter, run the place. Despite the wife and kids, Tony can't keep his hands off the waitresses, which probably explains the rapid turnover during the short time, three or four weeks, the driver has been dropping in.

He's seen the skinny blonde twice since she started working here a couple of weeks ago. She took his supper order the first time, the second time topped off his coffee. She didn't say any more than she had to either time, but the smile damn near knocked him off his stool. Her smile and her ass—the driver, who believes he has a keen eye for such things, would argue that a combination like that is maybe one in a hundred, or five hundred, or a thousand. The Greek's too cheap to buy tags for the girls, and the driver doesn't have the nerve to ask her name. He picks up, though, on the details. She bites her nails and wears a tiny diamond ring on the third finger of her left hand.

Sipping his heavily sugared coffee at this end of the counter, the driver feigns interest in that afternoon's *Star* and pictures Tony lurching up behind the blonde in the kitchen or down the basement where they keep the groceries, running his hands up the front of her uniform and shoving his crotch against her ass. The driver pictures her closing her eyes and smiling. Tony, who's probably in his early thirties, is not a bad-looking guy, short and square with the neck of a stevedore and a thick head of curly black hair. Maybe the idea of a war wound excites the girl. The driver imagines that she likes the attention, yet is wary of being caught in flagrante by Tony's old man. The Greek, all business and always in a foul mood, has no time for shenanigans. And if there was trouble, he'd blame the girl, not his horny son.

"Said she's got a toothache, Pop," the driver hears Tony say.

Frowning, the old man grabs a spatula and scrapes the grill as though the congealed grease and baked-on fat are the sins of the world. He doesn't bother to reply. These girls are a dime a dozen. They come streaming out of the Greyhound depot on Seventh Street, a couple dozen a week, fair-haired farm girls from outstate Minnesota and the Dakotas and dark-eyed miners' daughters from the Iron Range. They come here for a job and adventure, not necessarily in that order.

Listening to the Zevoses' palaver, the driver learns that the skinny blonde hails from Dollar, North Dakota, wherever the hell that is. He pictures a windswept spot-in-the-road with a shuttered movie house, a couple of crummy bars, and three or four grain elevators standing like old ghosts beside the railroad tracks. Maybe an out-of-business five-and-dime and a worn-out Catholic church attended by a half-dozen old-timers. The kids have fled to the cities—Bismarck, Fargo, Minneapolis—where they believe a more exciting life is waiting for them.

The driver knows, too, that the skinny blonde, formerly of Dollar,

North Dakota, now lives with her sister in this seedy south-of-the-Loop neighborhood of Minneapolis. He's picked that up listening to the conversation.

Tony, now a girl short at dinnertime, refills the driver's cup and removes the chipped pie plate with its purple streaks of congealing blueberry filling. A dirty fork slides off the plate and clatters on the drab linoleum floor.

"Where does a person go to get a toothache fixed on a Friday night?" the driver asks. It's a reasonable question, nonchalantly stated, something a guy might wonder about in casual suppertime conversation, masking his prurient interest.

Tony looks at him as though he just noticed the customer who's been sitting on the stool behind the coffee and pie for the past thirty minutes. The driver appreciates the fact that he's one of those people other people walk past and don't remember three seconds later. What's to remember? There's no Jimmy Durante nose or Dumbo the Elephant ears, no stammer, drawl, or highfalutin vocabulary. He's neither tall nor short, beefy or gaunt. There's no swagger, hop, or buckle in his walk. If he didn't drive a bright yellow car with a light on top, you wouldn't notice him at all. Even then, it's the car—Canary Cab No. 313—that you look at, not the driver.

"There's a Jew dentist on the next block, open nights and weekends," Tony says, dragging his bum leg in the direction of the kitchen door. "That's prolly where she went."

He dumps the driver's pie plate and fork into a tub of greasy water behind the counter. "Do I give a shit?" the driver hears him mutter. "Not hardly."

The girl's name is Teresa Hickman, and at this moment—five minutes to seven, on Friday evening, April 8, 1955—she's killing time until her seven-thirty dental appointment. Teresa's sister, Grace Montgomery, put her on to Dr. Rose. Grace has gone to him a dozen-odd times during the past year. She went to him at first because her teeth needed work and because his office was around the corner from the

Montgomerys' apartment, and later because she developed a relationship with the man.

Tonight will be Teresa's fifth visit to Rose since she moved to Minneapolis in December. The first time, in January, her jaw was sore and swollen; she had an infection that required urgent treatment. The second time, ten days after the first, she said she was still having pain, though the swelling was gone. The third and fourth visits she had no complaints and hasn't mentioned the visits to Grace. This evening she told Grace she has another toothache and called the luncheonette to say she can't come in on account of it. Grace thinks she's probably lying, but decides not to make it an issue.

"I hate the dentist," Terry said before the first visit, in January. She wasn't referring to Dr. Rose, whom she hadn't met, but to the dentist as a scary archetype, like Jack Frost, the Headless Horseman, or the Devil, though she wouldn't have thought to use the word *archetype*.

Grace had laughed and said, "Everybody hates the dentist, sweetie."

Physically, the sisters have little in common. Grace has a mop of tightly curled ginger hair, unremarkable brown eyes, and twenty pounds more than blonde, saucer-eyed, lithe and lissome Terry. Grace is twenty-seven, so almost seven years older than Terry, and, by most accounts going back to their Dollar public school days, at least marginally smarter. As if that was any kind of advantage.

The sisters share a small-town experience that included visits to a sadistic silver-haired dentist in the neighboring town of Hartford (there has only recently been a three-day-a-week dentist with an office in Dollar), who instilled in them, their two brothers, and their local contemporaries a fear of Dr. Piet Vermeer at least equal to the man's malice and shaky incompetence. Vermeer, as it happened, had it in for the children of Walter and Marva Kubicek, treating them, even more than his other young patients, rudely and rough, often withholding the novocaine. The popular explanation for this extra nastiness was an unrequited love for Marva, a high school classmate, and cancerous jealousy of Walter, another classmate, who married her.

This evening, after Grace's husband, Bud, leaves for his night shift at the Moline tractor factory on East Lake Street, the sisters wait without fear for Terry's seven-thirty appointment. Terry's eighteen-month-old toddler is fussing with his bottle, and Grace is in an off mood, but they can't resist some reminiscence.

"I'll never forget those stairs," Terry says from the bedroom, where Harold Hickman Junior sucks on his bottle's nipple. Vermeer's office was situated above Hartford's Main Street hardware store. To reach it, you'd climb sixteen steep, linoleum-clad steps, the fumes becoming more pungent with each step. The insect whine of the dentist's drill grew louder, too, and as you neared the top you'd sometimes hear the poor sap in the dentist's chair let loose a blood-chilling scream.

Neither sister has to mention the experience at the top of the stairs: the windowless waiting room with only a stack of used-up coloring books to take your mind off the horror to come and crabby, blue-haired Mildred Rasmussen behind the receptionist's desk. Then, through another door, there was the big white-and-black chair, the corded drills, and tray full of hooks and needles and clamps, and Vermeer's scowling hatchet face, his tiny eyes like green marbles behind rimless spectacles, and Sen-Sen on his breath.

If Vermeer said anything at all to the whimpering patient during the ordeal that followed, it was, "Sit still, child! And, for the love of Mike, be quiet!"

"Dr. Rose isn't like that," Grace had told Terry in January. "He's odd, but nice. If he thinks you need it, he'll give you a pill that puts you to sleep, or almost asleep. You'll feel funny afterward, but you won't feel any pain. And when he's done, you'll be rid of your toothache."

Now Terry returns from the bedroom with her son in the crook of her arm. The child is red-eyed and squirming, his upper lip glazed with snot. With her free hand, Terry reaches for Grace's cigarette, takes a drag, and hands it back. She's run a comb through her hair and freshened her lipstick. This evening she's wearing a green pullover, plaid skirt, and black pumps. She has straight white teeth and a dazzling smile.

Grace stares at her sister through the cigarette smoke. She knows

Terry better than anyone in the world, certainly better than their parents and their brothers ever did, and better than Terry's husband does now. Grace knew about the "secret" boyfriends back home, and that trouble at the Hartford Ben Franklin that disabused Grace of the belief that she was the only shoplifter in the family. Then there were the summer nights when Terry and her pal Connie Canfield stripped naked and walked down County Road 6 in the headlights of Cullen Hanson's pickup, and the time Terry got "drunk and crazy" with Kenny Landa's married brother and a couple of the brother's Navy friends when Kenny was in a Grand Forks hospital with appendicitis.

Still, there have been the occasional surprises. Two days ago, while Terry was at work, Grace came across a half-dozen photographs tucked beneath the bras and underpants in Terry's dresser.

That evening, after Bud left for work, Grace dropped the photos on the coffee table and fanned them out in front of her.

"Where did these come from, hon?" she asked.

Terry actually colored a little.

"A guy I met at the Palace," she said. "His name is Richard, and he does weddings and yearbook photos. Some fashion stuff on the side."

Grace looked at the photos again, one after another.

There is Terry perched on a tall wooden stool with a cheesy-looking curtain as a backdrop. She's wearing a sleeveless blouse and tight white shorts that Grace recognized but hadn't seen for a while. In one of the photos the blouse is unbuttoned and Terry is barefoot. In another she's wearing high heels, has turned her back to the camera, and is looking over her bare shoulder like Betty Grable in the photo that a million GIs tacked up in their barracks during the war. The photos are black and white, and, in Grace's opinion, not very accomplished for a professional.

"'Fashion stuff,' huh?" Grace said, handing them to her sister. She smiled knowingly, the way a big sister would smile in this situation, but knew that her face betrayed her envy.

"Hal's been begging for pictures," Terry said with a shrug. "So when Richard asked if I wanted to pose, I said, 'Sure. Maybe I'll send some photos to my husband.' We went over to Richard's place in Stevens Square. The studio, so-called, was just the little living room in his apartment, with a sofa bed, a couple of chairs, and that stool. But he was nice and didn't charge me. Afterward, he said, 'You owe me,' and I said, 'Don't worry, I'm good for it.'"

"Hal's not going to like them," Grace said, thinking about the unbuttoned, barefoot shots and wondering if there were other poses that this Richard kept for himself.

"Hal will be jealous," Terry replied with that smile. "But that's okay."

When Terry leaves for Dr. Rose's office, Grace checks on the baby, lights another one of Bud's Pall Malls, and in her mind's eye follows her sister downstairs, out the front door, and around the corner onto Nicollet Avenue. She can't see Terry from her windows, which face Fifteenth, but in her mind's eye she sees her clearly. Grace knows the short trip by heart.

Terry walks a half block south on Nicollet, wending her way through the leering drunks and drooling stumblebums idling in front of the Whoop-Tee-Doo Club, drawing wolf whistles, catcalls, and, if she doesn't move quickly enough, their grabbing, grasping, pinching hands. Loud music pours out of the club's front door, driven by a thumping bass and chased by a saxophone's carnal shriek, along with shouts and hollers and the kind of language you hear in a Navy yard. Another few steps and she sees a short list of businesses and professionals on a pair of double doors, including H. DAVID ROSE, DDS, and hurries inside.

Terry will run up a narrow flight of stairs that reminds her of the steps leading to Piet Vermeer's torture chamber in Hartford. When she reaches the top, the street noise has faded a little. There's a door with the word WELCOME stenciled on the frosted glass and beyond that door a short, dimly lit, faintly chemical-smelling corridor with two more doors on either side. The first, on the left, says A. O. FISCHER / CHIROPRACTOR, the second REYNARD & RIDGEWAY /

DANCE INSTRUCTION FOR ALL AGES. Across the hall there's a door with no markings at all, and finally there's Dr. Rose's.

The only sound, at seven-thirty on a Friday night, is the raucous music, up here muffled by the beams, trusses, and plaster walls and ceilings of a prewar commercial building, from the club downstairs. The other second-floor offices are dark and silent behind their closed doors.

Terry opens the last door and steps into a small waiting room. There's no whining drill, no fish-eyed receptionist, only a slipcovered settee, three or four wooden chairs, a small end-table bearing stacks of *Readers Digest* and *Saturday Evening Post*, and a spindly floor lamp weakly illuminating a worn brownish carpet. The chemical reek is faint, but unmistakable.

Terry will be mildly surprised—as she was on previous visits, as was Grace on *her* visits—that the waiting room is empty. Above the muffled noise from downstairs, the stillness is thick as cotton batting. Then, almost immediately, there's a soft footfall in an adjoining room and yet another door opens and, in the doorway, a slightly stooped, dark-haired, long-faced man in a white jacket appears, smiling.

"Teresa, dear," Dr. Rose says. "Won't you come in?"

At the apartment, Grace sits down, rubs out the cigarette, and closes her eyes.

The driver hauls a flatulent middle-aged businessman from the Curtis Hotel on Tenth Street to the airport, twenty minutes away, and then heads back downtown with the windows lowered in his empty cab. He hopes he's had enough coffee to stay upright behind the wheel until ten or eleven, at which time he'll either go home or hit an all-night diner for another shot of joe.

Cruising through Uptown and then north on Hennepin toward the Loop, he sees plenty of what he looks for this time of night: girls and young women, between fifteen and thirty, with or without an escort, and with that ineffable look that tells him they would enjoy what he has to offer. But it's early April, so it's still chilly in the Twin

Cities, and the girls are still bundled up in overcoats and kerchiefs. This time of year he kicks himself for not living in Florida.

He ignores a couple of fares waving at him along Hennepin, and then returns to Nicollet, where he parks near the corner of Fifteenth Street, kitty-corner from the Whoop-Tee-Doo Club, rolls the windows up, and turns off his roof light. It's only a quarter to ten, but he's done with taxi business for the night.

He parks here because he learned before leaving the Greek's place that the dentist the skinny blonde might be visiting this evening works out of an office above the club, maybe where lights glow in a pair of second-floor windows. The supper trade, such as it is at the Palace, was over, both Tony's old man and his ugly wife had left for the day, and Tony was talkative.

"I'll be goddamned if some Jew's gonna stick his fingers in *my* mouth, but I heard Rose does all right," the gimp said. "They say a lot of his trade is working girls who go to him in the evening and on weekends—when dentists generally ain't open for business. Anyways, I've seen the lights on up there late, and his car parked around the corner, on Fifteenth, always the same spot, a black Packard Clipper. Someone pointed it out once, said it was his."

The driver was careful not to ask too many questions. The gimp's obviously a firecracker. Unpredictable. Volatile. Maybe dangerous. You never know what a guy like that might tell the cops if it came to it. Like, *Yeah, there was this guy, a regular fuckin' nosy Ned, always asking about the girls.*

Of course, the driver can't be certain the lights he sees in the windows above the Whoop-Tee-Doo are the dentist's, much less if the skinny blonde is on the premises, much less what he should do if she is. Lights burning in second-floor commercial windows on a Friday night have a way of inspiring impure thoughts, but the driver doesn't have the guts to go up there for a look-see, what with the crowd milling around on the sidewalk out front and no plan of action except to snoop. Snooping is usually excuse enough, but not tonight. Despite the coffee, the driver is tired and tentative.

From where he parks, using one or the other of his mirrors, he can keep an eye on both the double doors that must lead to the offices upstairs and the black Packard parked where the gimp said it would be, around the corner on Fifteenth. The driver is okay parked where he is. No one pays attention to a cab when its roof light is off.

The driver turns on the radio and listens to the news. Eisenhower this, Eisenhower that. The driver's got nothing against the president, but he's tempted to vote for Stevenson if he runs against Ike next year, mainly because he knows that the stingy, stuffed-shirt businessmen who make up the majority of his fares vote the Republican ticket. Plus he doesn't like Nixon, Tricky Dick, Ike's Number Two. Then again, the driver didn't bother to vote for anyone in 'fifty-two, and probably won't in 'fifty-six, either. He doesn't see that it makes much difference.

He lifts and shakes his Thermos jug though he knows it's empty, and then drops it on the floor. Listening to Eisenhower droning on about Berlin and the Suez Canal, he takes off his peaked cap and sets it beside him on the seat. Then, with no intention of napping, he turns off the radio, drops his head back to rest his eyes, and falls asleep.

Forty-five minutes later, he's roused by a drunk rapping on his window. The drunk is standing in the street and hanging on to his girlfriend, both drunks leaning against his car and peering at him through the glass like a couple of circus clowns.

Rolling his window down far enough to smell the booze, the driver says, "You fuckin' blind? The roof light is off. That means the car ain't in service."

The man straightens up and sways away from the window, clutching his girlfriend's arm. The driver notices a large stain on the front of the man's trousers. Trying to focus his eyes on the roof light, the man says, "Well, shit, fella, you're still a taxi, aincha? We demand a ride."

"Take the bus, asshole."

The driver rolls his window up and rotates his stiff neck. He looks at his watch—it's almost ten-forty. When the drunks stagger off and it occurs to him to check the mirrors, he sees that the Packard is no longer in its parking spot. And, when he looks toward the Whoop-Tee-Doo Club, the second-floor windows are dark.

"Son of a bitch!" he shouts, slapping the steering wheel. He starts the car and pulls into the Friday-night traffic. He turns left on Fifteenth and proceeds down along the south side of Loring Park, where a dozen girls stand on the sidewalk facing the street, their coats open to show what they have to sell.

But the driver doesn't like whores. Whores are used merchandise, dirty and worn-down and mean. It's not a whore he's looking for tonight.

For want of a better idea, he turns back toward Hennepin and heads south.

Nearly two hours later, on the same April night, a young man, naked as a newborn, stretches his arms and legs and squints at the luminous hands and numerals of the alarm clock on the dresser. He reaches for his glasses, which he'd shoved under the bed, so he can get a better look.

"You have to go, Bobby," says the young woman beside him. "Karl'll be on his way pretty soon."

In the spring of 1955, Robert Gardner has just turned twenty-three and been hired by the United Press wire service bureau in Minneapolis. He is single and lives—temporarily, he assures them—with his sister and her husband in a two-bedroom apartment on Forty-fourth Street in Linden Hills. Today, Robert worked, as he has for the past three months, the three-to-eleven shift in the bureau's downtown office. For the lion's share of the last hour, he's been fucking Pamela Brantley. Karl Brantley, Pam's husband, is an intern at Hiawatha General Hospital downtown.

"Jesus," Robert mutters, stretching out on his back.

The back bedroom of the Brantleys' second-floor apartment, two blocks west of Robert's temporary lodging, is not much larger than a walk-in closet, and its air is thick with the musk of their lovemaking. Pam, naked as Robert, slides off the damp sheets and pushes open the room's single window, letting in a welcome rush of chilly night air. Looking at her sweat-slicked back, plump ass, and short but nicely shaped legs, he wants to fuck her again, this time from behind, braced against the window frame.

It is sheer coincidence—he will go to his grave believing it's the definition of "happy accident"—that he and Pam are together, much less lovers. Pam is the twenty-one-year-old younger sister of Janice Jones, whom Robert dated while attending high school in Rochester. Robert and Karl Brantley's kid brother, Ted, were teammates on the junior varsity basketball team. For much of their high school careers, Robert and the Brantley boys were casual friends.

Though they dated exclusively for more than two years and talked about marriage after college, Robert and Janice never let themselves go beyond the serious petting stage. Each had reasons for restraint: Janice's hellfire Baptist faith and Robert's fear of scandalizing his staid, socially conscious family, pillars of Rochester's medical aristocracy. They broke up a month after their high school graduation, and then headed off in different directions. The last time Robert saw either Janice or Pam— until he encountered Pam at the Butler Brothers drugstore in Linden Hills—was at Pam and Karl's wedding reception eighteen months ago.

"What are *you* doing here?" Pam exclaimed. She and Robert had literally bumped into each other in front of men's toiletries near the back of the store. Born dark-eyed, olive-skinned, and sultry, she had a body that was made for the tight sweater and short skirt she wore that day.

"I live here," Robert replied. "Around the corner, off York."

"Me, too!" Pam said. "On Forty-fourth and Abbott. Karl works downtown."

Not yet a ladies' man, Robert was flattered by Pam's exuberant response to seeing him. Though he hadn't seen her since her wedding, he'd been enjoying the occasional Pam Jones fantasy since he dated Janice. Robert is tall and conventionally handsome, though he could stand to put on another ten pounds. He's also intelligent, well educated, and self-possessed in the way you'd expect of the son of an eminent thoracic surgeon. Pam Brantley, whose parents run a failing dry-goods store several miles beyond the shadow of tony Pill Hill, exudes a self-confidence that's easily his equal. But what Robert discovered soon enough is that Pam is an unhappily married woman.

She told him so when, at her suggestion, they met for coffee at a France Avenue cafe the day after their accidental meeting.

"It was a mistake," she said softly. "Karl couldn't get enough of me before we were married. Now I think he couldn't care less. All that matters is his work."

Robert, his throat dry, said he found that hard to believe, that *he* couldn't imagine ever getting enough of her. Pam smiled and reached under the table and spread her fingers on his leg. She told him he was sweet. Then she slid her hand up a couple of inches and told him that Karl worked late most nights.

"Maybe you could come by," she said.

That was a month ago, and Robert and Pam have been torching the sheets in the Brantleys' back bedroom ever since. So far, there have been no close calls nor need for extraordinary measures—scrambling under the bed, leaping from a second-floor window—and Pam insists that Karl, absorbed in his medical training, is none the wiser. Robert has yet to run into him in the neighborhood and is sure that Karl has no idea he lives nearby. On the nights they meet, Robert steps off the bus at Xerxes Avenue and joins Pam by eleven-thirty. An hour later, spent but happy, he walks to his sister's apartment, slinking along the abandoned trolley tracks that run behind and below the modest apartment buildings, duplexes, and storefront businesses facing Forty-fourth Street. If Robert's sister ever asks where he's been so late, he'll say he had drinks with colleagues downtown.

Still, Robert is a cautious young man, a worrier like his mother and a stickler for detail like his father, both of whom, it goes without saying, would be outraged if they knew about his midnight adventures. Majoring in journalism at the University of Minnesota was heartbreaking enough—he was supposed to follow the family line into medicine. Seeking and apparently enjoying the work of a vulgar news hound have been all but unbearable to his parents. Now a furtive adulterer as well, he's taken to wearing a black jacket and dark trousers on his tryst nights, believing himself, like a cat burglar, difficult to spot in the shadows.

The abandoned right-of-way is weedy and littered with worn-out automobile tires, pieces of broken furniture, and discarded paint cans—rubbish that a person could break an ankle on if he isn't careful—not to mention clumps of dog shit, a used condom or two, and other waste that he wouldn't want to drag into his sister's place. He wonders if he should carry a flashlight, but decides the light would attract attention.

Tonight's exit is no different from the previous ones. Hurriedly dressed, Robert kisses Pam, who will put on her nightgown, crawl into the double bed in the other room, and feign deep sleep when her weary husband trudges in. The lovers kiss again, and again, until she pushes him away. There are no proclamations of love, not yet, but Robert believes, and believes Pam does, too, that they've already become essential to each other's happiness and will be together soon, the disapproving world be damned.

It is well past midnight when Dr. Rose returns home, scarcely half a mile, as it happens, from Robert and Pam's love nest on Forty-fourth Street.

Rose also resides, with his wife and two pubescent daughters, in the Linden Hills neighborhood of southwest Minneapolis, but instead of overlooking derelict streetcar tracks, the Roses live a block off scenic Lake Calhoun. From their master bedroom, they can see a sliver of the city's most popular lake through a small forest of elms, birches, maples, and poplars. Several other professional men—doctors, dentists, attorneys, and corporate executives—live on the same block, across the street, or in the immediate vicinity. There are two or three more exclusive neighborhoods in the city, but none more comfortably "livable," to use a word relentlessly employed by local real estate agents.

The Roses' girls—Margot and Lael—have been in bed for hours, but Ruth is up when David comes home. She is a short, solid, chestnut-haired woman of forty, plainspoken, humorless, and unassuming, though she comes from significant family money. Ruth is always up when David comes home.

The Roses will have been married for seventeen years come September, and Ruth likes to tell friends that she's never had a regret and is certain that he hasn't either. Her friends smile, knowing full well that he, at any rate, has no reason for regret, not the way Ruth takes care of him. Ruth buys the groceries, pays the utility bills, hires the yard work, even sees that his Packard's oil has been changed and the tires rotated. More important, she keeps Margot and Lael, fine young ladies anyway, on the straight and narrow. And David—well, her friends say, Ruth is simply everything to him: nurse, caretaker, confidante, and, once or twice a month, if he requests it, lover.

Tonight—it's actually early morning—Dr. Rose walks in the back door exhausted and disoriented, as though he's entered a stranger's house. His exhaustion is frequent and understandable, given his long hours at work and peculiar eating habits. Even the disorientation is not uncommon, probably for the same reasons. Rose is a tall man, six foot two or three, though he's round-shouldered and somewhat stooped, the price he's paid, Ruth insists, for bending over patients for nearly twenty years. He has a long, gaunt face, sad dark eyes, a meticulously maintained mustache, and a full head of glossy black hair. If the hair were thinner or showed the slightest sign of gray, he would look much older, given his posture and pallor.

Rose stands in the middle of the kitchen and looks around as though he'd dropped in from Mars. Ruth steps around him and eases off his overcoat and then the jacket of his suit. She can't reach his gray fedora and, in any case, wouldn't dream of trying to lift it off his head, which would be not only difficult given the difference in their height but disrespectful as well. In a minute or two, he will realize he's still wearing his hat and remove it himself.

In another moment he looks at his wife, blinks his long-lashed eyes, and says he drove his last patient home, then returned to his office and lay down in the waiting room.

"I must have fallen asleep," he says, though it always strikes her as preposterous, a man of his dimensions getting comfortable enough to doze on that settee.

"Are your knees bothering you?" Ruth asks.

"Not so much tonight," he says.

"You haven't eaten, have you?" Ruth says.

He looks at her as though he's thinking about the answer.

"I don't suppose I have," he says at last.

"Ronnie was here for supper," she says, referring to her brother, a thirty-year-old bachelor lawyer and frequent dinner guest. "There's beef stew I'll put back on the stove."

Rose eats in silence, head bent over his plate, while Ruth sits silently across the table and waits. When he's finished, he will thank her and, without another word, climb the stairs to the master bedroom on the second floor. She will rinse off his plate, drinking glass, and silverware, and follow him a few minutes later.

Upstairs, after he washes his face and brushes his teeth, Rose slides into bed beside his wife. Both wear flannel pajamas—his striped, hers dotted—and black sleep masks, though neither will have trouble dropping off tonight. Rose reaches out and takes hold of Ruth's hand, and in another moment both appear to be asleep.

Robert Gardner, in his stocking feet, eases himself down the back stairs of the Brantleys' building and out the back door. He sits down on the stoop and puts on his shoes. The night is quiet save for the sad, ragged barking of a dog somewhere in the neighborhood. The waning moon, as insubstantial as a nail clipping when it appears through the broken clouds, offers negligible illumination.

Robert walks carefully down the cracked sidewalk to a short flight of uneven stone steps, then through ten feet of ankle-deep weeds, brush, and trash, and then onto the former right-of-way. Though unused for two years now, the tracks gleam with a dull sheen in the yellow glow of a streetlight. Robert walks between the double row of tracks, stepping carefully between the rotting ties, and wonders what he'd do if somebody jumped him. He's a lover, he tells himself with a smile, not a fighter. One night last week, he spotted a couple of kids making out in the shadow of a garage. He pretended he didn't see them and picked up his pace. He doubted if they noticed.

Suppose Karl Brantley waited in the shadows.

The notion also makes Robert smile. Karl is not a fighter, either. A deferential, perpetually smiling beanpole, Karl was voted Rochester High's Mr. Nice Guy of 1946. Granted, nice guys can change, wise up, and stop smiling. *Some* nice guys—but probably not Karl. Robert feels bad about fucking Karl's wife, so he tries not to think about Karl any more than he has to.

Robert is sated, bone-tired, and eager to crawl into his own bed, meaning the narrow roll-away he's using at Gwen and her husband's apartment until their baby arrives. He earns enough for a cheap place of his own, but wants to wait until he can buy a decent used car, which should be sometime this summer. (Robert's father made it clear that once he moved to the Twin Cities and got a job with the wire service, he was on his own, ineligible for parental gifts, loans, or subsidies. Gwen lost her meal ticket when she married a Catholic.) If there's an extra bottle of Grain Belt in his sister's refrigerator, he will drink it, but he will skip a late supper and hit the sack. He expects to have a wet dream about Pam.

Later, he will ask himself what caught his eye, what it was that snatched his mind away from Pam and that cold bottle of beer and drew his attention to the woman's body lying on the south side of the tracks. The woman was wearing a dark green or blue coat and what looked like a plaid skirt. One hand, pale and thin, with chewed nails and a ring on the third finger—he can see the glint of a tiny diamond in the weak light—is thrust out, protruding from the brush a few inches onto the gravel track bed. It must have been the hand with its glinting gem that he spotted in the semidarkness.

He stands a few feet from the body, staring. A moment later, his heart pounding, he looks in both directions, and then takes another step. He stops and leans forward, not quite over the body, but close enough to see more. He looks for movement or a sound, a moan or a whisper begging for help. But there is nothing. The woman is dead. Though he covered a couple of fatal car accidents during a year at the Rochester paper, he's never seen a corpse up this close. He sure as hell has never discovered one. He is sure, though, that this woman is dead.

He knows enough not to touch the body or turn it over to get a better look at the victim's face. He's a newsman, paid to be curious, but at this moment fear and what little he knows about crime-scene protocol tamps down his curiosity. He realizes that he's shivering, though that could be the chilly night. He straightens up and looks around. Though he sees no blood or signs of a struggle, he presumes that the woman was murdered. Nothing runs on these tracks anymore, and they're fifty yards from the street, so there's no chance she was hit by a trolley or a car. What could it be except murder or maybe a suicide, though if it was suicide how would she have done it—he sees no weapon or bottle of pills—and why here?

Could her assailant be nearby? For no good reason, Robert doubts it. The body seems rooted in the weeds, an organic part of the scrub and detritus that line the track bed. That helps him believe her killer is gone.

Robert takes another, short step toward the body. He squats, extends his right arm, and touches the woman's exposed hand. Impulsively, he strokes the back of her hand with his forefinger, and then traces a slightly raised vein just visible in the dim light. His finger maintains contact with the woman's hand for only a moment, but he will remember the cold, wax-like sensation—he will compare it to the feel of a discarded candle—for the rest of his life.

He believes, though he has no way of knowing without a better look at her face, that the woman was beautiful.

CHAPTER 2

Arne Anderson is still sleeping when Lily Kline pinches his shoulder and says, "Downtown's on the phone." He rolls over, rubs his eyes, and tells Lily to tell Downtown to fuck themselves. Lily, who's already dressed and probably still angry about last night, snaps the shade up and walks out of the bedroom. "I told Mel you'd call him right back."

The phone is in the short hallway that connects the Chicago Avenue apartment's single bedroom with the bath, kitchen, and a minuscule living room. Anderson, barefoot and yawning in his boxers and sleeveless undershirt, makes the call and scratches his back against the stuccoed hallway wall while waiting for Mel to pick up at the office. He can hear Lily in the kitchen, frying eggs and making toast. He figures she can't be too angry if she's fixing breakfast, and tries to remember what she might be angry about anyway. She's been angry a lot lately.

It's a chilly Saturday morning, not yet eight o'clock if the worn-out Westclox on the dresser hasn't stopped.

Melvin Curry, Anderson's Homicide Squad partner for the past three years, tells him that the body of a white female, probably in her late teens or early twenties, has been found along the streetcar right-of-way in Linden Hills. A couple of patrol cars responded to a citizen's call half an hour ago. "Hessburg and LeBlanc will be waiting for us, plus the new guy from the coroner's office," Curry says. "Considering the victim and the neighborhood," he says, "I wouldn't be surprised if Augie and Big Ed are on their way as well."

Anderson straightens up and scratches himself between his legs.

"You said Linden Hills?"

"Strange but true."

Arne coughs.

"When was the last time we had a body down there?"

"Before my time, unless we're counting a couple suicides," Mel says. "I'll pick you up in ten minutes."

When Curry arrives in an unmarked Chevy sedan, Anderson climbs in, balancing a plate of fried eggs, a slice of buttered toast, and a couple of browned sausages in his right hand. He carries a fork between his teeth the way a pirate carries a dagger. Mel, who's no doubt been up for hours and enjoyed a proper breakfast with his fetching new wife, smiles and shakes his head.

"Don't let me forget the plate and fork somewhere," Arne says. "Things are touch-and-go with Lily as it is."

Traffic is nonexistent this early on a Saturday morning so Curry doesn't bother with the red dashboard light and siren. Even so, they're at the crime scene—a stretch of deserted tracks behind three or four blocks of small apartment buildings, modest duplexes, and small, storefront businesses—in ten minutes.

For decades, the Twin City Rapid Transit Company operated one of the finest public transportation systems in the country, and electric-powered streetcars the color of French's mustard jars covered the Twin Cities like a blanket. This route, Line No. 1, carried riders from downtown Minneapolis through the populous south and south-west precincts of the city all the way out to the lakeside town of Excelsior in the far western suburbs. Then a cabal of shady businessmen, corrupt politicians, and organized-crime figures sold off the cars, ripped out most of the tracks, and turned the routes over to a fleet of diesel-powered buses that fouled the air and did little to improve service, traffic flow, or safety. In the spring of 1955, this forlorn scrap of track is one of the few vestiges of the trolley system in the city.

"There was nothing wrong with those streetcars," Arne says. "I hear there are a lot of them on the streets of Mexico City."

Mel parks a car length north of where the tracks cross Zenith Avenue, behind Sid Hessburg and Frenchy LeBlanc's Chevy, a white Chevrolet station wagon driven this morning by the coroner's assistant, and the black Buick sedan bearing Detective Captain August Fuller and Fuller's boss, Inspector of Detectives Edwin Evangelist. Black-and-white prowl cars are parked at odd angles on Zenith and York, effectively blocking those streets.

The focus of the dozen-plus uniformed and plainclothes police and the coroner's man is a bundle of winter clothing lying in the weeds off the south side of the tracks about halfway between the crossing streets. Behind them a dozen or so civilians, presumably neighborhood residents, stand in clusters of twos and threes, speaking in hushed voices and staring at the bundle in the weeds. The sun is up but hardly a factor behind a scrim of gray clouds, so Anderson is glad to see officers holding flashlights.

Fuller, his unshaven moon face as dark and grisly as a Gateway wino's, stands with his hands shoved deep in the pockets of his tweed overcoat. "You got this one, Arne?" he says without bothering to look at his best investigator.

"Do I, Captain?" Anderson says in a flat voice. That's neither self-deprecation nor false modesty. He's simply not one to take things for granted.

"Yeah," Fuller says. "You do."

"And too fuckin' bad for you, Anderson," says Evangelist, who's lighting either his first cigar of the morning or the remains of last night's. The fat bureaucrat is a political appointee despised for his inopportune appearances at crime scenes and his flaccid support of the department's detectives. "This one's gonna be a bitch."

Anderson steps forward and hunkers down alongside the body.

It's too early in the season for flies, but already there's the unmistakable stink of death rising from the body. As an infantryman in George Patton's Third Army during the Battle of the Bulge, Arne saw plenty of young corpses, many of them gruesomely bloodied, mangled, or dismembered. The bodies of a few females, too—stripped, abused, and murdered, or merely collateral damage. One snowy morning, he spotted Patton standing in an open Jeep, hands on his hips, looking at the same scatter of lifeless bodies, the bodies lying at odd angles, grotesquely contorted or oddly peaceful, as though only asleep.

As a street cop and homicide detective, Arne has seen his share of civilian dead and dying, too, though this is Minneapolis, not Chicago or Cleveland or Kansas City, so not *that* many. But this body is out of the ordinary. It's the body of a slight young white woman, fully and appropriately dressed, maybe a college student or a shop clerk, almost certainly not a barfly or a prostitute. She was small enough for her killer—most likely a man—to easily carry her body the one hundred–odd feet from either Zenith or York and dump it here.

The woman is wearing a hip-length, dark green winter coat or jacket, but no cap, scarf, or gloves. An extended hand, her left, is white and cold, its delicate fingers already stiffened by rigor mortis; there's a small diamond engagement ring and thin wedding band on the ring finger. She's wearing white anklets, but missing her right shoe. She's also wearing what looks like an inexpensive necklace and matching bracelet. Anderson looks more closely at the rings, which appear to his untrained eye no pricier than the necklace and bracelet. Nevertheless, she's still wearing them, which means she was probably not murdered during a robbery or mugging.

He stares at the tiny diamond and wedding band. Where, he wonders, is her husband?

Detective Sid Hessburg, eager to offer his opinion, squats down beside Anderson and says, "No purse in sight, but there was a billfold in her coat pocket. There's a North Dakota driver's license with the name Teresa Marie Kubicek—"KOO-bah-chek," he pronounces the last name, correctly it turns out—of Dollar, North Dakota, "wherever the hell that is." He reads off the driver's license. "Five foot two. One hundred pounds. Date of birth: 9/2/33."

Anderson stands up and looks around.

"Anything else in her pockets?"

"A pack of Pall Malls," Hessburg says, standing, too. He holds up a familiar dark-red package. There are three cigarettes left. "Pall Mall— that's a guy's brand. I don't know any women who smoke Pall Malls. Maybe she swiped 'em."

"Find her other shoe?" Anderson asks him.

"Not yet."

Arne takes the red, imitation leather billfold from the young detective. He glances at the driver's license and flips through a half-dozen two-by-three-inch snapshots in their cloudy glassine sleeves. There's a studio shot of a baby, a headshot of a young man in an Army uniform, and photos of another young man in civilian clothes, a bare-shouldered young woman in a wedding gown, and an elderly couple grinning from behind a decorated layer cake. Either the soldier or the young civilian could be the victim's husband, assuming the victim is in fact married. The woman in the wedding dress is pudgy and curly-haired, definitely not the victim, but maybe a sister or a friend. The old couple are no doubt parents or, more likely, grandparents back in Dollar, North Dakota.

There's a tightly folded sheet of pink paper in the last sleeve, a small typewritten document of some kind. In the zippered change pocket: a folded sawbuck, three crumpled singles, fifty-three cents in change, and a pair of bus tokens.

Anderson waits for an MPD photographer to shoot the scene from this angle, and then squats down again beside the body. He, Mel, Sid, and Dr. Alois Jensen from the coroner's office turn the woman face up. They might as well be lifting a child, the body is so light. Mel shines his flashlight on her face. Her mouth is slightly ajar, what little lipstick remains is smudged off her lower lip, and her pale, gray or green eyes are half-open and dull, staring at the sky but seeing nothing. One slightly rouged cheek bears traces of the unkempt ground it's been pressed against, but there's no sign of physical stress or violence.

"Wow!" Hessburg says softly, admiringly, peering at the young woman's face.

Dr. Jensen reaches between the unbuttoned flaps of the woman's coat and gingerly probes the body inside.

Anderson stands and looks down at the corpse. "This was a very pretty young lady," he says to no one in particular.

"You can say that again," Hessburg murmurs.

"You're assuming she was a lady," Evangelist, standing behind them, says out of the side of his mouth.

"Doesn't look like a sexual assault," Jensen says, writing something in a small notebook as he speaks. "Her clothes are damp, probably from lying in the weeds for several hours, but I don't see any rips or tears. No visible bullet holes or puncture wounds." Jensen's boss, Hiawatha County Medical Examiner Fred MacMurray, will likely want to perform an autopsy as soon as possible this morning.

"No visible blood, either," Jensen continues. "But there's a mark, some bruising maybe, on the left side of her neck."

"Have a guess as to how long she's been here?" Anderson asks.

"I'm thinking she could have died anytime late last night into early this morning. Probably not here. We'll get a better idea downtown."

Other than Hessburg, the detectives are reluctant to offer their two cents' worth until they're sure Evangelist and Fuller have offered theirs. Oddly, neither of the senior officers says a word. Big Ed is hung over. He's literally swaying in the weeds beside Augie, a safe distance from the corpse and rheumy eyes focused elsewhere. Augie, who's been fighting a spring cold, doesn't look very chipper, either.

"Sid, we're talking to the neighbors, aren't we?" Anderson says to Hessburg. "You and Frenchy, take five or six uniforms and keep at it. Go three blocks east and west, on both sides of the right-of-way. See if anyone saw or heard anything last night. Keep your eyes out for her other shoe."

"Unfamiliar cars, maybe unusual activity down here along the tracks," Hessburg, an overgrown Eagle Scout, says needlessly.

Anderson smiles.

"Yeah, Sid. All of that," he says.

Fuller clears a phlegmy throat and says, "It's possible she didn't live in the neighborhood, but maybe her killer does."

Six months ago, Augie, who is third-generation MPD, ran Forgery and Swindle; before that, he was Auto Theft's second-in-command. He has the probational respect and affection of the murder cops who work for him today. He tries hard to make a point that his charges will appreciate, and occasionally he does.

"If that shoe isn't in the immediate vicinity, she probably wasn't murdered here," Anderson says. "Unless the killer took it with him."

"Somebody needs to find her old man," Evangelist says. He's right, of course—the husband is the prime suspect at this point in most investigations of murdered married women—but there isn't a cop in the world who needs a bibulous hack like Big Ed to tell him that.

Jensen, Hessburg, LeBlanc, and a young uniform Anderson doesn't recognize are placing the woman on a stretcher. Jensen then pulls an army blanket over her body and draws it up to cover her face. Arne looks around as Fuller and Evangelist turn back toward their car. The brass will be happy to let him handle this one for now. If the woman's death turns out to be something more than a run-of-the-mill homicide, they'll have second thoughts and want their names on the public statements and in the newspaper features, prepared, of course, to back off again if the investigation gets messy. For the time being they're happy to let Anderson and his crew kick the can down the road.

"Where's the guy that found the body?" Anderson asks.

Hessburg nods toward a thin, bespectacled man in a corduroy jacket and matching cap standing next to a uniformed officer beyond the semicircle of detectives. The man has gray hair and looks to be in his forties. He's holding a cigarette in one hand and a leash with a handsome Dalmatian tugging against it in the other. His name, Hessburg says, is Gerald Bergen. Citizen Bergen is looking at Arne and smiling self-consciously.

Anderson walks over, introduces himself, and guides Bergen to one side, out of earshot of the other civilians. Both men are aware of the growing number of the curious, many of whom must be acquainted with Bergen, and the arrival of a gaggle of downtown reporters and photographers who will be eager to introduce him, along with the late Teresa Marie Kubicek, to the rest of the city.

At nine forty-five this Saturday morning, Dr. Rose is just getting up. This is not unusual. After a late night, the doctor almost always sleeps in. He typically doesn't schedule patients before one in the afternoon. He's always preferred afternoons and evenings to mornings. He believes that later in the day he's more alert, focused, and adroit—demonstrably more dexterous—and in the past several years he's developed a comfortable practice with working women and women with small children who can't get away for appointments during daytime office hours.

Today, he plans to go in before noon, to give himself time to tidy up the office before the afternoon's first patient arrives at one.

He removes the sleep mask and walks stiffly to the bathroom. His joints ache; his parents' arthritis is an unfortunate inheritance. He is, among other things, a man of purposeful and unvarying routine. He will sit in the big claw-footed tub for fifteen minutes, his bony knees poking out of the sudsy water like a pair of Pacific atolls. He will then follow the precise and unalterable protocol taught him and his brothers by their father back in Vincennes—preparing the lather with the porcelain mug and boar-bristle brush, then scraping away his thick beard with one of his father's bone-handled razors (properly stropped while the lather softens the beard), then rinsing and drying his face with a clean towel, and slapping on the Barberry Coast bay rum that he's been buying since college.

Before all that, however, he stares in the mirror at his long, almost comically somber face as though it belongs to a stranger.

It's the face, sans mustache, wrinkles, and pouches, that he's had all his life, its features shared by his father and paternal grandfather, uncounted uncles and cousins, and, to a somewhat lesser extent, his two brothers, yet it's a face that inevitably surprises him when he leans over the bathroom sink and peers into the mirror.

He would never describe himself as a handsome man, certainly not by gentile standards, especially here in the German- and Scandinavian-dominated Upper Midwest, but there's a presence about him that indicates a serious, sensitive, substantial man. His well-groomed hair, combed straight back from his forehead, and soulful eyes are no doubt his best features, and, though not everyone in the family agrees, he believes that the neat mustache he has worn since dental school adds gravitas to his appearance.

Today, in the privacy of his toilet, he's inspired to take a close look at his naked body in the full-length mirror attached to the bathroom door. His stooped shoulders and bandy legs belong to an older man, no denying that. But the ropy musculature of the arms, especially the hairy forearms, the pale torso free of the moles and keratoses that cling like barnacles to many middle-aged men, and the long, circumcised penis, thick as a ship's rope, that shows signs of life as he stares at it— all of that speaks of a vital man still very much in the prime of his life.

Meanwhile, his hands—large, white, and neither scarred nor blemished, with extraordinarily long, sturdy, well-shaped fingers and neatly tended cuticles—mark him, in his eyes, as an artistic man as well.

Not that he expects to find any, he nonetheless looks closely for scratches or bruises on his body, especially on his face, neck, arms, and hands. Satisfied with the inspection, he steps into the clean pair of undershorts his wife has laid out for him and wonders which necktie he should wear to the office.

Ruth Rose, who's always needed less sleep than her husband, has been up for hours.

Margot and Lael have a cousin's birthday party to get ready for, and Ruth has the usual Saturday housecleaning to do. Though her husband has offered to pay for one, Ruth insists she neither needs nor wants a housekeeper, not even a woman who would come in once a week to dust, vacuum, and take care of the laundry. She believes that having hired help is ostentatious and undemocratic. She believes that dedicated and progressive Jews who vote for the likes of Humphrey and Stevenson and contribute to the NAACP don't keep "servants."

Rose looks at his wife from the kitchen door. He has shaved, bathed, and dressed for the office—he selected the blue-and-green-striped tie she gave him on his last birthday—and is ready for breakfast. Breakfast is on many days the only meal he eats for twelve or fifteen or twenty-four hours.

"That's how he stays so thin," Ruth tells friends.

"As a matter of fact," the doctor often interjects, "food is usually the last thing on my mind during the day. I hardly even think about it."

"Except in the morning," Ruth adds with a wry smile, rounding out the discussion.

From the kitchen door, the doctor says, "Ruth, you are an exceptional woman. My life would be unimaginative without you."

Ruth doesn't hear such words every day, though her husband is not averse to sharing his feelings when so moved, often including an unintended malaprop. She knows he loves her and is reasonably certain he's been faithful all these years, as she has been to him, but he often seems to have so many other things on his mind. The practice, of course, is paramount. She knows, because she's heard it from sources she trusts—namely, his brothers—that he is not the most admired or popular dentist in town. He's always had detractors, even back in Vincennes, where he practiced fresh out of the university, but then name a dentist, or a physician for that matter, who doesn't. He reads the journals and attends the conventions and does his best, she knows for a fact, to stay up to date on both the technical and business sides of the enterprise.

"Dave's a student of the game," his brother George, also a dentist, has said more than once.

Everyone agrees that the technical side of the "game" is his strength. He has large, sure, steady hands, a passion for precision, and the knowledge and experience to operate confidently on his own. His bookkeeping, he will admit, could be improved.

"Well, I manage," he says when he and his wife have this discussion.

Ruth, who grew up in her father's *very* successful Oshinsky Brothers liquor business on the North Side, replies good-naturedly, "Oh, David, stop. Your books are a mess."

She has offered to straighten out her husband's accounts at least as often as he has offered to hire a cleaning lady, with the same effect. Neither one of them will say it, but the doctor clearly believes that the hands-on practice of dentistry requires the sensitivity and technique of an artist while updating the ledger is an accountant's work and, frankly, beneath him. He believes, as he tells his wife, he can manage those pedestrian tasks without outside help.

In the past few years, Dr. Rose has researched and now specializes in "sedation dentistry," in which, following the administration of a large capsule combining several legal pharmaceuticals, the patient is rendered blissfully unaware during even a long and complicated procedure. *Complete Dental Care While You Sleep!* is the intriguing if not entirely accurate tagline he has "borrowed" from a Chicago practitioner for a yet-to-be commissioned advertising campaign that he intends to run on select Twin Cities radio stations in the fall.

He hasn't told Ruth that he's hired Grace Montgomery, one of his regular patients, to help spread the word of the practice among young working women in the area. He wants to see how Mrs. Montgomery works out first. But he can envision a "squad" of engaging ladies—energetic and personable and proud of their bright smiles—talking up Dr. Rose among their peers at Dayton's, Young-Quinlan, First National, and sundry other stores, shops, banks, and offices in and around the downtown Loop, dispelling the hoary negatives about dentists and explaining the appeal of dental care while they "sleep." For each new patient one of them sends his way, he will hand the recruiter a crisp five-dollar bill.

Grace Montgomery has been his patient for almost a year. A typical child of the rural Midwest, she is reasonably pretty albeit a few pounds overweight, though her appeal was compromised by a youth and early adulthood of indifferent or incompetent dental care, which Rose has taken steps to correct. She has been working for Rose for only a couple of months and has directed three other women—one of them her sister—his way. If she becomes more productive, he may not need additional recruiters. He may also have to figure out a way to pay her less than five bucks for each recruit. He's enough of a businessman to know that much.

He drinks the black coffee Ruth puts in front of him and eats a bowl of Cream of Wheat with a piece of lightly buttered toast, the extent of today's breakfast. He feels vaguely unsettled this morning, and he's not entirely sure why. He has gauzy, weirdly disturbing images behind his eyes that he assumes to be remnants of last night's dreams. Rose dreams often and luridly, though he must not talk much in his sleep because Ruth, a light sleeper, rarely mentions anything he's said the next morning. Now, when he tries to remember what transpired last night before he came home, went to bed, and commenced dreaming, his recollections are as unsubstantial as the fragments in his head. He will do his best to forget them.

He thanks Ruth for breakfast and kisses her on the cheek. Then he walks into the living room, with its large bay window overlooking Zenith Avenue, the baby grand piano they bought for the girls, carefully matched overstuffed chairs and sofa, a fieldstone fireplace, and a floor-to-ceiling walnut bookcase. He has a few minutes to kill. He fills and lights one of the several meerschaum pipes he keeps in a rack on a side table and considers sitting down at the piano on which he was once reasonably proficient. Instead, he sighs deeply and puts Rachmaninoff's *Piano Concerto No. 3* on the big Magnavox phonograph Ruth gave him at Christmas.

From the kitchen he hears Ruth talking over the swelling music and turns down the sound.

"I forgot to tell you, David," she says, "an ambulance and police car drove past while you were sleeping. But they didn't have their sirens on, so maybe it wasn't anything important."

Fred MacMurray—Hiawatha County's chief of pathology, not the Hollywood film star—performs the autopsy midmorning.

He's a loose-limbed, good-looking, middle-aged man who, like the popular actor, seems almost preternaturally fit and happy, often humming a show tune as he supervises the plumbing of a decedent's stomach or sawing off the top of its skull. Today, though, even Dr. Fred, as he's known among the cops and his colleagues, is glum and terse.

Assisted by Alois Jensen, he bends over the lifeless body of Teresa Marie Kubicek Hickman, of Dollar, North Dakota. According to the document detectives found in her billfold, she was the wife of one Harold V. Hickman, a U.S. Army private stationed in Stuttgart, West Germany. Speaking into a tape recorder as he reviews the appearance and condition of the naked corpse, he describes her as a young, fair, slightly underweight Caucasian woman, five foot two and one-half inches tall, one hundred and two pounds. Aside from her nibbled fingertips, she bears no noticeable scars, birthmarks, or other visible imperfections, and would seem to have been constructed to lead a long and healthy life. She has beautiful teeth—white, straight, and reasonably well cared for—at least what he can see of them. ("The anterior portions of the anterior teeth," he will put in his report.) The rigor mortis prevents him from opening her jaw wide enough to make a comprehensive evaluation of the decedent's dental health.

When Dr. Jensen cuts into Mrs. Hickman's thorax and abdomen and removes one by one the woman's internal organs—he looks as though he's lifting produce out of a shopping bag—MacMurray can see the evidence of her demise. While her heart appears normal, her lungs are filled with fluid, which suggests suffocation. Her brain reveals trauma usually caused by an interruption in the flow of oxygen. Looking at her bruised throat, he notices that the hyoid bone, a tiny component of the larynx, has been crushed and there's been bleeding at the site.

Then MacMurray steps away from the table and pulls off his mask. "Death by homicide," he says for the record. "Cause of death: asphyxia due to manual strangulation."

He says this, too: "The victim was three months pregnant, and there's a trace of semen in her vagina, which tells us she had sex within a few hours of her death."

Robert Gardner is wolfing down a fried-egg sandwich in his sister's kitchen when the phone rings. The sudden noise shakes him out of a very pleasant erotic reverie.

"It's for you," Gwen says, handing him the receiver.

A chill runs up Robert's back. Nobody calls him here. If Pam wants to talk to him, she calls the bureau. What about Karl? Karl doesn't know he's here, much less his sister's number. Robert is being silly.

He's only slightly less nonplussed when he hears Miles Mckenzie's gravelly voice on the other end of the line. He experiences a familiar sinking feeling in the pit of his stomach. He's supposed to be off today, his first free day since last Saturday, and he's been looking forward to doing little more than dreamily reliving his newfound love life and fantasizing about its next installment.

"You live in Linden Hills, don't you, kid?" Mckenzie says.

"Uh, yeah," Robert replies. "For the time being anyway." Something else pricks the lining of his stomach.

"Well, a girl got murdered down there last night," Mckenzie says. "A guy walking his dog along the streetcar tracks stumbled across the body early this morning. If you look out your window, you'll probably see the cops knocking on doors."

Robert woke up half an hour ago with nothing but visions of Pam Brantley dancing in his head. But gradually, like a face emerging from a photographic negative, the image of the dead woman coalesced behind his eyes, pushing his lover aside. Lighting a cigarette and pouring himself a cup of coffee, he said good morning to Gwen, who was still in her curlers and bathrobe, and hoped she wouldn't ask about last night.

He wanted to think that the corpse was a bad dream, a nightmarish counterpart to his sweet dreams about Pam. But, no, it was real. It *is* real. Its ugly factuality has just been confirmed by the United Press bureau chief.

Before falling into a fitful sleep last night, Robert lay in bed and listened to Ray, his brother-in-law, saw logs, and his sister, now in her fourth month of pregnancy, go to the toilet a couple of times. He knew he couldn't call the police, much less tell Gwen and Ray, much less give the scoop to his employer. He *should*, of course, but he can't, not without having to explain what he was doing on the streetcar track at that hour, two blocks from where he was expected to be, and nowhere near the direct route he might have taken from the bus stop to his sister's apartment. He would run the risk of revealing the affair, destroying the Brantleys' marriage, and shaming himself in the eyes of his family. It's not inconceivable that he would also become a suspect in the girl's death.

"Gardner!" Mckenzie says. "Are you there?"

"I'm here, Chief."

Robert smiles in spite of himself. No one calls Mckenzie "Chief," but Robert can't bring himself to call the man either "Miles" or "Mr. Mckenzie." He's pretty sure it will be "Miles" when he can build up the nerve and if he has the job that long.

"Get out there and start talking to people," Mckenzie says. "I sent Pullman to the coroner's office, and Hickok's talking to the murder cops at the courthouse. That leaves you to sniff around the crime scene. Get some detail, some color. How are the neighbors dealing with a murder in their backyard—'Nothing like this ever happens around here,' that sort of thing. See if the girl lived in the vicinity, or if anybody was up and about that might have seen her. I got no one else to send down there right now. You're our man on the scene!"

Robert wonders if he should write down Mckenzie's instructions, not that the instructions weren't obvious and easy enough to remember. He'll have to wash up and brush his teeth and put on a sport coat and tie before he goes out. He's all at once both terrified by the possibilities and excited by the prospect of covering a murder, the first of his career. He could use another cup of Gwen's strong coffee, but he doesn't want to take the time.

"Gardner!" Mckenzie barks. "The guy who found the body—his name is Gerald Bergen, and the address I got for him is Thirty-three-eighteen West Forty-fourth Street. Talk to him first."

The folded sheet of pink paper stuck in the victim's billfold is a form from the Red Cross in Minneapolis, a voucher for the amount of $12.50, paid to Mrs. Harold V. Hickman, of Nine East Fifteenth Street, Apartment 204.

Anderson hands the paper to Curry, who reads it and smiles at his partner. The detectives are just leaving Hiawatha County General Hospital, where they watched MacMurray and his men disassemble the woman's body and render a preliminary judgment. To Sid Hessburg, who is trailing behind but not out of earshot, Anderson says, "Call that Red Cross office. The number's on the form. If they've got a file on the Hickmans, tell them we want to see it."

Mel passes the voucher to Sid, and Arne says, "If they don't want to give it to us over the phone, tell them we'll come down and get it."

Then to Curry he says, "Let's the two of us go see what we can see on Fifteenth Street."

On the sidewalk, Anderson spots a couple of familiar newspapermen and a photographer, notebooks and Speed Graphic at the ready, hustling self-importantly but without a clue toward the hospital's main entrance. The *Star*'s police reporter, a fat, red-faced man in a checkered hat named Oscar Rystrom, sees the detectives before they can duck around the corner and hollers, "Hey, Sarge, whadda we got here? A homicide? Rape? Who the fuck gets murdered in Linden Hills?"

In the considered opinion of Anderson and most of his colleagues, Rystrom, while no dummy, is a pain in the ass and so are most of his pals.

"A girl died," Arne says over his shoulder. "That's all I know, boys. Best of luck."

* * *

Grace Montgomery is in a snit.

She has called Dr. Rose's office three times this morning and gotten no answer—she could look up the doctor's home number in the phonebook, but she wouldn't have the nerve to call him there—then tried the Palace, where the Greek said he hadn't seen Terry since Thursday night. "She said she have a toothache," he told her and hung up.

Grace dug the photos out of Terry's underwear drawer and checked the backs to see if the photographer had written his name and phone number. He hadn't. It occurred to her to call Kenny Landa's folks back home, on the odd chance that Kenny had driven down to surprise her sister, and then thought that was a foolish idea for several reasons and would only cost her the price of a long-distance call, which Bud wouldn't be happy about when they got the phone bill.

The left side of her face, where Bud smacked her when she couldn't get Terry's baby to hush up this morning, has darkened and swelled. An hour ago she dumped the last of the ice cubes into a dishtowel and pressed it against the pain, and all she has now is a wet dishtowel dripping on her faded flowered housedress and the relentless throb of the bruise. The baby has been asleep for a couple of hours now, but that won't last much longer. He'll need a clean diaper and a bottle in another hour. Thank God Bud left early for wherever it is he goes this time of day.

If she had Dr. Rose's home number, she thinks now, she *would* call it, no matter how angry that might make him, or his wife if she answers the phone. Calling him at home would probably cost her the referral job, but she really doesn't care, she's that mad herself. In fact, at this hour, almost ten-thirty in the morning, after hardly two hours' sleep, she's angrier than she is worried. It wouldn't be the first time, after all, that "something came up," as Terry likes to explain her random absences and delays, having left the baby in Grace's hands and showing up the following morning smudged and disheveled and smiling.

As usual, Grace's righteous anger about her sister is curdled with jealousy. Whoever Terry may be with, including Dr. Rose, the guy most certainly would be an improvement over Bud. Once more, Grace burns with resentment of Terry's almost magical appeal to men of all ages, and jealous of Terry's blithe self-assurance and willingness to take chances. And, yes, she's jealous of Terry's baby, even though she feels she spends more time with the child than Terry does. Her own maternal experience has been limited to a hush-hush pregnancy and abortion several years ago.

Grace closes her eyes and listens to Harold Junior as he begins to fuss in the other room; then, after a few minutes, the baby quiets again. She may have dozed off herself when the apartment's doorbell buzzes.

"Police!" a man's voice calls out.

Grace's first thought is Bud. He's finally done it. He's gotten in a fight with a bigger, tougher guy, smashed up the car, or sassed off to a cop who stopped him for spitting in the street. She expects to open the door and see her husband slumped and bloodied between a pair of husky patrolmen.

There are two policemen all right, but they're wearing suits and Bud is nowhere in sight. One of the officers, the larger and older-looking of the two, holds out a leather case with a silver shield pinned to it, and introduces himself as Detective Sergeant Anderson of the Minneapolis Police Department.

"This is Detective Curry," he adds, nodding toward the shorter, dark-eyed, very handsome man beside him. She opens the door wider, steps to the side, and asks them to come in.

The men's hats and overcoats remind Grace that it's chilly outside this morning. They both look like her vision of big-city detectives—square-jawed, broad-shouldered, and formidable, direct in manner and gaze. Before either she or they can say another word she somehow knows what this is about.

It's not about Bud.

It's about Terry.

Terry is dead.

"Are you Mrs. Henry Montgomery?" Sergeant Anderson asks her.

For a split second she thinks, No, this *is* about Bud. When she says she is, the detective says, "We got your address from the Red Cross. They told us Teresa Hickman lives here. They said she's your sister. Is that correct?"

Grace backs into the room and sits down. She thinks she's going to throw up. "What about her?" she says.

The large detective doesn't answer right away—he's staring at the bruise on the side of her face. But she was right. This is about Terry. Terry is dead. Idiotically, she hopes it will be the dark-eyed detective who breaks the news.

Anderson says, "Your sister is dead, ma'am." He pauses, watching her, and then adds, "We think she was murdered."

No one says anything for a moment.

"We'd like to ask you some questions, if you don't mind," the dark-eyed detective, whose name she's already forgotten, says. "It's a homicide, so we need to move fast."

She nods and, always the pleaser, tries to smile.

"Your sister's body was found early this morning in the Linden Hills neighborhood," Anderson says. "The coroner says she'd been strangled."

Grace stares at him. She doesn't know what to say.

"Do you have any idea why she would be down in that part of town last night?"

"No," Grace manages. "Lincoln Hills? I don't even know where it is."

"*Linden* Hills," Curry says. "It's in the southwest corner of the city, out past the lakes."

Anderson says, "What happened to your face, ma'am?"

She reaches up and touches the bruise. She's all too aware of the pain, but the amount of swelling surprises her. "Oh," she says. "I slipped on the back stairs and bumped my head against the bannister." It occurs to her to be embarrassed by her bitten fingernails. Like Terry, she's never been able to break the habit.

The policemen look at her skeptically.

"Where's Mr. Montgomery?" Anderson asks.

"He drove over to his mother's," she says. "She lives in South St. Paul, and he goes over there on Saturdays."

"Did he hit you before he left?" Curry asks.

"No," she says. "I told you—I bumped my head on the stairs."

She would love to tell him the truth, but doesn't dare. It dawns on her that it's going to be safer, and probably easier, too, to lie to these men about almost everything. So that's what she decides to do—to lie at least as often as she tells the truth.

She is truthful when they ask if her sister has been living here since moving to Minneapolis, that the baby now squalling in the other room is Terry's child, and that Terry's husband, Harold Hickman Senior, is an Army private stationed in West Germany. She is truthful, too, when she tells them—after pausing to change the baby, heat his milk, and bring him into the living room, where she cradles him in the crook of her left arm while offering him the bottle—that her sister recently went to work at the Palace Luncheonette, a couple of blocks down Nicollet. When she's asked why her sister turned to the Red Cross for money, she truthfully explains that Private Hickman's monthly military allotment didn't arrive in February and she needed emergency cash for baby formula and diapers. She watches with some satisfaction as the dark-eyed detective writes down what she tells them in a notebook.

She catches her breath when Detective Anderson pulls the red billfold out of his overcoat.

"Does this belong to your sister?" he asks, and she nods. The billfold originally belonged to her, one of those precious teenage possessions that get passed down to younger siblings and become ugly and unfashionable in the process. Anderson opens it and holds the photo sleeves out toward Grace.

"I take it this is you," Anderson says, pointing to the young woman in the wedding dress.

Grace feels herself color.

"My first wedding," she says truthfully. "That was six years ago."

"And the soldier? Is that Private Hickman?"

"Yes," she says. "That's Hal. Right after basic training."

She looks at the snapshot of the old couple sitting behind a large cake. "Our Kubicek grandpa and grandma in North Dakota. This was their wedding anniversary ten years ago. They're both gone now."

All of this is the truth.

But when Anderson points to the photo of the other young man, the one in civvies, she says she doesn't know who it is, though of course she does. It's Kenny Landa, and she doesn't know why she lied about him. "It might be a guy Terry knew before she got married," she says, backtracking a few steps.

She closes her eyes and thinks about Kenny and starts crying.

"Terry," she says with an embarrassed smile, "knew a lot of guys. She's always been very popular." *Was always very popular.* But she doesn't bother to correct herself.

When the detectives ask about last night, Grace says she believed Terry went to work at the Palace. She says that's where Terry told her she was going. When Curry asks if her sister was wearing her waitress uniform when she left, Grace says she can't remember, but was pretty sure she was. When he asks if Terry had plans for after work, Grace says not that she knew of.

"Well," Anderson persists, "is there any place she liked to go when she wasn't working? A bar or the roller garden or a friend's apartment?"

Grace shakes her head. "She liked to be here at home, with me and the baby."

Anderson says, "Were you aware, Mrs. Montgomery, if your sister was seeing any men here in town? Did she have a boyfriend?"

Grace shakes her head again, her eyes filling with tears.

"No," she says sharply. "She loved her husband."

Maybe startled by the tone of Grace's voice, the baby starts to cry. The detectives exchange glances.

"When do you expect Mr. Montgomery home?" Anderson asks.

Grace says she isn't sure.

Curry looks at his watch, and Anderson says they'd like to look at her sister's things. Grace shows them into the apartment's second bedroom, which is hardly large enough for the three of them, what with its single bed, four-drawer dresser, and the bassinet that Grace says they borrowed from the landlady and hauled upstairs. A pair of cheap-looking suitcases are visible under the bed.

Grace knows it won't take the detectives long before they find the cheesecake photos among Terry's delicates. She will lie when they ask her about those, too, insisting that this is the first time she's seen them.

While Anderson pokes around in the bedroom, Curry walks into the bathroom, opens the medicine cabinet, and looks inside a narrow linen closet. He peeks into the kitchen and opens the door leading to the back stairs. Finally, he steps into the larger bedroom. Grace is embarrassed because the room is a mess, the double bed unmade and littered with clothing, both clean and dirty. There are also clothes on the rug, and God knows how many months' worth of dust on the floor beneath the bed.

She lies once more when she apologizes for the disarray and tells the dark-eyed detective that she's been under the weather for the past several days and is just now beginning to feel like herself again.

Curry doesn't seem to hear. Or maybe, she thinks, he doesn't care. He's no doubt seen bedrooms far worse than hers, bedrooms spattered with blood and gore and strewn with battered bodies. Then he looks at her and asks, "Did your sister get along with your husband?" She notices that his top two front teeth are not as white as the others. Probably replacements.

"She hated him," she says without thinking. "We all do."

She told the truth, more or less, and immediately wishes she hadn't.

At noon, Robert Gardner is on the No. 1 bus en route downtown. He needs to file a story, or at the very least combine what little he got from his desultory inquiries around the neighborhood with the presumably more substantial information Milt Hickok and Tommy Pullman picked up from the coroner and the police.

In the space of an hour he talked to a dozen individuals. Nobody had much to say beyond reiterating what a quiet and peaceful part of town the Linden Hills neighborhood has been for as long as anyone can remember. No one knew, or knew of, Teresa Marie Kubicek (he wasn't aware of her married name). No one saw or heard anything unusual last night.

Robert didn't know what he would have done if one of those citizens said he or she saw *him* beside the right-of-way between midnight and one o'clock this morning. He didn't need to worry. No one showed the slightest sign of having recognized him, despite the fact that he's been coming and going to and from his sister's place for the past few months.

Of course he would have loved for Pam—Karl, too, for that matter—to see him doing the work of a wire service reporter, but he knew he couldn't trust either Pam or himself to act surprised to see each other, as though less than ten hours earlier they hadn't been going at it like a pair of rabbits in the Brantleys' apartment. The more he thought about it, in fact, the more he feared bumping into either one of them. He therefore steered clear of the Brantleys' building, working the residences east of the crime scene and then staying on the north side of the streetcar tracks.

When he rang the bell at the address he'd been given for Gerald Bergen's apartment, he was told, presumably by his wife, that Mr. Bergen had been driven down to police headquarters for a statement.

On the bus downtown he wonders what Pam must be thinking, assuming a police officer or another reporter has knocked on her door. She knew that Robert left her building by the back door and would likely have walked down the dark right-of-way behind the buildings. Would she wonder whether he had seen either the victim or the killer—or maybe the murder itself? Would she have been worried about him? The thought of her concern both warms and excites him, and then freezes into a stab of panic that she might have said something without thinking, either to the police or afterward to Karl, that would raise suspicion not of murder but of adultery. She's a smart girl, he tells himself, but she has a tendency to say things without thinking, especially when she's excited.

"Oh my God," he imagines her exclaiming, her fingers splayed against her cheeks, "what if Robert saw—"

Oops!

Then he remembers that Karl would have returned to the apartment not long after he crept out the back. When the Brantleys learned about the murder, they surely would have considered the possibility that *Karl* might have seen something, unlikely as that would have been because he habitually walks from the bus stop via Forty-fourth Street and enters their building through the main door in front.

Maybe Pam will call Robert at the office—though how would she know he's at work? Last night he told her he was off today, and she knows better than to call him at Gwen's.

His head swims with possibilities as he gets off the bus at Fourth and Hennepin and jogs through the thin Saturday crowds—shoppers mainly—to the bureau's shabby office across the street from the *Star* and *Tribune* building on Portland. As he climbs, two at a time, the long, steep stairway to the second floor, it occurs to him, not for the last time, that he should be thrilled to be working on the first big story of his career. Instead, he's unsettled by the thought that the murder of that girl might ruin him.

Anderson and Curry leave the Montgomerys' apartment and drive along the Nicollet Avenue dogleg to Twelfth Street, where the Palace Luncheonette, a cheerless hole-in-the-wall that reeks of garlic, fried onions, and cigarettes, occupies the southeast corner. Faded color photos of the Acropolis, Parthenon, and other glories of ancient Greece scissored out of travel magazines, stuck in cheap frames, and hung too high on the dingy yellow walls provide the sole ornamentation. When the detectives walk in, the Saturday lunch crowd has shriveled to a pair of solitary diners reading the paper.

Curry flashes his shield, and Anderson asks the lone visible employee, a youngish woman with henna hair, to see the owner.

Saturday is the one day of the week Anatoli Zevos takes off, so his son, Tony, steps out of the kitchen dragging his bad leg and wiping his hands on a gray dishtowel.

Curry shows his badge to Tony and asks if Teresa Marie Hickman worked there.

Tony says, "Still does, though if she doesn't haul her sweet ass in here pretty soon I'll have to decide if she's still got the job. She had to see her name on the schedule."

Anderson steps around the counter and pushes Tony through a swinging door into the kitchen. As though on cue, the kitchen's only occupant, a swarthy short-order cook in a sweaty T-shirt and greasy apron, ducks out the back door into the alley.

"Hey!" Tony says. "What's this about?"

Curry is right behind Anderson.

"Teresa Hickman is dead, shitbird," Mel says. Mel is the Homicide Squad's "sweetheart" until something—and it doesn't have to be much—gets under his skin. Then you notice the outsized shoulders, meaty hands, and wide nose flattened by three-plus years in Golden Gloves.

Young Zevos looks at the cops. He's dark-complected, dark-haired, dark-eyed, and oily. To a Swede and an Irishman, he looks guilty of *something*. "I don't know nothin' about it," he says. He's also the kind of knucklehead who sounds as though he's lying even when he's not.

"She work last night?" Anderson asks him.

"No," Tony snaps.

He looks from the big cop to the smaller one, who, despite their four-inch, twenty-odd-pound difference, looks more dangerous at the moment.

"No," he says again, calming down a little, re-establishing, at least in his own eyes, a slice of the authority that comes with running a restaurant, even a dump like this one. "She was supposed to, but called in late afternoon, just before her shift started. Said she had a toothache."

"A toothache," Anderson says. "So she said she was going to stay home, go to bed, or what?"

Tony says, "She didn't say. She just said her tooth was killin' her."

He looks at the detectives with a smirk. "Maybe it was her tooth that killed her."

The detectives stare at him. They obviously don't have a sense of humor.

Anderson wants to ask the little greaseball if he ever fucked Teresa Hickman, or at the very least shoved his hands down her pants, willing to bet good money, judging by the looks of him and by what Arne has learned about the world, that he has—which may, but more likely may not, be relevant in this instance. Instead he asks, "Is there anybody in the neighborhood who can fix a toothache on a Friday night?"

Tony gets an odd look on his face, almost a look of amusement, as though it's a question he is asked a lot. He fumbles in the pocket of his wilted white shirt and pulls out a Lucky Strike.

"I don't know where she went," he says, patting his pants pockets for his lighter, "but I know there's a dentist a couple blocks up Nicollet who works nights and weekends. A Jew named Rose." He grins. "A Rose is a Rose is a Jew—ain't that what the man said?"

"Rose," Anderson says, ignoring the rest.

"Up the street above the Whoop-Tee-Doo Club," Tony says, smirking now at whatever crude allusion he attaches to the idiotic name.

Anderson glances at Curry, who looks over his shoulder at the deserted counter area out front and nods. Mel punches Tony Zevos in the face, knocking him on his back.

Tony looks up at Mel, blood bubbling in his nostrils and grouting his teeth.

"Jesus Christ!" he cries. "What the fuck you do that for?"

Curry massages the knuckles of his left hand as though contemplating additional action. "General principle," he says and follows Arne toward the front door.

CHAPTER 3

Waiting for the early edition of the *Star*, the driver cruises west on Thirty-eighth Street to Nicollet, hangs a right, and proceeds north. It's half past one on Saturday afternoon, and he's more than a little curious about the location of a certain black Packard.

He spent the morning in the single-car garage behind the stucco bungalow he shares with his wife and six kids on Bryant Avenue. There was nothing he *had* to do—the snow was gone so there was nothing to shovel or pull off the roof, and it was too early to cut the grass, what little of it might have survived the winter. He changed the Plymouth's oil the previous Sunday, and washed the car on Monday.

The garage is his refuge. Margaret knows better than to bother him out here, and the kids are spooked by the venomous spiders and giant centipedes he's convinced them lurk in its dark corners. He keeps a ratty canvas lawn chair and wobbly floor lamp inside, and after backing the car halfway into the driveway, he has room to read the paper and peruse the adult books and magazines he brings home from Shinders News and stashes behind the stacked snow tires.

When Margaret asked if he was going to Mass that afternoon, he told her he was working. "I'm running light this week," he said, not exaggerating, though he's always happy to have an excuse to avoid church. "Gonna work all weekend."

That morning, in bed, at the kitchen table with Margaret and the oldest kids, and then by himself in the garage, he kept thinking about what happened last night. Was it real or had he dreamed it? Was it another one of his "visions"—one of the waking fantasies that both excite and unsettle him?

In the car at noon, Cedric Adams, on the radio, announced that the body of a young woman had been found along abandoned streetcar tracks in south Minneapolis. Murders are still big news in the Twin Cities, especially if the murder takes place in a comfortable part of town and if the victim is a young, presumably attractive white girl or young woman. But Adams has nothing more to report than that. He doesn't have the victim's name or age or any information about the circumstances or cause of death, much less any possible suspects. Maybe the newscaster has the information, but is honoring the cops' request to withhold it for the time being.

Well, fuck Cedric Adams, the driver muses. And fuck the cops—bumblers and bullies all of them, the ones he's encountered. The afternoon's *Star* will surely provide at least the victim's name, and maybe her age and what caused her death.

Crossing Franklin, he keeps an eye peeled for the dentist's Packard. The Whoop-Tee-Doo Club is already open, but, by the looks of it, not doing much business yet, and the other businesses along this dreary avenue are either closed for the weekend or serving minimal traffic. And then, sure enough, he sees the black sedan, just where it was parked last night before he dozed off, on the south side of Fifteenth Street a few car lengths west of Nicollet. That must mean that Dr. Rose is upstairs, seeing patients.

The driver continues down Nicollet. At Fourteenth, he turns left and doubles around the block and a few moments later approaches the Packard from behind. There's no place to park so he stops alongside. The Packard's windows are rolled up so all he can see through the lowered passenger-side window of the cab is his own face and the reflection of the gray sky and the dingy brick building on the other side of the street.

For a moment, though, he sees the Packard as he saw it last night, after he woke from his drowse, realized the dentist and—he feverishly believed—the skinny blonde were no longer in his office above the nightclub, and set off to find them. He'd headed south on Hennepin and eventually wound up in the shadows along the east side of Lake of the Isles, among the several cars lined up on what in those days served as a lovers' lane.

He sees himself returning to the spot fifteen minutes later, after circumnavigating the lake and slipping into the spot vacated seconds earlier behind the dentist's sedan. As it happens, this is an area where he often parks between fares, to drink coffee from his Thermos, listen to dance music on the radio, and maybe see what he can see in the lovers' cars. Tonight he feels uncharacteristically lucky. What are the odds he'd find the Packard in this very spot?

He sees two people in the Packard's front seat, a man and a woman, sitting close but apparently not touching, only talking. It's a chilly night and the windows are rolled up so he doesn't hear their voices, yet it seems obvious, given the animated way they're speaking to each other, that they're arguing about something. He has no doubt that the man is the Jew dentist and the woman is the waitress from the Palace. The man in the car is tall, sitting high up behind the steering wheel, with dark hair (if he has a hat, he's not wearing it) and what seems to be, when he turns toward the girl, a long face, prominent nose, and mustache. The girl is bareheaded, but seems to be wearing a coat.

Then he sees the front passenger's door open abruptly and the girl step out. The man leans toward the door as though trying to keep her from leaving, but it's too late. He is saying something, though she doesn't seem to be listening if she can hear him after she slams the door. The driver watches her walk along the boulevard beyond the curb, past another four or five parked cars, their steamy windows opaque in the cool night air. But the girl doesn't look at the other cars, and who knows if their occupants, in their own heated entanglements, notice her as she passes.

As the driver watches, the girl walks to the corner, where Euclid Place juts away from the East Isles Parkway. She disappears from his line of sight and presumably heads up the hill toward Twenty-sixth Street and Hennepin Avenue beyond.

Now, on Saturday afternoon, a car behind the taxi honks, snapping the driver out of his reverie. Glancing at the impatient face in his mirror, he proceeds back to Hennepin, where he turns left into the sluggish downtown-bound traffic. He tries to return to the Lake of the Isles scenario, but can't reclaim it while he's driving.

Wide awake now and almost supernaturally alert, he decides to stop at the Palace on the odd chance that it was *not* the blonde who was murdered last night and he's either crazy as a shithouse rat or he's just had one hell of a titillating vision.

To Arne Anderson's surprise, when he and Curry reach Dr. H. David Rose's office above, no joke, the Whoop-Tee-Doo Club on the Fifteen-hundred block of Nicollet, Detectives Ferris Lakeland and Charlie Riemenschneider are already there. The detectives—large, loud, ursine men, all the larger in their shapeless fedoras and tatty storm coats— all but fill the dentist's small waiting room, leaving little space for Anderson and Curry.

"Where'd you come from?" Anderson asks the other pair, prepared to be angry if a couple of "his" men were operating outside his immediate direction.

"We've been over to the Red Cross on West Broadway," Lakeland says. He has an exceptionally wide, flat nose that, like Curry's, has been broken multiple times, though Ferris's injuries were sustained while walking a skid-row beat as a young cop. "Their records showed that a Dr. Wallace Ralston, who has an office on East Hennepin, saw Teresa Hickman a week ago—the Red Cross covered the cost—so we called him at his office."

Riemenschneider, his colorless eyes squinting behind round spec-

tacles, says, "He said he couldn't talk to us, doctor-patient confidenti-
ality and all that shit, but I told him we were investigating a homicide
and didn't give a rat's ass about doctor-patient this or that. He said,
'Okay, I'll tell you what I know.' He said that Mrs. Hickman was three
months pregnant and she'd told him that her dentist—none other
than Dr. H. Star-of-David Rose—was the baby's daddy. She told him
that Rose put her to sleep with a pill and then banged her."

Anderson has the not-unusual sensation of running alongside a
moving train, keeping up but just barely. The name Ralston rings a
bell, and he recalls a Dr. Ralston caught up in an abortion bust a few
years back, which probably explains the good doctor's sudden willingness to cooperate when Charlie raised his voice.

"Have you talked to Rose?" he says, nodding toward the closed
door off the waiting room.

"He's taking care of a patient," Riemenschneider says. "He stepped
out to see who it was, and we told him that one of his patients, Teresa
Hickman, had been murdered."

"What did he say?"

"He asked us to wait out here," Lakeland says. "I said, 'Sure.' There
ain't no back way out of this place, unless you count the fire escape. He
said we could look around while we waited. Not that there's much to
look at."

Riemenschneider says Rose's suite comprises the waiting room, a
slightly larger room with a single dental chair and the usual cabinets
and equipment where Rose sees his patients, plus a small room, more
like a closet, with shelves filled with chemicals and medications, and
yet another room, not much larger than the medicine closet, with a
wooden desk, a swivel chair, and a four-drawer filing cabinet.

The waiting room is warm. Lakeland sits down, pushes his hat off
his forehead, and grabs a six-month-old *Saturday Evening Post* from the
table. Riemenschneider and Curry light cigarettes and look around for
an ashtray, which is on a stand and stuck between an uncomfortable-
looking chair and a small sofa. The dusty ashtray looks unused.

Curry absently rubs the knuckles of his left hand, wondering, he'll tell Anderson, why exactly he hit Tony Zevos, knowing the answer and then forgetting the question. He'll tell Arne he thinks about the girl they knelt beside in the weeds this morning, and the naked corpse they watched the coroner cut apart a couple of hours later.

Arne will understand. He's been investigating homicides for almost eight years, yet will admit that he doesn't seem to be figuring it out.

Sometimes there's zero information to go on and no realistic expectation of a solution. Sometimes there's too much data, and the possibilities seem capable of overwhelming him. True, there aren't that many homicides to investigate in Minneapolis; there will likely be only a dozen by year's end, a small fraction of the totals racked up in bigger cities and cities with more mob activity and larger colored populations. Here, most of the homicides are simple matters, involving a berserk husband who comes home after losing his $3-an-hour job on the railroad and finds his wife in the spare bedroom with the landlord or a couple of dope-addled niggers who came out on the shitty end of a crap game. Both types are easily closed, and the rest of the city doesn't give a damn.

Then, on rare occasions, there's a homicide like this one, with an unlikely victim and an unlikelier location. A young, pregnant white woman, the wife of a GI serving in Europe and the mother of a toddler, is found in the weeds in one of the Twin Cities' tidiest precincts. How much info Arne and his men will be able to accumulate in the next few days remains to be seen, but the public's expectations, and therefore the expectations of the press and the politicians and the MPD brass, will hit them like a tidal wave.

The piercing whine of a dentist's drill and a sudden squeal from the other side of the closed door turns the detectives' heads. The whine stops, then starts up again and lasts several seconds, cutting like razor wire through the hundred years of collective memories in the waiting room.

Lakeland laughs.

"Fuck me if there's a worse sound in the world," he says.

The drill whines again behind the door.

Curry says, "I used to hide in the neighbor's fruit cellar. My ma and a couple of my aunts would walk up and down the block looking for me. Ma used to whip my ass when she found me, but I didn't mind the whipping half as much as the drill."

"I ran away from home once to avoid it," says Riemenschneider. "Another time I begged my brother to yank out a bad tooth with pliers, which he did, thinking I wouldn't have to go to the dentist, which I did anyways. Turned out my brother, the dumb shit, yanked out the wrong fucking tooth."

"Our dentist, old Doc Wessel up on Johnson Nordeast, would shortchange us on painkiller," Lakeland says. "I told my old lady once, 'Ma, Wessel didn't give me the novocaine,' and she said, 'Of course he did. You just have a low threshold for pain.'" Ferris laughs. "Low threshold, my ass! That fucker was a sadist!"

Arne says nothing, but he has vivid memories, too. His stepfather marching him up the stairs to Dr. Jurgensen's office above the Sailor Tap at Forty-second and Cedar, shoving him through the door, and holding his skinny bicep in a vice grip while Arne surveyed the dismal waiting room, usually occupied by a school acquaintance or two, all of them sniffling and trying not to show how afraid they were. There was a bowl of penny toys—a tiny plastic airplane, a whistle in the shape of a race car, a scotty dog—that a young patient could pick as a "prize" when the appointment was over, not that anyone wanted anything more than getting out of that place.

Anderson tries to remember what happened to Dr. Jurgensen after Arne enlisted and left the neighborhood. Word had it that he fell out of a boat and drowned on a fishing trip up North, though Arne preferred the speculation that an unnamed patient tied the dentist to his chair and bored the largest drill at hand into his forehead, skipping the novocaine.

The door to the inner office swings open. A tall, slightly stooped, middle-aged man with a long face and a mustache stands back while a large woman in a polka-dot dress with perspiration stains under the arms walks out, holding a hanky up to the left side of her mouth.

Dr. Rose glances at the men in his waiting room, but doesn't appear unsettled by their presence.

He says to the woman, "The anesthetic will wear off in a few hours, dear. Take a couple of aspirin if the pain persists. You may also wish to put some ice in a towel and hold it against your jaw. If the extraction site still hurts on Monday, please come back in."

Ignoring the officers, Rose waits with his hands folded while the woman roots around in her purse.

"Ten dollars," he says, as though he's just sold her something nice for her table and needs to remind her of its cost. He thanks her when she hands him two crumpled fives. "Enjoy the weekend," he says as the outer door closes behind her.

Rose is wearing a white shirt and striped necktie beneath his starched white jacket. Anderson notes that he has large, well-formed hands. He appears tired, but not in the least bit worried or frightened.

Arne holds out his leather-bound shield, thinking that this will be the first time he's ever questioned a dentist about anything.

"We'd like you to come downtown with us, Doctor," he says. "We also want to look around your office and take a peek inside your car."

He wonders if Rose will want to see a warrant. Rose doesn't.

Rose's dark-eyed gaze moves from one detective to another. He appears curious and even mildly amused, as though he's been invited to take part in a stunt of some kind. He says, "This has to do with Mrs. Hickman, the officer told me," he says, nodding toward Lakeland. "Well, yes, of course. Mrs. Hickman was a patient of mine. I saw her last night. It's terrible what happened."

He fumbles in one of his pants pockets and withdraws a ring of keys.

"These are for my car, a black Packard Clipper parked around the corner on Fifteenth," he says. "This one is for the office door. Please turn the lights off when you're finished."

This is not an arrest so there's no need for handcuffs. It will be a "conversation" between investigators and a cooperative witness, Anderson tells the dentist. Arne hopes, of course, that it will be more.

While Lakeland and Riemenschneider begin to poke around the office, opening cabinets and drawers and riffling through papers on the dentist's desk, Anderson and Curry follow Rose down the long flight of stairs and out into the gray afternoon. They can hear the jukebox in the Whoop-Tee-Doo Club—the Crew Cuts singing "Sh-Boom"—though it's nothing like the cacophony that defines the place after dark.

Lakeland will tell Einar Storholm to pick up Rose's car keys and drive the Packard downtown for a going-over by the forensics crew. Presumably, Hessburg and LeBlanc are back from Linden Hills, maybe with some helpful information, though Arne isn't optimistic. The victim didn't live there, and the odds of anyone coming forward with anything useful are shrinking by the hour.

He wonders why Grace Montgomery didn't say anything this morning about her sister's dental appointment. It's inconceivable that she didn't know about it, especially if Teresa Hickman's toothache was bad enough for her to skip work and make an afterhours appointment. He wonders if Grace called Rose after he and Mel left her apartment. He wonders when Bud Montgomery will come home from wherever he's been keeping himself. Grace's surprise at the detectives' news seemed to be genuine, but her apparent lack of curiosity about details might indicate a foreknowledge of events. Until Arne learns differently, Bud is as credible a suspect as Dr. Rose.

He'll station Curtis Wrenshall and a couple of officers outside the Montgomerys' building to pick up Bud when he shows himself. He will also send Sid and Frenchy to talk some more to Tony Zevos and his employees about last night and the luncheonette's clientele.

Everybody on the eight-man murder squad plus what other bodies Augie Fuller can commandeer will be involved in this one.

Suppose, Arne muses, that Teresa Hickman was walking along Nicollet Avenue after her appointment and some scumbag leaving the Whoop-Tee-Doo followed her down the street and around the corner and attacked her in the shadows between buildings. But it was Friday night and the streets around the club were no doubt crowded. If her assailant had forced her into a car, her clothes would likely have been in disarray, and there would have been marks on her body. But she hadn't been roughed up or beaten. There were no broken bones (besides the hyoid) and nothing on her skin except the bruise on her neck. She'd had sex with someone not long before she died, but there was no sign of the sex being forced. So she probably went willingly, on foot or in his car, with someone she knew at least casually.

It will take ten minutes to get from Rose's office to police headquarters in the courthouse. Mel drives while Arne sits in back with the suspect. Arne sees Mel looking at Rose in the rearview mirror. Arne himself glances at the dentist when there's a reason to look in his direction. Rose is not panicking and does not seem to be anticipating and rehearsing what he must surely believe will be more than a casual conversation. He did not seem surprised or inconvenienced when told about Teresa Hickman's death and the need to go downtown in the middle of a Saturday afternoon. He said he didn't have another patient scheduled today, but this couldn't have been the way he expected to finish his workweek.

Anderson tries to remember the last time he interrogated a Jew. It was probably one of Bunny Augustine's hoods, though Arne can't recall who or when. (He's seen but never spoken to the Northside crime boss himself.) One thing for sure: Arne has never seen anyone who looked more like a Jew than Rose. It's almost comical—the long face, the large nose, the dark hair, and sallow complexion. In fact, now that he thinks about it, you could throw a towel over the man's head and put him in a robe, and he'd be the spitting image of one of the Pharisees in the picture books Arne used to page through in the basement of Calvary Lutheran Church when he was a kid.

As Mel turns onto Fourth Street and looks for a parking spot in the lee of the fortress-like courthouse, Arne wonders what he's going to say to Lily when he gets home this evening. Lily is the Jew he sleeps with, the Jew he once thought he loved, and the Jew who's capable of making this case more complicated than it probably is already.

He will say nothing about the case to her tonight and hope there will be reason to arrest Bud Montgomery in the morning.

Responding to a sudden inclination that he attributes to self-preservation, the driver decides to skip the Palace and proceed instead across the river and onto the University of Minnesota's East Bank campus. School is still in session, which means there will be a lot of girls around, strolling down the streets in twos or threes or on the arms of boyfriends, or lounging in front of one of the bookstores or at the soda fountain in Gray's drugstore in Dinkytown.

He finds a parking spot a few doors down from the drugstore and grabs the last free stool at the lunch counter. He picks up the *Star*'s first evening edition, orders a cup of coffee and a slice of devil's-food cake, and reads about the young woman found murdered early this morning in south Minneapolis.

Besides the woman's name, age, and address, the brief article at the top of the front page has little information. Teresa Marie Hickman was the wife of Army Private Harold V. Hickman, who is reportedly en route to Minneapolis on emergency furlough from West Germany, and the mother of an eighteen-month-old child, Harold Hickman Junior. She was a graduate of Dollar High School, in Dollar, North Dakota, was living with her sister and brother-in-law, Mr. and Mrs. Henry Montgomery, until she could find permanent lodging, and worked part-time at the Palace Luncheonette on Nicollet Avenue.

Teresa Marie Hickman. He'd guessed the girl's name was either Susan or Sally—who knows why? Unlike most girls who catch his fancy, this one didn't remind him of anyone else, say one of the neighborhood girls he'd followed around or stared at during Mass at Holy Name, or one of the nubile teens Margaret has once in a while hired to watch their younger kids. A couple of them have been Susans and at least one was a Sally.

According to the paper, the police are saying nothing about the investigation, other than that all available personnel have been assigned to the case. An MPD bigwig, Inspector Edwin Evangelist (speaking of names!), is quoted as saying, "This heinous crime will be promptly solved, and its perpetrator will be apprehended. The citizens of Minneapolis can count on us."

An even shorter story, enclosed in a box alongside the main story and carrying a United Press byline, describes the "shock, bewilderment, and outrage" of the "sleepy" Linden Hills neighborhood where the victim's body was found. Gerald Bergen, who lives on West Forty-fourth Street, found the body alongside the streetcar tracks behind an apartment building while walking his dog, a six-year-old Dalmatian named Jocko, shortly after dawn this morning. Bergen told the reporter that he at first mistook the body for an "armload of old clothes." A traveling pharmaceuticals salesman, Bergen says he saw no one else out and about at the time, approximately six-fifteen a.m.

Other residents said they couldn't recall the last homicide in the neighborhood, although there'd been a couple of suicides and at least one accidental drowning in Lake Harriet during the past few summers.

For want of anything better to do, other than cruise the campus for a while, the driver will stop at the company's garage near Seven Corners and get the cab washed inside and out. It hasn't been a week yet, but the construction sites he's driven through left enough dust and grime on the Plymouth's canary finish to justify another hose-down. When he inspected the interior earlier today, he found only a used lipstick tube, a couple of Juicy Fruit gum wrappers, an unwrapped Ramses-brand condom (which he tucked away in his billfold), and a man's monogrammed (*JDM*) handkerchief. Still, a thorough cleaning seems a good idea.

His brother-in-law, Fat Jack O'Shaughnessy, who owns the company with a couple of downtown businessmen, gives him the stink eye when he pulls in. If a driver gives him the opportunity, O'Shaughnessy will bug the guy about how few fares he's been carrying and how the guy's got to put in more time on the street, as though any of his twenty drivers could keep up with the bigger outfits nowadays. Before O'Shaughnessy can collar him—"Hey, Juice! Let's talk about your numbers!"—the driver slides back behind the wheel and exits the garage.

Even if he picks up a fare or two, he'll be home in time for supper, though too late to join Margaret at five o'clock Mass.

It's almost three p.m. before the small group of policemen, a single civilian, and a department stenographer assemble in the office of Detective Captain August Fuller on the third floor of the courthouse.

Fuller, looking uncomfortable as usual, sits behind a large, nearly empty wooden desk. Dr. Rose sits in a straight-backed wooden chair directly in front of the desk. Detectives Anderson and Curry sit on either side of him, far enough away to dispel any impression that Rose is a prisoner, but close enough in case he forgets that he is. A petite spinster named May Grey sits off to one side of the desk, a steno pad resting on her bony knee. Inspector Ed Evangelist stands in the office doorway, his bloodshot eyes swimming in his bloated face, the elephant not quite in the room.

"Dr. Rose," Augie Fuller begins, "nobody here is accusing you of a crime. You may end this, *uh,* conversation at any time, and, of course, you are free to call an attorney."

Rose sits with one long leg crossed over the other, his large, white hands folded atop his right knee. Arne is quite sure the man hasn't changed his expression since he left his dental office almost an hour ago.

"I understand," Rose says.

Fuller, glancing down at the paper in front of him, leads Rose through the basic data while May Grey, the picture of fussy competence, takes her meticulous shorthand off to the side.

"For the record, your full name, please."

"My name is H. David Rose. The *H.* is for Herschel." He turns his head toward the stenographer and smiles slightly. "That's *H-E-R-S-C-H-E-L,*" he says. "Herschel with a *C.*"

May Grey casts him a glance, looking not especially grateful for the help.

"Date and place of birth, please."

"June 18, 1908. Vincennes, Morrison County, Minnesota."

"Are you married?"

"Yes. To Ruth Evelyn Rose. Maiden name Oshinsky. With a *Y*. We've been married for almost twenty years and have two daughters, Margot and Lael—*L-A-E-L*, Margot with a *T*—ages thirteen and eleven, respectively."

"And your home address?"

"Thirty-nine-fourteen Zenith Avenue South. Minneapolis."

The detectives know exactly where he lives, of course—five blocks north of where Teresa Hickman's body was found.

"You're a dentist."

"Yes. I maintain a practice at Fifteen-twenty-eight Nicollet Avenue South, second floor. I've had a solo practice at that address since I moved to the city in 1940."

"What did you do during the war, Doctor?"

"I tried to enlist, but was rejected because of inherited arthritis in my shoulders and knees."

"Is yours a general practice, Doctor?"

"Yes. Men, women, and children."

"But I understand the majority of your patients are women. Is that correct?"

"Well, that's possible, I suppose. I couldn't give you an exact percentage."

"Is it kosher to call you 'Doctor,' Mr. Rose?" This is Big Ed butting in from the doorway.

Rose turns his head in Evangelist's direction, surprised, and perhaps for the first time in the past hour a bit annoyed.

"My diploma from the University of Minnesota avers the fact that I'm a Doctor of Dental Surgery."

"But that doesn't make you a real doctor, does it?" Evangelist says. "Not like the guy who listens to my ticker and every once in a while checks my plumbing." He winks at the stenographer and grins. "My apologies, Miz Grey."

Rose looks back at Fuller, who momentarily shuts his eyes, a sign of either weariness or exasperation.

"That individual," Rose says, "would be an MD. A Doctor of Medicine."

"A *physician*," Evangelist persists, pleased to have made the point.

May Grey has stopped writing. She looks at Fuller as though for a sign.

Augie says, "Did you have a patient named Teresa Marie Hickman, Dr. Rose?"

"Yes," Rose replies. "But she's listed in my office ledger as Mrs. Harold V. Hickman."

"How long was she your patient?"

"Well, for a couple of months, or a little more. Since sometime in January or February. I know it was after Christmas."

"Christmas?" From the doorway Evangelist clears his throat, a loud, phlegmy hack. "So you celebrate our Savior's birth?" he says.

This time Rose doesn't turn toward the inspector. Looking straight ahead, he says, "We put up a Christmas tree for our daughters, who have many Christian friends, and exchange gifts amongst ourselves. So, yes, we celebrate Christmas."

"But you *are* a Jew, aren't you?"

"Ruth and I describe ourselves as nonobservant Jews. We don't attend services on a regular basis."

"You're circumscribed, I presume," Evangelist says.

"Yes, I am."

"How would you describe your sex life?"

Rose sighs, smiles slightly, and says, "Not what it used to be." Making Big Ed laugh.

Fuller, in high color now and eager to regain control of the conversation, says, "What brought Mrs. Hickman to your office in January, Doctor?"

Rose says, "Her sister, Grace Montgomery, has been a patient of mine since last fall. She referred me to Terry—I mean Terry to me. Mrs. Hickman, I'm talking about."

Augie pauses, lifts the top sheet of papers on his desk, then pulls a well-used handkerchief out of a back pocket and blows his nose before pushing on.

"You treated Mrs. Hickman last night, didn't you?"

"Yes, I did. She had a seven-thirty appointment."

"How long would you say she was in your office?"

Rose appears to be thinking. "Oh, I'd say she was in the chair for two and a half or three hours."

"Three hours?" Fuller and Anderson say at the same time. May Grey looks up from her notebook. Curry looks past Rose to make eye contact with Arne.

"Permit me to explain," Rose says. "I practice a technique, not uncommon in the profession, called sedation dentistry. For patients who need a significant amount of work, or for those who have a low tolerance for pain or a high level of anxiety, I make up a pill—a capsule—usually containing one and a half grams of Seconal, which is a barbiturate derivative, and the contents of a common headache remedy, such as Anacin. I provide the capsule instead of, or in addition to, an injection of novocaine."

"And this capsule puts them out?" Fuller asks.

"It puts the patient in a deeply relaxed state."

"For three hours?"

"Sometimes for even four hours or more. A procedure rarely takes that long, but the patient will be drowsy for a while afterward. If it's late and I don't feel they can safely navigate their way home, I will arrange for a taxi or, in some instances, escort the patient home myself."

"How did Mrs. Hickman leave your office last night?"

"Well, I helped her down the stairs and walked her to the entrance of her apartment building around the corner. I thought the fresh air would pep her up."

"What time was that?"

"I can't say for certain. Probably about eleven. I don't wear a watch"—Rose raises his left arm, exposing a bare wrist—"but that's probably pretty close."

Anderson says, "You walked her to the entrance of the building where she's staying with the Montgomerys?"

"Yes."

"Then what?"

"I watched her go into the building and up the stairs to her sister's apartment. I waited for about a minute—enough time for her to enter the apartment—and walked back to the office. I needed to catch up on my books. And then, probably because I hadn't eaten all day and felt a little woozy, I sat down and dozed a while on the settee in my waiting room. I do that sometimes, before driving home."

"So the last time you saw Mrs. Hickman she was entering her sister's apartment building at approximately eleven p.m.?" Fuller says.

"Yes."

"Do you remember what she was wearing?"

"Well, it was chilly last night, so I know she had a coat on. A short coat or a jacket. I believe it was either dark blue or dark green."

Fuller stares at Rose and clears his throat. Anderson knows his boss isn't sure how to proceed. Augie has spent most of his police career investigating property crimes and has only since last fall been running the homicide unit. He's sure as hell never overseen a case like this one.

"Did you know that Mrs. Hickman was pregnant?" Augie says at last.

Rose says, "I always ask my patients about their general health. Last night, Mrs. Hickman volunteered that she'd missed her period. She didn't seem very concerned, even though her husband has been overseas for several months."

Fuller's office is silent for a moment. The room is stuffy, and there's a feeling of restlessness among its occupants. Augie says, "Well, that's right. If Mrs. Hickman was pregnant—and according to her autopsy this morning she was—Private Hickman, over there in West Germany, could hardly have been the father." He pauses, and then asks, "She didn't happen to say who the father might be, did she?"

"Well, she said she thought it might be me," Rose says.

The room is silent for another moment.

"What did you say to that?" Fuller asks.

Rose, his legs crossed, his immaculate hands sitting atop his knee, raises his eyebrows and says, "I told her I didn't understand how that could be possible."

"And why couldn't that be possible?"

"Because I've never had sexual relations with the woman."

Evangelist, after a few moments of quiet, can no longer restrain himself. "*Dr.* Rose," he says, "did you murder Teresa Hickman?"

"Of course not," Rose says. "Why on earth would I murder one of my patients?"

In the ensuing silence, all eyes stare at the dentist. Not even Big Ed says a word.

Finally, Rose looks around the room at his interlocutors and says, "If that will be all, Captain, I should return to my office. I still have that paperwork to catch up on."

Augie sighs and says, "That will be all, Doctor. Your car is downstairs."

Grace Montgomery sits in the late afternoon gloom with the baby, who's content for now to sleep in his aunt's ample lap. Bud has not returned to the apartment. He is not, despite what she told the detectives, visiting his mother in South St. Paul; his mother lives with her latest boyfriend in Hudson, Wisconsin. Grace isn't sure why she gave the policemen false information. But then she's not sure of anything right now, including her husband's actual whereabouts.

Grace, always the "responsible" sister, has taken care of business since the detectives left. She called her widowed father in Dollar and tracked down Kenny Landa through his sister, one of Grace's school chums, who now lives in Grand Forks. Grace gave her father the few details she had about Terry's death as straightforwardly as she could manage, and, after a few moments of silence, he responded in kind. Hanging over her like a gravid cloud was the knowledge that her father had always doted on Terry while only tolerating her. A man of few words, he said little in response to Grace's news and asked few questions, almost as though

Grace's bad news was not news at all, or anyway didn't come as much of a shock. He thanked her for the call and hung up before she could.

Kenny Landa, when she finally reached him in Fargo, where he'd recently taken a job at a used car lot, was, by contrast, thunderstruck. Kenny wasn't the brightest boy in North Dakota, but Grace was surprised to have to explain and repeat the news as though she was describing a complicated world event to a third grader. When he didn't reply for a few seconds, she realized that he was crying.

"Kenny," she said, waiting for him to collect himself, "will you do me a favor and pick up my dad in Dollar and drive him to Minneapolis if he wants to come down? I don't trust him driving by himself anymore." Kenny, bless his heart, said that he would, though, as it turns out, she won't see either Kenny or her father until Terry's funeral in North Dakota.

Someone at the Minneapolis Red Cross told her that the organization had begun the paperwork to fly Hal Senior home from West Germany. Apparently, the local authorities had alerted the organization. Factoring in logistics, the international time changes, and the vagaries of the weather, a kindly woman told Grace on the phone, Private Hickman should arrive in the Twin Cities no later than Tuesday evening.

Grace turns on a lamp and spreads a blanket on the living-room rug. She checks Hal Junior's diaper and puts him down on the blanket, then lights a cigarette and goes to the window. The cars on the street have switched on their lights, and the few people on the sidewalk are moving briskly in the gloaming, their coat collars turned up and their necks drawn into their collars. "April," she remembers learning in school, "is the cruelest month."

For the first time today the tears roll freely down her cheeks. She loved Terry as much as she hated her, admired her as much as she envied and resented her and wished she was dead.

As the oldest of the four Kubicek kids, Grace was the leader when they were little, but her authority had evaporated by the time they reached adolescence.

The two boys, duplicitous Albert and oafish Lyman, either ridiculed or ignored Grace while celebrating "baby Terry." Grace struggled with her weight, a difficulty telling the truth, and a temptation to take things that didn't belong to her, which got her into trouble in town. Terry stole stuff, too—lipstick and movie magazines and Butterfinger candy bars from the Dollar Rexall—but Terry rarely got caught and, if she did, could usually wiggle her way out of the bind, especially if her accuser was a man. When Terry turned twelve and began attracting serious male attention, her brothers kept a protective eye on her. No one bothered about Grace until local ne'er-do-well Otto Garley knocked her up after the '47 Harvest Whirl, quietly paid for an abortion in Mandan, and then moved to parts unknown under threat of death from her brothers.

Their mother, a tiny, temperamental beauty who believed she could speak in tongues, spent much of her time, once the kids were old enough to fend for themselves, traveling the Dakotas, Montana, and Canada's western provinces with a Pentecostal tent preacher from Winnipeg named Inman Akers. Despite a rumored relationship with the raven-haired Bible-thumper, Marva Kubicek taught her daughters that sex was painful and dirty and even in marriage must be indulged only for procreation. If Marva noticed the attention her younger daughter was beginning to attract, she apparently believed she could pray it away.

Not coincidentally perhaps, more than one of the older men around Dollar in those days observed that Terry looked a lot like Marva had in her teenaged years—a small, sleek, fair-haired siren whose big eyes, sly smile, and provocative gait could make the most righteous man think salacious thoughts. Grace, meanwhile, had the springy reddish hair and thickset body of their father's family. Like most everybody in those days, three of the four Kubicek kids had crooked teeth riddled with caries and the occasional abscess, while Terry alone, though not immune to cavities and toothache, was, like her mother, blessed with a beautiful natural smile.

Then, one after another, Grace's mother and brothers died. Albert was killed in action in Korea on Christmas Day 1950, and

Lyman suffocated after falling into a corn-filled silo during the late summer of 1953. Marva, who was always susceptible to infection, contracted pneumonia during an Akers "crusade" in Alberta and died in a Calgary hospital almost halfway between the passings of her sons. Grace had taken some satisfaction in delivering the news of Albert's death to Terry, interrupting her sister's pleasure in the backseat of Kenny Landa's Pontiac one snowy night outside of town.

Six months after Lyman died, Walter Kubicek sold the farm to a neighbor and moved into a tiny bungalow in town. Terry moved in with Kenny for a while, then met and six weeks later married Kenny's slightly older, taller, better-looking cousin, Harold Hickman. The newlyweds settled down in the knotty-pine-paneled basement of his parents' house in Grand Forks, where Harold Junior was presumed to have been conceived. The couple stayed there unhappily—Harold's parents made it clear that they never trusted Terry—until Hal enlisted and went off to basic training in Kansas.

Grace was gone by that time. The day after she turned twenty-one, she married another hometown no-account, Riley Read, whom she divorced after six months of mutual indifference. A few weeks later, she took a Greyhound bus to the Twin Cities, where she got a job clerking in the credit department of the JC Penney store in downtown Minneapolis and shared an efficiency apartment with a girl from Dollar. She met Henry Montgomery at Jax Cafe, where she had taken a second job waiting tables at night. Bud was the bad-tempered son of an alcoholic Minneapolis fireman, but he had broad shoulders, an attractive smile, and a taciturn manner that reminded Grace of *her* father.

For reasons having more to do with nostalgia than anything else, Grace insisted, when she married Bud a few months later, that the nuptials be held in Dollar. At the drafty little Lutheran church no one in the family had attended for years, Terry was the maid of honor and, because Bud had no brothers and none of his few Minneapolis friends made the trip to North Dakota, Kenny Landa served as best man. During the reception in the church parlor, Bud told Terry that *she* was the Kubicek girl he wanted to fuck that night.

But now Grace is thinking about Dr. Rose.

Was he the last person to see her sister alive?

Terry was sure she was pregnant and that the baby was his. Terry told Grace that she and Rose had sex during her appointment in late January, and that's undoubtedly when it happened. Terry said she was going to tell him about the baby last night, after he took care of her toothache. That was odd, actually kind of comical, Grace thought, but that was Terry for you. Maybe Terry liked Dr. Rose, was not put off by his age and his Jew looks, and when he'd finished in her mouth last night maybe they had sex again. Grace's jealousy flickers on and off like a defective lightbulb.

Then, before she can sink too deeply into her anger and hurt, she hears an unmistakable sound on the stairs. Even in the carpeted hallway, Bud's footfalls sound like the hammer blows of doom.

It's half past seven this Saturday evening when Arne Anderson returns to the apartment on Chicago. Lily isn't home, and her unexpected absence makes him uneasy. Then he remembers that she was doing a friend a favor and took an extra shift—she's one of three staff librarians at Mount Sinai Hospital—and then planned to have dinner with her ailing mother in St. Louis Park.

Arne is drinking whiskey out of a water glass and reading the *Star*'s sports page when Lily gets home at nine-thirty. She looks tired, but not unhappy to see him, seemingly in a better mood than when he left this morning. (He remembered to bring home his breakfast plate and silverware, and to rinse them off in the kitchen sink.) He's happy to see her and wonders if she's up for sex tonight.

"That murdered girl in the paper this afternoon—is that where you were today?" she says, after pouring herself a glass of red wine and sitting down beside him on the couch.

"Afraid so," he says, looking at her.

Lily Kline will be thirty-five in September. She is slightly built and dark-eyed, not particularly attractive, but sensual in the vaguely exotic, Eastern European way that Arne associates with Jewish women.

"Have you arrested anyone?"

"No," he says.

He wonders, for maybe the tenth time in the last hour, what he's going to tell her about Dr. Rose. "We're looking at a handful of suspects. A guy where she worked and a brother-in-law who beats up her sister. Maybe some of the knuckleheads that hang around the neighborhood, too."

"Was the girl raped?"

Arne shakes his head, taking a sip of his whiskey. "Didn't seem to be," he says softly, thinking about Teresa Hickman's still, small form on the coroner's gurney and also the cheesecake photos they found in her dresser. "She had sex not long before she died, but MacMurray said he didn't think it was forced. She was dressed when we found the body, and her clothes weren't torn or disheveled. She was missing a shoe, is all."

"Poor thing," Lily says.

Arne takes another swallow. This one drains the glass. He knows he shouldn't, but he can't help himself, so he pushes on.

"She had a dental appointment last night. A dentist named H. David Rose, on Nicollet Avenue south of the Loop. Ever hear of him?"

She gives him a look.

"Why? Because he's a Jew?"

Arne shrugs. He's relieved to hear her chuckle.

"We don't all know each other," she says.

Arne gets off the couch and pads into the kitchen for a refill. Lily has lived here for almost three years, Arne not quite six months, though he feels as if it's been longer than that. He doesn't give any thought anymore to either Charlotte or Marianne, his ex-wives—luckily, for everyone, there are no children—much less to the several apartments and the one cramped bungalow he and Marianne rented on the North Side. He has shacked up with a couple of other women, too, in various locations around town, but he can hardly remember either the women or the addresses.

"I just thought, you know—all the doctors at Mount Sinai—"

"All the *Jew* doctors at Mount Sinai, you mean," she calls after him, seeming to enjoy this in her way.

He appears a moment later with his tumbler half-full. "Yeah, that's what I meant."

"Well, no, I've never heard of *that* Jew," she says. "You know, of course, the difference between a physician and a dentist? The dentist wasn't smart enough to get into medical school."

It's an old joke. Arne forces a smile.

"This dentist strikes me as pretty smart," he says, sitting down again. "We brought him downtown and had a long talk, Augie, Mel, fucking Ed Evangelist, and me. He told us about this procedure of his—sedation dentistry, he calls it. He gives the patient a barbiturate and a headache remedy that knocks them out for several hours. Ever hear of anything like that?"

"No," she says, looking at Arne over her wine glass. "But what do I know about dentists, except I hate them? Well, did you arrest the dirty Jew and give him the third degree?"

Arne sighs. It's been a long day. He's tired and now halfway drunk. He wants to fuck Lily, or somebody, and go to sleep.

"No," he says. "But we have reason to give him a good look. He told us that when he saw the girl last night, she accused him of being the father of the baby she was carrying. We're going to talk to him again tomorrow."

"So whoever murdered the girl murdered a child, too—the unborn baby?"

Arne closes his eyes.

"The fetus doesn't count, Lil, as you well know. Maybe someday, but not now, not under the law. Give me a break, will you? One victim is enough."

CHAPTER 4

When Anderson arrives at the Hiawatha County Courthouse a few minutes before ten on April 10—Easter Sunday—Charlie Riemenschneider is waiting for him. Mel, Ferris, and the
other members of the squad are on their way in despite the holiday, but
for the moment Arne and Charlie have the office to themselves.

Charlie, grinning his gat-toothed grin and squinting behind his
glasses, holds up a brown paper bag. "Guess what I got, Sarge?" he says.

Arne sits down at his desk and scans the cluttered surface for
anything new—callback slips from the front desk or directives from
upstairs. He is thinking about Lily. Lily last night. Lily in bed. Lily
different and indifferent. He wonders if he is falling in love with Lily
at the same time Lily is falling out of love with him. Then again, when
did she ever say she was in love with him?

"Pastrami on rye," he says absently. Arne hates guessing games.
"How the hell should I know?"

He looks up and sees Riemenschneider open the bag and turn it
upside down. A woman's low-heeled, black leather shoe clatters on the
top of his desk. The single empty shoe looks odd on the desk. There

should be a foot in it, or there should be a pair of them, and they should be on the floor.

"A citizen on Euclid Place flagged down one of our cars last night, said he found it in the street," Charlie says. "I'll lay you three to one this belonged to our dead beauty."

Anderson unlocks his desk and pulls open the bottom drawer. He takes out another paper bag and withdraws a woman's left shoe—sure enough, a match with the right shoe Charlie dropped on his desk. He holds the shoes up, one in each hand, and looks them over as though he knows something about women's shoes other than what he likes or dislikes on attractive women. The shoes—size five and a half, according to the tag inside, bought at a JC Penney's department store—look neither new nor expensive, but they aren't badly worn or scuffed. Arne can imagine Teresa Hickman wearing them out to a movie in the evening, or to a dental appointment. He holds each up, looks closely at the insides, and slides his thick fingers into the toes. He resists the temptation to sniff them.

"Euclid Place," he says.

"A block up from the lake," Charlie says, meaning Lake of the Isles.

"That's a couple of miles from where the body was found," Arne says. "Less than a mile from Rose's office."

Also on his desk is a report from Donald Forsberg, the head of forensics. A thorough search and vacuuming of Rose's Packard, front and back seats, floor, glove compartment, and trunk, yielded nothing other than what everyone else has in their cars. No sign of blood or semen or other bodily fluids. The only fingerprints were Rose's—on the steering wheel, gear shift, front doors, glove compartment, and trunk handle. There were a couple of long blonde hairs on the back of the front passenger seat, possibly Teresa Hickman's. But if Mrs. Hickman was in the car, where are her fingerprints? Rose must have wiped down her side after she either got out of the car or was murdered.

The squad's other members are present by ten-fifteen.

"He is risen!" Ferris Lakeland declares by way of a wise-ass Easter Sunday greeting.

"Big fuckin' deal," Riemenschneider growls in response. "*I've* been up for three hours."

Anderson senses a rare energy within the group. Even sluggish Einar Storholm, marking time until his end-of-the-year retirement, and legendary malingerer Curtis Wrenshall seem more than casually interested in the Hickman homicide. And why not? The case has the makings of an old-fashioned—and, in real life, exceedingly rare—who-dunit. What's more, the victim was a pretty young woman, a pregnant mother, and possibly a party girl, whose body was discovered in one of the city's quieter corners, and one of the suspects—hell, the prime suspect at this point—is the victim's Jewish dentist.

Arne assigns Storholm and Wrenshall to grab a couple of patrolmen, including the officer who brought in the matching shoe, and start canvassing the blocks around Euclid Place and the east side of Lake of the Isles. He sends Hessburg and LeBlanc to interview Rose's Zenith Avenue neighbors. When the Whoop-Tee-Doo Club opens tomorrow, they can talk to the club's staff and customers as well as Rose's second-floor neighbors.

Riemenschneider and Lakeland will go see if Bud Montgomery is home yet (he didn't come home last night, according to the stakeout), and if Grace Montgomery has anything more to say. "Bring them both in," Anderson says. "If Bud falls down the stairs and bumps his head en route—well, those things happen."

As Anderson and Curry get ready to leave for Rose's house, Arne notices a yellow call slip he overlooked amid the clutter on his desk. The slip says a man phoned in early this morning to report having seen a "young-looking male" walking along the streetcar right-of-way about one a.m. Saturday. He was "skinny and wore glasses" and "seemed to be interested in something in the weeds," the caller said. Unfortunately, the caller didn't leave his name or phone number or say how he happened to see the "young-looking male" strolling along the tracks at that hour. No one else has mentioned a skinny guy with glasses. Arne sticks the slip in his notebook.

Rose's home, three doors off the southwest corner of Thirty-ninth

Street and Zenith Avenue, is a two-and-a-half-story, red-brick structure bearded with English ivy. Later described in the papers as a Tudor Revival built in the early 1920s, it is not the largest or most ostentatious house on Zenith Avenue, but, like most of its neighbors, it is a house that a professional man and his family would be happy to call their own.

The house boasts a nicely landscaped front yard shaded by two fifty-foot American elms and a gently sloping backyard. A double garage is attached to the rear of the house and opens on a tidy alley that runs the length of the block. It is early April, so the yards, though likely free of snow for the season, will need another month, two or three inches of rain, and consistently warmer temperatures to green up and sprout their flowers.

Anderson and Curry, warm enough in their overcoats and fedoras, ring the front doorbell while a squad car idles at both ends of the alley. Arne would be flabbergasted if Rose tries to make a run for it, but protocol demands the backup.

Ruth Rose, a short, stocky, plain-faced woman Anderson figures to be about the dentist's age, answers the door. Anderson extends his shield, but she knows who they are, if not by name then by their appearance. She appears as unruffled this morning as her husband seemed to be at the courthouse yesterday afternoon. Anderson was half-expecting a uniformed maid.

"David said we should expect you," Mrs. Rose says, holding open the door.

Dr. Rose and a younger man are standing in the spacious, thickly carpeted living room to the left of the foyer. Rose is wearing a starched white shirt with a blue dotted necktie and pinstriped suit pants. His wingtip shoes gleam in the low light. He extends his right hand to each of the detectives and turns to the other man.

"May I introduce Ronald Oshinsky," Rose says. "Ronnie is my brother-in-law and, for the moment, my legal counsel."

Short, sturdy, and sobersided, Oshinsky is obviously Ruth's kin. Unblinking behind a pair of plastic-rimmed spectacles, he looks like a well-dressed owl.

Anderson is angry with himself for not hustling Rose downtown before the dentist could hire a lawyer. At the same time, he's relieved that this lawyer is not one of the high-octane defense attorneys that usually attach themselves to cases like this, headline-grabbing, cop-hating legal eagles, like Avery Kerr, Harry Hall, and Dante DeShields. Arne has never heard of Ronald Oshinsky.

The house smells of roast beef, fried onions, and furniture polish. A string quartet plays softly on the radio or phonograph in another room. Otherwise the house is silent.

Anderson says, "We want to take you downtown, Dr. Rose. To continue our conversation."

Oshinsky says, "Is he under arrest?"

"No," says Curry. "But we need more information."

"Why not talk here?" the young man wants to know.

"Orders from the top," Anderson says with a little smile, the usual bullshit response.

"That's perfectly all right," Rose says. He seems incapable of fluster, and it occurs to Anderson that the man is probably a pretty good dentist. Calm, self-confident, and steady.

Rose says, "May my wife and brother-in-law join us?"

Before Curry can say no, Anderson says, "If they can get themselves downtown and back on their own."

Robert Gardner sits in Miles Mckenzie's cramped office, seriously sleep-deprived and hungry for another adventure in Pam Brantley's bed, whenever that might be.

Mckenzie's "private" office is enclosed on three and a half sides by four-foot-high partitions topped with a foot of frosted glass and has hardly room enough for the bureau chief's messy desk, squealing chair, and battered Remington typewriter, plus a pair of straight-backed metal chairs facing the desk. The entire bureau, maybe twelve hundred square feet crammed with mismatched furniture, dented file cabinets, incessantly ringing telephones, and a platoon of clat-tering teletype machines, stinks of cigarette smoke, burnt coffee, and a dozen-odd men for whom personal hygiene isn't always the highest priority.

Because there's no door on his cubicle and because the walls rise only so far, there's no respite, even for the chief, from the mechanical chatter of the teletype machines that receive, print, and spit out tightly spaced rolls of news from around the world twenty-four hours a day. Bells announce the arrival of a new item, the number of bells signaling the urgency of each.

Mckenzie, in his bargain-basement short-sleeved white shirt and tartan tie that not quite reaches the bottom of his paunch, sits behind his desk looking at sheets of sliced-off teletype paper. He wears his watch on the inside of his right wrist and smokes incessantly. He is a United Press lifer, a newsman out of the movies, hoarse, gruff, and all business if you don't count bad puns and corny wordplay.

Bespectacled and prematurely bald, twenty-five-year-old Tommy Pullman sits in the chair beside Robert, furiously chewing Beech-Nut gum and fuming. Sunday is not Tommy's day to work. There's no bureau policy or union rule that gives him Sundays off, but Tommy, though with only a year and a half of seniority, carries a veteran's aura of entitlement and simply presumes a Sunday-free schedule. When pressed, he will explain, in unabashedly personal terms, that he's reserved the day for his newly married wife. Robert has met Bonnie Pullman, a slinky, six-foot-tall redhead, and has no trouble imagining how the couple spends their Sabbath.

"That was a decent sidebar in last night's *Star*," Mckenzie says to Robert. The men sitting around the desk know that Robert only contributed to the short piece Mckenzie wrote to accompany the *Star*'s front-page story. They know that Mckenzie is going to be the lead on the Teresa Hickman story, directing the bureau's coverage and writing both the features and the breaking-news reports that go out on the wires, and slapping his byline on top of most of them. The bureau's five full-time reporters, including Pullman and Gardner, will do the grunt work, wear down the shoe leather, and be content with reflected glory.

Milt Hickok, the foghorn-voiced veteran who's worked at the bureau (and the one-man state capitol office in St. Paul) almost as long as Mckenzie, has just called in from the courthouse. Milt told Mckenzie that the cops are going to arrest the dead woman's dentist. His source at the courthouse says Arne Anderson's homicide unit questioned a Dr. H. David Rose yesterday afternoon and is picking him up at his home today.

"That's all?" Pullman asks.

Mckenzie, lighting a Viceroy, says, "Shit, buddy, if that's true, this ain't some run-of-the-mill mugging arrest. This is a professional man, for chrissakes. A doctor of fucking dental surgery. Maybe the girl was a patient and he was filling more than her oral cavities."

"Rose," Pullman says. "That's a hebe name, isn't it?"

Mckenzie shrugs. "Sounds like it. Easy enough to find out."

Robert says, "Does that make a difference?"

"In this town it does," Tommy says. "The national press says we're the, quote, 'anti-Semitism capital of America.'"

Still learning the ways of the city, Robert has read about the real-estate redlining that has kept Jews and Negroes out of the city's better neighborhoods, and that Jewish doctors had to build their own hospital, Mount Sinai, because they couldn't get operating privileges in the city's established institutions. He's heard that the city's venerable country clubs and business associations and even the local YMCA have a history of denying Jews membership. But the anti-Semitism capital of America? He wonders if that can be true. Maybe once upon a time, but today? How would he know? He's pretty sure he has never knowingly spoken at any length to a Jew, either at home in Rochester or here in the Twin Cities.

"Rose might not be the only suspect," Mckenzie says, the cigarette bouncing between his lips. "Someone told the cops they saw a guy standing over the body by the trolley tracks. A young guy with glasses, according to the source."

Robert feels the blood drain from his face. *Jesus Christ! Someone did see him after he left Pam's apartment!* This is what he's been worried about—someone having spotted him near the body and the police suspecting that he had something to do with the murder.

He takes a breath and says, "Is that all? A young guy with glasses?"

He's relieved that neither Tommy nor Mckenzie bothers to look at him.

"That's more than you got, Bobbo," Tommy says.

"Mr. Gardner," says Mckenzie, as though suddenly inspired. He leans back in his noisy chair, which shrieks like a stuck pig under the torque and stress.

"I want you to run over to the courthouse and give Hickok a hand. Introduce yourself to Sergeant Anderson, tell him you're new on the beat. That'll be to your advantage because Anderson hates the reporters he knows around town, including yours truly. To Arne we're all parasites, bottom-feeders—or worse. Tell him you're just off the bus from East Overshoe, Manitoba, some place where the press takes the cops' word as gospel. See what he'll tell you about the Jew dentist and the skinny kid with glasses."

Then the chief looks at Tommy and says, "*You* can go home and pleasure your bride, pal. Tell her you're the Easter Bunny."

Robert, on his feet now, wonders how Mckenzie knew the kid with glasses was skinny.

"You need to know, Dr. Rose, that anything you say may be used against you in court," Captain Fuller says, after the two men and Detectives Anderson and Curry take their seats behind and around Fuller's desk on the third floor of the courthouse. May Grey, clutching three freshly sharpened pencils and her steno pad, has joined the circle as well. Ruth Rose and Ronald Oshinsky have been directed to chairs along the wall behind the others. No doubt owing to the fact that it's Easter Sunday, Ed Evangelist—not a religious man despite the name and yesterday's provocations, but a man who fervently believes in his weekly day of rest—isn't present.

"Do you understand?" Augie says.

"Yes, I do," Rose replies.

Rose has assumed the identical posture, expression, and disposition he displayed here yesterday. By the looks of him, Arne muses, the dentist might have spent the night in that chair.

Investigators won't be required for another eleven years to inform a criminal suspect of his Sixth Amendment rights—that he is not obliged to incriminate himself *and* has a right to have a lawyer present during an interrogation. But Fuller believes he owes a professional man a modicum of courtesy, and, in any event, he said nothing about the suspect's right to a lawyer. Rose *has* a lawyer, of course, but on the drive downtown the dentist told Anderson and Curry (who told Fuller on their arrival) that Ronald Oshinsky, though "a bright young man with a promising future," has handled only divorce and traffic cases in his short career and is present as a favor to Mrs. Rose.

"He won't be any trouble," Dr. Rose assured the detectives, as though Oshinsky was a child permitted to remain at the dinner table while the grownups talk business.

Fuller begins with questions about Teresa Hickman's Friday evening appointment, her general appearance, her mood, and the specific reason she had made her appointment with the dentist.

Rose answers each without hesitation or the slightest sign of discomfiture.

"She was an attractive girl, I would say," he says. "Not beautiful, actually a little on the thin side of the specter, but she had pretty eyes and an engaging natural smile. A dentist can't help but appreciate a smile like that, especially when the patient grew up in a rural part of the country and probably didn't have access to regular care.

"She was in a good mood, or at least as good a mood as can be expected from someone with a toothache," he says. "The infected tooth was an upper lateral. She told me it hurt like the dickens when she tried to eat something or even just touched it with her tongue."

He says he gave her an injection of two percent novocaine and one of his capsules, and then removed the existing filling, which had apparently been put in several years earlier. An unpleasant odor indicated infection and told him to proceed with a root canal, using his drill, reamers, and a flush of light peroxide.

"Then I blew the thing dry and put in one or two cotton points and went ahead and used a medication on another cotton point, just put it up in there, put a little soft cement over that, then put in a soft porcelain on top of that, then after it set drilled into it so that any gas that formed would escape."

Arne glances at Miss Grey, who seems to be getting it all and is not put off by the clinical details. No one in the room could have understood a word Rose said.

"Did she talk to you during this process?" Augie asks him.

"Well, I had a saliva syringe and cotton in her mouth, so it would have been difficult for her to speak while I was working. But both before and after I'd say she was talkative."

Anderson catches Fuller's eye, and Fuller nods.

Arne says, "When did she tell you she thought she was pregnant? Before or after you fixed the tooth?"

Rose turns his head.

"Afterward," he says. "I'd helped her out of the chair and led her into the waiting room and encouraged her to lie down on the settee, until the medication I'd given her began wearing off."

Curry asks, "What did you do while she was on the settee?"

"I went back to the operatory and cleaned up."

"There was no one else in the office at the time? No other patients waiting or anyone helping you?"

"No. Mrs. Hickman was the last patient of the day. And, as I believe I told you, mine is a solo practice. I work by myself."

Arne can hear Mrs. Rose and her brother stirring behind him, the clearing of a throat and the shuffling of feet on the worn linoleum. The implication of Mel's questions was obvious. Arne forms a picture of the dentist sitting down beside Teresa Hickman, who is supine and semiconscious and maybe blithely acquiescent, and sliding his hand under her skirt. But maybe, Arne muses, that is only what *he* might have done.

"How long was she unconscious?" he asks.

"She was never unconscious," Rose replies. "She was in a semicon-scious state."

Fuller says, "She was talking to you while she was lying on the settee?"

"I was in the other room most of that time. It was probably another half hour to an hour before she sat up and started to talk."

"And that's when she told you she'd missed her period."

Rose seems to be thinking. "Well, no, not right away," he says. "We talked about other things, as I recall. I inquired about her sister, who's also a patient of mine, and her husband in West Germany and her little boy, whose name I can't remember."

"Harold Junior," Curry interjects drily. He gives Anderson a look. Mel is already convinced that Rose is a murderer.

"She told me she and her husband, when he gets out of the service, want to open a little motor hotel outside of Grand Forks."

"Just a little run-of-the-mill chitchat," Augie says.

"Yes," Rose says. "She asked if I minded if she smoked. I told her I don't allow smoking in the office, for obvious reasons. I'm sure she knew that, so it was odd that she asked. She wasn't entirely lucid yet."

Arne wonders what those "obvious reasons" are. A little tobacco smoke might help mask the medicinal, hot-drill stink of the place. Fuller's cramped office, as it happens, is thick with cigarette smoke by this time, though the doctor either doesn't seem to notice or doesn't mind. Maybe it's only his own nest he doesn't want to foul, though yesterday the detectives smoked without any objections in his waiting room.

"So her statement about missing her period came out of the blue," Augie says.

"Well, actually, she'd mentioned it earlier, before I started to work on her, when I asked about her general health."

"But she didn't say at that time she thought you might be the father."

"She did not. That was afterward. In the waiting room."

"What exactly did she say in the waiting room?"

"Well, she said she believed I'd gotten her pregnant after I sedated her during her appointment in January."

Augie glances at the papers in front of him, and then looks up. "What did she say when you told her that was impossible, that it couldn't have been you?"

"She said, 'Well, I can't think who else it could be.'"

"What did you say to that?"

"I said, 'Well, you need to think a little harder.'"

"And she said?"

"She said, 'I've thought a lot about it already. I think it was you.' She said, 'You gave me that pill, and now I am pregnant.'"

"Did she raise her voice?"

"No."

"Did you?"

"No. It was a civil conversation."

"Her accusation had to make you mad."

Rose thinks this over.

"I was perturbed," he says finally. "I'm sure my wife and brother-in-law will confirm that it takes a great deal to make me angry."

Fuller stares at Rose, whose posture and expression haven't changed since they started. Rose might as well be talking about the weekend weather.

Augie, who has a notoriously weak bladder, says it's time to take a break. He stands, and the others, except May Grey, still jabbing at her steno pad, follow suit.

Anderson glances back at Ruth Rose and her brother. She looks as unperturbed as her husband. Young Oshinsky, on the other hand, is clearly agitated, twisting in his chair and jiggling his legs, though it's impossible to tell whether his discomfort is the result of his brother-in-law's narrative or the direction in which the detectives' questions are heading.

In the men's room down the hall, Anderson and Curry watch Fuller relieve himself in front of one of the rust-streaked urinals.

Mel glances toward the men's room door and says, "The guy's a cool fucking customer."

Shaking himself off and stepping away from the pisser, Augie says, "You ask the rest of the questions, Arne. He's our guy, but you're more likely than I am to get him to say so."

After their break, instead of taking his chair, Anderson sits down on the edge of Fuller's desk, at six foot three and two hundred twenty-plus pounds an intimidating figure, all the more so in this elevated position.

"So then, Dr. Rose," he begins, looking down at the suspect, "after another several minutes you led Mrs. Hickman out of the office and down the stairs and back to the Montgomerys' apartment around the corner. Isn't that what you told us yesterday?"

Rose pauses for a moment, and then says, "Well, that may not have been entirely accurate. I *drove* her back to her apartment."

"You *drove* her?"

"Yes. She seemed a little wobbly on her legs, so I led her down to my car, which was parked around the corner. I've done that for other patients—driven them home—especially when it's been late or the weather's been bad and the patient's still under the influence of the medication."

Anderson and Curry exchange glances. Anderson hears Augie clearing his throat as he thumbs through the notes on his desk.

"What time did you take Mrs. Hickman down to your car, Dr. Rose?"

"Well, as I believe I mentioned yesterday, I don't wear a watch," Rose says. "But I suppose it was by this time about ten or ten-thirty. Maybe eleven."

"And you drove her home. But her apartment—the Montgomerys' apartment—is right there where you're parked, isn't it?"

Rose sighs.

"Yes," he says. "Let me start again. Terry told me she wanted to talk about her pregnancy. Now she was adamant about it, in fact, and

I didn't feel I had much choice but to discuss the matter with her. So I didn't drive her home."

"Where did you go?"

Arne, surely no more than anyone else in the room, was not expecting this. He does his best to keep from looking at Mrs. Rose seated behind her husband.

Rose says, "I'm not sure. South on Nicollet or maybe Hennepin, away from downtown, in the direction of the lake. Lake of the Isles. Or Lake Calhoun."

"Can you be more definite, Doctor?"

"I'm afraid I can't," Rose says. "I know we eventually parked by one of the lakes, where I thought we could talk."

Ronald Oshinsky is on his feet.

"We need to stop here, gentlemen," he says. The young man's face is red and he looks self-conscious. He has to be as surprised as everyone else, and even with his limited experience he has to know that the discussion is lurching into dangerous waters.

But Rose looks placidly over his shoulder and says, "There's no need to stop now, Ronnie. The cat's out of the box and there's no reason to beat behind the bush. I took Mrs. Hickman, perhaps unadvisedly, for a ride in my car and we stopped to talk. That's all."

Oshinsky looks at his sister, who says nothing, and sits back down.

Anderson feels the energy changing in the room as it sometimes does during an interrogation.

"Did you argue at that point?"

Rose sits silent for a moment.

"Well," he says, "we probably did. I'm having difficulty recalling the specifics. It was very late, and I remember beginning to swoon in my weariness."

"Swoon?" Anderson says. *The cat's out of the box. There's no reason to beat behind the bush.* Rose has an interesting way with the language.

"The poor man hadn't eaten all day!"

This, at last, is Ruth Rose jumping into the conversation. "Dr.

Rose often forgets to eat. He goes all day without a meal, then suffers the effects."

Nobody says a word for a long moment. At last Anderson asks, "When did you finally drop Mrs. Hickman at her apartment?"

For the first time, Rose displays some emotion. "I don't know," he says. He seems genuinely perplexed. "I don't remember driving back toward downtown, and I don't remember dropping her off at her apartment. I seem to have blacked out, and when I came to my senses she wasn't in the car. I didn't know where she'd gone."

Anderson has heard hundreds of alibis, but never anything quite like this one, from a suspect quite like Dr. Rose.

He says, "Where were you when you came to your senses?"

"Well, only a block or two from my home. On Xerxes Avenue, at the south end of Lake Calhoun."

"And what time do you think it was then?"

"I don't know. Perhaps about midnight."

Fuller says, "You didn't know what had become of Mrs. Hickman?"

Rose takes a deep breath and says, "Mrs. Hickman and I were in the car, and the next thing I knew she was gone."

Curry asks, "Do you remember driving—or stopping—near Forty-fourth Street? Forty-fourth and Zenith, or Forty-fourth and York?"

"No."

"Do you remember driving on or across any streetcar tracks?"

"No, I don't."

"Do you recall walking on or stepping across any streetcar tracks?"

"No."

"Did you kill Mrs. Hickman, Doctor?"

"I did not. Well, I don't remember. Not that I know of."

When Anderson, now sweating like a prizefighter, lifts himself off the desk, Fuller and Curry stand up, too. Then so does Dr. Rose, slowly and laboriously, as though his back and legs are arthritic, and then so do Ruth Rose and Ronald Oshinsky. Arne hears Oshinsky tell his sister that he's going to make a phone call and watches the lawyer hurry out of the room.

Ruth catches Anderson's eye and says, "I'm afraid my husband's memory is not always very reliable, Sergeant. Maybe it's his diet and all the pressure at the office. David is a perfectionist, and he doesn't get enough rest."

Augie Fuller, coming around from behind his desk, says, "Dr. Rose, I'm arresting you on suspicion of the murder of Teresa Hickman."

Rose looks at his wife and stands there, expressionless and awkward-looking, as though he no longer knows what to say or what to do with his hands.

The following morning, after a breakfast of oatmeal, dry toast, and black coffee, Rose is fetched by Mel Curry and escorted in handcuffs down a flight of stairs to a small, untidy office on the second floor of the courthouse. After his arrest late yesterday, he was booked, issued a bedroll, and assigned a cell in the courthouse tower. The jailer, a blimpish sheriff's deputy named Miller Haskins, told Curry that he had no complaints about the prisoner.

"Didn't hear a peep," Haskins said. "Far as I know, he slept like a baby."

The office, according to the name on the frosted-glass door, belongs to James P. Jerecki, Deputy Director, Weights & Measures. It wouldn't occur to Rose, a naif in such matters, but Jerecki's unassuming venue has been selected to provide cover for the investigators, lest reporters get wind of developments and before Ruth Rose and Ronald Oshinsky can send an actual criminal-defense attorney to the courthouse.

"We need another hour to ourselves," Anderson says to Riemenschneider and Lakeland as he ushers them into Jerecki's office. Neither the Weights & Measures director nor his secretary is present (Fuller has made the necessary arrangements), but Homer Scofield, the thirty-two-year-old Hiawatha County attorney, is leaning against one of the desks when the detectives arrive. Scofield is new to the job. This is his first county case of any kind, never mind his first homicide prosecution. He has a mop of red hair, a pale, freckled face, a long, bony frame, and Coke-bottle glasses with colorless plastic frames. His oversized suit makes him look like a ten-year-old pretending to be his father. He is here to decide whether to call his first-ever grand jury.

Augie, who just met the new prosecutor, introduces him to the others as "Herbert Wakefield," and then red-faced, hastily and with the prosecutor's help, makes the necessary correction. "Sorry about that, sir," he says. "I went to Patrick Henry High with a Herbie Wakefield."

Scofield smiles uncertainly.

Curry brings Rose in and directs him to a large table the contents of which—stacks of files, ledgers, and three-inch-thick technical manuals—have been shoved to one side. May Grey, unnoticed until now, opens a fresh steno pad and steadies it on her knee.

After a few tepid pleasantries, Anderson, facing Rose across the table, says, "Were you aware that Teresa Hickman had sexual relations shortly before she died Friday night?"

"No," Rose says. He wears this morning only a white dress shirt, beltless suit trousers, socks, and shoes, pending the issuance of regulation jail garb. He looks alert if somewhat rumpled and disoriented. "No, I wasn't."

"Did *you* have sexual relations with Mrs. Hickman?"

"No, I didn't."

"Either in your office or in your car?"

"No." He pauses, and then adds with a rare flash of impatience, "I did not."

"Yesterday, when I asked if you killed Mrs. Hickman, you told us that you didn't remember. 'Not that I know of,' you said. Is it possible that you don't remember having sex with her, either?"

"Well, I suppose it's possible, but I doubt it. It would be a violation of my professional ethics."

"You said the two of you argued when you were in the car," Anderson says.

"I suppose we did," Rose replies, sounding uncertain, either forgetting or disregarding what he said yesterday.

"What did you argue about?"

Rose suddenly rolls his shoulders, as though easing out the kinks of having spent the night on a mattress the thickness of a couple *Saturday Evening Post*s. Arne recalls Rose's comment about arthritis.

"Her pregnancy, no doubt," he says.

"Was she making demands? Did she want you to pay for an abortion, or to help with the child once it was born?"

"I don't remember."

"Did she threaten to tell people about her situation, threaten to go to the police, or make a complaint to the state dental authorities?"

"I don't remember," Rose says quietly. "If she did, I wasn't going to stand for it, I can assure you of that."

"You have a good reputation in this community, don't you, Doctor?"

"I believe I do."

"During the drive, Doctor—"

"The drive was her idea," Rose says. "She wanted to talk about her pregnancy. I think your proposition is correct, though I can't be certain I'm recalling this correctly. I think she wanted to ask me for money."

"*Did* she ask you for money?"

"Well, I can't say for certain. But I'm pretty sure that's what she had in mind."

Arne looks around the room, but avoids eye contact with his colleagues and the county attorney.

"Did she in fact ask you for money that night?"

"I don't know."

"You don't know or you don't remember?"

"I'm not sure I understand the difference."

Arne looks down at his hands, which are folded atop May Grey's typed transcript of yesterday's interrogation. "What's the last thing you remember before you blacked out Friday night?" he says.

"All I can recall with any certitude is coming out of it near my home," Rose replies.

"And Teresa Hickman was not in the car when you did?"

"No, she wasn't."

"She was sitting beside you in the front seat of your Packard, possibly threatening you with blackmail, and then, sometime later, when you looked in her direction, the seat was empty and she was gone."

"Yes."

"Mrs. Hickman was manually strangled," Anderson says. "According to the pathologist who performed her autopsy, there was a bruise on her neck and the hyoid bone in her throat had been crushed. She also had semen in her body, indicating recent sexual intercourse. Her body was dumped in the weeds a half-mile from your home. Does any of that information ring a bell, Dr. Rose?"

Rose stares at Anderson, and then makes that little rippling motion with his shoulders.

"As a professional man myself, I have to respect the opinion of another professional man," he says. "If the pathologist says she was strangled, I have to accept that she was strangled. If he says she'd had sexual intercourse, she must have had sexual intercourse. I won't argue with another doctor's report."

He sounds tired, Anderson muses, maybe from a bad night's sleep or maybe because he's finally out of gas.

"It was just the two of us in the car, and the girl made me angry so I can see why you might wonder if I lost control," Rose says quietly. "But I want you to know, Sergeant, I am not a violent man. I have no memory of laying a hand on Terry Hickman—of doing anything to her or with her, in any way harming her—and, frankly, I doubt very much that I did. I have not deliberatively hurt so much as an ant or a ladybug in my lifetime. I am not a murderer."

He manages a weak, almost apologetic smile and doesn't say another word.

That evening, the *Star* runs the story along the top of the front page below a headline set in sixty-four-point type:

CITY DENTIST HELD IN WOMAN'S DEATH

Under Oscar Rystrom's byline, the story reiterates the basics of the case, the coroner's findings, and the arrest of H. David Rose, a Southside dentist, providing, as the papers routinely do at the time, the home addresses of both the victim and the suspect. Rystrom quotes MPD Captain of Detectives August Fuller saying that Teresa Hickman had been Rose's patient, and that the police believe he was the last person to see her alive.

An unidentified "well-placed" source is quoted as saying that in interviews with the police on Sunday and earlier today, "The suspect has all but confessed to the crime." None of the detectives Rystrom interviewed, however, would confirm or deny that statement on the record.

Rose has hired "flamboyant local defense attorney" Dante DeShields, Rystrom notes. DeShields immediately issued a statement, calling the arrest "totally unjustified" and concluding, "David Rose is an eminent doctor of dental surgery, a law-abiding citizen, a loving husband, and a conscientious father. To suggest that he had anything to do with Teresa Hickman's murder is outrageous. Dr. Rose is innocent. He has 'all but confessed' to absolutely nothing."

A rudimentary map of the Linden Hills neighborhood, extending from West Forty-fourth Street to the south end of Lake Calhoun and including Rose's Zenith Avenue home five blocks from the spot where the victim's body was found, accompanies the story. There is a photograph, no doubt from her high school yearbook, of Teresa Hickman and a studio portrait of Dr. Rose.

Teresa Hickman is smiling. Dr. Rose is not.

CHAPTER 5

R obert Gardner sits bare-assed on the edge of the narrow bed and
    tries desperately to think about other things: the pathetic three-
legged mutt that hobbled around his Rochester neighborhood when
he was a kid, the *Life* magazine photo of a Japanese soldier about to
behead a blindfolded American airman, his grandmother's elaborate
funeral. He tries to picture the five-fatality car wreck on Highway 14
he helped cover for the *Post-Bulletin*—anything that will keep him
from exploding in Pam Brantley's mouth.

He manages to hold on for another few seconds before the past is
swallowed by the present and he comes in a mighty rush and exclama-
tion.

It was Monday night and it's now very early Tuesday morning, the
first time he's seen or talked to her since Teresa Hickman's murder.
Pam said when he arrived a few minutes before midnight that they
have "all the time in the world" because Karl is working an extra shift
at the hospital. So they made love once, then twenty minutes later a
second time, and then Pam went down on him, another first in his
rapidly expanding portfolio of sexual experience.

This night, like the several nights they've trysted before it, has seemed too good to be true, though Robert can't help but listen, at least during pauses between lovemaking, for the door at the bottom of the stairs to open and Karl's footfalls on the steps. *What if Karl changes his mind and heads home after his first shift?* Robert worries, too, about Gwen waking up in *her* apartment and noticing it's nearly two in the morning and her little brother hasn't come in yet. Nothing, not even this wild carnal pleasure, is without complication and concern.

Robert wonders if he can fuck Pam a third time tonight. Nothing in his experience, or, for that matter, in his many years of sexual fantasy, has prepared him for the opportunities his seemingly insatiable lover is giving him—so different from his two years going steady with her cautious, abstemious sister.

Pam, lying beside him, is now snoring softly, like a child, her face turned toward him and her legs partially open as though inviting his return. The dark triangle between her thighs looks damp in the pallid light from the window. He wonders if he should repay the favor, if he should go down on her, wondering what she would taste like, wondering at the same time if the taste of her is something her husband knows, wondering if she has done to Karl what she has just done to him, and what Karl has done in response. He feels himself begin to stiffen.

When Pam, a moment later, stirs and sits up, Robert tells her that he saw the dead girl on the tracks after their lovemaking that night.

He says it just like that, in so many words, without forethought and without a plan. They have not talked about the murder at all tonight. Somewhat to his surprise, Pam hasn't brought it up, and damned if Robert was going to say anything that might chill the erotic temperature level in the apartment.

Later, when he tries to find a way to explain his foolishness, he will tell himself that his secret had become too much to carry by himself, that he had to tell *someone* and there was no one else he could tell under the circumstance. Maybe sharing the secret with Pam might somehow lessen—what?—his cowardice in not telling the police and his boss.

It was entirely possible, he would tell himself, that whoever reported seeing the skinny young man with glasses leaning over the body could identify him. The possibility has been on his mind since the Sunday meeting at the bureau—blocked out only by the intoxicating prospect and then the reality of another couple of hours with Pam—and maybe telling Pam is his way of dealing with that fear, which makes no sense whatever, he realizes as soon as he thinks it.

He will prefer to rationalize his mistake by telling himself that he has fallen crazy in love with Pam Brantley, and that sharing secrets is something lovers do, whether it makes sense or not.

Pam is looking at him quizzically.

"You saw *what?*" she says.

He knows he's made a mistake, but, like a skier who's launched himself over the lip of a precipitous hill, there's no turning back.

"That murdered girl. Teresa Hickman."

"You saw her get murdered?" Pam says. Her wide-eyed, bewildered expression almost makes him laugh.

"No," he says, "but I might have been the first person to see her afterward. That was five or six hours before the guy who the police say discovered the body said he came across it."

He isn't sure what reaction he expected, but Pam, sitting up beside him, simply stares at him, nonplussed. It occurs to him that their love-making is finished for the night.

"What did she look like?"

Robert shakes his head.

"She looked *dead*," he says sharply. He is annoyed by the witless question and angry with himself for being an idiot. "I don't know," he says in a softer tone. "She was lying on her stomach, so I didn't get a good look at her face. It just was obvious that she was dead."

Pam says nothing for another moment. He's never seen her in what he would describe as a contemplative moment, or looking confused and uncertain, as though someone has said something important in a foreign language. He's seen her elated and angry, aroused and then sated, but never in a serious situation such as this, all the more unlikely and absurd because the two of them are stark naked and sitting in the sticky aftermath of their sex.

Pam says, "You told the police, didn't you?"

Robert lies back against his rumpled pillow and drops his arm across his eyes. He's cold now, the sweat on his chest and thighs chilling him unpleasantly, but he doesn't try to pull her against him for warmth.

"No," he says. "I haven't told anybody, not even my sister or my boss. I'm afraid if I do, I'll have to explain what I was doing down there at that time of night, and that would put the two us in jeopardy. So, no, Pam. You're the only one."

Pam looks at him uncertainly.

He says, "Now we have *two* secrets." But if that's an effort to calm the waters, it doesn't seem to be effective. She says he better go.

En route to his sister's apartment a few minutes later, Robert steps out the front door of the Brantleys' building, not the back, and walks quickly down the sidewalk that runs along the north side of Forty-fourth Street in front of the apartments and other buildings. He is wearing a tan jacket and khakis, not the dark combination that he wore the night of the murder.

A yellow taxi passes heading west, but that's the only car he sees going in any direction at this hour. He pats his breast pocket where he's stashed his glasses.

Detective Ferris Lakeland and a representative from the Minneapolis office of the Red Cross greet Harold V. Hickman near dusk on Tuesday afternoon at Wold-Chamberlain Field. Private Hickman is a tall, lean, pale-faced man who would need another dozen pounds to make his dress greens fit properly. Even his envelope-shaped garrison cap looks a size too large. Presumably, as a North Dakotan, he's been to the Twin Cities before today, but he looks bewildered and uneasy, as though he stepped off the plane in Timbuktu.

After offering the widower their condolences, Lakeland and the man from the Red Cross lead Hickman through the busy baggage claim (he has only his Army-issue duffel bag) and toward the terminal's front door. A couple of newspaper photographers, somehow alerted to his arrival, fire off their Speed Graphics as the men pass, the flashbulbs on the big cameras popping like firecrackers.

"Stay the hell away from us," Lakeland snarls at the photo boys, flashing his badge and dragging the skinny soldier out the door. The sun is still shining, but in a desultory, grudging way.

Lakeland directs Hickman into the backseat of an unmarked Plymouth, and then slides in behind the wheel next to the Red Cross official, a balding, bespectacled man named Jerry Ingram. Arne Anderson told Ferris to talk as little as possible during the twenty-minute drive downtown. "Tell him he can see his son later this evening or first thing tomorrow," Arne said. "Tell him the kid is doing fine with his auntie." If Hickman wants to see his wife's body, Arne said he could arrange that later, too, after the two of them talked. If Hickman wants to see the man they arrested—well, that was out of the question, at least for now.

Anderson and the rest of the murder squad have been busy during the past few days. Besides interrogating Dr. Rose, they brought in for questioning Bud Montgomery, Anatoli and Tony Zevos, and a freelance photographer named Richard Ybarra, and interviewed the chiropractor and dance instructors who occupy the office space across the hall from Rose's practice and a dozen-odd bartenders, waitresses, and hangers-on from the Whoop-Tee-Doo Club downstairs.

"Go over your lists," Anderson told the squad. "Anybody out there on parole or who otherwise might look interesting, find them and bring them in, too."

A dragnet is standard operating procedure in a high-profile homicide case, but not everyone on the third floor of the courthouse believes that it's necessary in this one.

"What's the matter?" Riemenschneider groused to Curry during the roundup. "Doesn't Arne believe the kike's our guy?"

In fact, with the exception of Bud Montgomery and Tony Zevos, none of the possibilities has offered much reason to believe otherwise.

Richard Ybarra, a curly-haired Romeo barely out of his teens, is a slippery hustler whose "professional portfolio" comprises mostly black-and-white photos of not particularly attractive, partially clad young women, the very attractive Teresa Hickman the notable exception. The cops spotted a couple of her photos on the street—obviously taken by the photographer who took the shots the detectives saw at the Montgomerys' apartment—and these, no doubt for promotional purposes, had his name and phone number stamped on the back. They caught up with him walking into the Greyhound station at Seventh and Hennepin, that oversize portfolio in one hand, a battered overnight bag and camera case in the other.

"Going when the going's good, eh, slick?" Frenchy LeBlanc said, shoving the startled shutterbug into the backseat of an unmarked squad car. In the car, LeBlanc began their interview with a forearm shiver to Ybarra's jaw. Once at police headquarters, however, while there was plenty to appreciate in the eight-by-ten glossies spread across a conference table, there was nothing to learn from either the portfolio or the photographer himself.

"Did you fuck Teresa Hickman?" Einar Storholm asked him, holding up a photo of the dead woman.

"No!" Ybarra whined. He was pressing a handful of wet tissues against his bloody mouth.

"I bet it crossed your mind," Storholm muttered, staring at the shot of Mrs. Hickman in the white shorts, smiling over her naked shoulder. "A fine ass like that."

Ybarra sniffed and attempted a just-one-of-the-boys smile. "Well, yeah," he said, as though the detective had asked him if he liked hamburgers. *Who wouldn't? Who didn't?* But the photographer said he hadn't seen Teresa Hickman since he gave her copies of the photos a week ago.

"April Fool's Day," Ybarra said. He then produced the name of a half-dozen family members and friends whose wedding party he photographed in Duluth, two and a half hours away, the night of the murder, and swore the alibi would check out. Ybarra hadn't left

Duluth for Minneapolis, deciding to hitchhike down Highway 61, until the following afternoon.

"Who gets married on a Friday night?" Storholm, with uncharacteristic persistence, wanted to know.

Ybarra shrugged. "I guess they couldn't get the church on Saturday," he says. "Ask the Cunninghams. I gave you their phone number."

The chiropractor and dance instructors confirmed the report that Rose's practice seemed to comprise a large number of women, and that their neighbor routinely worked evenings and weekends.

The chiropractor, Artemis Fischer, said Rose was always cordial and polite, but not especially outgoing, rarely initiating even casual conversation when they encountered each other in the building or on the street.

LaVerne Ridgeway, one of the dance masters, said he didn't think he or his partner had exchanged more than a dozen words with the dentist beyond the occasional "Hello" and "Good evening." "I don't think he cares much about anything or anyone if they don't involve his practice," Ridgeway told Curtis Wrenshall. "He didn't seem eager to make new friends."

The Whoop-Tee-Doo crowd, meanwhile, had nothing substantive to offer. To the detectives' surprise, given his solitary, conservative nature, Rose occasionally stopped by the club for a "cordial" before going home at night. The club's manager, a one-armed Guadalcanal survivor named Buster Haswell, said that when Rose comes in, maybe twice or three times a month, he's always alone, rarely speaks to anyone after ordering his drink, and the drink is always a single Grand Marnier Orange.

"He looks at the talent," Haswell said, "but I've never seen him talk to anybody other than his waitress and the hatcheck girl, coming or going. He'll sit at a table near the back of the room, nurse his drink for a good half hour, then leave. Not a bad tipper for a Jew, but a strange guy, I'd say."

"Have any of the girls been a patient?" Wrenshall asked.

"Not that I know of," Haswell said, "which is odd, since he's right upstairs. Maybe they're afraid of him, or vice versa. Feel free to ask around."

Wrenshall said that maybe he would. And he did. That night, he chatted with five or six girls sitting at the bar before the show, but only two seemed to know who Rose was and neither of them said she'd had any contact with the man. Wrenshall, who had all he could do to keep his hands to himself, especially when speaking to the brassy redhead in a sparkly halter top and net stockings, thanked them profusely and happily added their names and addresses to his detective's notebook.

Anderson and Curry spent a couple of hours with both Bud Montgomery and Tony Zevos, but learned nothing they didn't already know—namely, that both men were crumbums and both deserved whatever rough handling they received. Both men, Anderson believed, were capable of forcing themselves on Teresa Hickman and then killing her, especially if she threatened to tell on them. It was possible, of course, that Mrs. Hickman, eager for male attention in her husband's absence, initiated the contact. It would have been convenient enough considering that she was staying in Bud Montgomery's apartment and worked for Tony Zevos.

Unfortunately, both men had alibis that allowed them to walk out of the courthouse with no more than a couple of whacks and the promise of worse if either one of them turned up in the squad's interrogation room again. Zevos produced the names of three individuals who would vouch for his presence at the luncheonette the night of April 8 and until four the next morning at a buddy's stag party in Robbinsdale. Bud's alibi—he insisted he was bar-crawling with a pal—was not as solid. Arne wanted more work done on that one.

Afterward, Anderson and Curry met with Augie Fuller in Fuller's office. Ed Evangelist hovered with no apparent purpose other than to butt in and annoy.

"Well," said Augie, "we all heard Rose confess, didn't we?"

"We did," Arne said, "sort of. And we arrested him. Then his family hired Dante DeShields, who said that what Rose told us doesn't amount to a confession. In any event, no doubt at DeShields's direction, Rose declined to sign his statement. His family will post bail, and Rose will go home."

"Fucking kike," Evangelist said.

Ignoring the fat man, Anderson said, "Everything, including his own words, points to Rose, but DeShields knows how to play the game. We know that from experience."

"So what's next?" Fuller wanted to know. As impatient as he can be, Augie likes to give his investigators room to operate as they see fit. So far, at least with Anderson, that hasn't gotten him in trouble.

"We rule out the alternatives and build our case," Arne said. "Grace Montgomery lied about Teresa's Friday night appointment and surely knows more about her little sister and her little sister's relationships than she's told Mel and me. MacMurray couldn't verify the dental work Rose said he'd done on Mrs. Hickman that night— the rigor mortis made it impossible to open her mouth wide enough during the autopsy. He could check again now that the rigor mortis has worn off, but I don't think it's relevant. I'm willing to take Rose's word that he worked on her tooth."

But something deep and for the moment inaccessible is troubling Arne. With no apparent eyewitnesses and no meaningful forensic evidence, the case against Rose has come together too fast and too easily, and for reasons he can't articulate he has doubts about Rose's role in the murder. There's a lot that bothers him about the dentist, but he has difficulty picturing him as a killer.

Now, early on Tuesday evening, Lakeland knocks on the captain's open door.

"Excuse me, Sarge," he says to Anderson. "Private Hickman is waiting. It's been an hour and a half, and he wants to see his wife and kid."

Arne Anderson walks down the hall, knocks on the door, and enters the smaller of the third floor's two conference rooms.

A gaunt young man in ill-fitting Army greens looks up from his folded hands, which are the only things on the conference-room table.

The mostly unadorned uniform speaks of a buck private with less than a year in service, with, however, a familiar red, blue, and yellow triangle on the left shoulder. Jerry Ingram, from the Red Cross, sits silently, apparently having run out of conversation with the soldier, at the other end of the table.

Arne extends his right hand. The soldier's right hand is moist and cold.

"First Armored," Arne says, sitting down and acknowledging the tricolor patch on the soldier's jacket. "I was an infantryman in the *Fourth* Armored during the war. Part of Patton's Third Army. I saw Old Blood 'n' Guts once, on the way to Bastogne."

He wonders if a twenty-three-year-old recruit will be familiar with the nickname—famous in 1945, but maybe not so familiar ten years after the war's end and the general's death in a car accident. He also wonders, too late, if bringing up the war and the aura of death, even if intended to open some common ground between them, was a good idea. Probably not.

Arne feels sorry for the kid, who has to be exhausted by a twenty-four-hour (or longer) trip from Germany and in shock over the death of his wife. The kid's eyes are red-rimmed but dry. He can't seem to decide what, if anything, he should say to the detective.

"Are you hungry?" Arne asks him.

"We had a bite downstairs," Jerry Ingram interjects. "That little place off the lobby."

Anderson stands up. "Let's, just the two of us," he says to the soldier, "go see your family."

Ingram rises and starts to say something, but Arne forces a smile and says, "I'll take him over to Hiawatha General and then to the Montgomerys' apartment. Give me his lodging information, and I'll see that he's there at a decent hour. Maybe we'll have a drink at the hotel. You can check on him in the morning."

Ingram's frown says he doesn't like the idea, that it's probably "against policy," but he's either intimidated by the big detective or doesn't care to argue.

For the next forty-five minutes Hickman says nothing. Arne doesn't try to make conversation, but simply nods or touches the soldier's arm when leading him through the corridors and down the stairs to the morgue in Hiawatha General's basement. Then he steps out of the way when one of Fred MacMurray's white-jacketed assistants raises the sheet and reveals the chilled remains of Teresa Hickman. Arne watches Private Hickman's shoulders; but if the soldier twitches or shudders, he doesn't see it.

Hickman says nothing. He merely stands there, his hands at his sides, looking down at the lifeless body, and then turns away. His pale eyes are still dry. There's nothing Anderson can tell him that he hasn't already been told, including the cause of death and the arrest of a suspect.

At the Montgomerys' apartment half an hour later, Grace awkwardly hugs her brother-in-law and says, "Our poor Terry." Her eyes are red and puffy. The apartment smells of fried onions and something sweet. Arne is not surprised that Bud Montgomery isn't around. There is a lot Arne wants to talk to Grace about, without Bud in the room, but that will have to wait. Bud, she says when he asks, is bowling with friends.

Then Grace tiptoes into her bedroom and returns a moment later with Harold Hickman Junior, who stirs in his aunt's arms but doesn't come fully awake.

"This is your daddy, honey," Grace says, tears sliding down her cheeks.

Private Hickman stands stock still, his arms still at his sides, when she holds the baby out in front of him. He doesn't take the child, but bends forward at the waist and leans over the red, fussing face as though he's inspecting a strange and maybe dangerous object. When Grace asks, "Don't you want to hold him, Hal?" Hickman says, "I better not."

Anderson watches. He wonders if Hickman would like a few moments alone with his son and sister-in-law, but by the look of the two adults—both staring at the little boy but neither saying a word— he doubts if either one of them wants that. Besides, he's reluctant, for investigative reasons, to leave them alone. If they have something meaningful to say to each other, he wants to hear it.

After a few minutes, Hickman, staring at Hal Junior in Grace's arms, says, "I'm very tired and should probably get some sleep. Thank you for looking after the boy, Grace. I'll take him off your hands when we go home for the funeral." Hickman says that with the help of the Red Cross he's made funeral arrangements in Grand Forks, where his parents live.

Grace looks at her brother-in-law as though he slapped her in the face. Whatever she might have been expecting, she apparently thought she'd be consulted about the arrangements. Anderson suspects that these are the sorts of families that don't talk much to each other in the best of times and not at all during crises. He wonders if Grace thinks she ought to keep the baby, or if she's relieved he will no longer be her responsibility. He thinks, not for the last time, that there is so much he doesn't know about Grace Montgomery, and he wonders how much of it matters. He supposes that he'll find out soon.

The Red Cross has arranged for Private Hickman to stay at the Talmadge, a small, clean, slightly down-at-the-heels hotel on the south end of Marquette Avenue. Waiting while the young man registers, Anderson is surprised when he turns and says, "I'll have that drink now, sir."

The two men sit in a corner of a nearly empty bar off the lobby and drink the whiskey that Anderson orders and pays for. Hickman seems more alive than he was an hour earlier, and Arne suspects that he's relieved to have seen his wife and son and can now relax. For the first time since he's been with the detective, and probably for the first time since he left Germany, he loosens his black, Army-issue tie and undoes the top button of his khaki shirt. The jukebox, for better or worse, is playing Patti Page.

Arne keeps one eye on the door in case someone has tipped off the press about the widower bunking at the Talmadge. If anybody's going to have a conversation with Private Hickman, it's going to be him. He is curious about military life in postwar Germany—curious about the ravaged landscape and certain places that they might have in common—but more interested in Hickman's late wife and the life the couple briefly shared.

"I'd like to ask you a few questions about Teresa, if you don't mind, Harold," Arne says. Hickman has asked for Canadian Club and 7-Up. Arne takes the CC on the rocks.

Hickman shrugs, so Arne begins.

"When was the last time you spoke with her? I assume you had a chance now and then to make a long-distance phone call."

Hickman shrugs again. "That wasn't so easy," he says, staring at the glass in his hand. "We don't have that much access to the phones, and calls are expensive. I don't think we've talked since Christmas."

"She'd moved down here by that time, right?"

"Yes."

"When did you get her last letter?"

Hickman doesn't answer right away. He stares into his glass and shakes his head.

"The first of March," he says.

Before Arne can point out the obvious—that the first of March was more than a month ago—Hickman says, "She told me she wanted out of the marriage. She said she wanted to meet other men or that she was dating them already, I don't remember which."

He picks up his glass and drains the rest in a gulp.

Wow, Anderson says to himself. He expected the young man to tear up and show some emotion, but he doesn't. Still, Arne wonders how far he can push the questions under the circumstances. He spots the bartender eyeballing their now-empty glasses and nods his head.

"Do you know," he ventures, leaning forward over the little table, "who she might have been seeing just before she died?"

Hickman sighs. His eyes are closed now, and Anderson worries that he will fall asleep in his chair.

Then Hickman says, "I don't guess that's something a cheating wife tells her husband—the names of the men she's sleeping with."

Arne wonders if Hickman is aware that his wife was pregnant

when she died. If he picked up a newspaper at the airport that afternoon he would know. Arne decides not to mention it for the time being.

"Did Teresa ever mention the dentist Grace referred her to—Dr. Rose?" he asks.

"No," Hickman says. "I don't know anything about a dentist."

"How about the place where she worked, the Palace Luncheonette, near the Montgomerys' apartment? Did she tell you about the job there or about her boss, a guy named Tony Zevos?"

"No."

"How about a photographer named Richard Ybarra?"

Hickman shakes his head. "She didn't tell me anything," he says quietly.

Arne waits a moment, and then asks, "How did Teresa get along with her sister? And with Bud Montgomery?"

For the first time in the past couple of hours, Hickman manages a laugh. A small, bitter laugh.

"Grace was jealous of Terry, how pretty and popular she was," he says. "Terry, I think, felt sorry for Grace, especially after she married Bud and put on more weight."

"Do you think Terry slept with Bud?"

Hickman closes his eyes again.

Very softly he says, "I wouldn't be surprised. Terry wasn't very choosy. She knew a lot of guys before we got married, and I guess she knew a lot of guys afterward, especially while I've been away. When she was sad, which was often, she counted on sex to make herself feel better."

Anderson can't get the conversation out of his mind as he drives through the late-night streets after making sure Hickman was safely tucked into his room for the night. He has assigned a patrolman to sit outside the soldier's door, just in case Oscar Rystrom or some other bottom-feeder from the papers manages to find out where he's staying or, for some reason, he decides to take a powder. Hickman will no doubt sleep soundly tonight, maybe feeling sorry for himself and for the child, but not sleepless with grief for his round-heeled wife. Still, it doesn't hurt to take precautions.

Anderson isn't sure how *he'll* sleep tonight. He's going to have the bed to himself because Lily is spending a couple of nights at her mother's house. Tomorrow morning, after checking on Hickman, he will pick up Mel Curry, go back to see Grace, and get her to tell them more about Rose, though, after Hickman's comments about his wife's activities, they have good reason to consider the other possibilities. He will ask Grace what he did not ask Harold Hickman this evening: Is Harold Hickman Junior the soldier's child?

The thought of Mel Curry sets something else off inside him, something unrelated to the Hickmans, and he turns right at Thirty-eighth Street and heads west a few blocks to Columbus. Cruising south now on Columbus, he drives past a neat, stuccoed duplex and cranes his neck to look up at the second-floor windows. A light is on behind the curtains, so he makes a U-turn at the end of the block and doubles back, more slowly than on the first pass.

He parks across the street under a leafless elm, cracks a window, and lights a cigarette. He's not certain what he expects to see in the Currys' bedroom window tonight, but decides then and there to send Mel to Grand Forks for Teresa Hickman's funeral.

The driver has given his usual haunts a wide berth since Teresa Hickman's murder, avoiding especially the Palace, the Whoop-Tee-Doo Club, and other locations on and around Nicollet Avenue between downtown and Franklin.

He's stayed clear of Lake of the Isles, too, especially the east side, spending more time in other parts of town, such as Powderhorn Park and Lake Nokomis and the U of M campus. Another couple of months and there'll be plenty to see, especially at the Big Beach of Nokomis, but for now there's nothing going on and nobody's likely to notice him on the prowl. For the time being, on the east side of town, he'll be just another faceless schmo driving a canary-colored cab.

He follows the Hickman case in the papers: the arrest of the dentist, the dentist's hiring of a big-shot lawyer, then the lawyer getting the dentist out on bail. If the cops are still looking at other suspects, the papers don't know about it or have agreed not to say anything that might queer the investigation.

On Wednesday, not quite a week since the murder, the *Tribune* runs an interview with the lawyer, Dante DeShields. What the hell kind of name is that anyway? the driver wonders. Probably another Jew, the way they stick together. The photo that accompanies the interview shows DeShields standing in front of a desk the size of an aircraft carrier on the tenth floor of the Foshay Tower. The lawyer looks awfully short, almost midget-short, with a large head wreathed in curly gray-black hair. His dark eyes bulge below heavy black eyebrows. There's a bulbous nose and jug ears poking out of the thick hair. He has a five-o'clock shadow every bit as prominent as Richard Nixon's. And he looks as though he'd like nothing better than to rip a guy's lungs out.

The *Tribune*'s headline runs big and black across the top of the front page.

LAWYER: DENTIST CAN'T GET FAIR TRIAL HERE

"Although no date has been set for the trial of a Minneapolis dentist accused of murdering a pregnant North Dakota woman, Dr. H. David Rose's lawyer says a fair trial in the Mill City is unlikely due to 'systemic anti-Semitism' that has drawn nationwide attention since before the war," staff writer George Appel writes in his opening paragraph. "According to defense attorney Dante DeShields, empaneling an unbiased local jury for his client, who is Jewish, will be 'virtually impossible.'"

The driver is sitting in his car in one of the parking areas along the West River Road, this morning's paper propped against the cab's steering wheel. After dark, the site is popular among amorous teens, who pack the space as though they're at a drive-in movie, the cars often rocking on their suspensions within minutes of their arrival. In broad daylight, he has the space to himself.

Appel notes that though Rose has not yet been indicted in the strangulation death of serviceman's wife Teresa Hickman, DeShields, "according to unnamed courthouse sources, seems to be setting the stage for a change-of-venue request or an appeal if the dentist is eventually convicted."

DeShields says Rose, while conceding that Mrs. Hickman was his patient the night of the murder, has not confessed to the crime. "Police sources say Rose admitted driving the victim around town after her appointment and discussing her pregnancy. According to detectives, the woman, whose husband is on active duty in West Germany, believed Rose was the father of her unborn baby." At some point during the drive, Appel's sources told him, Rose "suffered what he described as a 'blackout,' and when he 'woke up' the woman was no longer in the car. Rose told police he had no idea what happened to her." The allegations appeared earlier in both the *Star* and *Tribune*. What's new is DeShields's pre-emptive strike.

Appel's story concludes, "Hiawatha County Attorney Homer Scofield, who is expected to convene a grand jury later this week, calls Rose's story 'not credible' and DeShields's suggestion of a biased jury pool 'insulting to the good citizens of this city. Counsel should be ashamed.'"

The driver carefully excises the story with a single-edge razor blade he keeps in the glove compartment, neatly folds the rest of the paper, and stuffs it into one of the trash bins on the edge of the parking lot. He's no expert, but he reads the papers and listens to the news and knows that the Teresa Hickman case will be a hot topic for weeks, maybe months, through the trial and beyond.

He recalls the comment he's heard several times over the years, something to the effect that, in high-profile murder cases, the victim is all but forgotten amid the legal wrangling and the focus is on the accused. That may be true, he muses, but *he* won't lose sight of the victim in *this* case. He knew her, after all. He's seen and talked to her. He's seen her up close. In the flesh.

He sees her now, in his mind's eye, moving back and forth behind

the Greek's counter, in and out of the kitchen, her perfect ass in per-
petual motion, usually within reach of the Greek's gimpy kid. He can see
her walking along the street in front of the Whoop-Tee-Doo Club, the
sidewalk trash whistling and catcalling and grabbing at her as she passes,
dying to get a feel for what's under the winter coat. Then he sees her dis-
appearing through the doors that lead upstairs to the dentist's office.

The next time he sees the girl she is sitting with the dentist in
the black Packard along the east side of Lake of the Isles. It's much
later, closer to midnight. What he sees now is much clearer––the
couple arguing in the Packard's front seat, then the girl exiting the
car and striding up Euclid Place, away from the lake and the car. This
time, however, the driver doesn't leave the lake and head back toward
Hennepin Avenue. He pulls out and around the Packard and follows
the girl past the other cars parked along the boulevard. Turning onto
Euclid Place, he spots her a quarter of a block away, her blonde hair
bouncing on her shoulders and her winter coat turning from black to
dark green as she passes under a streetlamp.

He switches on the cab's roof light and creeps along behind and
then alongside the girl. He leans across the front seat and cranks down
the passenger-side window. The girl, not five feet away now, stops,
turns, and looks his way. He can see her smile.

CHAPTER 6

Teresa Hickman's funeral was scheduled for eleven o'clock on the morning of April 15, on the outskirts of Grand Forks, one week after her murder and two days after her body was released by Hiawatha County authorities to her husband. Without a word to anybody in either her family or his, Private Harold Hickman made arrangements for her service to be conducted at His Will Baptist Church, where they were married, and interred in the cemetery out back.

Arne Anderson, alluding to the widower's arrangements, said to Mel Curry, "Well, at least he'll know who's she with." Mel laughed, though Arne didn't mean it as a joke.

Arne decided that Curry and Hessburg will be the eyes and ears of the Minneapolis Police Department at the funeral. They will drive to Grand Forks Thursday afternoon, set up shop at a local hotel, and attend the services Friday morning. They will speak to Teresa Hickman's father and any other family members and acquaintances they can connect with, most importantly the boyfriends and sundry admirers who may feel compelled, or be persuaded, to articulate their obsessions. Arne tapped Hessburg rather than Lakeland, Riemenschneider, or any of the other more senior squad members because Sid, his relative youth notwithstanding, has shown an ease and self-confidence talking to people in stressful situations. Of course, Mel's good at talking to people, too, though that's not why Arne sent him away.

Miles Mckenzie assigned Robert Gardner to attend the rites on behalf of the United Press's Minneapolis bureau. All four of the Twin Cities dailies as well as the UP's archrival, the Associated Press, will be represented by senior reporters and feature writers. Mckenzie figures a small-town funeral will be a simple enough event to cover, even for his least-experienced staffer; the bureau chief and his senior reporters will be better utilized digging up dirt closer to home. In any event, Mckenzie will rewrite everything that Robert files from Grand Forks.

Robert has spent the past couple of days talking to employees of the Whoop-Tee-Doo Club and Palace Luncheonette as well as to Rose's neighbors in his building, learning nothing new about either the dentist or his practice. With Sergeant Anderson's permission, Milt Hickok pored over the doctor's practice records from the past two years, surprised by Rose's sloppy bookkeeping, but likewise learning nothing important.

"North Dakota might be our best chance for a scoop, kid," Mckenzie told Robert, clapping him on the shoulder, "all those horny bachelor uncles and sex-crazed farm boys—find out what *they* have to say about Teresa and her crowd."

Robert is put off by the idea of digging up dirt on the girl, but understands that dirt is often a component of a journalist's job. He decides, however, that he's going to do something grander, nobler. He's going to write the "definitive portrait" of a small-town girl who journeys to the big city looking for work and excitement, only to wind up pregnant, dead, and debased. (The phrase *definitive portrait* glows like a neon sign behind his eyes.) It's exactly the kind of riveting cautionary tale that he read and reread in the U of M's journalism school library, rich in human emotion and provocative detail, and has since dreamed of writing himself. He hasn't told anybody about the idea, least of all

Mckenzie. Better, Robert figures, to simply drop the finished story, a fait accompli, on the boss's desk when he's finished.

On Thursday morning, after receiving Mckenzie's marching orders, Robert jogs downstairs and calls Pam Brantley from a pay phone on Third Street. He figures that this is a good time to call because Karl is almost sure to be dead to the world in the couple's bedroom and Pam hasn't left for lunch or whatever the hell she does during the day.

Pam picks up on the first ring, and he quickly tells her about his assignment. "This will be my first major feature," he says, hoping he doesn't come across as pompous and self-important—that is, like his dad. "I'll be up against the guys from the big papers and the Associated Press, but I'm pretty sure I'm up to it."

"That's great, Bobby," she says in not much more than a whisper. She sounds uninterested or distracted.

"Is something wrong?" he says. "You don't sound like yourself."

But instead of answering him, she says, "I've got to go—why don't you call when you get back." And hangs up.

What was that about, he wonders, standing on the busy street, the phone still pressed to his ear, its dial tone competing with the thrum and rumble of downtown traffic. Maybe Karl was stirring. Or maybe she has another guest, though he's pretty sure it wouldn't be another man this time of day. Maybe her mom or sister is visiting from Rochester.

Then a more depressing thought occurs to him: Pam is angry about their last meeting, when he told her he saw the dead woman along the tracks. Their tryst ended unpleasantly that night, Pam clearly bothered by his revelation that not only had he discovered the body, he hadn't called the police or told his boss—someone in authority. Robert left her apartment angry, not floating on the postcoital cloud their love-making usually placed him on.

Pam knows nothing about the rules of responsible journalism and wouldn't care less if she did. Robert, now unkindly, doubts whether a woman who so enthusiastically violates her wedding vows would worry much about either professional ethics or civic duty. If anything, he was, at least until that moment, reasonably sure that she would think about what he told her and be happy he'd kept his discovery—and their relationship—a secret.

He thinks about calling her back, and then rejects the idea.

"Fuck it," he says out loud, startling a pair of elderly women who happen to be shuffling past on the sidewalk. "Fuck *her*." He immediately feels ashamed of himself, not yet accustomed to spouting obscenities in public.

But, as he heads back to the office, he realizes that the emotion he's feeling most acutely right now is neither anger nor shame. It's hurt.

Like many young journalists, Robert begins to write his story before he sets foot on the story site or speaks to his first source. Fortunately, the four-hour train ride from Minneapolis to Grand Forks, crossing endless dun-colored fields awaiting spring planting, is conducive to daydreaming. An hour shy of the Red River, Robert decides he likes this lede:

As a teenager growing up in tiny Dollar, North Dakota, pretty Teresa Marie Kubicek was little known beyond the town's borders. As a twenty-one-year-old murder victim returning home from the big city for burial, she is a tragic celebrity. The image of the murder victim's waxen corpse lying in the weeds beside the streetcar track hovers behind the words.

And, like many journalists young and old, Robert is surprised when hardly anybody or anything is quite the way he's pictured it.

His Will Baptist Church, for one thing, is not in Grand Forks, but sits by itself on the edge of a potato field three miles southwest of town. Imagining a quaint whitewashed building with lancet windows, peaked roof, and soaring steeple, Robert sees instead, when he and his travel mates in a rented car round a bend on a two-lane county road, a squat brick building with small, square windows and no steeple at all. Its only visible religious symbol is the small cross atop a white sign in the scrubby front yard welcoming *ALL VISITORS* and advertising the church's Sunday and midweek services. From the gravel parking lot on the side of the building, Robert can see a small cemetery, its markers visible beyond a rusty iron fence.

Another surprise: the large number of cars and pickup trucks already filling the lot and parked bumper-to-bumper on both shoulders of the county road that runs in front of the church. Men, women, and a handful of children stand in the parking lot and on the yellow lawn, the church itself, according to one local, already full to its modest capacity. Several dozen folding chairs have been set up in the basement, where speakers will broadcast the words and music from upstairs. A couple of sheriff's deputies in blue caps and fur-collared jackets are stationed outside the church's front doors, where a Chrysler hearse and two black Cadillac limousines are parked. A man with an orange hairpiece and officious manner informs the crowd that only family and "personal friends" have been allowed inside for the service.

It's a bright, cool day, and standing in the elements is not intolerable, but the locals make no attempt to disguise their disdain for the out-of-towners, especially the journalists, easily identified by their notebooks and cameras and shiny suits. The journalists huddle on the edge of the parking lot, cupping cigarettes in their hands and glancing at their watches. Among them, George Appel and Oscar Rystrom from the Minneapolis dailies, and Martin Rice from the Associated Press. Robert is surprised to see Mel Curry, the Minneapolis detective, standing behind Rice.

At five minutes to eleven, six men of varying age and posture line up behind the hearse and wait for the undertaker's men to slide the taffy-colored coffin out of the vehicle's rear door and carry it up the low concrete stoop and into the church. A reporter from the *Grand Forks Herald* helpfully identifies the principals following the coffin and pallbearers, pronouncing the names *sotto voce* as family, neighbors, and "personal friends" shuffle inside.

"Grace Kubicek Montgomery and her husband," the hometown newspaperman says.

"Teresa's father, Walter Kubicek, accompanied, I'm pretty sure, by his sisters.

"Connie Canfield, a school chum of Terry's.

"Kenneth Landa, reportedly the favorite among Terry's boyfriends."

None of these individuals looks like any of the characters that Robert Gardner imagined.

Harold Hickman, in his green uniform and garrison cap, arrives with his middle-aged parents and a young woman the *Herald*'s man identifies as Hickman's kid sister. The Hickmans don't look bereft so much as harassed and annoyed. At the church's front door, ginger-haired, bowlegged Walter Kubicek offers Private Hickman a picket-fence smile and an awkward military salute, but Hickman responds with only the slightest nod of acknowledgment. Hickman's family seem determined to keep some space between themselves and the Kubiceks, and Robert imagines that among the differences is a city-country divide between the comparatively urbane Grand Forks Hickmans and the Kubicek rubes from Dollar.

The biggest surprise is Kenneth Landa. He is not the rugged, broad-shouldered field hand that Robert imagined, but a slight, nervous-looking young man with black-rimmed glasses who could pass for a high school sophomore. He stands to the side, apart from both the Kubiceks and the Hickmans, though Robert knows that he and Harold Hickman are cousins. He heard that Landa and Hickman became rivals after Kenny made the mistake of introducing Teresa to Hal, at the time a sophomore and ROTC dropout at the North Dakota Agricultural College in Fargo.

The service is mercifully brief. No attempt is made to broadcast beyond the church's walls whatever words and music are employed inside to bid farewell to the deceased. The reporters hear only an occasional muffled exultation from the pastor and the high-pitched skirl of the church's organ. Just before the service ends, the officious man in the orange toupee informs the journalists that there will be refreshments in the church parlor upon the service's conclusion, but only for family and friends.

"Grand Forks has several establishments that will be willing to serve you," the man tells the reporters and photographers. He looks at them as though he's talking to a scrum of lepers.

"Fuck you," Oscar Rystrom says under his breath. "And your ugly wife."

George Appel guffaws—an odd sound at a funeral.

"How do you know his wife is ugly?" Marty Rice asks Rystrom.

"You can tell," Rystrom says.

As most of the outsiders either head back to their cars or make plans to hang around and try to talk to family members after the burial out back, Mel Curry asks Robert Gardner if he wants to ride with him to Dollar. Detective Hessburg stayed in Grand Forks in order to speak to the police and other possible sources about the Hickman clan, and Curry tells Robert that he wouldn't mind a "little company" on the sixty-mile drive into the North Dakota hinterlands.

"The truth is, I don't have any sense of direction out here," he says. "All by myself I could wind up in Canada."

Robert is surprised and flattered by the invitation, whatever the detective's real motive. He finds Curry attractive and interesting, though they've exchanged only a few words since the Hickman investigation began. He admires Curry's intensity and soft-spoken manner, which doesn't gibe with his tough-guy-with-a-hair-trigger-temper reputation, and sets him apart from the other cops Robert has met on the job. "Anderson is a loner, hard to approach and get close to, a combat vet with demons," Mckenzie told him during a brief primer on the MPD's homicide detectives a few days earlier. "Lakeland, Wrenshall, and Riemenschneider are old-school boom and bluster, probably on the take, and can't be trusted. Hessburg and LeBlanc are inexperienced and ambitious, out for themselves. Curry's a good guy, reasonably trustworthy. He's also volatile, maybe a trifle unbalanced. Don't get on his bad side."

Robert doesn't like the country, either, and is easily disoriented even in the unevenly populated farmland of southeastern Minnesota that surrounds Rochester, where he grew up. He smiles at the idea of finding his way with Mel Curry, a pair of city slickers trying to navigate the wilderness.

He wonders, briefly, sitting beside the detective in the unmarked Chevrolet, if there are professional guidelines he ought to keep in mind—if sharing a ride with a cop in the middle of a murder investigation, a ride initiated by the cop, is proper. He quickly decides that it is, so long as he doesn't become the cop's source of information instead of the other way around. Robert is mindful, of course, of his own secret and the possible consequences of revealing it, not to mention the temptation he will no doubt have to fight to keep from sharing it with a friendly cop.

He wonders how exactly he should talk to Curry, if, pen and notebook in hand, he should ask questions about the Hickman investigation or if he should be more circumspect and make general conversation, about the crime rate in Minneapolis, for instance, and the challenges of postwar police work. What would more experienced reporters such as Milt Hickok and Marty Rice do in this situation? Then he tells himself it doesn't matter because *he's* the one sitting beside Mel Curry on the road to Dollar.

"Christ," Curry mutters about twenty minutes into the drive. "I'd put a bullet between my eyes if I had to live out here." He doesn't sound as though he's kidding.

The detective tells Robert he grew up on the Near North Side of Minneapolis, attended Vocational High School downtown, worked on the Milwaukee Road while doing some prizefighting around the Midwest, and joined the MPD after returning home from three years in the Merchant Marine. "Other than that time at sea, I've never lived anywhere but in the middle of a city," he says. He married his high school sweetheart, got divorced, then married again, got divorced, then married a third time—"this one's a keeper"—on Valentine's Day, two months ago.

Though the detective doesn't ask, Robert is eager to maintain the conversation. He offers his own private history, slightly more detailed.

"My dad and three of my uncles are surgeons at the Mayo Clinic," he says. "I attended public school in Rochester, then broke my parents' hearts when I went off to study journalism at the U of M." ("Who could blame them?" Curry interjected, seriously or not.) "I worked a year at the *Post-Bulletin*, then came up to the Cities and got the job at the United Press bureau. I'm staying with my sister in Linden Hills until I find my own place."

Curry, one hand on the wheel, turns his head.

"Linden Hills," he says. "So you know the area where the girl was found."

Robert blinks. Why did he mention Linden Hills?

"Well, kind of, I guess," he says. "It's a block from my sister's apartment." Not to mention, he *doesn't* say, a few steps from the apartment where I was fucking my girlfriend the night of the murder.

It occurs to Robert that, despite his fears, there could be some benefit in telling the detective about his discovery. It could give him an importance unique among local reporters. It could also make him a suspect.

Looking out at the empty highway, Curry says, "You didn't see anything important that night, did you?"

Once more, Robert can't tell if Curry is making a joke. In his mind's eye, he sees the girl's hand protruding from the weeds. It takes him a moment to find his voice.

"No, I didn't."

The detective and the journalist say nothing for several minutes. Robert would now give just about anything to be somewhere other than in a car with Mel Curry. God knows what Curry is thinking. Robert hurriedly conjures up the picture of Pam in the back bedroom, Pam in her black bra and underpants and then Pam slipping out of them, and is relieved when he feels the familiar stirring. Maybe Curry is having a similar daydream about his third wife, the "keeper," who, Robert guesses, given the detective's good looks, is a sexy woman in her own right.

* * *

The town of Dollar, when it suddenly materializes on the North Dakota prairie, *is* pretty much what Robert anticipated.

The sign says *DOLLAR Pop. 950*, though, on this Friday afternoon, none of those residents appears to be out and about, either on the short main drag or among the dozen-odd blocks of modest homes that look, the few that Robert sees, forlorn and needing paint in sere, mostly treeless yards. The three-block-long main street—U.S. Highway 2, reduced to a fifteen-mile-per-hour speed trap through town—is home to a Philips 66, a drugstore with a tin Greyhound bus sign swaying in the breeze out front, an out-of-business Ben Franklin emporium, a couple of storefront saloons facing each other across the street, a derelict movie house, a mortuary, a Catholic church, a Lutheran church, and a two-story frame building that advertises a doctor, dentist, and lawyer. All the establishments except the doctor and dental offices seem to be closed for the day.

"Everybody went to Grand Forks for the funeral," Curry says. "We beat 'em home."

The dental office makes Robert think of Dr. Rose, but when he and Curry step inside they learn that its owner, a Dr. James A. London, is a recent University of North Dakota grad who didn't arrive in town and hang out his shingle until the first of the year and, according to the woman behind the receptionist's window, is currently vacationing in Florida. His predecessor, the woman confides when Curry shows his badge, died "by his own hand" two years earlier. "That's not unusual, dentists committing suicide," she adds in a whisper, though there appears to be no one else around to hear her. "I read in a magazine article once that dentists take their own lives far more often than other professional men, though I don't remember if the article said why." She tells Curry that until *that* man's arrival, most Dollar residents, including no doubt the Kubiceks, drove to Hartford or Grand Forks for their dental work. She says, however, that she remembers Terry Kubicek, "may she rest in peace," and that Terry had a "lovely smile."

The visitors split up and spend an hour knocking on doors, sticking their heads in an open establishment when they find one, asking their separate but probably similar questions.

Back in the car, Curry grins and says, "I'll tell you mine if you tell me yours." But neither man has learned anything he didn't know, or hadn't heard, already: Teresa Kubicek—everyone calls her Terry—was a "very popular" girl. She had a lot of friends both boys and girls, did okay in school (Grace was "the brains in the family," they heard more than once), had a "pretty" singing voice, loved to dance, and never got into "serious" trouble. It was unclear whether the latter reflected the speaker's ignorance of or indifference to the reports of shoplifting and flights of "wild" behavior that were by now common knowledge among Twin Cities investigators and reporters.

The pastor of Our Savior's Lutheran Church, now semiretired, told Robert that Terry was confirmed in 1948.

"She was a nice girl, always considerate of others," the Reverend Evert Thomason said. "But she had a careless side, too. She made bad choices sometimes. I worried about her." He declined to elaborate.

Everyone the visitors spoke to knew and expressed regret about her murder, though not everyone seemed especially surprised.

"The Kubiceks have been cursed since Marva ran off with that Holy Roller," a muscular middle-aged man who worked at one of the grain elevators off Main Street opined, citing the untimely deaths of Terry's brothers and Marva herself. "Poor Walter—he never knew if he should shit or shine his shoes," the man, J.D. Fessler, said. "Still doesn't, you ask me. All those deaths in his family left him permanently shell-shocked."

A pair of fiftyish women who might have been twins mentioned rumors that Terry had divorced Harold Hickman and secretly married Kenneth Landa.

"Kenny was her one true love," said the first woman, and her mirror image nodded. The women identified themselves as the Hamblin sisters and said they lived down the block from Walter Kubicek on Third Street. "That's after he sold the farm and moved into town," the second woman said.

A young man in a double-breasted suit refueling a yellow DeSoto at the town's lone filling station spoke darkly of a rumor that Terry had become a "top-dollar prostitute" in the Twin Cities. "I'm not sure I believe that," the man, who declined to give his name, told Robert, "but I knew Terry in high school, and I can tell you it wouldn't be beyond the realm of possibility. She had the looks and a way about her, that's for sure. At the same time, I think most of the gossip about her has been wishful thinking on the part of a lot of guys around here."

"That include you?" Robert ventured.

The man grinned.

"That's for me to know and you to find out," he said.

The Kubicek farm, now reportedly owned by a Hartford family, is in obvious disrepair behind a ragged evergreen windbreak that flanks the gravel approach off the highway. Curry drives up to the house, but neither man can find any sign of life, human or animal, on the property. Robert feels himself shiver in the chilly gloaming as he looks around, hands stuffed deep in the pockets of his overcoat. On their way back toward town, he sees a cluster of barren trees bordering a meandering creek and wonders if the sheltered space once provided cover for Terry and her boyfriends.

At their Grand Forks hotel that evening, Robert calls the bureau from a pay phone in the lobby and reports what he's learned, prefacing his remarks by saying that neither the Kubiceks nor the Hickmans have been willing to talk to reporters, hoping he is right about that.

In Minneapolis, Miles Mckenzie says, "Well, goddammit, then you'll have to stay another day. Try to talk to the girl's old man and that ex-boyfriend, Leander or Landreau or whatever his name is. Her husband, too, if he isn't on his way back to Deutschland already. Call in what you get and find a way back tomorrow night or Sunday morning. I'll probably need you Sunday afternoon."

Before hanging up, Mckenzie tells him that Rose was indicted that afternoon and will be arraigned the next morning. "Then he's expected to post bond and go home," he says.

Curry is drinking whiskey with Sid Hessburg in the noisy lobby bar. He looks up, but doesn't invite Robert to join them. Robert thanks the detective again for the ride out to Dollar and then joins the half-dozen Twin Cities reporters hunched over their drinks and complimentary bowls of shelled peanuts at a long table next to the wall. Nobody is excited about spending the night in Grand Forks.

Oscar Rystrom, already slurring his words, is speculating about the "rampant inbreeding out here in the boondocks," and George Appel, who's heard this before, seems to be struggling to stay awake. Robert glances at his wire service rival, Marty Rice, who's enjoying a Seagram's 7 and 7. Rice rolls his eyes and smiles at Robert. Not a bad guy for the competition, Robert thinks.

Robert wonders how he's going to get back to Dollar, assuming that's where he'd catch up with Walter Kubicek, then decides to stay put in Grand Forks and try to find Kenny Landa and one of the Hickmans, preferably the widower. Mckenzie will be okay with that. Then he'll take the train back to Minneapolis on Sunday morning.

He's no longer thinking about the "definitive portrait" of the small-town girl who comes to grief in the city. Instead, he wonders when he'll see Pam Brantley again.

At four o'clock Saturday afternoon, Dr. Rose sits at the desk in his private office, looking with little interest at the numbers in the clothbound ledger in front of him. Following an unusually swift grand jury proceeding yesterday, he was indicted on charges of first-degree murder in the death of Teresa Marie Hickman. This morning, after entering a plea of not guilty, his lawyer, Dante DeShields, posted a $15,000 cash bond and Rose went home. Having nothing else to do, and with a vague notion of putting his affairs in order prior to what he expects to be a prolonged hiatus, he then drove himself to his office.

He can hear what he'd describe as "mambo music" from the dance studio across the hall and the pounding jukebox racket from the club below, but pays no attention to either. Breaking his own stricture against tobacco smoke in the office, he packs, tamps, and lights his pipe, always a pleasing ritual, and wonders what he's supposed to do with himself in the absence of patients. This will be the most difficult phase of his "situation," he muses. The inability to practice dentistry is almost impossible for him to comprehend.

Thanks to Ruth, talking to his daughters was not as painful as he feared it would be. She told the girls, "Your father never laid a malicious hand on that poor young woman and had nothing to do with her death. Mr. DeShields will make that perfectly clear if and when the case goes to trial. Your father is a good and gentle man and would never do anything that would besmirch the family or damage his practice. But our lives will be different, at least for a couple of months, and in the meantime we must carry on as best we can."

She could have added, but didn't: "Our people have survived far worse than this."

Of course the girls cried, especially Lael, the younger of the two, but they take after the Oshinskys, a tough, stolid, and when necessary combative family, and will soldier through this crisis. Ruth has already confirmed plans for the girls' six-week summer camp in northwestern Wisconsin that begins shortly after school lets out in mid-June.

The appointment cancelations began the Monday after news of Rose's arrest appeared in the papers, then continued through the new week and didn't stop until there were no appointments left to cancel. With her husband's approval, Ruth hired a woman who worked for her family's business to sit in his shuttered office and answer the phone while Rose, on his lawyer's advice, speaks to no one and keeps a low profile at home. On the legal pad the woman left for the doctor are sixty-seven canceled appointments beginning on April 11, representing nearly every woman, man, and child on his active patient list.

Most of the threats have come by way of phone calls, to both the house and the practice. Anonymous and all but two or three a male's voice, the worst cursing Minnesota's abolition of the death penalty more than forty years earlier and wishing Rose at least a life sentence at "backbreaking labor." Several letters bristled with anti-Semitic language, often accompanied by crude drawings of large-nosed men, nooses, daggers, and swastikas. The most unusual mailing was a supposedly comical rant against dentists that had been cut from a yellowed men's magazine and clotted with scurrilous handwritten marginalia.

Ruth's brother Ronnie, who had begun staying at the house, collected everything in a large cardboard box that he kept in a closet in his bedroom. "If one of these morons resorts to more than words," he explained to his sister, "the police will want to look at this shit."

"Just be sure the girls don't see it," Ruth replied. "And let's not use that language in the house."

Ronnie is a help and a comfort, but he has a way of making both Ruth and his brother-in-law nervous. (They suspect, but don't know and don't want to ask, that he carries a loaded handgun in his briefcase.) After the first of the threatening calls, he suggested the family request a police presence at both the house and the office. But when he called the MPD, he was told that DeShields had already made the request and it was rejected. Whoever Ronnie talked to said the department would "consider" increasing its patrols in the neighborhood, but nobody in the house has noticed any squad cars on either Thirty-ninth or Zenith during the week. Ruth says she hasn't seen a police car on Zenith since she spotted one that she believes was en route to the crime scene at the trolley tracks.

Now, a few minutes before five *this* Saturday—a week since Teresa Hickman's body was discovered—Rose is surprised when Detective Sergeant Anderson knocks on the outer office door.

"It's a good idea to keep it locked," Anderson says when Rose lets him in.

"Well, I don't have to worry about turning away patients," Rose says, his idea of a small joke. "I don't have many left. None of my regulars, to be exact."

The two men stand in the windowless waiting room, where the time of day or night is indeterminate, neither man seeming to know what to say next. Rose notes that Anderson is alone and that it's a nice enough afternoon for him to have left his overcoat at the office or in his car. When the detective removes his fedora, Rose notices perspiration on his broad forehead.

"Come in, Sergeant," Rose says. "Have a seat if you wish. What can I do for you?"

Is it possible the detective has a toothache? The big man has smiled only once or twice in the dentist's presence, but that was enough to suggest that, like most middle-aged, working-class Americans, Anderson has been indifferent about his dental hygiene. He suspects Anderson is a year or two on the bright side of forty and, though ten or fifteen pounds overweight, appears generally healthy. There is, Rose noted on their first meeting, a vigor and physical strength about the man that's shared by his younger partner, Curry, but not by the other detectives—large, bulky, slow-moving men—that he's met during the past week.

There's a quiet solemnity about this detective, too, Rose observes. He hasn't encountered enough policemen in his life to hazard a generalization, but he's seen a similar melancholy in ex-servicemen he's dealt with since the war. He guesses that Anderson is a veteran who saw his share of combat.

Anderson sits down in one of the waiting-room chairs and says, "This is off the books, Doctor. Neither my superiors nor your lawyer would be happy to know I'm here. What you say to me today will not be used against you in court, I promise."

The detective pauses, and Rose wonders if he's struggling to decide if he should say what he came here to say. Could this be a ploy to trick him into stating, in no uncertain terms, that he murdered Teresa Hickman? Should he take the detective at his word?

"I won't tell if you won't," Rose says, sitting down himself. He surprised himself. He's not given to flippant remarks even with family and close friends—so why, he wonders, is he making a joke now? Surely, he doesn't want to come across as disrespectful or, worse, unmindful of the allegations against him and the seriousness of a young woman's death.

Anderson, leaning forward, his thick hands clasped between his knees, says, "I've had the chance to watch Dante DeShields at work. He's an excellent lawyer, maybe the best criminal lawyer this side of Chicago.

But, trust me, Doctor, you're going to lose this case in court. You will be convicted of murder and sentenced to twenty years in prison."

Arne pauses again, and then says, almost under his breath, "But I'm not convinced you're guilty."

"I'm pretty sure I'm not," Rose says.

"Well, a jury will decide you are," Anderson continues. "Partly because you're a Jew, and partly because the circumstances you described during our conversations are preposterous. Even a juror who might not care if you're a Jew—or a Jap or a colored—if there is such a person in this town, is going to laugh out loud when your lawyer says that you blacked out in the car with Teresa Hickman and when you woke up she was gone."

Rose thinks about DeShields's insistence on silence and wonders what he could say. Anderson is not taking notes, so the dentist isn't sure what, if anything, could be used against him if the detective went back on his word. He realizes, with a small sense of surprise, that he likes the man. Despite Ronnie's offhand comment about a brutality complaint, Anderson impresses him as an intelligent, honest, even considerate man. Rose suspects that he can speak candidly, at least when the two of them talk one-to-one, in such a familiar setting, without a roomful of police, a prosecutor, and a stenographer who's writing everything down.

The two men stare at each other across the small room. Neither seems to be aware of the Latin music shimmying in from the dance studio across the hall or the thudding bass from the jukebox downstairs. When Rose relights his pipe, Anderson strikes and holds a match to a Camel. So much for the office rules.

"You need to tell me exactly what happened that night," the detective says.

"I told you," Rose replies.

"Tell me again."

Anderson says, "Tell me about your relationship with Grace and Teresa, Dr. Rose."

Rose draws thoughtfully on his pipe.

"Well," he says, "I've known Mrs. Montgomery since last fall. She came to me because she needed a root canal and because my office was around the corner from her apartment. I've treated her for various concerns maybe three or four times since. I've also hired her to solicit patient referrals, for which I agreed to pay her a modest amount."

"Did she provide any referrals?"

"Yes, she did. Two or three, I believe."

"One of those referrals was her sister, wasn't it?"

"Yes."

"Did you ever see Mrs. Montgomery outside the office?"

Rose seems to think about this for a moment. Finally, he says, "Not that I recall, though, since she lives nearby, it's possible we have encountered each other on the street. A couple of times, I felt I had to help her return to her apartment after a long procedure because she was slow coming out of the sedation. On those occasions, I walked her downstairs and around the corner to her building. It would've been dark and maybe slippery on the sidewalk. Sometimes there are unsavory men lingering outside the club."

"'Lingering'? Do you mean 'loitering'?"

"Well, hanging around, watching the women—that sort of thing."

"Did you ever go inside with her?"

"Once for sure. I was afraid she couldn't make it up the stairs."

"Was Mr. Montgomery at home that evening?"

"Not that I was aware of. She said he worked late hours at the tractor plant."

"Did you spend any time in her apartment?"

"She made me a cup of Nescafe. I stayed long enough to drink it."

"Would you say you developed a friendship with Mrs. Montgomery, Doctor?"

Rose sucks on his pipe, and then takes it out of his mouth.

"She is, or was, a patient of mine. You could say we were friendly, but I'm not sure that made us friends."

Anderson stares at the dentist. He notices that while *he* is perspiring in the stuffy anteroom, Rose is not. Rose looks as crisp and comfortable as he must have looked driving away from Zenith Avenue that morning.

"If and when you and Grace Montgomery talked about personal matters, what would you talk about?"

Rose uncrosses and then recrosses his legs.

"Oh, I don't know," he says. "She would tell me about her family and talk about her life in North Dakota and her trouble finding a good job in the Twin Cities. She didn't seem to like it here, and I got the impression that she was unhappy with her marriage. Unhappy with just about everything, or so it seemed to me."

"Have you met her husband?"

"No. And I don't think I'd care to. He sounds like a brute."

"Did you ever have sex with Grace, Doctor?"

"Sexual relations with a patient would violate my professional ethics, Sergeant," Rose replies evenly. "I thought I made that clear. So, no, I have not."

"Did Grace talk about Teresa?"

Rose sighs and shakes his head.

"She mentioned a sister, but didn't say much about her until she called one afternoon after the first of the year and said her sister was in town and needed to see a dentist. She said Teresa had a toothache."

"What were your initial impressions of Teresa Hickman, Doctor?"

"Well, Sergeant," Rose says, the hint of a smile playing on his lips, as though he is speaking of someone they both knew well, "she struck me immediately as very different from her sister. Physically different, that's for sure, but in her manner as well. I'm not certain I would have thought of them as sisters if I hadn't known they were."

Anderson tries to picture Teresa Hickman presenting herself in the dentist's office the first time, a pretty young woman with large eyes, a trim, provocative figure, and a smile that makes a dentist swoon. He imagines a cold night, a couple of inches of fresh snow on the sidewalk and maybe flurries in the air, though Rose's office is uncomfortably warm, the big cast-iron radiators in both rooms hissing and clanking.

Because she has a toothache, the young woman presses a handkerchief against her cheek, but the discomfort doesn't depress her. In fact, there's a liveliness about her that her older sister doesn't have and that animates her physical appeal.

"She struck me as a young woman who knew how to enjoy herself," Rose says. He pauses as though to fix the picture in his mind's eye. "That seemed apparent the first time I met her."

"Did you have sex with Teresa Hickman, Dr. Rose?"

"No." He sighs and shakes his head. "I repeat: I don't have sex with my patients."

"Did you *attempt* to have sex with Teresa Hickman?"

"No."

"Did you *consider* having sex with her?"

Rose is quiet. He seems to be thinking. Or trying to remember. Or wondering what he should say.

"I suppose you could say that I considered it," he says at last. "She led me to believe it was something we both would enjoy."

Anderson stares at the dentist.

"She propositioned you?"

Rose sighs again.

"Not in too many words," he says. "But I felt she was flirting with me. She led me to believe she would not be opposed to the idea."

"How did you respond?"

"I'm sure I told her that that would be against the rules."

The conversation goes on long enough for Rose to tell Anderson that he had seen Teresa five or six times, always in his office and always in the evening, and that only two of those visits—the first time in January and the last time the night she was murdered—were actual dental appointments.

"She would come by to talk," Rose says quietly. "She'd call first and come up if I didn't have a patient. She could do that because she lived close by. We'd sit in this room. Sometimes she seemed sad and confused. She laughed a lot, but she cried, too. She'd be talking about something—her husband or her child or someone at home—and I'd notice that her eyes were brimmed with tears. She said she'd married the wrong man and hated living with her sister and wanted to move somewhere warm, like California."

"Did she tell you why she didn't like living with her sister?" Arne asks. The shadowed image of Bud Montgomery looms behind the question.

But Rose shakes his head.

"Teresa would say something and then either take it back or refuse to explain," he says. "That's the way she talked."

"Was there any physical contact between you at all, besides the dental work, during her visits?"

Rose sighs.

"Well, I might have given her a hug."

"A hug? That's all?"

"I might have kissed her once."

"Just once?"

"I don't remember."

Anderson lets this sink in.

"Did she ever ask you for money?"

"If she did, it was only during that last visit."

Rose makes a strange face, his lips pursed as though he's about to whistle. It's an expression that Anderson hasn't seen until now. Rose says, "I felt sorry for the girl, Sergeant. She was sad behind her smile. I think she was very unhappy." He shook his head, and then added, "Folks think we're heartless people, but that isn't true."

Arne considers those last few words.

Was Rose talking about Jews or about dentists, he wonders.

CHAPTER 7

The driver doesn't have to buy the *Star* on the following Monday because a fare left everything but the sports pages on the backseat when he got out in front of the Farmers & Mechanics Bank downtown. Maybe the cheap asshole, a crabby business type who looked like he could do better, figured the paper would be his tip. Anyhow, that's where the driver gets the evening news today, and as soon as he pulls it into the front seat at a stoplight, he sees the skinny blonde's face staring back at him.

It finally feels like spring. There's a bright blue sky with a fragrant breeze from the southwest, and the sun warms his left arm, which, shirtsleeve rolled above the elbow, he dangles out the driver's-side window.

He turns off the roof light and drives south on Portland, takes a left at Thirty-eighth, then a right onto Chicago, and drives another block. He likes to park here, alongside a large playground and ball field, in the valley between Chicago and Park avenues that runs south from Thirty-ninth Street. He parks on Chicago, across the street from an imposing yellow-brick church, and walks down the steps to a bench near the wading pool. The pool is empty and the benches otherwise deserted, this being only April, but when school lets out in a few minutes, Central High girls will stroll through the park in chattering, giggling twos and threes, with their winter coats off or at least flung open, promising good things to come.

FAMILY, FRIENDS SAY GOODBYE TO SLAIN NODAK WOMAN, the *Star*'s eight-column, top-of-the-page headline reads. Below the headline are two stories, one by the *Star*'s Oscar Rystrom and the other by Miles Mckenzie of the United Press. (The driver pays attention to the bylines. He once fancied himself going to college and becoming a newspaperman, and then decided it would be more work than it was worth.) For several minutes, however, the driver can't get past Teresa Hickman's photo, which looks in its posed primness very much a high school graduation picture, which of course it is, courtesy, according to the photo credit, of the 1951 Dollar High School *Greenback*.

There are other photos as well, two on the front page and two more inside on the jump. They were taken on Friday, before and after the funeral in Grand Forks, according to their captions, and show the girl's soldier husband and farmer father and a cluster of "family and friends," heads down and eyes averted, coming out of the church after the service. Only one man in the group, an angry-looking little guy with black-rimmed glasses, glares at the photographer. Maybe one of the girl's brothers, if she had any, or a cousin or a boyfriend. They all look like hayseeds in their bad-fitting suits and outback haircuts. Even in uniform the girl's husband looks like a hick.

There was a packed church and an "uplifting" Baptist service, according to Rystrom's account. The pastor, whose sermon had been mimeographed and distributed to the press, talked about spring being the season of "hope and renewal." While Teresa was murdered on Good Friday, his remarks concluded, "Easter Sunday—Resurrection Day—followed only two days later. Could that be a coincidence? I don't think so. It tells us that life will triumph over death."

"What an idiot," the driver mutters.

According to witnesses, Teresa's sister, Grace Montgomery, attempted to give the eulogy, but was "overcome by grief and returned sobbing to her pew." Walter Kubicek, the sisters' father, then "rose from his seat, turned to face the congregation, and shouted in a hoarse voice, 'Terry was a good girl, always neat and punctual, and respected her elders. I don't think she deserved what happened to her.'"

The driver laughs out loud. "Neat and punctual!" Hell, he thinks, I could have done better than that half-witted bohunk, and I didn't know the girl. Not officially anyway.

The United Press sidebar begins, "As a pretty teenager growing up in Dollar, ND, population 950, Teresa Marie Kubicek was little known beyond the small town's limits. Now, as a twenty-one-year-old murder victim coming home from the big city, she is famous."

The story describes Dollar and a handful of its residents, clearly implying that anybody in his or her right mind would have done what Teresa did and head for the bright lights of the city as soon as he or she could pay for bus fare.

Pretty Teresa Marie.

The writer got that right.

Harold Hickman, the widower, didn't speak to reporters, nor, apparently, did any of *his* family in Grand Forks. According to a one-paragraph statement issued on the family's behalf, Harold and Teresa's toddler will remain in the care of Hickman's family when he returns to West Germany at the end of the week. A couple of Teresa's friends, Kenneth Landa and Constance Canfield Bannister, were quoted, but neither said anything the driver found interesting.

Wrestling with the paper when the breeze rattles it in his hands, the driver returns to the girl's photo on the front page. This is not what she looked like at the Palace or on Euclid Place that night—at least it's not the way he remembered, or imagined, her. The large, pale eyes are unmistakable, but the posed and practiced expression in the yearbook photo is not the face that is burned into his brain. He can't help but wonder what expression she wears in her grave.

The driver reminds himself that he has his own photos of Terry

Hickman—her friends called her *Terry* in the newspaper story and so, from now on, will he—a trio of eight-by-ten black-and-white glossies taken by Richard Ybarra, whom the driver met at the luncheonette and has visited at his Stevens Square "studio." The driver paid fifteen dollars for the three prints, which was highway robbery, but, truth be told, he would have paid three times that much if he'd had to.

He'd love to keep the photos with him, clean and undamaged in the large manila envelope he lifted from the Canary Cab office, so he could look at them on his breaks, but he knows that he'd be in big trouble if they were ever discovered. So he keeps them with his magazines and books and other photos stashed safely away in his garage at home.

He looks up from the paper and smiles at the pair of comely Central girls passing at the moment. But if they notice him at all, they pay no attention.

Fuck 'em, he tells himself. Neither one of them can hold a candle to Terry.

Over a late lunch at the courthouse coffee shop, Anderson and Curry brief each other on their interviews of the past three days. An early edition of the *Star* sits on the counter next to their coffee cups, the crumbs of their ham-and-cheese sandwiches, and a bite or two of a disappointing peach cobbler.

"It's too early for peaches," Mel grouses. "Those should have stayed in the can."

While Curry was in North Dakota, Anderson, Lakeland, and Riemenschneider revisited the Greek and his son, the staff and assorted hangers-on at the Whoop-Tee-Doo Club, and Rose's office neighbors. Storholm, LeBlanc, and Hessburg went back to Forty-fourth Street and recanvassed the apartment- and duplex-dwellers along the trolley tracks with instructions to determine the source of the report about a skinny guy with glasses at or near the crime scene shortly after midnight on April 9.

"No one came up with anything fresh," Arne says, raising his cup and then setting it down again. "Storholm says there's a girl in one of the apartments—a hot little number, or so he says, you know Einar—who turned red and acted funny when he asked about the guy with glasses, but insisted she was sleeping and saw no one outside that night. Anyways, her apartment windows face the street out front, not the tracks in back. Her husband, who works at one of the hospitals downtown, said he didn't get home until almost three that morning and didn't see a thing."

Curry says that he talked briefly to Teresa Hickman's father, a handful of the Kubicek and Hickman family members and friends, including neighbors and former beaus, but no one would say much about anything.

"I had that new wire service reporter with me for a while—gave him a ride out to Dollar and back," Mel says, lighting a cigarette. "Nice kid, but green, trying to find the spine to talk to people. Of course, the people up there didn't much want to talk to people from down here, least of all reporters."

"What about that Landa kid?"

"With the exception of Kenny Landa. *He* talked. He says he knew Teresa better than anyone except her sister. But he struck me as crazy as a tick on a dog's ass. He ranted and raved and even started crying, but wasn't very helpful. I couldn't figure out, for instance, if Harold Hickman stole Terry away from him or vice versa, but I did confirm Landa's alibi for the night of the murder. Landa was in Devils Lake, North Dakota, staying with another cousin and working on their cars, all that weekend."

Anderson lights his own cigarette and looks around the room, at everyone except his partner. He pictures Mel knocking on doors and bracing Kenny Landa while Arne raps softly on the Currys' apartment door and fifteen minutes later commences to fuck Janine on the Currys' sofa. Their liaison was not something Arne planned, but was something he'd been thinking about since the Currys returned from their New Orleans honeymoon in February and he and Lily joined them for celebratory drinks at Harry's Cafe. He's no longer sure, for that matter, if Janine's availability occurred to him before or after he decided to send Mel to North Dakota. At any rate, he doesn't want to think about any of that, or about Lily, either, so he returns his focus to Teresa Hickman's unblinking gaze on the paper's front page.

"It will be easier to talk to the Montgomerys down here," he says. "Assuming they're back in town already."

Now Mel is looking at Arne and frowning.

"What do you expect they're going to tell us?" he says. "That Bud did it? That Bud scooped Teresa off the street after her dental appointment that night, drove her someplace dark and secluded, then raped and strangled her? C'mon, Arne. Bud might be a goon, but Rose is our killer. He probably didn't rape Teresa, but he sure as hell murdered her. He all but told us so. What more do you want?"

Arne signals for the check from the counterman.

What more do I want?

I want Rose to make a full and signed confession and a guilty plea that would spare me not only the burden of legal proof but the burden of Lily Kline's questions.

What more do I want?

I want to fuck your wife tonight and tomorrow night and maybe every night for the rest of my life.

"Everything" is what he says.

But when they knock on the Montgomerys' door a half hour later, they find only Grace, who's been drinking and says there's nothing more she can tell them. They can't help but notice a fresh bruise over her left eye and a swollen upper lip.

Anderson is tempted to ask if she worries she will end up like her sister, only without the sex first. Instead he says, "Why didn't you tell us that your sister had an appointment with Dr. Rose that night?"

Grace stares at them with a drunkard's eyes. "'Cuz I didn't know that 'til after," she says without conviction. "She lied to me. She said she was going to work."

"Why didn't you tell us that Private Hickman isn't Harold Junior's father?"

Anderson is making an educated guess that surprises even Curry. Not that the boy's paternity is particularly relevant, but he noticed that the child's eyes are dark brown, almost black, not at all like Private Hickman's icy blues.

"News to me," Grace replies with even less conviction than accompanied her first lie.

Arne takes a deep breath and exchanges glances with Curry. The woman is the link between Rose and her sister, but she's no good to them in her current state and may never be.

"Tell us what your sister told you about Dr. Rose," Curry says.

Grace says, "I told you everything I know."

Anderson asks where her husband is at the moment.

"Out," she says, "I know not where," and giggles at the poetic phrasing.

After leaving the Montgomerys' apartment a few minutes later, Arne tells Hessburg and LeBlanc to take turns staking out the place.

"Call the minute you see him," Arne says, knowing that the other detectives are rolling their eyes at the request, as though Bud Montgomery is still a suspect while every cop in the city except, apparently, Arne knows the killer's identity.

But when Frenchy calls ninety minutes later, Anderson sends Curry home and brings Charlie Riemenschneider back to the Montgomerys' apartment. Bud is coming down the stairs, on his way out again, when the detectives open the building's front door. Spotting the cops, he turns on his heel and starts back upstairs, but not quickly enough. Anderson hooks both ankles with a one-armed tackle that cuts Bud's feet out from under him—not unlike the plays he made as an All-City end on the undefeated Theodore Roosevelt varsity in 1936. Riemenschneider, a South High tough two years Arne's senior, piles on, grabbing Montgomery in a headlock and yanking him down into the main-floor vestibule.

"Let's go round back," Arne says, seizing Bud's right wrist and twisting it sharply, forcing an audible snap and a loud yelp. Riemenschneider removes his spectacles and tucks them into his vest pocket.

When the detectives have Bud out back, they shove him against the building's sooty brick facade, Riemenschneider's huge paw clamped on Bud's throat.

"Didja rape Teresa Hickman, shitbird?" Charlie says.

"No!" Bud struggles to say.

"But you tried, didn't you?" Arne says, moving in close.

"Uh-uh," Montgomery whimpers.

With his free hand, Riemenschneider yanks the sap out of his coat pocket and slaps it hard against Montgomery's privates. Bud gasps and falls forward against the detective.

"Come again, asshole?" Charlie says.

Bud, gasping and drooling, finally says, "Okay, I fucked her. But it wasn't rape."

The detectives grab Montgomery's arms and jerk him to his feet.

"Three or four times," Bud says, babbling, eager to please now. "Just before bedtime, when I wasn't working. She let me come in her room after Grace fell asleep."

Anderson and Riemenschneider glance at each other, and then back at Bud, who looks stupid and afraid, but proud of himself as well. Charlie smacks his right ear with the sap, drawing blood.

Arne puts his face up close and hisses, "Did you kill her, mother-fucker?"

"No!" Bud squeals. "Why would I do—"

But before he can finish, Anderson drops him with a fist to the solar plexus.

There's a cellar door down a short flight of crumbling steps, and that's where the detectives drag Montgomery. For the next several minutes, in a dank room filled with muddy garden hoses and rusty hardware, they beat him senseless. Arne has all he can do to keep from pulling out his revolver and putting a bullet between the man's eyes.

He leans over Bud's bleeding, heaving body and says, "Hit your wife again, asshole, and we'll cut off your balls and throw you in the river."

As he and Riemenschneider, both breathing hard and sweating,

146   THE SECRET LIVES OF DENTISTS

trudge back up to the alley and around the building to their car, Anderson knows that Bud Montgomery had nothing to do with Teresa Hickman's murder. But Bud is a despicable human being. Arne is quite sure he wouldn't feel any worse dispatching him than he did about killing Hitler's troopers on the way to Bastogne.

It's almost midnight on Tuesday before Robert reconnects with Pam. To his enormous relief, she's either extremely glad to see him or at least as sex-starved as he is, because she wastes no time pulling him into the back bedroom and onto the bed.

After they quickly reach a rousing climax, Robert kisses her shoulder and says, "I was afraid you'd still be angry."

"About what?" she says.

"You sounded angry when I called the day before my trip. About what I told you the night before." He doesn't want to go through it again.

"If I sounded angry, I'm sorry," she says. "I'm not anymore."

But she is different tonight. After the sex, she is distracted, maybe annoyed, despite what she said. He stares at her sex kitten's body. Their lovemaking tonight was as good as ever, or nearly so, yet he can't help but think that something has changed.

He has been reluctant to tell her that he loves her, but now he wonders if he should, even though he wouldn't mean it—not yet. He doesn't think he needs to say it in order to fuck another time tonight, but he may say it anyway, with an eye on the future. He's pretty sure that she won't say it back; she's not the type any more than Janice, whom he did believe he loved and told her so, but who only shook her head, looked away, and said she wasn't "there yet."

Lying beside Pam, he wonders if she's told anyone his secret. He doesn't know whom she would have told, with the possible exception of her sister, if she was going to keep their affair to themselves. But, judging by her comments over the past few weeks, she and Janice are no longer all that close and not likely to share a confidence, least of all one that could break up a marriage. No, Robert tells himself, he doesn't think he has to worry about that.

He rolls her over on her back and kisses her deeply, his right hand sliding down her body to the dewy patch between her legs. She responds the way he hoped she would, her body stirring beneath his touch while his cock stiffens against her.

"I don't think we have time," she whispers, but he's fully aroused again and isn't going to stop.

He mounts and pushes inside her as she wraps her legs around his flanks. He pumps her for what seems like a very long time before he comes. He can tell without her saying so it was good for her, and he's filled once again with self-confidence.

Ten minutes later, after she disappears into the bathroom and he reaches under the bed for his socks, he touches and then pulls out a pair of men's eyeglasses. The glasses are similar to his own, and for a moment he wonders if they're his—but, no, these have tortoise-shell frames and belong to someone else.

"Has Karl started wearing glasses?" he asks when Pam comes back from the bathroom, wrapping herself in a terrycloth robe.

"No, why?" she says, a second before it dawns on her why.

"Give me those, please!" she says, and snatches the glasses out of his hand.

Robert doesn't know what to say. He was hoping to tell her about his North Dakota trip and ask if she read the *Star*'s United Press sidebar he reported and all but wrote, never mind Mckenzie's byline, but that isn't going to happen now. There was another man in Pam's bed while he was away, and that other man, in his haste to scram before her husband got home, left his glasses on the floor. He thinks, irrationally no doubt, about the "skinny young guy with glasses" that Mckenzie and the boys were talking about at the bureau, another person the detectives investigating Teresa Hickman's murder are interested in identifying. So Robert isn't the only one of Pam's lovers who is skinny and nearsighted.

Then a more urgent question: Would Pam have told this other man Robert's secret? Robert retrieves his own glasses from the bedside table and reaches for his underwear at the foot of the bed.

He doesn't know what to say so he says nothing. He dresses quickly, offers Pam a forced smile, and walks out the door before she can respond. It's a beautiful night, moonless and chilly, but redolent of the coming spring, yet as he hits the front sidewalk on his wobbly legs he's afraid he's going to be sick.

By the last week in April, the handsome Zenith Avenue home of Dr. H. David Rose—like several of its neighbors built with enough faux Tudor embellishments, including the thick, spreading ivy, to suggest an English manor house—has become a fortress of sorts.

Ronnie Oshinsky has moved into a second-floor bedroom and conducts his own legal business (divorce work mainly) from the writing table beside a window overlooking the alley. A dozen-odd additional Oshinskys—in-laws and cousins and other members of Ruth's extended mercantile family—quietly come and go as needed.

Other Oshinsky cousins, scions of the original Oshinsky Brothers, Jacob and Bernard, have arranged for the private "operatives" who spend four-hour shifts sitting in a pearl-colored Chrysler Imperial out front. Three generations of cousins have provided security for Oshinsky family interests since before the Depression. While they haven't shut down the crank calls and poison-pen letters, there's been no garbage thrown on the lawn or other demonstrations of disapproval since they arrived.

Rose's two brothers—Samuel, a gynecologist currently practicing in Duluth, and George, a dentist carrying on the family's Morrison County practice in Vincennes—are frequent visitors. Sam long ago changed his surname to Ross. He became a very wealthy man after inventing and patenting an improved speculum. It was Dr. Ross who put up the $15,000 that freed his younger brother on bond.

David Rose no longer goes to the office, even when he can think of nothing else to do. If he had a patient, he would, but he doesn't, so he relies on the woman from the Oshinsky enterprises to sit in his shuttered office, answer the occasional phone call, and collect the mail.

He is by turn bemused and unsettled by all the coming and going.

He's grateful, of course, for the moral support and financial aid from his family, but understands that his acceptance is a tacit admission that his practice is small potatoes relative to his brothers'. Seven years younger than George and nine years Samuel's junior, he has never been close to the brothers (there are no sisters), who have picked on and patronized him his entire life. Like Ruth, he is nervous about *her* brother bivouacked upstairs. And he worries about what the neighbors must think about the omnipresent Imperial and its hulking occupants parked out front.

Since his arraignment, Rose has not been contacted by the police. He sometimes wonders if that peculiar Saturday afternoon visit by Sergeant Anderson was a figment of his imagination. In fact, he dreams about the big detective as often as he dreams about Teresa Hickman, both of them in unlikely scenarios and at least once sharing the same one. He has dreamed about a baby, too, though *whose* baby isn't clear. Ruth says that he's become a restless sleeper, often talking out loud about this or that, none of his outbursts making sense to her.

Dante DeShields is a regular visitor, parking his white Cadillac behind the gray Imperial and spreading a growing archive of documents across and under the dining-room table. Rose is intrigued by the famous lawyer, even though he's viscerally afraid of him, reminding him of a handsome but dangerous bulldog or German shepherd. (Rose has never owned or even lived in a house with a dog and knows nothing about them. Still, that's his impression.) The papers say that DeShields is "well connected" in state and city political circles, mentioning Hubert Humphrey and other Democratic Farmer Labor Party luminaries, but Rose, who, unlike his wife, has never been much interested in politics, can't decide if that's helpful or not.

Presuming *Dante* to be an Italian name, Rose supposes DeShields is a Catholic. Who knows what *DeShields* is—French, Dutch, English?—and he's not about to ask. At any rate, the diminutive, beetle-browed attorney and Michael Haydon, his fair-haired assistant who doesn't look old enough to shave let alone possess a law degree, are usually the only Christians in the house. Rose is aware, of course, of DeShields's comments to the press about the dire prospects of a fair trial in Jew-hating Minneapolis, but the dentist has no firsthand reason to worry about a biased legal system. Like apparently everyone else, he assumes that the lawyer is positioning the case for a change of venue, an eventual appeal, and ultimate relief.

One evening, after a couple of glasses of wine, Ronnie tells the Roses that DeShields will never ask David if he murdered the girl.

"He'd consider the question disrespectful and insulting," Ronnie explains, one lawyer purporting to describe the mentality of another. "He wants you to believe that he believes in you. Of course, it's irrelevant what a lawyer thinks or believes regarding a client's guilt or innocence. His job is to mount the best defense he possibly can and make the government prove its case—if it has one."

Dr. Rose, who isn't drinking, says nothing in reply, not certain how he feels about his defender's opinion. When he welcomes the lawyers into his home the following afternoon, he's not certain, as far as that goes, whose idea it was to hire DeShields in the first place. The decision seemed to have been made by a committee comprising Ruth, Ronnie, and Rose's brothers, with Rose himself merely observing— but maybe that's a dream, too. All he seems to know for sure is that he both likes and fears the scary little man and is glad he's here.

DeShields sits at the head of the table, either making a point or indifferent to the fact that the head of the household, not his attorney, typically occupies that chair. He rarely smiles, never makes small talk, and holds his Herbert Tareyton cigarette gangster-style between his thumb and forefinger. He has the heaviest five-o'clock shadow Rose has ever seen—yes, heavier than Nixon's—and could use a peroxide treatment to whiten his smallish, crooked teeth. Rose usually sits to DeShields's right, and Michael Haydon (who has beautiful teeth, doubtless the result of a straightening appliance purchased by affluent parents during his adolescence) faces him across the table, only infrequently looking up from the notes he scribbles on a growing stack of yellow legal pads. The fourth chair, on the end closest to the kitchen, is often occupied by Ruth, who sees to the men's coffee and occasional Fanny Farmer assorted chocolates, and doesn't say a word until DeShields has left for the day.

Ronnie often slips into the room and sits down with his own pen and legal pad in a chair pushed back against the wall next to the built-in buffet. But he doesn't interrupt or interject himself into the conversation. If DeShields notices him at all, he doesn't acknowledge him, a snub or at least an indifference that Rose can't help but wonder reveals the lawyer's own anti-Semitic bias.

The conversation today, as on most days since they began meeting, is about Rose's practice, especially his relationship with his patients, especially his female patients. DeShields's unseen and never named investigator has not yet uncovered any formal complaints with state or county dental boards, nor any informal accusations of improper or unprofessional behavior, nor any allegations of criminal behavior or civil suits alleging paternity—only a few vague, unsubstantiated rumors that add up to nothing but hearsay. The county board does have in its files a half-dozen complaints about unfinished procedures and billing mistakes, but nothing, even in these litigious times, that could damage a dentist's reputation and career.

DeShields has more than once pressed Rose on his evening and weekend hours and his recruitment of female patients, but Rose has no problem answering the same questions several times. He admires, in fact, the lawyer's attention to detail and insistence on precision, which, of course, are qualities he prides in himself. In his starched white shirt, polished agate cufflinks, striped tie, and pressed suit pants, Rose sits perfectly still other than to cross and uncross his legs, his hands folded in his lap or in front of him on the polished table. During a break he may light or at least fiddle with one of his pipes and a leather pouch redolent of Mixture No. 79.

This afternoon, though, DeShields mentions for the first time Rose's late-night visits to the Whoop-Tee-Doo Club, and Rose feels himself color, grateful that Ruth is at that moment in the basement tending to the laundry. He has never mentioned the club visits, innocent as they've been, to his family, though Ruth, who's no stranger to the office, can't be unaware of the raucous establishment on the street below. DeShields has obviously been briefed on Rose's occasional afterhours stops there by the investigator, whom Rose imagines to be a sobersided sleuth in the mold of Humphrey Bogart, surely more urbane and sophisticated than the tag teams of Northside palookas sitting in the big sedan out front.

Rose has nothing to be ashamed of or even embarrassed about regarding the club, yet he is both. The Whoop-Tee-Doo is the kind of establishment his parents and brothers would not approve of, garish and loud and chock-a-block with men and women who would never be invited into a Rose living room. The Oshinskys are more tolerant than the Roses and have at least a dozen rough characters among their brood, including the men out front, and Rose wonders if Ruth would in fact be amused to learn that he was among the club's customers.

DeShields apparently senses Rose's discomfort because he looks up from his notes and says, "I ask about the club because the police have been there and the prosecution will ask questions, if only on a fishing expedition, and maybe cast aspersions. More importantly, it's not inconceivable that another suspect could emerge from among the club's clientele."

Rose nods.

"Of course," he murmurs.

Still, he's relieved when the lawyer moves on to another subject moments before he hears Ruth's footsteps coming up from the basement.

It's now one o'clock in the morning, on the first day of May, and Grace Montgomery is celebrating her twenty-eighth birthday by herself. Bud is home, but he's unconscious on the daybed, snoring like a Cossack, in what used to be Terry's room, where he's been sleeping for the past three weeks and where he collapsed upon returning home from another toot, God knows where and with whom.

Grace is drunk, or nearly so, herself, sitting in a foot and a half of tepid water in the rust-stained tub in the apartment's tiny bathroom.

The decrepit tub, behind the locked bathroom door, has become her refuge. So has the booze. She holds in her left hand a pint of Four Roses bourbon, which she lifted that afternoon from Shorty's Holiday Liquors across the street, and in her right the damp but still burning Pall Mall she snatched from Bud's stash on his dresser. There's an inch left in the bottle.

Grace believes she's lost everything in the past month. Mentally, behind her swimmy eyes, she ticks off the losses as though taking inventory after a burglary:

Her sister and her sister's baby, who felt as much hers as he was Terry's, if you counted the amount of time she spent with him.

Her friendship and part-time job with Dr. Rose, who has closed his office and doesn't answer the phone. (When a crabby-sounding woman answers, Grace hangs up.)

Even her sexual relationship, bruising as it was, with her husband, who, ever since that night he literally crawled into the apartment, bloodied and broken and minus three teeth, has avoided all physical contact and hardly dares speak to her.

"Happy birthday, kiddo," she says out loud, then downs the last of the whiskey, drops the empty bottle in the water, and watches it bob on its side between her spread legs. She struggles to get up, then, laughing at herself, sits back down in the water, then tries again and manages to throw her right leg over the edge of the tub. Her wet foot slips on the tile floor, and as she pulls her left leg out of the water, she slides and sits down hard on the tile floor, missing the ragged yellow bathmat and laughing even harder.

Wet and cold, she stares at her stubby feet sticking out in front of her. She begins to shiver and then to cry.

She thinks about the newspaper story that appeared after Terry's funeral, the one in which the writer talked about young women coming to the Twin Cities from small towns around the Midwest, hoping to find a good, or at least a better, life, yet often ending up disillusioned and unhappy and, in at least one noteworthy case, dead. She and Terry already had husbands, such as they are or were—one an abusive drunk who fucked her sister, and the other a cold fish who lived thousands of miles away—but the jobs they managed to find didn't amount to much, and life here was not so good or even much better than it was back home.

Terry's appearance just before Christmas seemed a good thing at the time. Watching her little sister step off the bus at the downtown depot with Hal Junior in her arms, Grace felt a wave of familial emotion she often didn't feel. She thought that at last she and Terry might have a chance of forming a more or less normal relationship. She did her best to ignore the long looks Terry drew from the men in the crowded depot—soldiers and sailors and traveling salesmen—and noted that Terry seemed genuinely happy to see her.

For her part, Terry seemed grateful for a place to stay and someone to help look after the baby, and she managed to stay out of Bud's clutches for a while. Grace took to Hal Junior immediately. She had given up on the idea of having children of her own, partly because she was afraid of the kind of father Bud would be, and partly because she was afraid that neither she nor Bud was physically able to conceive one. Until the Army screwed up Hal Senior's monthly dependent allowance, Terry was self-supporting and no drain on the Montgomerys' modest resources, and then she was able to pick up the slack when she got the job at the Palace.

Then there was Dr. Rose.

Grace was startled at first by his advances—"I know a better way to take off your lipstick, dear," he told her after she was ensconced in his big operatory chair and asked for a Kleenex to remove her makeup—but managed to leave after that initial evening appointment, groggy from the sedation but confident that she hadn't given in to his advances. Then she agreed to return when he called her at the apartment, apologized for "any misunderstanding or personal discomfort" he might have caused, and offered to complete her dental work (a root canal and a crown) free of charge. He also hinted at an employment possibility. After her third, purely social visit—it was a wintry November evening—they became lovers.

All told, they had sex, in his office and in his Packard, maybe a dozen times during the fall and early winter. He was twenty years older than she was and if not exactly homely, then at least very *different-looking* from the men she was accustomed to, but he was always gentle and considerate. He didn't force her to do anything. He never insisted she completely undress, for which she was grateful, and he never did more than lower his trousers and shorts. He smelled of pipe tobacco and bay rum. He had a pleasant smile, but she wondered if he ever laughed. He had enormous hands, surprisingly soft but strong and sure, and the largest penis she had ever seen, let alone allowed inside her. He made no painful or unnatural demands and never used filthy language. He was so unlike Bud that Dr. Rose and her husband might have been natives of different planets.

When Terry arrived in December, Grace couldn't resist telling her that she'd taken a lover. She didn't say her new man was her dentist, let alone a middle-aged Jew with a wife and kids. But the idea of having *two* men, counting Bud, when her irresistible sister had none, not counting Hal, tickled her. Terry hadn't begun sleeping with Bud—at least not to Grace's knowledge—and had not yet visited Dr. Rose. Tonight, bereft of all three, Grace wonders when she knew she was going to share both her husband and her lover with the sibling she both loved and hated.

It was another snowy night, this time in January, scarcely a month after Terry's arrival in town. Terry had been complaining about a toothache for a couple of days and asked Grace if she knew a dentist. Grace could have feigned ignorance of the dentist around the corner who was available at night and on weekends, especially to young women, but she didn't.

"I know someone we can call," she said instead.

When Terry came home after the first time, it was almost eleven. She was helped up the stairs by the doctor, who smiled like an old friend when Grace opened the door and held onto Terry's elbow until she was safely inside. The two of them had snow on their heads and shoulders, their winter coats radiating the outside cold. Terry was heavy-lidded and wobbly and eager to lie down. Grace, of course, knew the feeling.

She knew that Terry would sleep deep into the following morning and probably not be good for much the rest of the next day. No matter; Terry didn't have a job yet.

Grace would be in charge of Hal Junior again, but she didn't mind. What was bothering her was the thought that Dr. Rose had been unable to keep those big hands off her sister once he'd sedated her and taken care of her bad tooth.

Standing now, holding onto the edges of the wash basin beside the tub, Grace avoids her reflection in the foggy medicine-cabinet mirror. She recalls Terry the afternoon following that initial visit to Dr. Rose, lying in the tub, her naked body sleek as a baby seal's, one slim, shapely leg protruding from the water and a pretty painted toe playing with the dripping faucet, smiling at something but telling Grace nothing. Terry wasn't going to gloat. She was no longer a randy teen determined to sleep with every able-bodied male in the county and make sure her sister kept score. She was now an adult, a wife and a mother, albeit as insatiable as ever. Grace knew what Terry was doing. She always knew.

Grace knew that Terry had been back to Dr. Rose three or four times between that first appointment and the last, each time telling Grace she had an urgent situation the doctor needed to treat. By that last visit, however, Terry was also having sex with Bud, plus the photographer, possibly her boss at the Palace, and God knows who else, all of them younger men who had to be more physically appealing than Dr. Rose. Maybe she was drawn to the Seconal, which she wouldn't get from her other lovers.

Grace and Terry said nothing to each other about their respective relationships with Dr. Rose, nor did Grace and Dr. Rose ever discuss Terry. Terry's latest pregnancy was news, though hardly a shock, and Grace, to this day, doesn't know if she believes that the unborn baby was Rose's, not when there were so many other possibilities.

But if the baby wasn't his, she wonders, why would he kill her?

SUMMER 1955

CHAPTER 8

People bitch about the snow and frigid temperatures of a Minnesota winter, but it's the summer heat and humidity that bring out the worst in the natives.

This year, in the three months between Memorial Day and Labor Day, Minneapolis will record six homicides, more than half the total for the year: two by gunfire on the same night in the same house on Fourth Avenue South, a fatal beating behind the Sourdough Bar in the Gateway, a domestic knifing in a Seven Corners rooming house, the intentional drowning of an infant in a Nordeast duplex, and the bludgeoning of Herman Goranski, a sixty-eight-year-old recluse in one of the city's few remaining tenements, kitty-corner from Holy Rosary Catholic Church on East Twenty-fourth Street.

The Gateway case, the domestic, and the infanticide were solved at the site before the bodies were removed; the Fourth Avenue shootout involved coloreds killing coloreds during a crap game, which is low- (or no-) priority downtown. Which leaves Herman Goranski, whose body was discovered by the building's absentee owner after other tenants complained about the stink.

On June 18, a Saturday, the temperature reaches the high nineties by early afternoon. Arne Anderson and Mel Curry are standing in the dead man's apartment, sweat liquefying their faces and handkerchiefs pressed to their noses and mouths. The corpse has moments earlier been removed by Fred MacMurray's crew, and Goranski's pathetic estate lies strewn across the grimy floor. Luckily, it's a small apartment—a single room, maybe fifteen by twenty feet, plus an alcove that passes for a kitchen, and a doorless closet. The toilet is down the hall, shared by the floor's other hapless denizens.

The old man's head has been crushed. Cause of death, Dr. Fred will declare, was blunt-force trauma. Anderson stumbles over a maple table leg sticking out from under the bed. He picks it up with a gloved hand and extends it toward Curry, showing his partner what both men are right away pretty certain are bloodstains.

"Whoever killed him he let in," Curry says, acknowledging the absence of forced entry. (Goranski's apartment is on the third floor; its only window is painted shut, and the flimsy wooden door was unlocked when the building's owner found him.) There are, according to Jordan Fanshawe, one of the city's more notorious slumlords, fourteen other tenants, twelve of them men, and the detectives will speak to all of them, except for one who's recovering from a broken hip in a nursing home, before the sun sets today.

With the shiny toe of his two-tone wingtip, Curry probes a pile of queer magazines and paperback novels, neither the names nor the authors of which mean anything to Mel, who looks only at smut showcasing women. Goranski's dresser drawers have been pulled out and dumped on the threadbare rug in front of it. The victim's worn-out billfold has been riffled and tossed atop the rubble. Even its unbuttoned change pocket is empty.

"Robbery seems to have been the idea here," Mel says. But the old guy was wearing only skivvies, and they were down around his skinny ankles. "Okay, money and sex. Or sex and then money if there *was* any money in the billfold."

"Couldn't have amounted to much of either," Anderson mutters behind his handkerchief. The heat and the reek are threatening to cost him his lunch. He's tempted to use the murder weapon, still in his hand, to smash the stuck window for a breath of fresh air.

"Let's get the hell out of here and let the lab guys find what they can find," he says. "I'll get Hessburg and LeBlanc to brace the other tenants."

When the detectives get back to the office, they'll check Goranski's name against the department's homosexual register and be surprised if he's not in it.

But the Goranski case is only a distraction. Anderson and Curry will poke at it over the next several weeks the way a steak-eater pokes at a side salad. Almost two and a half months have passed since Teresa Hickman's murder became an obsession, but it might have been yesterday.

For one thing, Homer Scofield, who, barring a second delay, will begin prosecuting H. David Rose on a charge of first-degree murder in Hiawatha County District Court in July, is determined that his first case as county attorney will end with a conviction. This means that, prior to the opening gavel, every possibility must be reviewed, rereviewed, and eliminated. The other possibilities currently include Bud Montgomery, Richard Ybarra, Tony Zevos, and the still-unidentified skinny guy with glasses. Fortunately from the cops' point of view, the skinny guy remains no more than the vaguest of descriptions, and the other three have more or less functional alibis for April 8 and 9.

The detectives were able to reconfirm Ybarra's and Tony Zevos's alibis. Bud Montgomery's alibi, the weakest of the lot, was provided by a coworker, who says the two of them watched a floor show at the Land O'Lakes Tap behind the Great Northern Depot, and then stopped for nightcaps at the Westerner at Hennepin and Lake. The coworker, a garrulous boozer named Allard Emmons, owns a car and told detectives he dropped Bud off in front of the Montgomerys' apartment at two-thirty the morning of the ninth.

"Triple check their stories," Scofield tells the detectives. "Make goldarned sure every one of them holds water."

Looming, figuratively speaking, over the prosecution is the specter of Dante DeShields, Rose's attorney, whose slashing attacks have sunk many a "watertight" prosecution. Scofield told his secretary, who whispered his words to her bridge partner May Grey, who confided in her lover Augie Fuller, who, leaning against one of the courthouse urinals alongside his lead investigator, told Anderson that the county attorney is "having actual nightmares" about facing DeShields in court.

Arne would love to destroy Bud Montgomery's alibi. He would love to destroy Bud Montgomery, though the reasons, when he tries to sort through them, are diverse and inchoate and buried in places Arne doesn't want to dig. Curry, like the MPD brass and every other member of the Homicide Squad, has "accepted the fact" that Rose strangled Teresa Hickman, but Arne, who now grudgingly agrees, isn't willing to let go of Bud for his own reasons, and continues to raise objections to the case against the dentist.

Mel and Arne bicker over lunch and in the car and while breathing through their handkerchiefs in a dead man's apartment.

"He had the girl in his car and was driving in the vicinity where the body was found," Mel says for the umpteenth time. "She was there beside him one moment, then gone the next. She was carrying his baby and making demands. They were arguing. We have all that in his own words, more or less."

"More or less," Arne replies. "That's the most cockeyed confession either one of us has ever heard, Mel. People *do* black out under pressure—I saw that in Europe. Bud Montgomery's alibi comes from a souse. And Bud was fucking Teresa. We have *his* confession, too."

"Oh, hell, Arne. With you and Riemenschneider on top of him, he would have confessed to killing Lindbergh's baby. Besides, he does have an alibi, which Rose doesn't, if we don't count the blackout. And half the male population on the South Side might have slept with Teresa Hickman since she hit town. There are even rumors that she was selling it."

Mel tells Arne that his judgment has been knocked sidewise by Lily Kline, who has both the inclination and the ability to get under

Arne's skin. But what Mel doesn't know, though he may be right about Lily's influence, is that Arne and Lily are on the outs, and that Arne, when the opportunity presents itself, is fucking Curry's wife.

Arne smiles wearily at his partner, who is also the closest of his few friends, all things considered.

"Say what you will, Mel," he tells him. "If the trial started today, my money'd be on DeShields."

On June 1, Robert Gardner moved out of his sister's place on Forty-fourth Street and moved into a fitfully air-conditioned, one-bedroom basement apartment in a newish building on Pleasant Avenue just south of Franklin, less than a ten-minute drive or bus ride from the bureau. He'd decided he was making enough money to live on his own and was tired of mooching off his pregnant sister and brother-in-law, as much as they pretended to enjoy having him there. Just as important, he imagined putting some distance between himself and both Pam Brantley and the spot where he stumbled across Teresa Hickman's body. He was and is kidding himself, of course, because he rarely thinks about anyone or anything else.

Though two months have passed since he's seen them, Robert can't get either woman out of his head. He dreams about them both, sometimes at the same time, in the same dream, fantasizes about them obsessively, and pounds out erotic fictions about one or the other on the Royal portable his parents gave him when he graduated from high school. (The idea, of course, was to use the typewriter for his med school assignments and writing letters home.) The stories, though never violent, are relentlessly graphic, an amalgam of his growing sexual experience and an overheated imagination, and he is ashamed of himself afterward. He burns the pages in the bathroom sink and flushes the ashes down the toilet.

At least once a week, usually on Sunday night, he dines with his sister and takes the opportunity to cruise past the Brantleys' building down the street, hoping, like every fool who has been similarly torched, to catch a glimpse of his erstwhile flame. He keeps his eyes peeled as well for the guy who left his glasses under Pam's bed. He can't help but think the mystery man looks like *him*—a tall, skinny young man with glasses—and sometimes imagines the guy was Teresa Hickman's murderer. When he's back in the neighborhood, he keeps an eye out, too, for Karl Brantley, having no idea what Pam might have told him.

The week before moving into his own apartment, he purchased, for $130 off a Lake Street car lot, a dark green '46 Ford coupe, and he imagines himself fucking Pam in its cozy backseat. At the very least, he'd love her to see him drive past in his "new" car, maybe with another attractive woman beside him, and let *her* imagination run wild. The trouble is, he doesn't know another attractive woman in Minneapolis, not counting his sister, Tommy Pullman's wife, and an auburn-haired freelancer who only the other day was introduced to him as Meghan Mckenzie, his boss's daughter-in-law.

Meanwhile, he is putting in more than forty hours a week at the bureau, reporting, writing, or rewriting wire stories about severe weather, auto fatalities, drownings, notable visitors, and the occasional serious crime.

On the third Saturday of June, Miles Mckenzie sends him to a murder scene on the South Side. An old man has been beaten to death in a dilapidated apartment building across the street from Holy Rosary church. The blue-collar, rough-and-tumble Phillips neighborhood has a parlous reputation—armed robberies, muggings, auto thefts, and sexual assaults if not a lot of homicides—so Robert is happy to park his little Ford behind a familiar Chevy sedan on East Twenty-fourth Street.

Detectives Anderson and Curry are hustling out of a rundown apartment building as Robert trots up the broken front walk.

"Nothing to see here, pal," Curry says with a wave of his hand and a wry smile that acknowledges the hoary cop-talk.

Both he and Anderson are red-faced and sweat-soaked, sucking in the relatively fresh air as though they just stepped out of a burning building. Both have slung their suit coats over their shoulders and tugged their ties away from their collars.

"Go in at your own risk," Curry says. "The body's been removed, the crime scene is closed. Only the bad air remains."

"What can you tell me?" Robert asks. "Victim's name? Age? Cause of death?"

Curry says, "Hey, Arne, this was my traveling companion in North Dakota. Roger Gardner—right?"

Robert corrects him with a forced smile, hoping Curry is only jerking his chain.

"*Robert* Gardner—sorry, kid," Curry says. "Okay, but only because we're pals. The decedent's name is Herman Joseph Goranski, spelled the way it sounds, but with an *I*, not a *Y*. Date of birth, according to his insurance papers, 23 April 1887. Next of kin, apparently nonexistent. It looks like he was assaulted with a blunt object, a club of some kind."

Robert fumbles with a chewed-on pencil as he tries to get it all in his notebook, knowing he'll have to call Curry later to check the details.

"Was it a robbery?" he calls after the departing detectives.

"Robbery or a fairy rape," Curry says over his shoulder. "Either or both. But don't quote me."

It will turn out to be neither, but on that day, and for weeks to come, that's the best guess. The next day, following Fred MacMurray's autopsy, Robert gets a firm determination of blunt-force trauma and a severely fractured skull, likely sustained three or four days previous, from the coroner's office. On Monday, he writes a seven-paragraph story that will be picked up by a few of the larger papers around the state, trimmed to three or four grafs, and forgotten.

"Just shows to go you," Mckenzie tells Robert on Wednesday. "A pretty white girl is murdered in a nice part of town and that's all anyone wants to read about. An old faggot is beaten to death in a shitty neighborhood and no one gives a damn. They're both whodunits, but only one has an outcome that means anything to anybody."

Over the next several days, however, a thought gnaws at Robert, one he's not about to share with his bureau chief or anyone else. He believes that he and Mel Curry have a relationship, the beginning of one anyway, and he pictures himself building on that relationship the way big-league reporters cultivate important sources. Robert, who has no actual brothers, can't help but fancy the two of them developing an almost kid brother-big brother bond that is both professionally and personally rewarding.

Now all he's got to do is figure out how to make it happen.

The driver has been waiting for the heat.

The house is unbearable, even with the screens on and the windows propped open and a couple of electric fans going full blast, and the garage turns into a Calcutta sweatbox when the temperature gets stuck in the low nineties for a few days. The cab is no refuge, either. Though he and the other Canary drivers keep telling O'Shaughnessy that within the next couple of years all the successful firms will have air-conditioned cars, Fat Jack, sitting in the air-cooled comfort of his office at the Canary garage, keeps saying that air conditioners create a drag on a car's engine, and take a huge bite out of fuel economy.

But it's the heat that brings the girls outside in their halter tops and shorts and sandals, that draws the teenage temptresses to the beach, where they can show themselves off to their boyfriends and whoever else might be watching. The driver, sitting in the car on the north side of Lake Calhoun, binoculars in hand, can't get enough.

When he was a junior at De La Salle High School, three years before Margaret got pregnant the first time, the driver (who wasn't a driver yet) flirted with a sexy, pint-sized sophomore named Judy Johansson, who, flirting back, said, "Do you ever go to the beach? I'm there all the time during the summer." She meant the main beach at Lake Calhoun, and he took her comment for an invitation, and all that summer and for years to come he fantasized about lying beside her on the scorching sand. They'd share a large bath towel, and he'd spread cocoa butter over her naked shoulders and the lovely round calves of her legs. In real life, he never did join Judy at the beach because he suffered from eczema eruptions on his chest and arms and was self-conscious when he took off his shirt. The eczema problem eventually went away, as did his chances with Judy Johansson, but to this day he is aroused by the seasonal perfume of tanning lotion and sun-basted human flesh, and the crowded, simmering, shimmering beaches of the city's famous lakes.

This summer, however, the driver, like many others who have somehow stumbled into her story, sees Terry Hickman wherever he looks.

Around the first of June, when he felt it was safe enough to loiter around Nicollet Avenue, the driver started talking to a new waitress at the Palace, a slim, dark-haired girl named Vondra. The Zevos kid had no doubt already had his hands all over her—it was a good guess the way they glanced at each other and interacted behind the counter when the Greek wasn't around, not having to worry about Tony's wife, who, the driver gathered from the small talk, had fallen down the stairs behind their apartment and would spend the summer upstairs in a cast.

The new girl was willing to talk to the driver when he sat at the counter with his sugary coffee and a scavenged newspaper. She had glossy hair, a nice build, and a showy ass, but the overall effect was ruined when she smiled. Her teeth were gray and mottled, as though her childhood diet had been deficient in some nutrient or she had a medical condition that affected her teeth. Her gimpy boss didn't seem to mind, but, as much as he admired the other parts, the driver was put off by that smile.

He was tempted to ask Vondra about Terry, what she's heard from Tony and the others, if there is gossip among the regulars, or any tributes to the dead girl—a photo tacked on the employees' bulletin board or a memorial fund—like you hear about sometimes after a young person's death. But Vondra (the driver never caught her last name) didn't seem to know or care much about her predecessor. Then, just like that, Vondra herself was gone, replaced by a heavily freckled scarecrow the driver finds not in the least attractive. And now the sunshine and heat have settled in. He decides to spend his breaks at one of the city's dozen-odd beaches that have opened for the season.

The papers have taken a breather from the Hickman case, maybe saving their ammunition for the trial that's expected to begin during the next few weeks. The driver religiously skims each edition of every paper he snatches off a park bench or lunchroom counter and, if there's something he hasn't read about the case, adds another clipping to the scrapbook he's begun keeping and hides behind the tires in his garage. Lately, there hasn't been much to clip.

Then he reads that the judge who will be trying the case has granted the defense a delay, postponing the trial's start from June 27 until July 18, presumably to give Rose's lawyer more time to prove that another man is, in the lawyer's words, the "real killer" of Teresa Hickman. The first time the driver sees the words "real killer" he catches his breath, then realizes that it's only a lawyer's trick and relaxes, and then begins to enjoy the idea that maybe there is more to the Hickman story than the public assumes.

His dreams have become a weird confusion of water and sunshine and a young woman in a green winter coat. He sees her, in one dream, striding along Euclid Place, but in the dream the night is hot and the lake behind them is Calhoun, not Isles. He shouts at the girl and she turns and smiles, but her teeth are mottled and repugnant. Waking, wet and agitated, he struggles to crawl back inside the dream, desperate to fix Teresa's smile and pull off her coat, to see her body unwrapped and warm and slathered with cocoa butter the way he might have seen her at the beach. He can't get back inside that dream, but he will dream similarly again during the next several weeks. Tossing and twisting, he calls and pleads, more loudly than he knows.

Finally, poor Margaret, his wife, looking more haggard than usual and a decade older than her thirty-five years, tells him that he has to use the Army cot in the basement because it's hard enough to sleep in this heat and God knows she needs her rest.

Lying by himself in the subterranean dark, he wonders what, if anything, he's given away.

On the morning of June 21, Dr. Rose receives a call at home from Buster Haswell, the manager at the Whoop-Tee-Doo Club.

Not one to mince words, Haswell says, "One of my girls needs a tooth fixed, Doc. I know things are up in the air right now, but I'm wondering if you could open the office for Geri. She won't be worth a damn down here until that tooth is taken care of."

Rose considers for a moment and then says, "Yes, of course."

He and Haswell agree on two o'clock this afternoon, before Haswell's employee begins her shift. Rose isn't certain, but he believes that "Geri" is the bottle blonde with a significant overbite who has waited on him a time or two when he's gone downstairs after work.

Ruth looks at him quizzically when he hangs up and tells her he has scheduled his first patient in more than two months.

"Are you sure that's a good idea, David?" she says.

Rose relights his pipe and says, "I don't see why not. I'm not a criminal. I still have my license. Nobody has said anything about my fitness to practice. And I can't imagine I need permission from DeShields."

In fact, DeShields, when he learns about the appointment, thinks it's a terrible idea. Unfortunately for the lawyer, it's now almost five o'clock. Rose has drilled out the decay in Geraldine Fiola's molar, disinfected the cavity, and filled it, all following only a weak injection of novocaine. After she handed him the ten dollars he and Haswell agreed on, he sat by himself in the operatory with the pleasant sensation of having returned to work after a long time away.

"Are you kidding me?" DeShields growls into the phone after Rose returns to the house. "What if the woman tells someone you touched her inappropriately, or tried to kiss her, or suggested the two of you go for a ride?"

Rose frowns and draws on his pipe.

"Why on earth would she do that?" he asks. He glances at Ronnie Oshinsky, who is sitting with him and Ruth at the dining-room table and can hear DeShields's excited voice on the other end of the line. Ronnie looks back at his brother-in-law, raises his eyebrows, and shrugs.

Tonight, after supper, with Rachmaninoff on the stereo, Rose sits by himself in his favorite living-room chair and reflects on this unexpected turn of events.

For an hour this afternoon he was a practicing dentist again, confidently moving around in the familiar environment in a starched white jacket, sterilizing and arranging his tools on the porcelain tray, and preparing the novocaine and Seconal if needed. With the patient in his chair, after the usual inquiries about her general health and specific complaint about the painful tooth, he worked with self-assurance and precision, probing, drilling, and completing the procedure with the proficiency borne of twenty-plus years of clinical experience. If the patient, who undoubtedly knows his recent history, was uneasy in the chair, or uneasier than most patients are during a dental procedure, she hid her discomfort well. Granted, Haswell was in the waiting room during most of the appointment, but that was for everybody's benefit, like a chaperone at a high school dance. It was Haswell's—actually the club's—money that paid for the work.

The important point is, Rose used the knowledge, skills, and tools to repair a patient's tooth. The woman may have been relieved to get out of the chair when he finished, but she did so without the pain that had plagued her and interfered with her employment for the past several days. He provided her with the relief from disease and pain he has always believed to be the dentist's mission, regardless of what the public thinks about dentists in general and now himself in particular.

Sadly, the larger situation hasn't changed.

Ronnie, nervous as a cat and presumably armed, is still a boarder, sleeping in the spare bedroom and taking most of his meals in the Roses' breakfast nook, and DeShields, accompanied by Michael Haydon, is an almost daily visitor, reviewing what seems to be every moment of Rose's life, not just the night and early morning of April 8 and 9. The Roses miss their daughters and worry about the cost of their extended stay at the Wisconsin youth camp, but they console themselves with the knowledge that the girls are safe and enjoying themselves 150 miles from the threats and gossip and worries at home.

For a while, from late May deep into June, though Rose rarely ventures outside, he and Ruth enjoy the sensation of an approximate return to normalcy. The number of ominous phone calls and anonymous letters has decreased appreciably, the bigots and the haters presumably having run low on vitriol and stamps, and the Chrysler Imperial with the large men inside makes only intermittent stops on Zenith Avenue. Ruth throws open the upstairs windows in the morning. It's almost—but not quite—possible to forget that the master of the house will soon be on trial for murder.

"Don't get too comfortable," DeShields, a dark cloud surrounding any possible silver lining, cautions the family. "As we get close to trial, the press will stir up the muck again. And when the trial begins, Katie bar the door."

On June 23, Anderson and Curry return to the Montgomery apartment on Fifteenth Street. Their focus today is Grace, so they wait in their car across the street until Bud, who, judging from outward appearance, has more or less recovered from his cellar beating (he still limps slightly), leaves the building before they go inside.

For the past several days, at Scofield's insistence, the homicide crew has been revisiting Rose's patients, past and present—all to no avail, at least so far as legitimate reports, complaints, and rumors of misconduct are concerned. Plenty of people believe that Rose is "unusual" or "a little odd," but nobody is either able or willing to say that he has done anything untoward with a patient. His Nicollet Avenue neighbors, upstairs and down, cast no aspersions, either.

Despite their lingering differences, Anderson and Curry agree that the most important witness, assuming DeShields won't allow Rose himself to testify, will be the victim's sister.

It takes Grace Montgomery a good five minutes to answer the door, and when she does she looks like hell, even worse than during their last visit. This time, though, her pathetic condition appears to be self-inflicted, the death's-door pallor and hollowed-out eyes the result of too much booze and not enough fresh air. The bumps and black-and-blue bruises are now the kind a drunk acquires while attempting to maneuver around the furniture and in and out of doors. She is smoking when she answers the door and is naked beneath her unbuttoned housecoat.

The apartment is closed and dark. It smells of heat, sweat, cigarettes, and something gone bad in the kitchen.

"You need to tell us everything you know about Dr. Rose," Curry says. "You can tell us here or downtown."

Grace sighs, shakes her head, and sits down on a messy sofa, shoving several days' newspapers onto the floor.

"Okay, shoot," she says. The idea of telling the cops to shoot makes her giggle. Much of her naked body, white and plump as a bedroom pillow, is falling out of the housecoat.

Anderson says, "First go put some clothes on, ma'am. We'll wait."

When she returns to the living room, she's wearing a wrinkled dress and a pair of well-worn carpet slippers.

Over the next hour and a half, she tells them, albeit haltingly and slurring her words, about her dental appointments, "friendship," and eventual intimacy with Rose, about sending Terry to the dentist to treat her toothache, Terry's evening visits to Rose after that initial appointment, the night of Terry's murder, and, most surprisingly, her doubts about Rose's guilt.

"You don't believe that Rose killed your sister?" Curry says.

Grace lights a cigarette from a fresh pack of Pall Malls she brought from the bedroom.

"There were a lot of men in Terry's life," she says.

"We know that, and we've talked to several of them," Mel says. "Including your husband."

Grace wearily waves away the cigarette smoke in front of her face.

"Didja talk to Richard Ybarra?"

"Yes," Curry says. "He told us he was in Duluth, or on his way up there, the night of the murder. His alibi checks out."

"Do you know better?" Anderson says.

Grace makes a face that might include a smile. She shrugs and says, "I know that Terry was sweet on him. I know he picked her up one night after her shift, and they were out until early the next morning. A day or two later she had a bunch of pictures he took and said, 'I think I'm in love.'"

"When was that?"

Grace ashes the cigarette and coughs into her hand.

"I dunno. March maybe, early April. Sometime before she died." She giggles, and then starts to cry.

Arne stares at the woman with a combination of pity and contempt.

"Ybarra had a car?" he says, recalling that his detectives had picked up the photographer at the bus station.

"It wasn't his," Grace says. "He'd borrow his buddy's, Terry said." She says she didn't know the buddy's name.

"Did you ever meet Ybarra?" Arne says.

"No. But I could smell his aftershave on Terry's clothes. He must've slapped it on real heavy. Bud said Terry came home smelling like a queer."

Grace Montgomery, Arne muses, is a lush and a liar. (Who isn't? he asked himself.) Still, if her husband doesn't kill her and she doesn't drink herself to death, she's going to be the center of attention when the Big Show starts next month.

Then he recalls his last conversation with Rose—that quiet Saturday afternoon in late April—and asks her, "Do you talk to Dr. Rose anymore, Grace?"

She looks at him, and again her eyes fill with tears. She shakes her head. From somewhere between the sofa cushions she pulls out a couple of wadded tissues.

"He told me the two of you are friends," Arne says, taking a leap, knowing the conversation is near its end. "Is that so?"

Grace's doughy face collapses on itself.

"Dr. Rose is a very nice man," she says, barely audible between sobs. "People don't want to believe that, but he is."

CHAPTER 9

No longer tied to the Linden Hills neighborhood by family and sex, Robert Gardner now spends most of his waking hours downtown.

He likes the rush and hustle and flashing neon of the bars and supper clubs that line Hennepin Avenue between the Gateway and the Auditorium and jut out in both directions along the busy cross-streets between Washington and Grant.

He likes what people call the "character" of the Loop's older structures: the ornate Metropolitan Life building (reported to be marked for demolition if the federal government's Urban Renewal program ever gets under way), the broad-shouldered Farmers & Mechanics, First National, and Northwestern National banks, the glittery Century, RKO Orpheum, Lyceum, Lyric, World, and State movie houses, the Curtis, Leamington, and Nicollet hotels, the clock-towered courthouse, neoclassical Federal Reserve, intimidating Great Northern Depot, and august Westminster Presbyterian Church. All of this is a big part of why he moved to the city, he tells himself while walking the hot, noisy, litter-strewn streets.

During working hours, Robert either chases fire rigs and ambulances around town in his Ford coupe or works the phones at the United Press office, confirming the identification of the city's latest drowning or industrial-accident victim. He and Tommy Pullman and whoever else is on duty at the time take turns recording for posterity the names, ages, and addresses of the day's traffic fatalities in a large, scruffy ledger they refer to as *St. Peter's Log*.

After work, he has become a frequent patron of Smokey's Bar & Grill on Fourth Street. In the summer of 1955, Smokey's remains the preferred afterhours hangout of Mill City detectives, prosecutors, criminal lawyers, and journalists, most of whom can thereby drink and schmooze only steps from their offices. Miles Mckenzie is a regular, often ducking in for a midafternoon bump after announcing that he's running downstairs to plug his parking meter. Milt Hickok helps shut the joint down after shuffling over from the police reporter's cubbyhole at the courthouse. Oscar Rystrom and George Appel will drop in after their papers go to press.

Dante DeShields occasionally holds forth at a corner table in the company of local political bigwigs, though he's rarely seen since going to work for Dr. Rose. Michael Haydon, when temporarily off DeShields's leash, makes an occasional appearance, showing surprising signs of a comic sensibility and an admirable capacity for Irish whiskey. Homer Scofield's notoriously bibulous predecessor, Ferdinand Twyman, now back in private practice, is often at or under another table, though Scofield himself, a teetotaling Methodist, has yet to darken the establishment's door.

One stuffy evening at the end of June, Robert finds himself sitting beside Meghan Mckenzie at a crowded table with her father-in-law, the AP's Marty Rice, and a trio of *Star* sportswriters who are drunkenly arguing about the Millers' pitching staff. Meghan, whom he sees up close and at length tonight for the first time, is a pretty woman in her late twenties or early thirties. He assumes that she's not a breathless nymphomaniac like Pam Brantley, but her quiet self-possession, not to mention her luminous green eyes and the auburn hair that cascades down her back, is very appealing. On this occasion, Robert learns that her husband, Miles's son Howard, is a copyright attorney who works for the papers and on this night is in Des Moines on company business.

Away from the bureau, Meghan turns out to be relaxed and friendly, a talker and a toucher, though not egregiously so. She has been nursing her Beefeater's-and-tonic for an hour, and keeps an eye on her father-in-law across the littered table, signs, in Robert's eyes, of a cautious, sensible personality. On his third Grain Belt, he begins entertaining thoughts of sleeping with her tonight. Those thoughts begin to evaporate when he notices Miles's gimlet eye on him from across the table, and disappear completely when Miles abruptly rises and shouts above the room's racket, "'Bout time I drive you home, Meg," and Meghan dutifully gets up to leave.

Many of the men in the vicinity turn their heads and follow her progress away from the table. Robert hears his boss saying, "You're lucky, honey. Five years ago, they wouldn't let a gal in here."

Watching Meghan wend her way toward the door, Robert wonders if he's destined to fall in love only with married women.

The following evening Robert and other late arrivals dash into Smokey's seconds ahead of a sudden thunderstorm. Meghan isn't there—nor, for some reason, is her father-in-law—but Mel Curry is, seated at a table next to an upright piano that Robert has never heard anyone play.

Curry sits with a small group of men and women, including, if Robert can judge from their proximity and body language, his newlywed wife, a diminutive, dark-eyed beauty in a tight dress. He recognizes Frenchy LeBlanc and Sid Hessburg from the MPD, but that's all besides Curry. LeBlanc sees Robert, but ignores him, probably unable to recall his name. Curry grins and hoists his glass in his direction before returning to the conversation around him.

Robert makes his way through the crowd, spotting several additional familiar faces from the courthouse, his eyes stinging from the thick tobacco smoke. He sees Marty Rice standing by himself at the bar and makes his way over, inserting himself between Marty and an obese copy editor from the *Tribune*. Robert and Marty have become friendly in the past several weeks. Both rent bachelor apartments on the same block of Pleasant (Rice is recently divorced) and occasionally share a ride downtown.

Despite working for the competition, Marty is open and encouraging. Both men have reported, written, or rewritten stories relating to the Hickman case and Rose's impending trial, though neither has dug up anything new or particularly interesting in the past couple of weeks. Robert admires Marty's understated confidence and facile prose.

They have little newsworthy to talk about during this lull in the case, so the topic is usually women, cars, or baseball. Tonight Rice says he's got a couple of tickets to the Millers-Saints game on July 3, and Robert says, hell, yes, he'd love to come along. He still hasn't been to a game this year (though he religiously tracks the box scores) and the season's almost half gone.

Coming out of the men's room a few minutes after midnight, he is surprised to find Mel Curry at his side, squeezing his arm, and pulling him out of the tipsy traffic in the hallway. The detective looks a little drunk himself, his eyes bloodshot and squinty, though that may be from the cigarette smoke.

"I want to talk to you," Curry says, clearly enough.

"Now?" Robert says.

"No time like the present," Curry says and directs Robert to the exit at the end of the hall.

The alley behind Smokey's is what you'd expect: a narrow, foul-smelling passage lined with overflowing garbage cans, sagging towers of empty cardboard boxes, and a couple of dozing tramps who've shambled over from Washington Avenue and will probably spend the night where they lie. Halfway down the alley, a sailor with the trousers of his summer whites down around his ankles is doing his inebriated best to penetrate his evening's rental. The thunder and rain have stopped, replaced by a damp, debilitating heat and a chain of large, oil-slicked puddles.

"Are you the skinny guy with glasses?" Curry asks Robert.

There's a harsh overhead light that casts the detective's face into shadow. He's let go of Robert's arm, but leaves the reporter, his back against Smokey's brick wall, no space to maneuver or even think about fleeing. Robert is sober enough to understand that the detective is serious, but sufficiently buzzed to believe that a clever response might be the ticket.

"Well, lemme see," he says, grinning broadly and slurring his words. "I'm skinny and I wear glasses. So you betcha, Kemo Sabe."

Curry drives his fist into Robert's midsection. He does it so swiftly that Robert wouldn't be sure he's been punched if it wasn't for the explosion of pain and expulsion of air from his body. Curry, clutching Robert's arm, keeps him on his feet. Struggling for breath, Robert wants to curse and demand an explanation and maybe sputter something about freedom of the press, but he doesn't have the wind to do any of that. He recalls, five seconds too late, that Curry was once a semi-pro fighter, maybe a good one, and that he and Anderson have been known for occasional rough stuff.

"Don't fuck with me, dickwad," Curry says. "Three things I know. One, you told me you were near the crime scene the night of the murder. Two, you're skinny and you wear glasses. Three, no other skinny guy with glasses has been identified and placed at the scene. And a fourth thing—our pencil-neck prosecutor won't get off our back until every goddamn report and rumor is accounted for."

Still in the detective's grip, Robert sags against the building. His shirt and sport coat are damp. Slowly he's regaining his ability to breathe and speak.

"Are you asking if I murdered Teresa Hickman?" he manages, barely.

"I'm asking if you were in fact in the neighborhood that night, and, assuming you were, if you have something more to tell me."

At that moment, Smokey's screen door flies open and half a dozen men and women tumble into the alley, laughing and pointing at each other and somehow managing to remain upright, most of them anyway, and hold onto their drinks. Robert recognizes a senior editor

from the *Tribune* and a county court reporter among the howling ine-
briates.

Curry tugs Robert away from the drunks.

"I was on my way home from work that night," Robert says, still
struggling for breath. "Someone must have seen me walking along
those trolley tracks."

More people come spilling into the alley, which now looks like a
scene in a Marx Brothers movie. Curry ignores the noisy slapstick and
stares hard at Robert.

"You were walking along the streetcar tracks about midnight?" he
says, his face three inches from Robert's.

"Yes," Robert says. He is trying not to pee in his pants.

"What time was it? Be specific."

"I don't know. Ten or twenty minutes after maybe. After midnight."

"Did you see anybody?"

Robert shakes his head, and then feels the warm flush of piss
coursing down his right leg.

"I swear to God, Mel. I didn't see a thing." He wonders if he made
a mistake by calling him "Mel."

Curry stares at him for a moment, and then lets him go. Robert
leans against the wall for maybe five minutes after the detective goes
back inside, and then walks stiff-legged and miserable past the revelers
and down the noxious alley, deciding not to go back inside and trying
to remember where in hell he'd left his car.

For reasons he will never understand, the driver sometimes fantasizes
about saving a young man from drowning.

He wonders if the fantasy is compensation for not serving during
the war. He also wonders if it means that he's a queer.

As fantasies go, the driver finds this one peculiar for a couple of
reasons. One, he can't swim and is afraid of the water (another reason
he never joined Judy Johansson at the beach). Two, despite the claptrap
he mumbles while standing beside Margaret at Mass, he couldn't care

less about the rest of God's creation and can't imagine risking his neck for anybody, least of all a total stranger.

So why, while he's parked in the dark near the north end of the Cedar Avenue bridge over Lake Nokomis on this sultry July evening, does this vision rise again behind his eyes?

A boy or young man, rail-thin and probably in high school, is walking toward him on the bridge. The kid is shirtless and barefoot; a belt cinched tight around his skinny waist holds up a pair of light-colored trousers. He has fair, tousled hair and wears glasses. Sometimes in the dream he is smoking a cigarette, sometimes not. Tonight he's not. Suddenly, near the middle of the bridge, he stops, hops up on the concrete balustrade, and somersaults backward into the darkness.

A moment later, the driver's Plymouth is the only car on the bridge, and, a moment after that, the driver is the only person leaning over the balustrade, peering into the black water. He sees the boy's head and naked shoulders, luminous in the dark, bobbing above the choppy surface. Their eyes meet—the boy is still wearing his glasses—though neither says a word.

The next thing the driver knows *he* is in the water. The cold wet is a shock on this hot night. The fact that he can't swim doesn't occur to him, and he somehow stays afloat. The boy says, "I am alone."

The driver says nothing. He knows the boy's story. In fact, twenty minutes earlier, he was watching the boy and his girlfriend—she is several years older than the boy, more experienced, and impatient—in the backseat of a car parked in the dark along the north shore of the lake. The boy is nervous, clumsy. The girl tells him to get out of the car.

Now, in the water, the driver grabs the boy's belt and begins to swim. A handful of passersby have gathered on the bridge. The driver is exhilarated. He believes he could swim the length and breadth of the lake if he had to, though Nokomis is the third largest in the city's Chain of Lakes. There's now a crowd on the bridge and along the shoreline, and he can hear their shouts. Grim-faced cops and firemen in helmets and rubber coats wade into the shallows to retrieve the boy, who sputters and vomits. Amid the noise and confusion, the driver climbs out of the water and walks unnoticed into the darkness.

The driver often wonders what the fantasy means. He'd love to get a better look at the girlfriend, whose name he somehow knows is Annette and whose imagined role excites him. He pictures her sitting in the car, a short, slim brunette. She is wearing white shorts, and her sleeveless blouse is unbuttoned.

If he had a good friend, dared speak to Father Dunne at Holy Name, or trusted O'Shaughnessy, he might bring it up over a couple of beers some night. He wouldn't dream, never mind the pun, of mentioning it to Margaret, who would blame the alcohol or the heat or the Devil for her husband's foolishness. But he relishes it all the same, especially the swimming. He pictures himself climbing out of the water, shirtless now himself, his dripping torso glowing in the light from the street lamps. He walks back toward his car.

Alone now in the parked cab, his eyes heavy, he sighs as the image fades and blinks out.

Arne says nothing to anybody about his and Lily Kline's breakup. Certainly not to anybody at the courthouse and not to Mel. He almost told Janine Curry after sex one night in early July—Mel was on a weeklong fishing trip in Ontario, and there would have been plenty of time to lay bare his pathetic domestic life to his new lover for whatever sympathetic ministrations that might encourage.

But what would he say? That yet again he screwed up a relationship, though he's not quite willing to concede it was all his fault? That Lily, as wonderful as she was in bed and the kitchen, when she felt like it, is as difficult a person to live with as he is—moody and demanding and angry much of the time? That her disdain for his work in general and his handling of certain high-profile cases in particular—notably, of course, the murder of Teresa Hickman and the indictment of H. David Rose—got to be more than he could handle? That, despite his denials that he dislikes Jews, he *doesn't* like Jews, including members of her family and the few friends of hers they saw socially, pushy and cliquish and superior every one of them?

Ordinarily, until recently, if he had to talk about his private life, he would talk to Curry over drinks at the end of a shift. He told Mel, for instance, about his personal Battle of the Bulge and the three German prisoners he executed—there is no other word for it—and the dreams he still has about the blood and bodies sprawled in the snow. But, even drunk, that kind of conversation would require, as far as Arne is concerned, an intimacy that he can no longer, now that he's sleeping with Janine, presume with Mel—not because of any scruple on Arne's part, but because it would be too easy to tangle the truth and the lies.

Arne Anderson, at the age of thirty-seven, has had two wives, a half-dozen serious relationships, and God knows how many booze-fueled one-nighters, backseat quickies, and red-light transactions here at home and in Europe, beginning in a Seven Corners whorehouse on his fifteenth birthday. Lily, whom he met during a chance encounter in the bar of the Waikiki Room downtown, belonged in the "serious" category for the better part of three years. But their relationship had been unraveling for months, even before the Hickman murder. Lily was too smart for him. He was no match for her university education, her irony and sarcasm and derision. She wasn't interested, after a point, in his wartime experience, harrowing and sometimes heroic as it was, more than once reminding him that she had uncles, aunts, and cousins who'd perished in the Nazi camps. She never liked the fact that he's a cop.

Even the intermittent sex wasn't enough, after thirty-odd months, to keep them together.

Sex was the magnetic force that pulled Janine Curry into his bed or vice versa. Arne does things to and with Janine that Mel, competent but unimaginative, would never think of doing to or with her. In the steamy privacy of the Currys' bedroom and sundry hot-pillow joints out past the city limits, she screams and shrieks and begs for more, scoring his pale skin with her manicured nails. Before and afterward, she is sweet-tempered and demure, uncritical, undemanding, and seemingly okay with his (and her husband's) occupation.

He refuses to think what he will do when Mel discovers their affair, which Mel will do, sooner than later.

While Mel's been in Canada, Arne has spent three nights in the Currys' bed in their carefully appointed duplex apartment on Columbus.

Janine talks about her days modeling apparel for Dayton's and Young-Quinlan, and shows him photos of herself in ads clipped from the Sunday magazines and pasted into an oversized scrapbook. The stylish suits, pretty dresses, and chic loungewear only hint at the compact eroticism of the body that lies beneath. Arne occasionally refers to the war—she has asked about the raised pink welts, thick as short lengths of clothesline, on his back and upper legs—but he doesn't tell her much. They speak sometimes about the MPD, the handful of officers she's met through Mel, and the Hickman investigation, but never about Mel himself. Arne knows she met Mel at a wedding nine months ago—he was divorced, she was recently separated, and it was, according to Mel, "love at first sight"—but that's all. If she has thoughts about her future with Arne, she doesn't mention them. He's content to make the most of the moment.

One night while Mel is gone they drink the Jameson whiskey Arne brought over in a paper bag and talk. They're lying in the Currys' bed after sex. It comes out of the blue: a question, apropos of nothing that's been said this evening.

"Why on earth would a man do something like that?" she asks him.

"What man? Do something like what?" he says. He's been admiring his lover's glossy legs protruding from her undone negligee.

"Murder that girl."

Arne takes a long swallow of the whiskey.

"The state will say he got her pregnant and she was blackmailing him to keep it quiet," he says at last. "That he strangled her either in a fit of rage or self-protection."

"Is that what you and Mel think?"

"Mel, yes. I'm still not sure."

This is the first time they've talked about the case and the first time this week they've mentioned Mel's name. Arne wonders, not for the first time, what Mel has said about him generally and about the Hickman case in particular.

"Why aren't you sure? Do you know something Mel doesn't?"

Arne is surprised by her questions. She strikes him as more than merely curious, almost provocative, or maybe she's teasing, though she's not one to tease. In either case, this is new in their relationship— echoes of Lily, baiting him about this or that aspect of his job. He doesn't like it.

He laughs and takes another drink. He doesn't want to discuss the case—not now, and not with his partner's wife in his partner's bed.

"No," he says. "I don't know anything the rest of the squad doesn't know. It's just a feeling I have. Anyway, whether Rose is guilty or not, Scofield is going to have to prove it in court."

Janine reaches for the pack of Winstons on the table beside the bed. The new filter-tipped brand, in what will become a familiar red-and-white package, has been on the market for only about a year. He decides to try one and motions for the pack.

After a moment, Janine rearranges herself against the bed's headboard and says, "I went to Dr. Rose a couple of times."

Arne blinks.

"What?"

He's not sure he heard her right. If he did, he wonders if she's putting him on, this entire conversation her idea of a gag. "You went to *this* Dr. Rose? When?"

She blows a plume of smoke toward the ceiling. She doesn't look as though she's joking.

"It's almost three years ago now," she says. "When Dr. Rose's name and picture were in the paper, I went back and looked at my calendars— I keep them, I don't know why, going back a few years. It was in the fall of 1952, during the presidential election. One of the other girls at the agency gave me his name. She said he was nice. Kind of weird, but nice. She said he was Jewish, though that didn't matter much to me."

Arne is looking hard at her now.

"So what happened? Did he give you a pill?"

When she shrugs, one of the strings holding up the peignoir slides off her shoulder.

"No, I'd just gone in for a checkup. He found a small cavity during the examination, as I recall. I needed a little novocaine when he filled it."

"Did he say anything off-color, or touch you where he shouldn't?"

"No. He was nice, but, like the girl at the agency said, there was something strange about him. I kept thinking it was odd, for instance, that both times I was there no one else was in the office or the waiting room."

"This was in the evening?"

"No. Both times it was late afternoon—four-thirty or five. He did say, though, that if it got late, he would drive me home. I was working downtown, but still lived with Bill, my ex, up off Stinson Boulevard. I thought that was strange—that my dentist would offer to drive me home—but it never happened and I forgot all about it."

Arne climbs off the bed and pulls his trousers over skivvies. He has the sensation of the world tilting a bit.

"You've never mentioned this to Mel?" he says.

"No."

"Why not?"

She shrugs again, and the string slides off her other shoulder.

"I don't know. If something had happened, if Rose had made a pass at me, I suppose I would have, but nothing did, so . . ." Her voice trails off.

"I don't tell Mel *everything*," she says, looking at Arne standing at the foot of the bed, watching her nightie fall away like the unveiling of a work of art. She knows she is beautiful, and when men look at her a certain way she knows she can have what she wants.

"A girl should have a few secrets, doncha think?"

The week of July 11, marking the last few days before the beginning of his trial, Dr. and Mrs. Rose open their Linden Hills home to the press.

The idea of "exclusive features" that would run in all four Twin Cities dailies and in the dozens of Upper Midwest papers served by the local wire service bureaus is Dante DeShields's. The lawyer is surprised that Homer Scofield hasn't launched his own public relations offensive and decides to throw the first punch in what will be, he likes to say with typical grandiosity, "a battle to the death for the hearts and minds of the citizens of this community." Meaning, more precisely, the Hiawatha County citizen pool from whom Rose's jury will be drawn.

DeShields is a practiced hand at press initiatives. He has the home phone numbers of the Upper Midwest's important publishers, news directors, editors, reporters, and photographers, and does his best to hide his utter contempt for the lot of them, knowing if he can get them on his side, he can use them to significant advantage, and, if he can't, they can add to the difficulty of his job. As always, he expects to win in the courtroom. He wouldn't take a case, even a tough one like this, if he didn't. And his detractors are right: like all prima donnas, Dante loves to see his mug in the papers.

"I've made preliminary arrangements with Appel, Rystrom, Joe Clayburg of the *Pioneer Press*, Doyle Hibbert of the *Dispatch*, Rice from the AP, and Mckenzie from the United Press," he told the Roses the preceding Saturday. "They'll each get a bio and fact sheet and an exclusive half hour one-to-one with you. Mike and I will prepare you and be present for every interview. You will find this unpleasant—I wouldn't want those barbarians in *my* living room—but it's necessary and we'll help get you through it."

"You'll do fine," Ronnie says from behind Ruth's chair. Nobody looks his way or acknowledges the comment. Like Michael Haydon, Ronnie is now almost always present at these discussions, usually silent, and generally as unobtrusive as the floor lamp in the corner. Even in the stuffy heat, he keeps his suit jacket on, probably to keep a shoulder holster out of site.

Rose himself, after the brief return to work three weeks ago, has sunk into a torpid funk that Ruth attributes to tedium as much as worry about the future. "I just wish David gardened or enjoyed nature hikes or would go out to Oak Ridge with one of my cousins," she tells Haydon as she refills his tumbler with iced tea. "Of course, he'd have to learn to play golf," she adds with a chuckle.

Imagining Rose with a five iron in his hands, young Haydon muses, smiling, is as difficult as imagining Ben Hogan with a dentist's drill.

At that moment, Dr. Rose—who has never played a sport, had the slightest interest in the outdoors, or enjoyed a hobby of any kind if you don't count his phonograph records and meerschaum pipes—is sitting in his preferred wing chair in the living room, staring out through the bay window at Zenith Avenue. Ruth is right about his state of mind (he can hear her talking in the kitchen), but he doesn't have the vaguest idea what to do about it. He doesn't believe he's depressed in a clinical sense—that has never been his problem—nor does he worry much about the pending trial. On the surface, he is a model of calm and equanimity, just as he's always been unflappable at the office, and, to the best of his knowledge, he is not very different underneath.

He rarely thinks about Teresa or Grace, either, and doesn't make an effort to revisit the night and early April morning that will be the focus of his trial. DeShields brings it up, often and insistently, but the lawyer has obviously come to understand and accept that Rose has said all he is able and willing to say on the subject. DeShields will construct his defense on the defendant's personal character and professional reputation and, by stark contrast, on the reputation of Teresa Hickman and the bungling of the police.

When the members of the press come trooping into the house this week—thank God it's not winter and it's been dry of late, otherwise the mess they'd make on the taupe carpeting might drive poor Ruth around the bend—Rose will not speak of the fateful night. DeShields, hovering like a watchful parent, will make sure of that, and if it does come up, violating the "ground rules" the lawyer has laid down for the reporters, he will stop the interview and show the offender to the door.

Ordinarily, arranging a press meeting with a client, DeShields would use his posh, mahogany-lined Foshay Tower office, but in this instance he wants to emphasize the Roses' genteel yet unpretentious home life, with the family photos on top of the baby grand, the tasteful if not especially distinguished artwork on the walls, and the doctor's classical record collection leaning against the phonograph—all of that in marked contrast to the disreputable, vagabond environments of Teresa Hickman. The pearl gray Imperial and the large men inside it will be parked out of sight in the alley.

Rose still insists that he remembers nothing of those fateful hours in April. "Blacked out" is, as it was when he was grilled by detectives, the most accurate way to describe his state of mind at the time of the woman's murder and to explain his ignorance and absence of memory of the relevant events. The passage of time has not lifted a corner of the opaque shroud nor shone any light under it. On the rare occasions when Rose sits behind the wheel of his Packard, nothing he sees, touches, or smells jogs more than the dimmest memory, certainly nothing worth mentioning, nor has anything he's read in the papers rung any bells. His brief return to the office in June brought back only professional nostalgia and pedestrian recollections of dance music and doors slamming and rowdy laughter from elsewhere in the building.

No matter. DeShields isn't going to let his client talk about any of that. The summer's lone patient, Haswell's girl, Geraldine Fiola, will not be mentioned. DeShields, moreover, has made it clear that Rose won't testify in his own defense when the trial gets under way next week.

CHAPTER 10

On Sunday, July 17, the day before the scheduled beginning of Rose's trial, major features—each dominated by at least three or four photographs and in a few instances a map of the Linden Hills neighborhood—appear on the front pages of newspapers throughout Minnesota, the Dakotas, Iowa, and western Wisconsin. The headline and kicker stretched across the top of the *Minneapolis Tribune*'s front page are typical:

CURTAIN RISES ON DENTIST'S TRIAL
Did Rose Strangle His Pregnant Patient?

Dante DeShields did everything but unspool the newsprint and lay out the pages. For many readers, the preview of the most highly anticipated criminal trial since the end of the war must seem predictable and tame, which was no doubt central to DeShields's plan. Even the driver, reading the *Tribune* on a bench in sun-dappled Powderhorn Park this Sunday morning, is disappointed.

The photos of the dentist and his wife sitting demurely in their living room, with a portrait of their virginal daughters on the piano behind them, were nicely staged and are surely faithful if not exactly flattering portraits of a middle-aged, middle-American, upper-middle-class family circa 1955. Ruth appears straitlaced and competent, the doctor placid and self-possessed if perhaps a tad aloof. The driver wishes the girls' photo was larger. It's difficult to determine whether they're pretty or not. Only the dentist looks unmistakably Jewish.

The driver, a slow reader, crawls through George Appel's text. This includes the case's chronology ending with Rose's arrest, a who's who of the attorneys, assistants, and presiding judge, a thumbnail sketch of the Honorable Haakon T. Nordahl ("a no-nonsense, twenty-four-year veteran of the district court bench," according to Appel), a panoramic photo of Courtroom No. 1 with the key players' designated positions boldly labeled, and a long list of possible witnesses, including the Nicollet Avenue characters the driver knows personally—Tony Zevos and Richard Ybarra. Reading the familiar names, the driver feels the shiver of excitement that people experience when they see a friend or relation on TV.

There is little discussion about courtroom strategy. But while County Attorney Scofield offers the usual huff about proving the defendant's guilt beyond a reasonable doubt, Defense Counsel DeShields, choosing more vivid language, says he's not only going to "dismantle, top to bottom, the state's specious case against this innocent man," he is going to "make it abundantly clear that, owing to police sloth, incompetence, and bigotry, Teresa Hickman's actual killer still prowls our streets, threatening other young women."

The driver decides that he will enjoy the trial in person. (Television sets are common in American living rooms in 1955, but no cameras of any kind are allowed in Minnesota courtrooms during trials.) From the *Tribune* story he learns, however, that Courtroom No. 1, though the courthouse's largest, has a seating capacity of only a hundred spectators, and Judge Nordahl will allow no standing. Thus, added to the problem of finding a way to spend time off the Canary Cab clock is the necessity of showing up by six o'clock on a weekday morning to have a chance of securing a seat.

Well, no fucking way that's going to happen unless Teresa Hickman herself is coming back from the grave to testify. The driver will rely on the papers, though he may try hanging around downtown to see what opportunities present themselves.

Miles Mckenzie and Milt Hickok will cover the trial for the United Press. Mckenzie, of course, conducted the bureau's interview of the Roses. He did his usual businesslike job, with Hickok and Pullman adding detail and color to the stories and updates that clattered over the bureau's teletype en route to regional clients. Mckenzie considers this one of the biggest stories of his career, certainly the biggest local murder case since Bunny Augustine rubbed out his erstwhile partner "Swifty" Platt in 1948 and walked free thanks to a hung jury. Robert Gardner is happy to pitch in and can't help but feel he's working a big story, too, though because his byline won't run atop any of the Hickman dispatches, if anybody is going to know he's part of the action, he'll have to tell them.

All such grumpy considerations vanish, at least temporarily, when on Sunday afternoon Meghan Mckenzie stops by the bureau to drop a manuscript on her father-in-law's desk and on her way out pauses at Robert's station, brushes his collar with her manicured fingertips, and inquires if he's free to join her for a drink when he finishes his shift.

"Do you know the Starlight on Highway 12?" she asks.

Hickok is preoccupied with something he's typing, and Johnny Dawson, the bureau's teletype mechanic, is tending to business on the other side of the room.

"Yes," Robert says.

He's never heard of the Starlight, but he'll find it.

Arne Anderson spends Sunday by himself, so hungry for Janine that his body aches. He thinks about driving by the Currys' apartment and coming up with an excuse to drop in, knowing he'll probably interrupt Janine and Mel in bed, which, according to Mel, is how they like to spend Mel's days off, and decides against it. He hasn't seen or talked to Lily Kline since they split, so despite the obvious reasons not to, he thinks of Janine as his woman, though he knows their relationship can only end bad.

Arne skims the *Tribune*'s trial preview. When he spoke to Homer Scofield on Friday, the prosecutor, sounding anxious and unsure of himself, said he expects jury selection to be contentious and take more than a week. Arne's job, and the job of his "colleagues," as Scofield always calls the investigators, is to make sure the state's witnesses are accounted for, available when they're needed, and "steady on their feet." Arne and his men have stayed close to Grace and Bud Montgomery, Richard Ybarra (who didn't seem to know who his "buddy" with a car could be, so the cops wondered if Grace had made the guy up), and the Zevoses, father and son. Harold Hickman, granted another emergency furlough, is flying in from Germany on Monday, and Walter Kubicek and Kenneth Landa are scheduled to arrive from North Dakota the following day.

Gerald Bergen, who discovered the body, and Fred MacMurray, the coroner, are on board. But Wallace Ralston, the physician who informed Charlie Riemenschneider that Teresa Hickman told him that Rose is the father of her unborn baby, has since been treated for alcoholism, abandoned his practice, and disappeared, supposedly somewhere out West. Ralston's hearsay testimony wouldn't seem to matter a great deal, however, inasmuch as Rose himself told the police that Mrs. Hickman had accused him of her fetus's paternity.

Arne daydreams about Janine taking the stand and describing for the court her experience with Rose, but it's only a daydream and not the most excruciating ones he has about her.

He is eager for the trial to start. He's now inclined to believe, more than he did a month ago anyway, that the dentist murdered the girl, but he still has trouble envisioning a convincing scenario. He knows DeShields's cross-examination will be hellish. DeShields will accuse Arne and his squad of botching the investigation, giving in to the department's—and the city's—historic anti-Semitism, and letting the real killer run free. It could be the worst experience of Arne's career that doesn't involve his fists or a gun. He decides to buy a new suit and tie for the occasion.

Dr. Rose, sitting in a fragrant cloud of Mixture No. 79, listens to Brahms and Schubert, the Sunday paper partially read and discarded on the glass-topped coffee table in front of him.

The memory of going to work on Monday, the beginning of a new workweek with its challenges and satisfactions, seems as distant as images of his small-town boyhood. He has spoken to his daughters on the phone and enjoyed a half-hour visit with the girls at a roadside diner just over the Wisconsin line. This evening he is calm and disengaged, neither worried about the trial's eventual outcome nor confident of the verdict.

If forced to describe his mood he would say he is saddened by everything he has lost. People don't understand all that is taken from a man when he's accused of a terrible crime, all that is lost. Time will tell what, if anything, can be reclaimed. He suspects that most of it is gone for good.

Ruth, who does understand, is finally showing signs of strain, snapping at Ronnie about some inconsequential matter and dropping a bowl of strawberries on the kitchen floor. Finally, she goes upstairs to "check on" her husband's wardrobe for the coming week.

That night Rose has a dream about Teresa Hickman, but he will remember only a fragment of it in the morning. Terry, it seems, had twisted her ankle and lost a shoe.

Anderson and Curry are about to head downstairs to the courtroom when Sid Hessburg, putting down the phone, gets their attention and says, "Herman Goranski."

Arne and Mel look at Sid. It takes a moment for the name to register, the murder of the old queer in a Phillips tenement, which, like the shootings of the two coloreds on Fourth Avenue, has been all but forgotten with the focus on the Rose trial. Hessburg scribbles something on a pad, tears off a sheet, and hands it to Anderson.

"Guy walks up to Dewey Ostlund's car in front of the White

Way on Cedar a half hour ago, says he knows who killed the geezer by Holy Rosary," Hessburg says, looking at what he's written on the pad. "'Yeah, who?' Dewey asks him. 'Me,' the guy says. 'Bashed his head in with a leg off a table.'"

Officer Ostlund and his partner, whose name Arne can't remember, are standing behind a sour-smelling, sorry-looking, middle-aged gent with a lazy eye in one of the interrogation rooms off the MPD's lobby. Walking over from Homicide, the detectives can hear the hubbub in the courthouse atrium at the bottom of the grand staircase, preparatory to the gavel falling in Courtroom No. 1.

"This here's Willard Woolworth," says Ostlund, a trim, pink-faced cop in his late twenties. "Says he clubbed his neighbor Goranski and knocked him dead."

"Woolworth?" Curry says. "Any relation to—"

"Sheee-it," the suspect says, shaking his head at the question's foolishness. "Do you think I'd be living in that dump if I was? Maybe a coupla generations ago there was a connection, but that never done me no good."

Woolworth, who can produce no identification but says he'll turn fifty on Labor Day, tells the officers he was having sex—"after a fashion"—in his pal's apartment when Goranski "started making fun of my equipment." Woolworth pulls a stiff, yellowed handkerchief out of his back pocket and loudly blows his nose. "I'd warned him about that crap, but once Hermie got going, he wouldn't let go." With that wandering eye, it's difficult to know whom Woolworth is addressing.

Anderson and Curry look at the man while the patrolmen make halfhearted attempts to stifle their snickers.

"Where'd the table leg come from?" Curry asks.

Woolworth fusses with his nose, which is bulbous and crosshatched with broken blood vessels.

"I brought it up from the alley."

"So you were planning to kill him," Hessburg says.

"Naw. I thought I'd see if there was enough scratch in his billfold to borrow some—I'd only smack him if he objected." He shakes his head. "Turns out there was only about ninety cents, so I thought, fuck it, we'll have a little fun instead and unbuttoned my trousers. Hermie would be alive today if he hadn't cast aspersions on my winky." Hard to know with his eye, but he seems to be talking to Anderson.

"That was more than a month ago," Mel says. "What took you so long to tell us?"

Woolworth pulls out the handkerchief again and says, "I was thinking about the old cocksucker this morning and realized I missed him. I thought maybe I should tell someone what happened, you know, for the next of kin." Goranski, the cops have learned, has a nephew in Colorado.

Arne tells Hessburg to book Woolworth on suspicion of murder and take him upstairs.

By the time Arne and Mel enter the courtroom Judge Nordahl has ascended to the bench and the lawyers are facing each other across the attorneys' table, two on each side. There are twenty-six reporters seated on folding chairs behind two long tables on the left side of the well while the two-tiered jury box on the far right side awaits the dozen jurors and two alternates. From the back of the room, standing alongside a half-dozen uniformed officers, Arne can see, seated in the front row of the gallery, Dr. and Mrs. Rose, Ronald Oshinsky, and two well-dressed couples Arne presumes to be the defendant's brothers and their wives. The ninety-odd other gallery seats are filled with spectators. Only the policemen and miscellaneous court personnel are standing.

Arne has been in Courtroom No. 1 several times and is always impressed. The big, high-ceilinged room, with its ornamental light fixtures, stained-glass windows, decorative columns, and heavy, dark wood, reminds him of the Calvary Lutheran Church he attended with his mother until he was out of high school. Most of the major criminal cases tried in Hiawatha County since the turn of the century have taken place here.

This morning's session, already under way, will comprise a numbing series of procedural issues between and among the attorneys, rulings by the judge, and anticipation replaced by boredom in the gallery as spectators, most of whom have been up since well before sunrise, stifle yawns, look at their watches, and wonder when the judge will declare a recess for lunch. Many, clutching brown paper bags, have brought sandwiches, carrot spears, homemade cookies, and apples, though Nordahl has made it clear that there will be no eating while court is in session.

Arne, standing beside Mel, wonders what Janine is doing at the moment, and damned if he doesn't feel, at the thought of her, the familiar thrill between his legs. Like a concupiscent high school kid during Sunday services, he tries to find another image to take his mind off the activity in his trousers. He settles on Herman Goranski and his red-nosed, wild-eyed killer, and that seems to do the trick.

Jury selection, the vital process the law dictionaries call *voir dire*, is, as Homer Scofield predicted, drawn out and contentious. There are the usual gaffes and buffoonery, which would be amusing if it didn't make a long process even longer.

An elderly Northside woman says, for example, she's had no personal experience with violent crime, and then recalls that her husband served a decade in the state penitentiary after an aggravated-assault conviction before the war.

A distinguished-looking man with a fashionable Kenwood neighborhood address is promptly selected, only to be promptly dismissed when he's overheard chatting about the case with the *Star*'s Oscar Rystrom during the lunch recess. (Rystrom throws himself on the mercy of the court and is fortunate to be allowed to keep his courtroom privileges.)

A retired Augsburg College classics professor is rejected when his pseudobulbar affect—unprovoked, uncontrollable laughter, later described to Arne as "emotional incontinence"—is determined to be a distraction.

DeShields rejects thirty-seven prospects when each admits to an "extreme fear" and/or "loathing" of dentists. Oddly enough to several observers, the defense asks no questions about the prospective jurors' feelings toward Jews, as though DeShields hopes to ignore the subject entirely or intends to fall back on a bias plea if the verdict is appealed.

After almost two weeks and the examination of ninety-two prospective jurors, seven men and five women, plus a pair of male alternates—ages twenty-three to sixty-four, all white and all Christian—are seated on July 29.

Opening arguments will begin on August 1.

The Starlight on Highway 12, a dozen miles beyond the Minneapolis city line, is a two-story, twenty-four-unit motor hotel with a detached knotty-pine bar at one end, across the small parking lot from the office. Robert Gardner and Meghan Mckenzie have met in the bar three times since the day before the trial opened and have so far resisted the temptation—though it's been discussed—to rent one of the motel rooms for their tryst.

Robert is taking his cue from Meghan, an older, presumably more experienced adulterer, and suspects the tawdriness of a motel room, even in a relatively clean and respectable-seeming establishment such as the Starlight, is below her.

She does not seem nervous about meeting him for a drink here, but comes across skittish as a sixteen-year-old virgin when he suggests booking a room. Howard and Meghan Mckenzie, she's told him, live twenty-some miles away, in the south Minneapolis suburb of Richfield, three blocks from Miles and Loretta Mckenzie, so the Starlight, on the edge of west suburban Wayzata, is distant enough from friends, neighbors, and in-laws to meet a guy for drinks. Why it's a step too far to rent a double bed on the other side of the parking lot remains a mystery.

So they have sex in the backseats of his Ford coupe and her more capacious late-model Dodge, off one of the heavily wooded back roads that snake around Lake Minnetonka minutes from the Starlight or, if time allows, in his modest but air-conditioned apartment in Minneapolis.

She doesn't invite him to her house, even when her husband is out of town.

Meghan fucks the way she walks and talks—purposefully and with a studied competence, as though she studied the erotic arts in grad school and is determined to follow the lesson plan. Her pale, lightly freckled, small-breasted body is beautiful in what Robert considers an austere, aristocratic sense, and he tries not to compare her with the voluptuous, olive-skinned, indefatigable, unmistakably hoi polloi Pam Brantley, whom, ironically, he misses with renewed passion since beginning his affair with Meghan.

But he's not about to pass up the opportunity to have sex with a beautiful woman, and he's filled with both affection and admiration for Meghan, the only child of a Pillsbury Company vice president and his socialite wife.

An English major at Northwestern University, Meghan might be the best-educated woman he's ever met, and surely the most widely traveled. She has studied in France, hitchhiked through the Balkans, and sailed around the Horn of Africa. She subscribes to *The New Yorker*, speaks knowledgeably about the reportage of John Hersey and Joseph Mitchell (Robert's gods since j-school), and is "intrigued" by the architecture of Frank Lloyd Wright and other modernists. She voted for Stevenson in '52—the first member of her father's family, she says, to vote Democratic in a presidential election—and vows to do it again if he runs in '56. (She also speaks enthusiastically about a handsome, young Massachusetts senator named John Kennedy.)

She doesn't raise her voice, curse, or use dirty language, even in the throes of their lovemaking, and he tries not to either when he's with her.

Meghan, of course, could cost him his job and God knows what else, but he's confident that she won't—she has too much to lose herself, plus he's pretty sure it wouldn't be her way to kiss and tell, much less confess to backstreet infidelity. She rarely speaks about her husband, as though to do so while with another man would be in bad form. Thus Robert knows little more about the couple than that they're childless and that "Howie," who lost an eye in a childhood accident, is an avid fisherman, which helps account for her availability on summer weekends. She talks occasionally about Miles and Loretta, but always in an affectionate and uninformative way.

He can't believe, given how easily their relationship blossomed, that he's her first or only lover, but he doesn't really care. He's confident, earlier thoughts to the contrary, that he is not going to fall in love with her, nor she with him. Best he can tell, they are only colleagues who enjoy each other in bed (or a backseat) and are content to leave it at that. The attitude pleases him as European and sophisticated.

Though she is by all accounts a facile and resourceful writer, her father-in-law has not assigned her to the Rose trial or to any case-related stories.

"He won't say it, but I know he doesn't think a woman can report and write like a man," Meghan says on a Saturday morning during the *voir dire*. "I also think he's trying to spare me the ugliness of the stuff journalists have to report on, such as the murder of a pregnant girl. He has an old-fashioned, sensitive side that he doesn't want you guys to see."

"No kidding," Robert says. "The way he shepherds you in and out of Smokey's—like you're a lamb passing through a pack of starving wolves. Is his son like that?"

Meghan shakes her head. "Howie's indifferent," she says without emotion. That helps explain, Robert thinks but doesn't say, why you're lying beside me in bed while your husband wets a line in a Montana trout stream. He also acknowledges that Meghan's rationale for her infidelity echoes Pam Brantley's.

"Does Miles say much about the case when you see him?" Robert asks.

"He thinks Rose is guilty, but isn't sure he'll be convicted," she says. "I agree, though all I know is what I read in the paper." She laughs at her feeble joke.

She is not especially curious about Robert. He's told her he's the son of a Mayo Clinic surgeon, which must be at least as prestigious, if not quite as lucrative, as a milling-company executive, but there's an unmistakable gulf between them, owing to what—her private-school education and refined sensibilities, or maybe her age (she'll turn thirty in October) and marital complications? He knows she finds him attractive and enjoys their lovemaking. For his part, he doesn't volunteer much about himself, has never mentioned Pam (she's never asked about other relationships), and is determined, this time, not to say a word about his secret connection to Teresa Hickman.

He does his best, certainly when he's with Meghan, not to think about his gruesome discovery along the trolley tracks. He pretends, when he can, that his accidental involvement with the Hickman murder is still unknown and will stay that way forever.

Dr. Rose survives the thirteen days of stultifying jury selection and now sits beside Ruth, his brothers, Samuel and George, Sam's wife and George's girlfriend (George has been widowed for ten years), and Ronald Oshinsky in the row just in front of the gallery, a few feet behind the table where the attorneys have begun their opening statements.

Rose tries to be attentive, but, God help him, he has all he can do to stay awake. He knows, because he's been advised by Ronnie and prepared by DeShields, that he will hear nothing new during these initial presentations, only the familiar arguments floated in the papers by County Attorney Scofield and discussed in his dining room by his lawyers.

So much of the experience, however, is new to Rose, a man who has never had to answer for so much as a traffic violation and has visited the courthouse only to pay his property tax.

Every day he will have to pass through a gauntlet of gawking, grinning, jabbering spectators waiting to claim a seat in the gallery as reporters shout his name and the name of his counsel—as though either he or DeShields is going to stop and chat—and the blue-white pop and hot stink of the photographers' flashbulbs fill the hallway. Police officers in leather jackets stand by, but Rose feels no physical threat from the crowd. Despite the occasional shouts of "Rapist!," "Killer!," and "Kike!," he understands that he is a curiosity these people are here to see, not to lynch.

Once seated, he will do little more than take in the surroundings of the grand chamber and its accouterments. He finds mildly interesting the faded portraits of late nineteenth- and early twentieth-century mayors, aldermen, and jurists, irregularly spaced on the cream-colored walls above the dark wainscoting. The gallery's long, oak pews have been buffed to a dull sheen by uncounted backsides over the past fifty-plus years, but the tables and chairs in the well are nondescript and temporary-looking, and the linoleum covering what he assumes to be the original marble floors is scuffed and worn thin in the high-traffic areas. The big room has the feel of a temple that is no longer quite equal to its original mission.

Then the players begin filing in: the pokerfaced court clerk and court reporter, the three bailiffs, and the four attorneys. Dante DeShields and Michael Haydon are now as familiar to Rose as his family, but Homer Scofield and his second chair, an older man in a rumpled suit and hideous flowered necktie named Rudy Blake, are not. Rose, of course, has seen the Hiawatha County attorney at an early interview and then at the grand jury proceedings. He reminds him of the Catholic farm boys he grew up among in Morrison County—all sharp elbows and knees, with a skinny neck and protuberant Adam's apple, skin white as parchment, and a wide mouth full of buck teeth. Blake, who looks to be in his sixties, is there, according to Ronnie, to add "experience and gravitas" to a prosecution needing both. He's wearing a silver hairpiece that doesn't quite match the dull gray that's visible beneath its edges.

Rose will learn later that DeShields worked under Rudy Blake when DeShields, not long out of the University of Connecticut's law school, was briefly employed in the Hiawatha County attorney's office. "The old man may not be as quick as he used to be, but he knows a lot and has a mean streak you wouldn't guess to look at him," DeShields told Ronnie.

DeShields himself is the picture of controlled ferocity at the attorneys' table. *Is* he a Jew? The possibility again occurs to Rose, who, besides his wife and siblings in the pew beside him, may be the only other Jew in the courtroom. The lawyer has revealed nothing, other than his East Coast education, about his background and personal life, and when referring to the Roses' Jewishness or the community's anti-Semitism, he's never suggested that he and his client have their heritage in common. A thin gold wedding band on his left hand suggests the presence of a wife, but she is never seen or mentioned. Rose has no idea where in town he lives.

When a bailiff shouts, "All rise! The Honorable Haakon T. Nordahl!," a tall, straight-backed, white-haired man with eyes so blue their color can be discerned from the last row of the courtroom emerges through a door behind the bench and steps up to his perch. "He's considered a prosecutor's judge," Michael Haydon said when Nordahl was named to the case earlier in the summer. A former county prosecutor himself, Nordahl, according to his official biography, is a member of the Interlachen and Minikahda country clubs, Mount Olivet Lutheran Church, the Sons of Norway fraternal organization, and the Twin Cities Torsk Club, among a dozen well-known local institutions.

Rose presumes that Nordahl is no friend of the Jews. Because the judge rarely smiles, it is difficult to speculate how he might feel about dentists.

On their way into the courtroom, Sam Ross's pretty second wife, Noreen, hands Rose a small notebook and a freshly sharpened pencil.

"It will give you something to do while you sit here," she tells him in a whisper. Her breath smells of cherry cough drops.

Now, as the razor-faced Viking in the black robe settles down behind the bench, Rose opens the notebook and prints in a neat, straight up-and-down hand, "God help me."

In the days leading up to the trial, Grace Montgomery is twice delivered by Anderson and Curry to Homer Scofield's office in the courthouse.

Grace stays sober on those days and does her best to look presentable in a clean dress and a touch of makeup. The most noticeable bruises have faded, and she avoids arguments with her husband, who, coincidentally or not, spends more time away from the apartment than usual. She knows the police are keeping their eyes on Bud, so she doesn't worry about him one way or the other.

Scofield reminds her of some of the homely boys she knew in Dollar, and can't help but be amused to think that one of them, or one like them, has such an important job in the big city. He tells her she will testify for the prosecution—"You must and you will," he says, sounding like the father of a five-year-old child—and "provide information about your sister and Dr. Rose that no one else can." The prosecutor doesn't use the term "star witness," but the papers do, and that amuses her, too. Terry would be jealous.

Grace tells Scofield and Scofield's assistant, who impresses her as a kindlier, more refined version of a couple of her Kubicek uncles back home, what she's told the detectives over the past three months. The prosecutors are most interested, of course, in her experience with Dr. Rose and her understanding of Rose's relationship with Terry. She will be asked to place Terry in Rose's office on the evening of April 8.

"Just answer the questions, dear," Blake ("call me Rudy") tells her, and pats her arm with a slightly tremulous freckled hand. "Don't reply to anything that isn't asked. Look at the jurors from time to time when you're speaking, as though they asked the question. Do your best to maintain your composure, but it won't be the end of the world if you shed a tear when you're talking about your sister."

Like her uncles, Rudy has an old man's yellowed smile and sour breath.

The prosecutors do not tell Grace that she is in for a long day, or days, on the witness stand. She is aware, as is most of the Twin Cities by this time, of DeShields's reputation, but all Scofield says is that her cross-examination by Rose's attorney will likely be "extensive."

On her second visit to Scofield's office two days after the first, the prosecutors lead her through a lengthy "dress rehearsal," in Rudy's words. She is sober and presentable, but visibly nervous, wringing her hands, licking her lips, crossing and uncrossing her legs.

"You need to control your emotions, Mrs. Montgomery," Scofield says after she stumbles over a few anodyne questions.

"Take a deep breath, dear," Rudy says. "We're going over the information you've already given to the grand jury. The trial jury will be on your side."

An hour into the rehearsal, Grace knows she won't be able to do this. She was never good at exams in school, smart as she was and even when she'd studied. She did not do well in the face of other people's expectations. Unlike Terry, she can't stand people staring at her, waiting for a response. Today her mind darts away from the practice questions like a fearful dog when someone tries to pet it. Her resolve to pull herself together, do her civic duty, and see to it that her sister's killer is punished has all but vanished.

She can tell by the lawyers' reactions that she isn't doing well. Scofield noisily pushes his chair away from the table where they're sitting, stands up, and turns toward the window, running a hand through his thatch of red hair.

"Focus, Mrs. Montgomery!" Rudy tells her, no longer so avuncular. "For the love of God, madam, *focus!*"

Then he lights a cigarette for her, and they continue. She does a little better, describing Rose's office and her visits there—but she knows it's no use. They can't say exactly when they will call her to the stand, but it will likely be a few days after the opening statements, following the testimony of the detectives and the coroner and the citizen who found Terry's body. It doesn't matter: she knows she won't be there when she's called.

She also knows she won't tell the lawyers or Anderson and Curry or whoever is assigned to "look after her" (Rudy's words) about her decision. She won't tell her father or Hal or any of the other North Dakota witnesses who have arrived in Minneapolis during the past few days and who she's managed to avoid, partly because the attorneys have cautioned her about speaking to other witnesses prior to her testimony, and partly because she doesn't want to see them. The only kin she'd like to see is Hal Junior, but the child is now and likely forever beyond her grasp, in the hands of Hal Senior's parents in Grand Forks.

She is overcome by the dizzying sensation that the life she's led during the past half year belongs to another woman, a woman she doesn't know, and therefore the names, dates, and places the lawyers are badgering her about have nothing to do with Grace Kubicek Montgomery.

She is suddenly, or maybe not so suddenly, very tired and sad. She wants to go home. She wants to have a drink. She wants to take a bath.

CHAPTER 11

First thing in the morning of August 2, Arne Anderson is back in Courtroom No. 1, but now he is sitting with Mel Curry and Sid Hessburg in a stuffy anteroom, waiting to be called to the witness stand.

Gerald Bergen, the Eli Lilly Company detail man who happened upon Teresa Hickman's body along the streetcar right-of-way behind West Forty-fourth Street shortly after sunup on April 9, is the prosecution's first witness. Bergen, Arne observed in the anteroom, seemed puffed up and pleased to be there—a hitherto anonymous middle-aged citizen thrust into the spotlight of his community's most talked-about event—then commensurately deflated when he returns to the anteroom ninety minutes later, following his plodding examination by Rudy Blake and a shorter, sharper-edged cross by Dante DeShields.

Bergen is followed by John James and Wyatt Campbell, two of the patrolmen dispatched in their radio car to Forty-fourth Street following Bergen's call to the MPD. Blake spends a combined fifteen minutes on the two of them, having decided to let the detectives provide the important details from the crime scene. DeShields, however, is just as obviously determined to launch his argument about police incompetence by reducing, over the course of an hour, James and Campbell, a pair of experienced if not especially quick-witted officers, to the level of the Keystone Cops.

Campbell, the junior partner, is crimson-faced and blinking back tears when he returns to the anteroom at eleven o'clock.

"Son-of-a-fucking-*bitch!*" he says, possibly loud enough to be heard in the courtroom.

Older and arguably wiser, James shakes his head and smiles sardonically at the two detectives.

"Good fuckin' luck to you boys," he says, anticipating *their* grilling by DeShields.

Arne isn't called until 1:00 p.m., after the hour-long lunch recess. He is wearing his new suit, a tan, double-breasted number, tight through the shoulders and chest, and a maroon, white, and blue-striped foulard, both items off the rack at Nate's Menswear, and enjoyed a decent night's sleep, waking, however, with the tatters of an unsettling dream about Lily Kline fluttering in his murky consciousness. He, Mel, and Sid, on notice from Scofield's office, spent the weekend reviewing their notes with Augie Fuller and other members of the squad, their encounter with DeShields looming like a scheduled tooth extraction.

As always when he's with Mel, Arne is hypersensitive to any mention or reminder of Janine, who he's seeing as frequently as he can, though not frequently enough. Some days his longing for her burns. On such occasions, he can't look Mel in the eye, can hardly bear to share a lunch-break sandwich with him, and can only hope that Mel attributes his heebie-jeebies to the pressures of preparing for trial. Is dreaming about Lily, whom he hasn't seen or talked to or, for that matter, even dreamed about since she called it quits, the sign of a desperate man? he wonders. Only when he's waiting in the anteroom four hours later does he recall that in the dream Lily was lying dead in the weeds beside a railroad track.

Seated on the elevated witness stand, Arne looks past the attorneys, the defendant, and the defendant's family to the hundred-odd men and women jammed shoulder to shoulder in the gallery pews.

The grand room is charged with an almost palpable sense of expectancy, as though finally, after the endless preliminaries of jury selection and technical motions and conferences in the judge's chambers, the actual trial, with important witnesses, is about to begin. He spots Private Hickman in his uniform and a doddering assemblage of elderly men and women whom he presumes, from the look of them in their blue serge suits and Sunday dresses, are relatives from North Dakota. He looks for but doesn't see either Janine or Lily, which simultaneously relieves and disappoints him.

He looks at Rose seated behind DeShields. The dentist, expressionless, is jotting something in a notebook.

Scofield will question Arne, the first important witness in the first important trial of the prosecutor's short public career. Scofield's voice is weak in the vast expanse of the high-ceilinged room, and when, at Judge Nordahl's request, he tries to raise it, he reminds Arne of a choirboy trying to sound like a man. Arne glances to his left, toward the jury box, where the seven men and five women are leaning forward as though by command, and wishes Rudy Blake, hardly a dynamo but at least capable of a commanding voice, would be handling the examination. But, for better or worse, this is Scofield's show, and Arne can't blame him for taking the leading role.

Scofield ushers Arne through the preliminaries: name, residence, age, rank, years with the MPD, and responsibilities as a homicide investigator. Then, looking down at his notes, the prosecutor pivots awkwardly to the events of Saturday, April 9, commencing with the investigators' early morning encounter with the young victim's body along the Linden Hills streetcar tracks. Scofield's slow march will make everybody impatient, but Arne figures the young man is terrified of making a mistake and opening the floodgates to DeShields, who glares up at his opposite, all but tapping on his wristwatch to speed things along.

Scofield reminds Arne of the twenty-two-year-old second lieu-
tenant—a shuffling, stuttering divinity-school washout from Greeley
Creek, Oklahoma—who briefly commanded Arne's platoon in
Belgium. That experience didn't end well, either.

Now, after a whispered conference with Blake, Scofield asks Arne
to describe the position and condition of Teresa Hickman's body,
its immediate surroundings when discovered, and the absence of
apparent witnesses and meaningful evidence at the site. He asks about
the decedent's identity, the coroner's findings later that morning, and
the identification, scarcely an hour after that, of Teresa's sister, Mrs.
Henry Montgomery. He asks about Grace Montgomery's professed
ignorance of her sister's whereabouts the night before and suggestion
that the detectives try Teresa's place of employment, the Palace Luncheonette on Nicollet.

It was, Anderson confirms for the prosecutor, the Palace's
manager, Anthony Zevos, who told the police that Teresa had called
in complaining of a toothache late that Friday afternoon.

Scofield pauses, this time with tactical intent.

"Did Anthony Zevos say he told Mrs. Hickman about a dentist
in the neighborhood who might be able to take a patient on a Friday
night, Sergeant?"

"No, he didn't."

"Did Anthony Zevos tell you about such a dentist when you spoke
to him the next day?"

"Yes, he did," Anderson replies.

"And that dentist's name was?"

"Dr. H. David Rose."

Oddly, Scofield stops there, and oddly (or not) DeShields
declines—"for now, Your Honor"—to cross-examine the witness.
Anderson steps down, and Scofield proceeds to examine Curry and
then Hessburg, mostly about the same points he reviewed with Arne.

DeShields declines to cross Mel, but rises behind the attorneys'
table when Scofield is done with Hessburg. It is Sid's first trial testimony in a murder case and, like the pharmaceutical salesman, he seems

pleased to have all eyes focused on him. The youngest son of the Twin Cities' largest tobacco distributor, he's the only member of the murder squad who grew up with any family wealth, and Arne attributes the young man's voluble self-assurance to his moneyed pedigree. Sid's handsome suit today came from Hubert White's downtown emporium, a long step up from Nate's, and his glossy, carefully constructed pompadour gleams under the bright ceiling lights. He smiles confidently at the jurors, particularly at one of the pretty young women in the front row.

DeShields says, "You made quick work of that crime-scene investigation, didn't you, Detective?"

Sid is surprised by the offhanded-sounding question. He won't grasp the intent of the lawyer's curveball until it's past him.

"Yes, sir, we did," he says with a toothy grin.

"A young woman is found dead, presumably strangled, in a highly unusual setting and circumstance," DeShields continues, his deep voice slipping into its Doomsday mode, "and the Minneapolis Police Department's crack homicide investigators take a quick look around, find nothing of interest, and move along. Is that correct?"

Hessburg's face is suddenly as red as Patrolman Campbell's was this morning, his mouth drawn tight, his eyes narrowed. He's not sure how to respond.

"Is that correct, Detective?"

"Well, no," Sid stammers. "You make it sound like—"

"Like heartless indifference, Detective?" DeShields barks. "How about gross incompetence?"

"No, sir! Like neither!"

Hessburg looks desperately at Anderson and Curry, who have taken seats behind the attorneys' table. Anderson returns his stare and shakes his head, hoping to stop Hessburg in his tracks. He has to hand it to counsel. Like a wolf stalking deer, DeShields let the stronger members of the herd pass by and then pounced on the weakest.

But Sid will not be taken down so easily. His chin jutting toward the lawyer, he says, "We launched an extensive investigation, and that afternoon we identified a suspect, Dr. Rose."

DeShields glowers at the witness.

"And I'd call *that* a shameful rush to judgment," he says. "That will be all, Detective."

"The prosecution is going after Dr. Rose," Oscar Rystrom wrote in that evening's *Star*, "while the defense, as Dante DeShields made brutally clear, has set its sights on the MPD. If today's fireworks are any indication, the prosecution should be worried."

At the United Press office a few minutes before six, Robert Gardner watches Milt Hickok hammer out a feed for the bureau's regional radio clients. Copies of the *Star* are scattered across several desks as Hickok punches the update into a chattering teletype machine. Everyone agrees that Rystrom hit the nail on the head. Unlike most of his newspaper and wire service competitors, the veteran courthouse hand has the freedom, at least in his periodic column, to pontificate on the events that everyone else is merely reporting, supposedly with cool objectivity. Everyone knows, even if they can't say it, that DeShields set Scofield back on his heels with his cross of Detective Hessburg.

Scofield tried to recover in the two hours before the day's adjournment with Fred MacMurray and Alois Jensen, who carefully laid out the grim details of the victim's condition: the fractured hyoid bone, the red marks on her throat, and the fluid in her lungs all pointing to a determination of death by manual strangulation. MacMurray went on to say, based on his analysis of the contents of Mrs. Hickman's stomach and degree of the body's rigor mortis, that the time of death was between eight o'clock on the night of April 8 and 3:00 a.m. on April 9. There was no sign of alcohol or other drugs—only traces of acetylsalicylic acid, the active ingredient in common pain relievers, and the sedative Seconal—in her system.

MacMurray is rarely challenged on the stand and never attacked, and he wasn't this afternoon. Neither was Jensen, his chief assistant, who identified the victim's clothing and underwear and testified to the presence of semen stains on her underpants.

The defense was also interested in the pathologist's declaration of manual strangulation and his later revelations that Teresa Hickman was three months pregnant and had sex shortly before her death.

"How do you know the victim wasn't strangled with a short length of rope, or with a man's belt or necktie?" DeShields asked.

"The marks on the victim's throat were consistent with a pair of human hands, forcefully applied, not any sort of ligature," MacMurray said, and DeShields set off in another direction.

"You can tell, Doctor, that a woman's fetus is three months along, but you can't provide us with the father's identity—is that correct?"

MacMurray nodded. "That's correct, sir. We don't have the means or the knowhow. Someday—maybe in only a few years or maybe in a decade or two—we will, but we don't yet."

"You can't determine the source of the semen, either. Is that correct, Doctor?"

"That's correct."

"And you concur with the investigators' determination that while the semen indicates the victim had sex not long before she was murdered, it's unlikely she was raped. Is that correct?"

"The fact that her body exhibited no signs of force or struggle besides the bruise on the neck and the broken hyoid bone, not to mention the fact that the body was fully clothed when discovered and the clothes, including her underwear, were not torn or even especially disheveled, all mitigate against a determination of rape."

Given the presumed sensibilities of a daily paper's readership in the mid-1950s, neither the *Star* nor the wire service accounts of the day's testimony included those verbatim exchanges, choosing to say merely that while the victim was three months pregnant and "likely had sexual relations" the night of the murder, "authorities did not believe she had been sexually assaulted."

Even Rystrom agreed that the prosecution had done better with the medical witnesses. At any rate, the examination and cross of MacMurray and Jensen ate up what was left of the afternoon.

Robert Gardner, who spent his shift reporting a four-alarm fire on the Near North Side, feels out of sorts. (Though the blaze caused an estimated quarter of a million dollars in damages, there were no deaths or serious injuries, and the structure, a little-used grain-storage complex, was hardly a community landmark.) While he's not a part of the bureau's trial team and has only a secondhand view of the proceedings, he still fears he may become part of the story––and not in a good way. The "skinny guy with glasses" has, according to the press coverage so far, not been mentioned in court, but the possibility remains out there like a landmine in a cornfield.

Robert has not seen or heard in more than a week from Meghan Mckenzie, who, at last report, was planning to vacation with her husband in Upper Michigan, and he can't help but wonder if Miles has been scheming to keep her away from the bureau and therefore away from him. He wonders, too, if she has tired of their relationship.

When he's not thinking about Meghan, he pines for Pam.

During visits to his sister's apartment, he drives past the Brantleys' building, both hoping for and fearing a glimpse of her coming or going. He tortures himself with images of Pam sunning herself on the patch of grass alongside their building or lounging around her no-doubt stifling apartment in a bra and panties or wearing nothing at all. On more than one occasion, he dials all but the last digit of her phone number, prepared, if he has the guts to dial the last one, to invite her to come enjoy his air-conditioned quarters.

Robert has not seen or talked to Mel Curry since that awful night behind Smokey's, though he thinks about the detective every time he takes a deep breath and looks at the purple bruise in the mirror. He can't believe that Curry or someone from the prosecutor's office hasn't contacted him since that night. Had he only imagined telling the detective that he'd walked past the crime scene, or had Curry, who was possibly as drunk as Robert on that occasion, forgotten Robert's remark? Or is the prosecution going to spring a trap during the trial?

Hickok, finished with his update, has pushed his chair back and hoisted his scruffy brogans on the desk. He lights a Camel and leans back in the chair.

"Why do you think Scofield didn't object when DeShields was pantsing Hessburg?" Tommy Pullman asks.

"Scofield's scared shitless of DeShields," Mckenzie says, "but I can't help but think—this is Rystrom's theory—that the farm boy doesn't mind seeing the MPD discredited, which can be his excuse if he loses the case. Nevertheless, he can put the girl in Rose's office that night and try to use Rose's statement to the cops that she was in his car that night and they were arguing. Plus the fact that the body turned up a few blocks from Rose's home. No matter how much he's worried about DeShields, Homer's still holding the good cards."

"Blake told me the girl's old man and husband will be on the stand tomorrow, to describe their pain," says Hickok. "Then the bereaved sister will describe the connection between Teresa and the dentist. Of course, DeShields will then have a shot at *her.*"

"Anderson and Curry will have to go back on the stand, won't they?" says Robert, standing on the periphery of the impromptu circle of analysts. Mckenzie, Hickok, and Pullman all look at him, as though they've forgotten that he's in the room.

"Yeah," Hickok replies, wearily. "And then DeShields will take *their* pants off and leave them bare-assed."

Despite his misgivings, the driver decides to take his chances, get in line at sunup, and see if he can wangle a seat in Courtroom No. 1.

He listened in last night while a couple of fares—half-in-the-bag lawyers he picked up outside the Flame Room after dinner—discussed the case. Probably because they were lawyers, they seemed to know what was going on. The driver decided there and then that a chance to see Teresa Hickman's next-of-kin, including her sister, would justify getting up at four-thirty, stashing the car downtown, and standing in line for three hours. It will be his secret. He'll tell Margaret he expects to be on the street all day and have her pack him a sack lunch. Later, he'll call the garage and tell Fat Jack that his sciatica is acting up again.

So here he is, in the second row from the back, squeezed into what looks and feels like the unforgiving wooden pews at Holy Name, craning his neck to see what he's here to see. He's surprised that the lawyers are all sitting at the same table, unlike the separate, side-by-side tables on the television dramas. DeShields, when he stands, is taller than the newspaper photo led him to believe—but not much. The Jew is also taller than he expected, or would be if not for that stoop, six feet two or maybe more. When he and his lawyer stand next to each other, who doesn't think of Mutt and Jeff in the comics? The driver is pleasantly surprised to see two comely young women in the jury box, cupcakes in their twenties who, before the judge comes in, smile and giggle as though they enjoy being looked at. They remind the driver of a couple of dollies in the Holy Name choir he looks for on the rare occasions that he accompanies his wife to Mass.

The proceedings begin at nine o'clock sharp, when the judge, black-robed and self-important as the archbishop, steps through a paneled door, and sits down behind his tall desk.

Teresa Hickman's father is called first. He's a small, bowlegged sodbuster in a brown suit he probably bought before the world war—the *first* one. The old man looks self-conscious in the formal setting, grinning occasionally at no one in particular and tugging at the collar of his overlarge white shirt. He reminds the driver of a jack-o'-lantern with those gaping spaces between his teeth.

Walter Kubicek says his daughter was a good girl who he'd warned against moving to Minneapolis.

"I told both my daughters that the cities was dangerous," he says, shaking his head. "We all heard the stories about young girls getting in trouble down there."

He's on the stand for less than ten minutes. DeShields doesn't bother to cross-examine.

The driver is more curious about Harold Hickman, the lanky sad sack in the Army greens, who the county attorney calls next. The driver is interested in his testimony because, of course, the soldier slept with Terry and presumably fathered at least one of her children. Hickman seems drawn and depressed, and so soft-spoken the gallery has to strain to hear him, hardly a match for the spitfire the driver imagines Terry to have been in their conjugal bed. He tries to picture the couple having sex, but can't.

Most of Hickman's twenty-minute testimony the driver can't hear, even after the judge tells the witness to speak up. He does hear, however, the following exchange between the soldier and DeShields.

"After your wife moved to Minneapolis, did she ever mention another man? A male friend or a fellow she might have met at work?"

Hickman sighs and looks up toward the ceiling. "Only Kenny Landa," he replies at last. "But he's my cousin so I knew about him already."

"Did she ever say anything about dental problems? A toothache maybe?"

"No."

"Did she ever mention Dr. Rose?"

"No."

Hickman is excused a few moments later, and Scofield calls the aforementioned Kenneth Landa, who identifies himself as both Harold Hickman's cousin and Teresa Hickman's boyfriend when she was Teresa Kubicek. The rube is not as tall as his cousin. And instead of sad-looking, he appears to be angry. He wears glasses with black rims and a tight-fitting blue-and-gray checkered sport jacket that's a bad match with his brown trousers.

The driver has as much trouble picturing Terry with Landa as with Harold Hickman, though he senses a wild fury in the guy that a girl might believe is passion.

Landa testifies that while he corresponded "a time or two" with Teresa after she moved to Minneapolis, she never mentioned the dentist.

"She had a perfect smile," he volunteers, as though challenging the presumption that Teresa would ever need dental work.

Then, on cross-examination, DeShields asks him if he'd had a "sexual relationship" with Mrs. Hickman.

Landa's face reddens, and Scofield jumps up.

"Objection, Your Honor! That's not relevant."

DeShields, on the opposite side of the lawyers' table, says, "Of course it is, Your Honor. Mrs. Hickman's sexual history couldn't be *more* relevant in this case."

Judge Nordahl overrules the objection, and a murmur ripples through the gallery.

"Answer the question, Mr. Landa."

The witness, red as a beet and looking even angrier than a moment ago, nods his head. "Hell, yes!" he says. "We had plenty of sexual relations! We were in love!"

Nordahl raps his gavel to silence the sudden chatter and widespread guffaws in the gallery. As the crowd quiets, a bailiff appears at the judge's elbow and hands him a folded piece of paper. After reading the note, the judge raps the gavel again and rises.

"We'll take a recess at this time," he says. "Counsel will join me in my chambers." The black robe flaring behind him like a raven's wings, he disappears through the door behind the bench.

The driver looks at his watch. It's only half past ten, too early for lunch, so obviously something's come up. While people on both sides of him get up, stretch, yawn, and look around, he stays put. He is titillated by Landa's testimony, by the idea of the little honyocker and the skinny girl having "plenty of sexual relations," and he pictures her in various states of undress in the backseat of a moonlit car or flat on her back in a dusty hayloft. The girl he pictures is younger than the twenty-one-year-old with the come-hither smile and suggestive poses in the photos he bought from Ybarra.

Then, fifteen minutes later, Judge Nordahl and the four attorneys return to the courtroom, heads down, lips pursed, distracted. The crowd, many still standing, goes quiet, all eyes on the bench.

"Owing to an unforeseen circumstance, the court is adjourned," the judge announces. "The jury will follow the bailiff to the jury room and await further instructions."

An excited, uncertain buzz fills the big room as almost everyone heads for the exits.

The driver lets his pew-mates squeeze past him. His erotic reverie dissolves like a dream upon waking. Everything he did to get a seat at this trial—the early wakeup, the lies he told Margaret and Fat Jack, the loss of a morning's earnings. Once again, he tells himself that life is fucking unfair.

As the courtroom empties, Anderson and Curry drive the short distance to the Montgomerys' apartment south of the Loop, the unmarked Chevy's siren wailing and red light blazing. The better driver of the two, Curry is behind the wheel, weaving in and out of the midday traffic like a kid in a dodgem car at the state fair.

Charlie Riemenschneider and Ferris Lakeland are already at the site, as are a half-dozen patrolmen, and Alois Jensen from the coroner's office. Assistant County Attorney Rudy Blake and a couple of sheriff's deputies arrive behind Anderson and Curry.

Riemenschneider is in the living room, smoking a cigarette and looking through the mess of dated newspapers, magazines, and articles of clothing strewn across the sofa and floor. When he sees Arne, he jerks his head toward the bathroom and says, "In the shitter."

Arne leads the delegation down the short hallway. The apartment is closed up and hot, much like the last time he and Mel were here. Lakeland has taken off his suit jacket and loosened his tie. In the bathroom the naked body of Grace Montgomery is lying supine on the floor alongside the tub. Someone, probably Ferris, has draped a colorless bath towel across her privates. The bathroom's cracked tile floor is wet and slippery.

"The water was up to the top when the uniforms got here," Ferris says, "and the faucet was still running. They pulled her out and pumped her chest, but she was gone."

Curry nods toward an empty Four Roses bottle under the sink. There's a bottle of sleeping pills, also empty, next to an empty water glass.

"Who called it in?" Arne asks, looking down at Grace's body. Her hair is wet and tangled as though she just crawled out of a swamp. Her dull eyes are partly open. She looks a few pounds heavier than the last time he saw her.

"Her husband," Lakeland replies.

"Anyone see a note?"

"Not I," says Ferris.

Dr. Jensen squeezes into the room and squats beside the body.

"Those are old bruises," he says, gently fingering the faded smudges on her chest and left shoulder. A contusion above Grace's right eye has gone a grayish green.

"Where is he?" Arne asks.

"Back bedroom," says Riemenschneider, standing in the bathroom door. As Anderson and Curry squeeze past, Charlie says, "We shoulda killed the fucker when we had the chance. I just reminded him that crime don't pay."

When Anderson walks into the back bedroom, Bud Montgomery, wearing a sleeveless undershirt and twill trousers, is sitting on the edge of the bed bent over his knees, his head in his hands. A veteran patrolman named Ralph Hitchens stands nearby, meaty arms folded across his chest.

When Montgomery lifts his head, the detective sees the bloody nose and swelling left eye, Riemenschneider's reminder about the wages of sin.

"I came home and found her," Bud says miserably. "I had nothing to do with it. She's been a mess since Terry got killed, drinking day and night, crying all the time, complaining she can't sleep. I haven't had a decent meal in three months."

Arne sighs. Once again the urge to throw the son of a bitch against the wall, or out the window, is difficult to resist. What a sorry excuse for a human being, he muses. Now that both Kubicek girls are gone, who would possibly miss him?

"Did she leave a note?"

Bud looks up and wipes his nose with the blood-streaked back of his hand.

"About what?"

"A *suicide* note, you stupid prick," Curry says. Mel is moving around the little room, picking through the junk atop the dresser and peering into the wastebasket beside it. "Saying she couldn't stand to live one more fucking minute in the same world as you."

Officer Hitchens turns away and coughs.

Bud says, "I didn't see no note."

The widower will ride downtown with Riemenschneider and Lakeland, wearing handcuffs and likely fearing for his life. Jensen will finish his preliminary examination of the decedent's body and its immediate surroundings, and accompany it downtown to the morgue, where MacMurray will be waiting. Before leaving the apartment, Anderson, Curry, and someone with a crime-lab kit and camera, if he ever arrives, will give the place a thorough going-over. They will make sure the sheriff's boys on the steps outside don't let reporters or photographers in the building.

First, though, the lead detectives, joined by Inspector Evangelist and Captain Fuller, confer with Rudy Blake, who's now minus a key witness.

"Homer will be beside himself," Blake says. "Already is."

Anderson thinks he sees a smirk on the old lawyer's face.

Blake, of course, has been around the block a few times. He's lost an important witness before, in more than one important case. Among them: a Northside rubout presumed to have been ordered by Bunny Augustine the week after V-J Day, and a leap, or push, off the Tenth Avenue Bridge of a notorious white-slaver two years ago. The second untimely death probably cost the prosecution a conviction, the first one probably not, at least not as much as the bumbling of Homer Scofield's alcoholic predecessor, Ferdy Twyman. Blake was Twyman's second chair at both trials.

"DeShields will use this to pump up a case against Montgomery. He'll say the asshole killed both women," Fuller says. "How much you wanna bet?"

"No doubt about it," says Big Ed, firing up the stub of a cigar.

"He was going to point at Montgomery anyway," Blake says, lighting a Viceroy. "Along with the hundred other possible suspects who aren't either a Jew or a dentist." He blows a plume of smoke into the smoky room. "Homer will think it's the end of the world, but I'm guessing Dante gains only marginally more from this than we lose."

Anderson lights a smoke of his own. Blake makes him smile in spite of the circumstances. Rudy reminds him of a baggy-suited, silver-haired physics teacher and assistant football coach he was fond of at Roosevelt High. Too bad the old man insists on wearing that silly toupee, which you can tell is a rug from a hundred yards away.

"We'll see what Dr. Fred thinks—murder or suicide," Arne says. "Or maybe the lady tried to kill herself with the pills, got drunk while she was waiting for them to kick in, then accidentally knocked herself unconscious on the edge of the tub and drowned."

"Fat fuckin' chance," says Evangelist.

But no one is paying attention.

Two hours after the news of Grace Montgomery's death is confirmed, Homer Scofield asks for and is granted a delay in the proceedings. The trial, per Judge Nordahl's order, will resume at 9:00 a.m. on Thursday morning.

Sitting around the Roses' dining-room table on Tuesday afternoon, Dante DeShields says the woman's death can only help the defense. "She would have been helpful to us, on cross, establishing, or confirming, Teresa Hickman's promiscuity, both back on the farm and once she moved to the city," he says. "Better yet, her death adds credence to the idea that Bud Montgomery might have been Teresa's killer. If the coroner rules Grace's death a homicide, Bud's the man."

DeShields says this in a growl that no one would mistake for celebratory. Still, Rose can't help but find his lawyer's remarks, even if it's positive news for him in the trial's context, disrespectful and unpleasant.

Rose is shaken by Grace's death. She was a nice woman, kind and reasonably intelligent. He felt sorry for her because he knew that she was unhappy. She rarely smiled or laughed, not in his presence anyway. Her clothes looked out-of-date, overly worn, and not always clean. He noticed the bruises on her neck and arms, once or twice a swollen eye or puffy lip, which he didn't feel it his business to ask about, but which he suspected had been inflicted by her husband. People would be surprised to know how many women—white women and women from good homes—are assaulted by their husbands or boyfriends. They may not want to talk about it, not to their dentist at any rate, but the abuse is often plain to see.

Yes, he'd had sex with Grace Montgomery—in his office at night, before Teresa's arrival last winter. The way Rose remembers it, the sex (he'd never call it lovemaking) was labored and rather awkward, always a mutual decision, but not especially satisfying for him and probably not for her, either. Rose felt bad for her and would sometimes hand her a five-dollar bill, even before he brought up the idea of referrals. To her credit, though she accepted what he handed her, she never asked for more. He had not seen or talked to her since her sister's death.

The trial, so far, struck him as a curious affair.

He knew, from his high school civics classes, reading the papers, and watching the occasional courtroom drama on television, what trials are supposed to look and sound like, but, as with many things in life, the reality, especially when you're in the middle of it, is something else. He is amazed, for instance, that so many people are involved in the process, presumably interested in the actions (or inactions) of a single individual, a total stranger to most of them. Listening to the lawyers on both sides of the table, he often drifts away, his mind wandering to unrelated subjects—and then he'll hear his name spoken and his mind snaps back to the here and now, and he's surprised to realize the judge or a lawyer or one of the witnesses is talking about him.

He's no expert, but it seems clear that Scofield is in over his head. The young prosecutor is jumpy, disorganized, and obviously intimidated by DeShields. Scofield's assistant, the much older and presumably wiser Mr. Blake, strikes Rose as too amiable and disinterested to ultimately secure a guilty verdict.

Rose took notes during the first couple days of jury selection, but then didn't see the point, other than, he supposed, to keep himself focused on the proceedings. (Not wishing to hurt his sister-in-law's feelings, he's kept the notebook in his lap. From where she sits, she can't tell if he's writing in it or not.) DeShields's assistant, Michael Haydon, occasionally leans over and asks how he's doing, but otherwise there's been little conversation with his attorneys when court is in session.

Back home in the evening, the lawyers eventually leave and the Roses, often including Ronnie Oshinsky and at least one of the doctor's brothers, have dinner. Ruth, as always, does the cooking—corned beef and cabbage, macaroni and cheese, a Cobb or Waldorf salad, a small dish of Jell-O pudding or lemon sherbet—with one of the other women helping out. DeShields doesn't want the Roses dining in public, not that they did a lot of that before the trial. The defendant, who has been free on bail since his indictment in April, is not considered a flight risk, but that's not to say some hotheaded bigot might not want to render his own twisted form of justice if given the chance. Apparently there was such a threat, during jury selection, because, though no one has mentioned it, he has spotted a maroon county squad car crawling past the house or idling in the alley. (The Oshinskys' gray Imperial is an occasional presence as well.)

For now, Rose is content to return home, listen to his lawyers and family members discuss the case, eat dinner, and peruse the several professional journals he subscribes to while listening to his music and sucking on one of his pipes.

His daughters are still at their camp in Wisconsin. Once a week, Rose adds a carefully written sentence to Ruth's letters and on Sunday speaks briefly to each of the girls on the phone. Every other week, Ronnie drives Ruth across the border to the town of Spooner, where they visit with the girls over lunch and take a walk along the lake. The trial is never discussed.

On her return to Linden Hills, Ruth says the girls are doing just fine and "send their love to Daddy."

First thing on Thursday morning, Judge Nordahl denies the prosecution's request for an additional delay to "allow Counsel time," said

Rudy Blake in his motion, "to reformulate strategy following the death of a key witness."

"You have plenty of witnesses, Counsel," Nordahl tells Blake, who looks as though he's going to respond, and then thinks better of it.

The judge also denies, for the second time, a defense motion for a change of venue.

Nodding toward the two-dozen scribes seated at the press tables, he says, "I'm quite sure these proceedings are front-page news all over the Midwest, Mr. DeShields. What's more, I strongly doubt that the anti-Semitism you've referred to in your public remarks—*if* in fact it's a significant factor in this city—would be any less so in Duluth or Fergus Falls or Rochester. So again, motion denied."

Fred MacMurray has declared Grace Montgomery's death a drowning, though whether by the woman's intent, an accident ("misadventure"), or a combination of both can't be determined. Neither the police nor the medical examiner found any sign of foul play. Following MacMurray's ruling, Bud Montgomery, whose alibi for that morning was corroborated by his boss, is released from his courthouse jail cell, and Frenchy LeBlanc drives him home to his empty apartment, leaving him at the curb with the admonition to "stay put until we tell you otherwise." A sheriff's deputy, pulling up behind Frenchy's car, will make sure that he does.

Scofield calls Anatoli and Anthony Zevos to the stand.

Anatoli, looking impatient and out of sorts, confirms that Teresa Hickman worked for him at the Palace Luncheonette on Nicollet Avenue between March 23 and April 7.

"She 'spose to work on the eighth," he says with his comical Greek accent, "but my son he say she call in sick."

Tony Zevos is clearly eager for the spotlight when he follows his father to the stand. He's wearing a yellow suit and a wide tie ablaze with Mediterranean colors. The jury and the gallery can't help but notice both the bum leg and the smirk on his dark, handsome face.

"Not *seek*," he says, mimicking his father. "She said she had a toothache. I thought, what the hell, so your tooth hurts. You can still pour a guy a goddamn cup of coffee, can't ya?"

Someone snickers in the gallery, and Tony grins in that direction. Judge Nordahl raps his gavel and tells the witness to watch his language.

"Did Mrs. Hickman call in sick very often?" Scofield asks.

"No more than the others," Tony says. "They come and go, these girls. They work for a coupla days, then decide they need a vacation. Their feet hurt or they've got the blind staggers or it's that time of month, so they call in sick." He glances toward the jury box, in particular at the two young women sitting side by side in the front row.

The smirk disappears when DeShields stands up at the attorneys' table and stares at the witness for a long moment before beginning his cross.

"Did the defendant patronize the Palace Luncheonette, Mr. Zevos?" DeShields asks.

"The dentist?" Zevos says. "I never seen him before today."

"Did Teresa Hickman ever mention him in your hearing?"

"No."

"When Teresa Hickman called in that Friday and told you she had a toothache, did you suggest she visit Dr. Rose?"

"I didn't suggest nothin'."

"Was Teresa Hickman popular with your customers, especially your male customers?"

"Maybe. I dunno. I never took a survey. One guy—I don't know his name, all's I know he drives a cab—he asked about her once or twice."

"Did *you* find Teresa Hickman attractive, Mr. Zevos?"

Tony doesn't reply for a moment. His face takes on the look of a feral animal sensing a trap. "Not especially," he says at last. "She was kinda skinny for my taste. Plus I'm married."

DeShields says, "Did you ever make a pass at Mrs. Hickman? Try to kiss her, or put your hands up her skirt? Back in the kitchen, say, or in the pantry, where your father or your wife couldn't see you?"

"Objection!"

Scofield is on his feet.

"The witness's actions are not the issue in this trial, Your Honor."

"Sustained," Nordahl says from the bench.

"No more questions," DeShields says and sits down without another look at young Zevos, who stumbles off the witness stand, flushed and perspiring, looking down at the floor, not at his wife and his father, who watch him with hard eyes from the gallery.

Robert Gardner, seated between Miles Mckenzie and Marty Rice at one of the press tables, a late replacement for Milt Hickok, says, "Wow!" under his breath. Mckenzie nods, acknowledging the rookie's response to DeShields's aggressive blade work.

Robert was at home last night, typing up another erotic fever dream starring himself and Pam Brantley, when Mckenzie called.

"Fucking Hickok," Miles said with more than his customary irritation. "The dumb son of a bitch fell off a ladder while fishing his kid's baseball out of a drain pipe. He's in traction at Deaconess Hospital for at least a week."

Before Robert can express his condolences (he likes Milt, though he's afraid of him), Mckenzie says, "Pullman's wife says Tommy has the flu, so it's you and me at the trial tomorrow. Be there by eight-thirty. And look halfway professional, for chrissake."

Robert was at the courthouse at eight-fifteen wearing, his good sport coat and a sharp dotted tie that he bought the day after he slept with Meghan Mckenzie for the first time. He stuck three ballpoint pens in a jacket pocket and holds a reporter's notebook in his sweaty hand.

Stepping past him on his way into the courtroom, Marty Rice clapped him on the shoulder and said, "You're in the big tent now, kid."

Robert watches Arne Anderson take the stand. Scofield has recalled the big detective to tell the jury what DeShields has decided that his client will not—namely, what Rose told the police soon after Teresa Hickman's murder.

DeShields reminds the court that the defendant never signed

his statement, which means that May Grey's transcriptions of Rose's April 9, 10, and 11 conversations with the detectives are inadmissible. DeShields asks the judge to bar Anderson's testimony.

"Overruled," replies Nordahl nevertheless, with the dry voice of a man declining cream with his coffee.

At the press table, Robert has trouble keeping up, though Anderson is speaking deliberately. He is intrigued by the detective and finds it difficult to take his eyes off him. He wonders if Mel Curry has told Anderson (or Scofield) about *their* interaction. His name was not on the probable witness lists when they were announced by both sides, and he's heard nothing more about it. As far as that goes, he has seen Curry only at a distance and has not had another word with him.

Curry must believe that Robert's statement about the skinny guy could only confuse, if not hurt, the case against Rose, so has chosen to keep it to himself. Maybe, Robert muses, Curry feels sorry for him. *The fuckin' kid can't hold his liquor.*

Meanwhile, Robert envisions Anderson in combat gear, a .50-caliber machine gun on his shoulder, trudging through knee-deep snow behind a racketing column of Sherman tanks and halftracks in southern Belgium. (He found Hickok's 1952 profile of the detective in the bureau's files, along with a story about the allegations of excessive force that resulted in his two-month suspension from the MPD in 1949.) *Solid* is the word he jots down in his notebook, describing both the man's physique and credibility. Anderson may have a short fuse, but it's difficult to imagine him lying to you. In fact, according to Hickok's story, he readily admitted his rough treatment of a couple of rape suspects and accepted without complaint or appeal the department's punishment. Robert is glad, all things considered, that it wasn't Anderson who confronted him behind Smokey's that night.

Answering Scofield's questions, Anderson recounts the three interviews with Rose preceding the dentist's arrest. DeShields then reminds the jury that his client's statements, as reiterated by the detective, are only hearsay.

Judge Nordahl stares balefully at the lawyer, but says nothing.

Rose sits stoically, long legs crossed, large hands clasped on top of his knee. He might as well be watching the drama on TV. DeShields scribbles on a legal pad and springs to his feet every few minutes. Nordahl overrules the objections, and Anderson's direct is finished in two hours.

Back at the office, Robert writes a three-hundred-word sidebar to accompany Mckenzie's feature and watches it clatter off to clients around the region. He has a pulsing headache and his back screams from spending six hours on a folding chair at the press table. His first long day in court has been exhausting, so he is relieved when Miles tells him that Pullman expects to feel good enough to help out in court the next day, "that tootsie he lives with permitting."

Robert joins Mckenzie, Appel, Rice, and a half-dozen other journalists at Smokey's. He drinks more than he should and goes home dyspeptic and depressed, a few minutes after midnight, scraping the Ford's whitewalls against the curb when he parks.

He's pretty sure he heard Miles say that Meghan is back from Michigan. Has been back, in fact, for several days.

CHAPTER 12

The next day, Curry corroborates Anderson's testimony and the prosecution calls Dr. Sutcliffe Cummins, a professor of psychiatry at the University of Minnesota, who tells the jury that the "temporary loss of consciousness—sometimes called a blackout—is neither novel nor unusual." Cummins's testimony is apparently the prosecution's attempt to raise and challenge Rose's blackout defense before his lawyers can bring it up.

"It often occurs during periods of emotional stress or after the patient suffers a blow to the head," says Cummins, a chesty man with a crown of glossy yellow hair and an incongruous dark mustache similar to Rose's.

"Are there warning signs or signs after a purported blackout that a layman might notice?" Rudy Blake asks from the attorneys' table.

"Not necessarily."

"Is a purported blackout likely to repeat itself in a given individual?" Blake continues amiably. "Is a patient who purports to have had a so-called blackout likely to have them over and over again?"

"Possibly. It is not a fully understood phenomenon."

"Is it possible for a person who has a purported blackout to drive a car and find his way around the city, or, say, find his way home while experiencing a purported blackout?"

"Objection," DeShields says, not bothering to stand. "Mr. Blake's repeated use of the word 'purported' is prejudicial and misleading to the jury. I ask that it be stricken from the record."

"Overruled," Nordahl says. "Answer the question, Dr. Cummins."

"Well, I'd say, from my personal observation, that it would be highly unlikely that a patient experiencing a blackout could manage all that. The patient's senses, including his eyesight, are, well, blacked out."

"Objection," DeShields says again. "The witness is speculating about something he admits he doesn't fully understand."

"Overruled," Nordahl responds. "The witness seems to be telling the court what he knows, even if it doesn't constitute full knowledge."

There's a line of titters in the gallery.

DeShields sits down and stares at the ceiling. Beside him, Michael Haydon scribbles furiously on his notepad.

Blake, sounding like a man who intends to have the last word on the subject, at least for the time being, says, "Is it fair to say, then, that a blackout is a phenomenon that may or may not have taken place in actual fact? That, ex post facto, its existence in a given instance can't be proved one way or the other, so we're forced, when an individual purports to have had a blackout, to simply take his word for it, same as if he says that he's just spoken to the Easter Bunny?"

Over louder laughter in the gallery, Cummins says, "Well, yes, without actually witnessing its occurrence, we can only rely on the patient's account. But, I must say, the Easter Bunny may be—"

"Thank you, Professor," Blake says. Turning from the witness to the judge, he says, "The prosecution rests."

DeShields declines to cross-examine the witness, and Nordahl adjourns the trial for the day.

As the courtroom comes alive with conversation and Nordahl departs, Rose stands up slowly, with apparent arthritic stiffness, and watches the psychiatrist step down from the witness box, appearing confused as to what to do next. A bailiff points to a door at the side of the room. Rose has only once been called as an expert witness. A young dentist practicing in Vincennes, he testified for the defense of another Morrison County dentist being sued for malpractice. Though that was a long time ago, he understands Cummins's disorientation. Rose recalls the sense of wondering if he provided anything of value to the cause of truth and justice. He doubted that he had.

Rose isn't certain whether Cummins hurt or helped his case. He makes eye contact with his brother George, who has been an expert witness in more than a dozen trials himself, but George merely shakes his head and shrugs. George looks as though he may have been dozing.

The trial continues to be an Alice in Wonderland experience. Rose still believes, as do Ruth, his brothers, and Ronnie Oshinsky, that he is ably represented by DeShields, though he thinks (he's not sure) that Blake raised significant questions about the blackout and the prosecutor's repeated use of "purported" created the impression that he, Rose, was making things up. He heard Ronnie tell Sam that the judge's refusal to sustain DeShields's objections was "ominous."

"Nordahl's just another blue-eyed anti-Semite," he heard Ronnie whisper. "I know for a fact that he's a member in good standing of the Minneapolis Athletic Club, which doesn't—or didn't until recently—admit Jews as members."

"That would be grounds for appeal, wouldn't it?" Sam replied. "Of course an appeal would only follow a guilty verdict—right?"

Ronnie didn't reply.

That night, Rose lies in bed and thinks about the April evening with Teresa Hickman. He has done his best to avoid such thoughts—to avoid, at any rate, the specific sights and sounds that make a remembered experience substantial and dangerous.

Unable to sleep as Ruth snores softly beside him, he thinks about kissing Terry. Once their lips touched, she seemed to open like an exotic flower, fragrant and irresistible. It was inevitable that one thing would lead to another, though it was also true that it was in his head to seduce her from the moment she stepped into his office that January evening. He just didn't expect it to be so easy. They made love—in his office or in the Packard—four times, and then again during her last visit.

Yes, they argued after that final time, but the emotion Rose felt then was not anger so much as—what?—dismay. Of course, it wouldn't have been surprising, after their lovemaking in January, if she had been carrying his baby, but the fact that she would be so sure of herself that she would demand compensation—logically or not, that disappointed him at the time and disappoints him now. He wonders if he should have brought up his own financial concerns, pointing out that not every professional man—not every Jew, either, if she had raised the point—is well-to-do. But she was an unsophisticated country girl so she probably wouldn't have believed him.

Did he in fact "black out" in the car?

The psychiatrist on the stand this afternoon, when discussing the science behind the phenomenon, left an opening for Blake to raise doubts about its legitimacy, reducing it in the end to the level of a make-believe character, a ridiculous joke. What actually happened that night in the car? He doesn't know—or doesn't remember, if there's a difference—but isn't that the definition, at least in this case, of a blackout? He's never given much credence to clinical hypnosis, as fashionable as it is in some circles, especially out East, but maybe a competent hypnotist could help uncover the truth about what happened during his "purported" blackout. Then again it might not be wise to dig too deeply in his subconscious. Who knows what somebody might find there?

When he finally slips into a fitful doze, Rose is enmeshed in an extremely graphic dream in which he first shouts at, then forces himself on and strangles Terry Hickman. When Ruth, wakened by his wild thrashing, calms him down, his pajamas are wet and he's shivering despite the warmth of the bedroom.

"It's only a dream, darling," she says, holding him close against her sturdy body. "That's all this is—a horrible dream."

* * *

Gwen Gilligan, Robert's sister, had her baby earlier in the week.

Dr. and Mrs. William Gardner drove up from Rochester to inspect their first grandchild, a seven-pound-nine-ounce boy called Raymond John after the baby's father and no one else in particular. The grandparents stay at the Leamington Hotel downtown and visit mother and child at St. Barnabas Hospital in the Elliot Park neighborhood nearby. They pronounce the boy a fine specimen—"definitely a Gardner, just look at the eyes"—and urge their daughter to promptly schedule the baptism at Rochester's First Presbyterian, the Gardners' church for three generations. But the baby's father is Catholic, which Gwen doesn't have to point out to her parents, so the issue of where, when, or even if—Ray Senior is in fact a happily lapsed Catholic—will be decided at a later date.

Afterward, the elder Gardners, noses in the air, briefly tour the bustling city and, in the early evening of yet another steamy summer day, agree to take a moment to visit Robert's apartment before heading home. Robert has cranked up the apartment's noisy air conditioner, but realizes he should have done it before he left for court in the morning. The apartment is almost, but not quite, stuffy enough to make the eminent surgeon loosen his tie.

While Vivian Gardner pokes around in the unit's little kitchen, Robert asks his father—it's either a joke or a dare—if he's been following the trial. "I'm pretty sure the *Post-Bulletin* carries our stuff," he says with a straight face.

"Such a sordid affair," William Gardner says, shaking his head. He's a tall, handsome man, though his swept-back graying hair is receding and he, like Dr. Rose, has developed a slouch in middle age.

"I don't know how you can listen to those horrible people all day," Vivian says from the kitchen. The apartment is small so she has no difficulty hearing the men in the other room.

"Not only *listen* to them, but *repeat* and *print* their stories in gory detail," Dr. Gardner says. "If I were you, Bob, I'd have to rush home after every session and take a long, hot shower."

"You haven't seen my shower," Robert replies. Only Robert smiles.

"Why on earth you want to be part of that seamy business I'll never understand," his father says.

Robert consoles himself with the knowledge that in a few minutes his parents will be on their way home. Also knowing that they would fall dead on his shabby carpet if they knew anything about his recreational life in Minneapolis—the "gory details" of his own sordid affairs. He considers asking about Janice Jones, Pam's sister who still lives in Rochester, and then decides against it. The Gardners would remember Janice from the time Robert dated her. Whether they'd remember her sexy little sister is doubtful.

"He's a Jew, isn't he?" his father says. "The dentist?"

"The *murderer*," Vivian says, huffing into the living room. "Have you ever cleaned that shower, Bobby? A little Dutch Cleanser and some elbow grease—"

"Yes, the dentist is a Jew," Robert says. "The jury hasn't decided if he's a murderer."

"You don't think there's any doubt, do you?" Dr. Gardner says.

Robert doesn't know what he thinks. He believes—in no small part because his colleagues at the bureau seem convinced—that the jury will vote to convict. Whether Rose *is* in fact guilty, well, that's another question. Robert can't make up his mind. There are too many other possibilities.

"I'm glad I'll only have to report the decision," he says. He sounds more like his father than he would like.

That morning the defense asked Judge Nordahl to dismiss the case against Rose for lack of evidence. Nordahl refused. DeShields then proceeded to call Ruth Rose, both of Rose's brothers, one of his long-ago mentors from the U of M's dental school, the executive director of the Minnesota Board of Dentistry, and two Nicollet Avenue neighbors.

The family members, like a practiced chorale responding to an accomplished conductor, created a tone poem about the shy, studious, hard-working boy who was inspired by his revered father—a medical doctor, not a dentist—to follow two uncles and an older brother into dentistry. David graduated in the top third of his university class, married his college sweetheart, and returned to his rural hometown to practice alongside his uncles and brother. After five years as a small-town professional, he established a solo practice near downtown Minneapolis while he and his wife began a family. That practice, if it has not made the David Roses rich, has provided the doctor, his wife, and their daughters a secure and comfortable life.

Ruth Rose said that while she'd never heard her husband speak of blackouts, away from the office he sometimes seemed "disoriented" and "confused," which, she said, "I've always attributed to his skipping meals and not sleeping as long and as well as a man in a stressful profession needs to do."

His brother Sam provided the most memorable comments from the stand. Grayer, shorter, and substantially beefier than his younger sibling, Dr. Ross described his brother's practice in terms that no doubt surprised much of his audience (the gallery was packed again today), including Dante DeShields.

"I'd have to say—and I know George would agree—that Dave's a better dentist than he is a businessman," Sam said. He did not seem to be speaking unkindly, but from a big brother's irreverent perspective. "I'm not sure he can tell you, off the top of his head, the name of his insurance agent or his pharmaceutical suppliers or the people that come in and clean the windows for him. He forgets names and numbers and gets tangled up when he's speaking, sometimes like English is not his native language."

Like some of the previous witnesses, Sam seemed to be enjoying his moments onstage.

"Those points aside, Dr. Ross," DeShields said, speaking over the laughter from the gallery and the rap of the judge's gavel, "would you hesitate to call on your brother if you personally needed dental work?"

"Absolutely not," Sam replied. "But it would have to be a serious problem. I love my brother, but, for crying out loud, it's a two-and-a-half-hour drive from Duluth!" He looked past both DeShields and the defendant at the tittering gallery, grinning like Milton Berle.

Speaking again over the laughter and Nordahl's demand for order, DeShields asked the witness, "Did your brother ever talk about his patients, including his female patients?"

"Of course not," Sam replied, straight-faced again. "That would violate professional ethics. And Dave is nothing if not ethical."

"Prior to Teresa Hickman's death, did he ever mention Mrs. Hickman or her sister, Mrs. Montgomery, if not as a patient then as an acquaintance?"

"No."

"Were you aware, Dr. Ross, of anything unusual or unorthodox about your brother's sex life?"

Ross laughed out loud.

"I didn't know Dave *had* a sex life," he said. "Outside of his happy marriage, that is."

"Did he ever mention having suffered a blackout?"

"I wasn't aware, until recently, that he had any of those, either."

At the press table, Robert Gardner felt Mckenzie's elbow in his ribs.

"Great stuff!" Miles whispered out of the corner of his mouth. "Who knew the Roses had a sense of humor? The blackout question was pre-emptive."

"During this time," DeShields asked his next witness, Dr. James J. St. Alban, the portly state dental board chair, "has there ever been a bad word spoken, or a formal complaint filed, against Dr. David Rose?"

"Not to my knowledge," St. Alban said. "I can tell you there is nothing of the sort—no legitimate documentation—in our files."

On the prosecutors' side of the attorneys' table, Blake murmured something to Scofield, who rose, after DeShields sat down, to cross-examine St. Alban.

"If an individual has a complaint of impropriety against a dentist, would she know to contact the dental board instead of, say, telling her pastor or the police?"

"The state board would be the logical place—"

"But not necessarily the *first* place she would think of?"

Heads turned at Scofield's uncharacteristic aggressiveness. Blake covered his smile while DeShields rose to his feet.

"Why must the complainant be a woman?" DeShields wanted to know. "The prosecution's use of the feminine pronoun is prejudicial."

"Overruled."

Emboldened, Scofield said, "Isn't it a fact, Dr. St. Alban, that two separate complaints about improper behavior on the part of Dr. Rose have been forwarded to you by, respectively, the Morrison County Sheriff's office and the Minneapolis Police Department? One involved a forty-two-year-old woman, last name Harrelson, and the other a much younger woman whose name was apparently lost or not recorded."

The witness cleared his throat and glanced at DeShields.

"When did you receive these complaints, Doctor?" Scofield persisted.

St. Alban's face colored dramatically. He twisted around in the witness box and crossed his legs like a kid in a dentist's waiting room listening to the whine of the drill.

"Those complaints, sir, were in fact only rumors—unsubstantiated reports at best," he said in a rush. "I was told they were looked into by the civil authorities and dismissed. I became aware of them only in the form of, well, chitchat at a couple of dental association social functions. That would have been, I don't know, maybe two or three years after the war."

"Then you are talking about hearsay, Doctor," said DeShields, on his feet again. "I move that the reference to 'rumors' and 'unsubstantiated reports' be stricken from the record, Your Honor."

"Sustained. The witness's last statement will be stricken."

Also that afternoon, a very tall, dark, doleful-looking man with long arms, large hands, and enormous ears—next to whose name two-thirds of the scribes at the press table immediately jotted down the word "Lincolnesque"—testified for the defense to the "irrefutable reality" of blackouts. The witness's name was Ovid Cowper, and he was a Harvard University professor of neurology who flew in that morning from Cambridge, Massachusetts—DeShields's expert witness.

"They exist, like migraine headaches and the occasional fainting spell," Cowper told the court. "Not well understood even by our best medical minds, but real nonetheless."

DeShields, standing with his arms folded across his chest, was obviously pleased with his expert.

"No two blackouts are the same, or can be described in exactly the same way," the expert went on to say, "no more than any two patients are exactly the same. It's impossible to say what Dr. Rose could or couldn't do—what he was capable of or not capable of doing—when in his particular state of un- or semi-unconsciousness. If Dr. Rose says he experienced a blackout, I believe we have no choice but to take him at his word."

"Would stress induce a blackout, Professor Cowper?" DeShields asked.

"Very possibly," Cowper said. "Patients who have reported blackouts have often described a period of extreme agitation prior to their onset. So can excessive physical exertion or a blow to the head or not eating for a prolonged period of time."

"The stress, or agitation, could be the result of a heated argument, could it not, Professor?"

"Theoretically, yes."

Cowper then put the courtroom to sleep with a thirty-minute digest of the known science pertaining to blackouts. The prosecution was content to let the expert ramble until, mercifully, the judge, swallowing a yawn, declared the trial adjourned for the day.

Robert was assigned to write nothing, and at four-thirty Mckenzie sent him home to have dinner with his parents.

Now, after dining at The President, the Nicollet Avenue chophouse across the street from the Millers' ballpark, and his parents' dispiriting inspection of his apartment, Robert sends them on their ninety-minute drive back to Rochester. At least his father picked up the tab at the restaurant.

The Gardners' midnight-blue Lincoln Continental is barely out of sight before Robert ducks back inside and dials Pam Brantley's number.

* * *

The driver is back in Courtroom No. 1 the following morning, having risen again at four-thirty and elbowed his way into the queue in the courthouse hallway, which already reeks of high-summer sweat and surly impatience, and finally, at eight forty-five, claimed his twelve inches of gallery pew. The maddening wait gave him time to read the morning's *Tribune* from front to back, doing his best to shut out the idiotic commentary of the trial addicts surrounding him.

In the *Trib*, George Appel, an erstwhile sportswriter, opines that the duel between the trial's attorneys "must be judged, at this stage, a toss-up." He writes, "Both sides have scored points, but neither has delivered a knockdown punch. Of course, the trial of H. David Rose is only in its middle rounds." The only really significant news is provided under an Associated Press byline. Martin Rice quotes Dante DeShields saying, "We're done with the doctors and professors and scientists. We've got other people who have a lot to say. This trial is far from over."

The driver, folding the paper, wonders who those "other people" are.

Grace Montgomery would have been an obvious witness, but she's gone. So who else? Maybe a few of the witnesses who testified for the prosecution—the Zevos kid, the hick from North Dakota—and maybe a surprise witness or two. In the movies, the lawyers are always pulling someone or something out of their hat. A cold finger runs up and down his spine and a vision of himself on the stand flashes behind his eyes. Then he sees the jury taking their seats, and again he zeroes in on the two sweeties at the near end of the front row. He's almost certain that the shorter girl, the one in the tight white blouse and short plaid skirt, made and held eye contact with him the other day.

Sure enough, first thing DeShields calls Bud Montgomery, who impresses the driver as a big, dumb plug-ugly you'd cross the street to avoid. He looks, however, like he's been taken down a peg or two by circumstances, which of course he has. He walks with a hitch and seems to be missing teeth. But if anyone expected DeShields to go easy on the new widower, he's mistaken. Within minutes, Rose's lawyer confronts Montgomery with his physical abuse of his late wife, accuses him of assaulting Teresa Hickman at the Montgomerys' apartment, and suggests the possibility that he murdered both women.

Typical is this exchange:

"Did you have sex with Teresa Hickman?"

"Once or twice."

"Did you rape her?"

"*No, goddamn it!* It was her idea!"

The judge pounds his gavel. "The witness will watch his language," he says, looking down at Montgomery. "Another outburst like that and I'll cite you with contempt."

Finally, the big lug—cursing, weeping, denying the charges all at once—is escorted out of the courtroom by a pair of sheriff's deputies.

Kenneth Landa, back from North Dakota, is called, technically another hostile witness, whom DeShields will use to pry open the Pandora's box that was Teresa Kubicek Hickman's sex life.

Landa has already admitted that he was Terry's frequent, if not sole, partner back in the day, and now, pressed by DeShields, he enumerates the teenagers' trysts in his '41 Pontiac, on a blanket beside a creek in the Kubiceks' pasture, and in his attic bedroom when his widowed mother worked late at a Hartford tavern. Landa has a solid alibi so DeShields doesn't suggest that he had anything to do with Mrs. Hickman's death, but there will be little doubt when the young man steps down that the victim was addicted to sex from an early age.

A prim, pretty brunette named Constance Canfield Bannister, formerly of Dollar and now residing in Minot with her schoolteacher husband, confirms Landa's accounts. She says that she and Terry Kubicek were best friends from sixth to eleventh grade, when Connie missed several months of school after coming down with undulant fever. She says she watched her friend attract and flirt with high school boys and even older men beginning in her early teens.

"It was like flies to honey," Mrs. Bannister, now a twenty-two-year-old homemaker, three months pregnant, tells the jury. "They would follow her around and take her for rides in their cars and even come by the house. Terry's mom was gone by that time, and Mr. Kubicek either didn't notice—he was always worrying about the farm and the turkey business he wanted to start—or didn't know how to deal with it. Later on, when Terry and Kenny were going steady, a lot of those guys were still coming around, you know, like Kenny didn't exist."

"Was Terry averse to the attention?"

"Not hardly," the witness replies. "I always thought she couldn't get enough of it."

In the silence that follows, Mrs. Bannister seems to be debating with herself about whether she should add another detail. She decides she will.

"Sometimes, when it was warm enough, Terry would strip naked and dance in the headlights of Cullen Hanson's truck. Later, Cullen joined the Army and was killed in Korea."

She doesn't bother to include the fact that she and another couple of Dollar girls would sometimes join Terry in those "high-beam shows," which were usually followed by a booze-fueled party in which the strippers joined the pickup's owner and his buddies on blankets in the country dark. Her blush and averted eyes give away, however, her likely participation in the events, at least in the minds of some members of the gallery.

By this time, the driver is thoroughly aroused—he keeps the copy of the *Tribune* on his lap—and considers for a moment following Constance Bannister to her hotel or wherever she'll be spending the night, assuming she isn't returning home today. He pictures her six or seven years earlier, showing off in the headlights with Terry, the two of them friendly but competitive, one blonde, the other dark, one skinny, the other "full-figured," as the magazines say, the both of them strutting their stuff in the cones of yellow light that illuminate the dark road. Maybe Mrs. Bannister needs a cab to get from the courthouse to wherever she's staying. It takes a moment before it occurs to him that Mr. Bannister might have accompanied her from Minot.

Then DeShields calls Richard Ybarra, and the driver decides to sit still. Lest Ybarra spot him in the gallery, he slides down in his seat.

The curly-haired photographer looks scared, intimidated by the surroundings, and likely terrified by what the man-eating lawyer is likely to ask. A petty thief and con man since junior high school, Ybarra has stood before a judge before, but never in a room like this one, and never, needless to say, as part of a murder trial.

DeShields gives him a few seconds to get his bearings.

"For the record, pronounce your name for us, please," the lawyer says, with what passes for a cordial smile. "Did I get it right?"

"Uh, yeah, no, Your Honor," the witness stammers. "Not Wy-BEAR-rah. Ee-BAH-rah."

"Ee-BAH-rah," DeShields says, exaggerating the pronunciation. "I'm not, by the way, 'Your Honor,'" he adds, nodding toward the bench. "His Honor is sitting up there."

Everybody but the judge laughs, and the witness turns red.

"Oh, yeah," he says. "I know that."

"And what do you do for a living, Mr. Ee-BAH-rah?"

"I'm a professional photographer."

"What or who do you photograph, Mr. Ee-BAH-rah?"

"Well, I've done weddings and private parties, even some baby photos," the witness replies.

"Have you ever taken photos of young women wearing swimsuits or just their underwear or maybe nothing at all?"

Though Ybarra, stupid as he is, must expect the question, he looks as though DeShields sucker-punched him in the gut. In the third row of the gallery, the driver sits up and leans forward, not about to miss a word of his pal's testimony.

"Well, sure," the young man replies, trying desperately to sound as though undressing women and snapping their picture is all in a day's work for a professional photographer.

"Were you acquainted with Teresa Hickman?"

Ybarra coughs into his fist.

"We met," he says.

DeShields turns to Michael Haydon, who hands him a sheaf of eight-by-ten photographs. "Exhibit numbers sixteen through twenty-two, Your Honor," he says, stepping up to the witness stand and handing Ybarra the photos.

"Are these familiar to you?"

Ybarra makes a halfhearted show of shuffling through the stack.

"Yeah," he says.

"Well, they should be. The police confiscated them from your apartment. Tell the jury who's in these photos."

Ybarra looks at the jury and mutters, "Terry Hickman."

"So I don't have to show the photos to the jury, who I'm certain will be outraged by their salacious content, please tell them, Mr. Ee-BAH-rah, what Mrs. Hickman is wearing in the top two photos."

Ybarra glances down at the glossies.

"A brassiere and underpants," he mumbles.

"And how about the next couple of shots?"

"Just the underpants."

"And the last couple?"

"Nothin'."

"What?"

"She's not wearing nothin'."

DeShields waits a beat, drawing out the effect. In the silence, the driver thinks, Goddamn him anyway! He never showed me the nudes.

"Did you have sex with Mrs. Hickman?"

"Yeah."

"How often?"

"Once or twice."

"It was more than once or twice, was it not, Mr. Ee-BAH-rah? More like a dozen times, usually at the love nest you called your studio in Stevens Square. Is that correct?"

Ybarra is trembling. A sheen of perspiration glosses his forehead and upper lip.

"I guess so."

"Tell the jury the last time."

Ybarra takes a deep breath.

"I think it was Wednesday, April fifth," he says.

The witness is barely audible, so Nordahl tells him to speak up.

"Wednesday, the fifth."

"Wednesday would have been the *sixth*," DeShields says. "Two days before Mrs. Hickman was murdered."

Ybarra ignores the last statement. He is obviously working up the nerve to reassert himself.

"She liked what we did," he says, an answer that followed no question. "Everything we did, right from the first. I didn't talk her into nothin'. She loved to get undressed and fuck, Your Honor."

Scofield is on his feet, demanding that the witness's "depraved language" be stricken from the record. The gallery sits in stunned silence, and Nordahl holds his gavel in midair, not knowing quite what to do with it at this moment.

DeShields takes the photos back from the witness and shakes his head.

"That will be all, Mr. Wy-BEAR-rah," he says.

At five o'clock on the same afternoon, twenty minutes after court was adjourned for the day, Arne Anderson stands on the southeast corner of Fifth and Marquette, waiting for Janine Curry to emerge from Powers Department Store. He's been standing there, kitty-corner from the store, pretending to be preoccupied by the midafternoon edition of the *Star*, for the past half hour, since spotting her coming out of Farmers & Mechanics Bank down the block.

This is risky behavior for several reasons. One, her husband, who spent the afternoon at the courthouse, will soon be on the street himself unless he's going directly to Smokey's. Two, there are any number of cops, lawyers, and other courthouse denizens who could spot him and wonder, since it's now public knowledge that Lily Kline dumped him, who he's waiting for outside Powers. And, three, Janine may well be on her way to Smokey's herself and won't be happy to see Arne or want anything to do with him this evening and maybe never.

Their last meeting, on a rainy afternoon in mid-July, ended bizarrely. It was still too hot to close the windows, and Arne could hear the wind flicking the rain against the screens. Mel had been sent down to Albert Lea, two and a half hours south of the Twin Cities, to confer with that city's detectives about a suspect in a Minneapolis murder case. The victim was a fifty-five-year-old homosexual whose beating death earlier in the week was similar to the murder of Herman Goranski in June. Yes, the MPD has a suspect who confessed to the Goranski homicide, but Willard Woolworth is certifiably crazy, so Captain Fuller said someone needed to drive down and take a look at the Albert Lea guy, "just to make sure there's no connection." Curry, Riemenschneider, and Lakeland drew straws for the honor, and Mel came up short. He would be gone all day.

When she and Arne finished that afternoon, Janine, out of the blue, told Arne, "I can't do this anymore."

Arne then surprised them both by saying, "I can't either. You're not the only one who loves Mel."

Janine didn't like his response, mistaking it for either a confession of queer attraction or a personal insult. It later occurred to Arne that Janine has never been the rejected party in a relationship. *She* would do the rejecting, thank you.

In fact, Arne will go to his grave not knowing why he said what he said that afternoon. True, Mel had become, more or less by default, his closest friend if he didn't count first Lily and then Janine, which he didn't. It has never been possible for him to consider a woman he sleeps with a friend. A friend is someone with whom you share everything important *except* sex.

He reckoned, when he thought about it, that he'd had no more than five real friends in his life. One died in a boating accident on Rainy Lake when they were kids. (Arne, always afraid of the water, had turned down his pal's invitation to join the boy's family on their vacation trip up north.) One, with whom Arne was close in high school, moved to Ohio after graduation and fallen out of contact. Two guys with whom he had bonded during advanced infantry training were casualties of war, one while wading ashore in Sicily, and the other after an artillery barrage on a freezing evening near Bastogne, while Arne tried to assure the suddenly faceless man that he was going to see another morning. The fifth is—was?—Mel Curry.

Yet, after an hour of passion, Arne believed that he would shoot Mel between the eyes if Mel walked in on him and Janine. He also believed that Mel would shoot *him* between the eyes if Mel got to his revolver first. Until that happened, they may have been the closest friends either one of them ever had.

This afternoon, Arne's ache for Janine has overtaken other considerations. He has not spoken to her since he left the Currys' apartment three weeks ago. He hasn't asked Mel about her or tried to glean intelligence about her through office chatter. Now, during the biggest trial of his career, he happens to see her on the street and, without much thought other than the three reasons he shouldn't be doing it, he does what comes naturally and begins to birddog the woman. He figures she will come out the door she entered because she'll either want to walk to the courthouse to meet Mel or catch a southbound bus for home on that corner. If she exits a different door, he'll be out of luck.

But she emerges through the revolving door closest to him, five minutes later. Petite as she is, he might have missed her in the crowd of shoppers coming out at the same time if she wasn't wearing her favorite red dress. She is beautiful and confident and perfectly coiffed, and she is smiling.

Arne catches his breath, suddenly excited as a schoolboy, as he watches her cross the street. But then he realizes that she is not smiling at him but at a man coming toward her on the other side of Fifth.

He steps back into the shadow of the building where he stands presumably unseen, ducking his head and slouching into the bovine herd of commuters waiting for their bus ride home. From there he watches Mel and Janine embrace and kiss and turn westward on Fifth, toward the bars and restaurants on Nicollet and Hennepin. He thinks about following the couple, and then rejects the idea.

His eyes shaded by his fedora, he heads off in the direction of Smokey's, where he intends to get good and drunk.

On August 10 and 11, a train of violent thunderstorms punches through the heat wave that has suffocated the Twin Cities since the middle of June.

Between midnight on the tenth and eight-thirty the following evening, more than seven inches of water swamp the region, and straight-line winds topple mature trees, rip the shingles off roofs, and turn somnambulant Minnehaha Creek into a roaring torrent. A pair of fourteen-year-old boys, seeking a thrill in a stolen canoe, are caught in the creek's fast-moving current and hurtled, moments later, screaming for their mothers, over the lip of Minnehaha Falls. Their bodies are recovered three days later, twelve miles down the Mississippi River, where they'd been deposited naked, battered, and dead.

For a couple of days the storm and the drownings are all anyone can talk about downtown, eclipsing the Rose trial, which Judge Nordahl recessed on the ninth to allow the defense time to identify and subpoena two additional witnesses. Nobody envies Fred Mac-Murray and his crew, not only having to process the drowned kids' ravaged bodies, but also having to remind citizens that water rushing over and between rocks the size of refrigerators and straight down a fifty-foot drop can yield nothing but a horrible death. He can't say it, of course, but the truth is, the thieving knuckleheads got what was coming to them.

"Sweet Jesus," Ferris Lakeland says in the squad room. "Us little dipshits used to do that all the time—push canoes down the creek when the water was running high after a hard rain. We'd hit rocks or slam into the bank and capsize before we got to the falls. Got a mouth full of water and broke an arm, but at least they didn't find our bodies halfway down to Red Wing."

That morning Scofield tells Anderson and Curry to bring in the reporter, Robert Gardner. After their "talk" behind Smokey's, Curry mentioned Gardner to the county attorney, but made it clear that he didn't consider the kid a suspect. Though he admitted to being in the vicinity on the night of the murder, Gardner could explain why he was in the neighborhood at the time, and there's nothing to show that he'd ever met either Teresa Hickman or Dr. Rose. He didn't own a car at the time and was living with his sister. Gardner is an accidental witness at best, Curry said, and if he's hiding anything, it has nothing to do with the case.

"He's banging a married lady in Linden Hills," Charlie Riemen-schneider says to the men slurping coffee in the squad room. "That or he's got a boyfriend he messes around with down by the tracks."

"He ain't a queer," says Lakeland. "I got it on good authority he's been boffing Miles Mckenzie's daughter-in-law. You know, the good-looking redhead with legs up to here—you see her over at Smokey's once in a while. She strikes me as a tight-ass, but sometimes they're the ones that turn out to be the fireballs."

The detectives have never identified the anonymous caller who reported the "skinny guy with glasses," never mind the skinny guy himself.

"Gotta be someone in the neighborhood," Einar Storholm says. "Maybe someone we talked to, but doesn't want his name in the papers or on DeShields's witness list."

"So did any of us talk to the guy down there?" Curry asks. The table remains silent. "No? I didn't think so."

"Maybe it's the killer himself," Riemenschneider says. "He's toying with us, taunting us, the way that kind of asshole likes to do."

"In the movies maybe," says Storholm.

"The last thing we want to do," Rudy Blake says, assuming a grownup's voice of reason, "is give DeShields another possible suspect to dangle in front of the jury. The more alternatives to Rose, the muddier the water and the harder it'll be to convict. And if we bring Gardner in on the QT, we run the risk of DeShields saying we've been holding back evidence."

"We know where to find Gardner if we need him," Anderson says, ending the discussion.

* * *

The driver is sweeping out his garage when a Hiawatha County sheriff's deputy named John Harrington sticks his head in the door.

"Julius Casserly," Harrington says.

The driver turns his head. When he sees the uniform, he stops sweeping and draws his arm across his sweaty forehead. He glances over his shoulder to make sure he hasn't left any photos out where people can see them.

"I told him you were busy, honey!" Margaret says. She is standing on her tiptoes behind the deputy, trying to see over his shoulder.

"What do you want?" the driver says, ignoring his wife. Despite the break in the weather, and even with the big doors open, the garage holds the summer heat, and he's sweating through his short-sleeve shirt. He pulls a handkerchief out of his back pocket, mops his face, and steps around the yellow Plymouth. He sees the large manila envelope in the deputy's hand.

"This is a subpoena issued by the Hiawatha County District Court," Harrington says. "You are ordered to appear at the Hiawatha County Courthouse at nine a.m. on Tuesday, August sixteenth. If you fail to appear at the designated time and place, Judge Nordahl will direct the sheriff to bring you in."

"Julius! What is this about?"

"Go in the house, Margaret!" the driver shouts.

She does, and he retreats into the garage and sits down in his canvas chair to think.

Fifteen minutes later, Deputy Harrington intercepts Robert Gardner as the reporter walks from his parked car toward the front entry of his apartment building. Robert carries a grease-stained sack with a Juicy Lucy and double order of French fries from Nib's Bar on Cedar, and a six-pack of Grain Belt from the grocery store on the corner.

"Robert Gardner? This is a subpoena issued by the Hiawatha County District Court," Harrington begins.

Robert was planning to eat, fortify himself with three or four bottles of beer, and then work up the nerve to call Pam again. Now he has to wonder why there's a subpoena sitting on the kitchen table beside his supper and how much trouble he can possibly be in.

Like several of the driver's grand ideas, this one comes to him as he cruises around Lake of the Isles in the cooling dark of late evening.

After supper, he picked up a quarreling middle-aged man and woman going to the airport and, at the airport, three brothers, Okies from the sound of them, looking for something cheap downtown. (He dropped the brothers at the Vendome on South Fourth Street and told them to talk to one of the colored boys about girls.) Then he turned off the roof light, found some dance music on the radio, and crossed Lake Street to Lake Calhoun, where amorous couples were already fogging the windows of their parked cars.

It had to be the Zevos gimp that put the authorities on to him—who else could it have been? Even then, it had to take some doing for the cops to track him down since, to the best of his knowledge, Zevos didn't know his name, nor did any of the girls who work there, or anyone else who's crossed his path at the Palace. Zevos no doubt saw the cab parked out front, maybe jotted down the number, and gave it to investigators who talked to O'Shaughnessy at the Canary garage. The fat asshole then directed them to his door without so much as a heads-up or how-do-you-do.

It wasn't the cops who tracked him down, though. A sheriff's deputy isn't, to the driver's mind, a cop—deputy sheriffs patrol the state fairgrounds and handle auto wrecks outside the city limits—so it must be Rose's lawyers who want him to testify. What the hell could they expect him to say, other than he'd met and exchanged a few words with the victim?

Then the grand idea occurs to him—the proverbial bolt out of the blue.

When he's called to the stand, he will tell the hushed courtroom that he saw Teresa Hickman sitting in Rose's Packard parked along the east side of Lake of the Isles on the night of April 8. He'll say that he could see they were arguing about something—he'll say they were talking "animatedly." Then, after a few minutes, he'll say he saw the woman "abruptly" get out of Rose's car and head up the cross-street alone.

Curious, and, yes, concerned for the safety of a young woman out alone in the dark—he has daughters of his own, he'll tell his rapt audience—he followed her up the hill, away from the lake, on Euclid Place. He intended to turn on his roof light and offer to drive the woman home free of charge.

But before he could do that, she crossed the street and walked over to a car parked on the east side of Euclid. There were two men in the front seat of the car—a late-forties, pale green Oldsmobile sedan. The men and the woman exchanged a few words. Then the man on the passenger side got out, grabbed the woman's arm, and pushed her into the car. For a moment, the man seemed to be looking for something in the street; then, cursing, he jumped back into the car and the car took off, its tires squealing. The car took a right at the corner, and proceeded in the direction of Hennepin.

"Can you describe the two men?" the nasty little lawyer will ask him.

The driver can feel the eyes of the entire courtroom staring at him. He'll look pensive for a moment, maybe glance away from the lawyer, maybe sneak a peek at the cuties in the jury box, before replying.

"I think I can," he'll say at last. "Maybe not the man behind the wheel—I didn't get a good look at him—but certainly the man who got out of the car and grabbed the girl. He was on the tall side, I'd say, at least six feet, maybe six one or two, and thin, with a narrow face and a pencil mustache. He was wearing a hat—so was the other man, I could see that much when the interior light went on—so I can't say anything about the color of *his* eyes and hair."

He imagines the carrot-topped prosecutor jumping up to ask how he knew that it was Dr. Rose and Mrs. Hickman before Mrs. Hickman got out of Rose's car.

"It was pure coincidence I parked behind them at the lake," he'll reply coolly. "And it wasn't until I saw their pictures in the paper the next day that I realized who it was that I'd seen."

"Why is it only now that you're coming forward with this information?"

This question is trickier, and the driver isn't sure how he should reply.

"Well, to tell you the truth," he might say, "I was afraid. What if the men in the Oldsmobile were gangsters? Would I be putting my family and myself in jeopardy by going to the police?"

No, even with the mention of his family, that would sound cowardly.

He could say, "Even after seeing the photos in the paper, I wasn't one hundred percent sure it was Rose and Mrs. Hickman. It was dark, and there was only the light from a streetlamp, which wasn't much help."

Or he could say that he was under a lot of stress at the time, wasn't sleeping well, and, frankly, didn't always trust his own eyes. He was having extremely vivid dreams—he dreamed, for instance, that he saved a boy from drowning in Lake Nokomis—and, though he never said anything to anyone, even his wife, he was having hallucinations. "So how could I be certain that I hadn't dreamt or hallucinated seeing Rose and Mrs. Hickman that night?"

The last explanation seems best, though he's not sure why.

However confusing this is right now, the idea of taking center stage—stealing the show!—at the biggest local trial of the year, maybe the decade, maybe *the century*, makes him giddy. One day he's just another schmo, anonymous and unimportant. The next, he's on the witness stand in the city's grandest courtroom, the focus of all present, including the sweethearts in the jury box and the two tables of newspapermen writing down his every word.

The facelessness that always worked to his advantage suddenly didn't have much appeal. Julius Casserly would be a star!

CHAPTER 13

The trial resumes, the defense calling its witnesses, on Tuesday, August 16. But it's been a busy several days since Judge Nordahl adjourned the proceedings last week.

The body of Grace Kubicek Montgomery was transported via the Great Northern Empire Builder to Grand Forks, and then by a Pontiac hearse to Our Savior's Lutheran Church in Dollar, accompanied by Bud Montgomery and Detectives Riemenschneider and Storholm. While only Anderson still harbored suspicions about the sullen widower's involvement in Teresa Hickman's death, most of the murder squad still felt he might have had something to do with his wife's death.

Meantime, Willard Woolworth, the lunatic who confessed to this summer's murder of Herman Goranski, botched a suicide attempt in his jail cell, first sawing off his penis with a table knife, then trying to choke himself on it. (On a scrap of notebook paper he also stuck in his mouth he had scribbled, apparently referring to his choice of weapon, "What good has it ever done me?") But, after Curry ruled out the possible Albert Lea suspect, the MPD was prepared to declare the Goranski case closed. Aided by a county-supplied attorney,

Woolworth is expected to plead not guilty by reason of insanity to Goranski's murder, and spend the rest of his life in the state madhouse at St. Peter.

Finally, in a development that shocked everyone who knew him, Fred MacMurray dropped dead of a heart attack moments after trimming a row of lilac bushes behind his Victory neighborhood split-level. Dr. Fred was only fifty, though it was learned shortly afterward that neither his father nor paternal grandfather had lived long past middle age, both dying suddenly of myocardial infarctions. The county announced that MacMurray's first assistant, Alois Jensen, will serve as medical examiner on an interim basis.

From his chair behind the attorneys' table, Rose watches the trial's resumption in his now-familiar posture, one leg crossed over the other, hands clasped atop his knee. He betrays no emotion, not even boredom, sometimes going long minutes without seeming to blink.

The defendant's "entourage" (George Appel's snide label) has thinned. His brothers and their partners have returned to Vincennes and Duluth; even Ruth's brother Ronnie is absent more often than not, having his own practice to tend to. Only Ruth, who even the most unapologetic anti-Semite would have to concede is the picture of a loyal, loving wife, stays close to her husband, smiling at him, stroking his arm, occasionally leaning over and whispering something in his ear. On those occasions, he will smile slightly, nod, and sometimes whisper a word or two in reply.

DeShields has made it clear that he will spend the lion's share of his time, having established Dr. Rose's good character and reputation, discussing Teresa Hickman's "susceptibility to the lure of sexual adventure" and the "sexual adventurers" who may have killed her. The lawyer has promised the Roses that he will not refer to Mrs. Hickman as a "whore," "slut," or any of the other ugly terms a person hears on the street these days. "That wouldn't be right, the poor girl not here to defend herself," Ruth has said more than once at the Roses' dining-room table.

The most recent witnesses DeShields has called have been, in Rose's eyes, men of dubious character. Grace's thuggish husband. The sex-addled boy and girl from North Dakota. The limping lunchroom proprietor. The oily pornographer. Who among that lot, with the possible exception of the childhood friend now married to a school-teacher, could an objective person consider anything but a rotten apple from the bottom of the bottle, if not a plausible murder suspect?

The current witness, a wan, shifty-eyed fellow named Julius Casserly, identifies himself as a "commercial driver" employed by the Canary Cab Company of Minneapolis. He says he's "a lifelong city resident currently living on Bryant Avenue South, a proud graduate of De La Salle Catholic Boys' High School, a husband for nineteen years, and the father of six children ages eighteen to seven."

Casserly, who says he's in his "late thirties," is the kind of person you could pass on the street a hundred times and not remember a thing about him. Yet here in court he has a curious studied quality—as though he's playing a witness in a theater production. Every once in a while he turns toward the jury box and smiles, apparently to ingratiate himself with the young women in the front row. (Rose has noticed the young women himself. He has watched them come and go, noted their smiles—both would have benefited from appliances during adolescence—and wondered about their lives beyond the basic data collected during the *voir dire*.)

"Mr. Casserly," DeShields says, getting down to business, "according to Anthony Zevos, you were acquainted with Teresa Hickman. Is that correct?"

"Well, I saw her at her place of employment—the Palace Luncheonette—and we'd chat when I sat at the counter."

"What would you chat about?"

Casserly smiles.

"Oh, this and that. Usually nothing of any consequence."

"'Usually,' but not always. Sometimes she *would* have something of consequence to tell you. Isn't that correct, Mr. Casserly?"

"Well, yes. In retrospect, I suppose that's true."

What Teresa Hickman had to say of consequence was this, he tells the jury:

Teresa Hickman was the "victim" (Casserly's word) of a "loveless marriage" (Mrs. Hickman's phrase, according to Casserly). Her child, Harold Hickman Junior, resulted, "miraculously" (her word, he says), from the "few times" (her words) she and Harold Hickman Senior slept in the same bed, which occurred during the week or two following their wedding. Private Hickman was a "decent fellow," but once their brief courtship ended in marriage, "the thrill was gone—he even seemed afraid to let me touch him." (All her words.)

"Terry had a boyfriend, Kenny Landa, she told me, and he would—well, see to her needs," Casserly continues. "There were other men, too, she said, both at home and here in the city, who she liked and spent time with."

As his testimony draws the predictable murmurs from the gallery, Casserly tries to keep the smile off his face, but it's obviously difficult. His eyes flick once or twice toward the pretty girls in the jury. Both his words and his audience's reaction to those words seem to add to the momentum of the narrative.

"Did Mrs. Hickman tell you about *other* men in her life since moving to the city—men who were *not* her friends?" DeShields asks.

"Yes," says Casserly. He is sitting on the edge of his chair, leaning forward, his words seeming about to lift him to his feet. He takes a deep breath, closes his eyes for a moment, and proceeds, gravely, with what seems exaggerated precision, his hands clasped between his knees.

"She was terrified of both Anatoli and Tony Zevos at the Palace. She said Tony touched her in a sexual manner and offered her cash bonuses in exchange for sex. She thought Richard Ybarra was her friend until he tricked her into posing for smutty photographs, some of which, she found out, he sold to other men. And her brother-in-law, Bud Montgomery, forced her to have sexual relations after she moved into the Montgomerys' apartment."

Now there is total silence, and a different look comes over Casserly's face. He appears uncertain and uncomfortable, as though he's afraid he's said too much.

DeShields pauses a moment, and then asks another question.

"Did Mrs. Hickman, during these conversations, ever mention Dr. Rose?"

"No," the driver replies. "Not once."

DeShields pauses again and then says, "But, earlier today, when we discussed your pending testimony, you told Mr. Haydon and myself that you happened to see Mrs. Hickman and Dr. Rose on the night of April 8. Isn't that correct?"

"That's correct," the driver says.

He describes parking along the east side of Lake of the Isles, behind a black Packard, observing a man and a young woman in the front seat, apparently having a heated discussion. He recognized Teresa Hickman from the lunchroom, but not her companion until he saw Rose's photo in the paper. He recounts Mrs. Hickman's sudden departure from the Packard, her walk up the hill away from the lake, and the Oldsmobile sedan with two men inside parked on Euclid Place. After a brief conversation with the men, he says, one of them jumped out of the Olds and forced her into the front seat, and then the car sped off.

Casserly says he could identify only the man who got out of the green car. He was tall, thin, and mustachioed, and wore a light-colored fedora.

He says he would have spoken up sooner, but was afraid for himself and his family. He realizes that he'd forgotten some of the detail he'd intended to tell the court, such as the man looking for something in the street and the Oldsmobile's squealing tires when it roared away.

"Thank you," DeShields says dryly. "Your witness."

Assistant County Attorney Blake stands, says something to Scofield, and stares at the witness. Not for the first time, Rose notices that Mr. Blake's uppers are ill-fitting and probably uncomfortable.

"That's all a load of hooey, isn't it, Mr. Casserly?" Blake says. "At least everything you told us after the ages of your kids." He pauses to give his mordant opening a chance to register with the audience. "Teresa Hickman never spoke to you at length and in detail, much less confided in you about her private life. You didn't see Mrs. Hickman with Dr. Rose on the night of her murder, and you didn't see two men whisk Mrs. Hickman away in a green Oldsmobile. What you didn't glean from previous testimony and the newspapers, you made up."

Casserly glares at the lawyer.

"Isn't it true that you had a prurient interest in Teresa Hickman, that you pestered her boss and coworkers about her whereabouts and activity when she wasn't at the luncheonette, and that you tried to follow her around afterhours?"

Before the witness can respond, Blake says, "Isn't it true that you purchased from Richard Ybarra your own set of suggestive photographs of Mrs. Hickman, which you hid in your garage at home and perused for your private enjoyment?

"And isn't it true that you were twice detained on peeping Tom charges when you were in high school, the charges dropped because you were a juvenile and through the intercession of a Brother Cecil Moreland, one of your teachers?"

"Objection!" says DeShields. "Mr. Casserly is not on trial here, Your Honor. What's more, we are unaware of any duly authorized search warrants pertaining to the witness's personal property and records."

"The pornography, at least a portion of it, was brought in unsolicited and voluntarily just this morning by Mrs. Margaret Casserly, the witness's wife, Your Honor," Blake responds. "Mrs. Casserly informed detectives at that time about her husband's peeping Tom arrests, which have only within the past hour been confirmed by police records.

"She also produced a carbon copy of what appears to be a doctor's letter dated November 14, 1942, alleging a trick knee suffered during a high school basketball game that would excuse Mr. Casserly from military service. Both the doctor and the trick knee, said Mrs. Casserly, were fictitious. Mr. Casserly dictated the letter, and Mrs. Casserly, who was doing part-time secretarial work in the Medical Arts Building downtown, typed it up on a doctor's stationery.

"So it would seem, Mr. Casserly, that you're a draft dodger as well as a liar and a fantasist."

DeShields, in sudden counterattack mode, thunders, "This

information constitutes a shocking violation of the discovery process, Your Honor! We should have been informed of anything relevant to the witness's history, record, and personal property."

"It was *your* responsibility, Mr. DeShields, to vet the background of *your* witness," Blake fires back, clearly pleased with himself.

"You're both correct, gentlemen," Nordahl says. For the first time since the trial began, the starchy jurist seems to be enjoying himself. "In any event, the jury will disregard Mr. Blake's references to pornography, the peeping Tom charges, and draft-dodging, said references to be stripped from the record. The jury will then decide whether Mr. Casserly's recollections about Mrs. Hickman, Dr. Rose, and the green Oldsmobile are credible or not. The witness may step down."

But the witness doesn't seem to hear the judge. He remains seated on the witness stand, eyes wide and slack-jawed, his body depleted like a punctured balloon.

If Robert Gardner's subpoena wasn't bad enough, there was a letter from Meghan Mckenzie in his apartment mailbox the same afternoon. There was no return address on the envelope, but he'd seen enough of her prim, backward-slanting handwriting to recognize it immediately.

Dear Bob, she wrote.

I want you to know how much I've enjoyed your friendship over the past several weeks. You are a sweet young man and a pleasure to be with in every sense of the word.

But I must tell you that Howie and I have recently spent a considerable amount of time (and money) examining and evaluating our marriage, which, as you can surely understand, has had its ups and downs this year. The bottom line is, we have after much introspection, discussion, and counseling rededicated ourselves to our marriage and to do our best to start a family. (Imagine me a mommy!)

I have no regrets about our time together, but now it must end.

Fondly, M.

P.S. Of course I will count on your continued discretion.

Ninety minutes and three Grain Belts later, Robert dialed Pam

Brantley's number. He was relieved when a man answered because he didn't have the vaguest idea what he was going to say to her, other than something slurred and stupid such as, "I'm going to commit perjury in court tomorrow, which is a felony punishable by several years in prison, in order to protect the two of us, so can I please get naked with you tonight?" He hung up and went to bed, having already laid out his sport coat and dotted tie and run his wingtips through the shoeshine protocol his father learned in the Army Air Corps and passed along to his only son.

The male voice that answered Pam's phone wasn't Karl's. Could it have belonged to the son of a bitch who left his glasses under the Brantleys' bed? Robert fell asleep wondering if he and the other guy looked alike, with or without their glasses and their clothes, and if the guy had pleased Pam in bed as much as he did.

Now, fourteen hours later, Robert is a witness in a first-degree murder trial in which he might be considered a suspect and may have to perjure himself. He almost has to laugh at this latest unlikely chapter in his unlikely autobiography. If there were such a thing, he'd call it *A Bumpkin Gets Fucked in the Big City*.

Surreal is the word right now. He sits in his spiffy clothes and spit-shined shoes a foot above the rest of majestic Courtroom No. 1 (not counting the judge and the two elevated rows of the jury box), fifteen feet from the Upper Midwest's most infamous murderer (alleged), the murderer's legendary attorney, and most of the region's first-string journalists—not to mention twelve citizens who will decide whether Robert is a liar, a truth-teller, or just another sap caught in the meat-grinder known as the American criminal-justice system. All of that plus a hundred-odd men and women (mostly women) whose lives are so boring they got up before sunrise, stood in line for several hours, and now sit cheek-to-jowl on unforgiving planks for several more hours to share the bad end of lives even sadder than theirs.

He does his best to avoid the eyes of Miles Mckenzie and Tommy Pullman at the reporters' tables (he has not yet been fired, but expects to be shortly) and scans the gallery for familiar faces: Meghan's, Pam's, Gwen's, or—God help him—those of Dr. and Mrs. William Gardner.

He sees none of them, but spots Detectives Curry and Anderson, who stare at him with cold eyes, as though he's either their prime suspect or they've never laid eyes on him, he can't decide.

He's been called to testify for the defense, to answer questions put to him by Dante DeShields. He conferred with DeShields and his assistant earlier this morning, going over the points they will cover.

"Just answer the questions," Michael Haydon told him. "Don't volunteer anything you're not asked to provide."

On the stand, after the first several innocuous questions from DeShields—name, age, current residence, occupation, employer— Robert begins to relax a little.

Then, responding to DeShields's questions, he describes his return to his sister's Linden Hills apartment shortly before midnight on April 8. He describes the weather conditions as best he remembers them— "dry, chilly, but not really very cold"—and his route from the bus stop on Forty-fourth and Xerxes to his sister's building a block away.

"Did you see anyone on the street at that time?" DeShields asks.

"No, sir," Robert says. "Maybe a car or two going down Forty-fourth, but no pedestrians."

"Did you notice any unfamiliar cars parked along that route, with anybody inside?"

"No. There were a couple of cars parked on Forty-fourth, but I didn't notice anybody inside them."

"Did you see the defendant?"

"No."

"Did you see a black, late-model Packard Clipper either moving or parked along the street?"

"No."

DeShields stares at Robert for a long moment, and Robert feels a chill inside his snappy jacket.

"At some point, Mr. Gardner, you decided to leave the sidewalk on the north side of Forty-fourth Street and proceed home instead along the abandoned trolley tracks that run behind the buildings on Forty-fourth. Is that correct?"

"Yes."

"Why did you do that?"

The question strikes Robert as harmless enough, but DeShields's tone is ominous.

"I'm not sure," he replies. "I guess because I usually go into my sister's building through the back door." So now he has told the court two lies.

DeShields cocks one of his formidable eyebrows.

"You could access that back door by simply walking from the front sidewalk around the side of the building, couldn't you?"

"Yes," he says. "That's usually what I do. As I said, I'm not sure why I came by way of the tracks that night."

"Did you see anybody or anything out of the ordinary at that time, Mr. Gardner?"

"No. It's pretty dark back there."

"A good place to not be seen, yes?"

Speaking of dark, Robert has a sudden sensation of descending a dark set of stairs. Slippery. Perhaps obstructed. Perilous.

"Yes."

"Do you have a girlfriend, Mr. Gardner?"

"No."

"Did you have a girlfriend on the night of April 8?"

"No."

Robert has perjured himself five times in less than a minute.

"What time did you leave the United Press office that night?" DeShields asks.

Robert knows he can't play fast and loose with this one, not with his colleagues sitting twenty feet away.

"I'm not sure," he says. "Nine-thirty, ten maybe. We don't punch a clock," he adds, casting a glance at Mckenzie.

"And you caught a bus, southbound on Hennepin. Is that correct?"

"I might have stopped for a drink or two first," Robert says. He has lost count of his perjured statements. Six now? Seven?

"You're not sure?"

"No."

DeShields sighs, picks up a sheet of paper, peruses it for a moment, and then puts it down.

"How tall are you, Mr. Gardner?"

"Uh, about six feet," Robert says. "Six feet, one-half inch, to be exact."

He manages a foolish smile. At least he's telling the truth this time.

"And how much do you weigh?"

Robert shrugs. "Last time I checked, maybe a hundred and forty-five, one-fifty."

"How would you describe your body type—thin, underweight, skinny?"

"I don't know," Robert stammers. "Thin, I guess. Maybe skinny."

"And, obviously, Mr. Gardner, you wear eyeglasses. How long have you worn glasses?"

"Since I was eight or nine. Since the fifth grade."

The judge peers down at the lawyer.

"Can this line of questioning possibly have an objective, Counsel?" Nordahl asks.

"I believe it does, Your Honor," DeShields says. "Earlier in this trial a police officer was heard referring to an eyewitness report of an unidentified male seen moving along the Forty-fourth Street trolley tracks late on the night of April 8 or early on April 9. The man was described as, and I quote, 'young, skinny, and wearing glasses.' Mr. Gardner is young, by his own account skinny, and he wears glasses. And he was in the immediate vicinity that night."

Now Rudy Blake is on his feet, crying hearsay.

"Your Honor, this witness has not been charged, much less indicted, in regard to Teresa Hickman's murder," he says. "I don't believe he's been questioned by the police or ever been considered a suspect. This is a diversion, another bald-faced attempt on the part of the defense to draw the jury's attention away from the evidence against Dr. Rose, who *has* been indicted and *is* on trial for Mrs. Hickman's murder."

"That's all," DeShields says. "I have nothing more."

Rudy Blake, who sighs and shakes his head, has three questions for the witness.

"Mr. Gardner, did you know or, to the best of your knowledge, ever meet Teresa Hickman?"

"No, sir."

"Did you murder Teresa Hickman or have anything to do with her murder?"

"*No.*"

"Do you have any knowledge at all about Mrs. Hickman's murder?"

"No, I don't," says Robert, lying one more time.

And then, at last, he is excused.

Over the course of the next two days, DeShields directs his fire at Anderson and Curry. The courtroom senses that he's building to the climax of the defense's case.

The fact that DeShields doesn't call Detective Inspector Evangelist and Detective Captain Fuller, never mind the MPD's senescent chief, sixty-four-year-old Orwin Samuels, could mean he holds the top brass in as low regard as the investigators do themselves. More likely, he wants to concentrate his attack on the two men closest to the Hickman investigation. DeShields's efficient pantsing of Detective Hessburg earlier in the month left little doubt about his intent and tactics.

He calls Mel first and lobs a couple of softballs about his background, education, marital status, and career path.

"Are you a religious man, Detective?" DeShields wants to know next.

"Not particularly," Curry says.

"You said you're a married man. May we assume you were married in a Christian church?"

"The Basilica of St. Mary. My wife and I were both raised Catholic. She takes it more seriously than I do."

"Do you believe that the Jews murdered Jesus Christ, Detective?"

Curry blinks. He has to have expected the question, or something along those lines, but when it comes he flinches.

"I haven't given it much thought," he says. "I guess that's factually true. The Jews or the Romans back then. Or the Jews and the Romans together. Whoever was in charge. But I don't know because I wasn't there."

There are snickers in the gallery, which the judge silences with a glance.

"Were you taught that as a kid, Detective—that the Jews killed Christ?"

"Well, that's what people said."

"What people?"

"The priests. The nuns. My parents. My friends' parents."

"You were brought up, then, thinking that Jews are evil. Christ-killers. Maybe other things, too. Underhanded, duplicitous, money-grubbing, not to be trusted. Is that true, Detective?"

"That I was brought up thinking that? I guess so. More or less."

"Do you still think that?"

"Probably not to the extent I might have as a kid."

"Do you have any Jewish colleagues, Detective? Are there any Jews employed by the Minneapolis Police Department?"

"I don't know of any Jewish detectives in the MPD," Mel replies. "I'm not sure about the entire department."

"Do you have any Jewish friends? Do you and your wife socialize with any Jews?"

Rudy Blake rises and objects.

"I don't see the relevance, Your Honor," he says. It's a pro forma objection, of course. Everybody in the courtroom knows exactly what these questions are about.

"Well, I do, Counselor," Nordahl says. "Let's see where Mr. DeShields is going. So overruled. Answer the question, Detective."

"My wife might have worked with some Jews when she was modeling, but I couldn't point to any by name."

"Surely you have dealt with Jews in your capacity as a police officer, Detective."

"Yes. Bunny Augustine and several of his associates, who we've arrested a number of times on racketeering, gambling, prostitution, and assault charges. Bunny Augustine is a Jew, and so is most of his gang."

"From your experience dealing with Mr. Augustine and his associates, Detective, and perhaps with another suspected Jewish lawbreaker or two over the years, have you updated your impression of Jews in general?"

Curry takes a breath. There's a slick of perspiration on his upper lip that's discernible from the first row or two of the gallery.

"The Jews you mentioned are liars, thieves, and murderers," he says evenly. "Which is why I got to know them."

"One moment, please, Your Honor," Blake interrupts. "I want to make it perfectly clear that the state has not in any way suggested that the defendant has anything to do with the gangster Arnold—aka Bunny—Augustine and his underworld confederates, or that Mr. Augustine and his confederates had anything to do with Mrs. Hickman's murder."

"What I'm suggesting, Your Honor," DeShields says, "is that Detective Curry and his MPD colleagues have a very narrow and inevitably prejudiced opinion of Jews."

"Mr. Blake's point is noted," Nordahl says. "The jury will understand that H. David Rose, not Bunny Augustine, is on trial in this courtroom today."

DeShields glances down at the table and says, "What do you think about dentists, Detective?"

Curry smiles.

"I try to avoid them," he says, and nearly everybody except the Roses laughs, though from a certain angle there appears to be a slight self-adjustment to Dr. Rose's blank demeanor. Miles Mckenzie will later describe it as the "faintest hint of a smile."

"You've had a negative experience with a dentist, then, Detective?"

Curry says, "I was scared of the dentist my mother dragged me to when I was a kid. So was everybody else. When I had a couple of teeth knocked out in Golden Gloves, I saw two or three different dentists and had a slightly better experience."

At that, several jurors lean forward in their seats, as though to get a better look at the witness's smile. Judging by a slight discoloration, the two front uppers are not the originals.

"How long have you been partners with Sergeant Anderson?" DeShields asks.

"Two years, a little more," Mel says. The smile disappears. "Closer to three."

"Are you friends as well as partners, Detective?"

"I would say so."

"You see each other when you're not on duty? Maybe in the company of your wives or girlfriends?"

Curry frowns, unsure where DeShields is heading.

"We get together sometimes for lunch or drinks after a shift, the two of us," he says. "A couple times we've brought our wives along to dinner or a movie, though Arne isn't married right now."

"So now it's just you and the current Mrs. Curry and Sergeant Anderson enjoying an evening together?"

"Arne had a girlfriend for the past couple of years."

"'Had'?"

"They broke up this summer."

"Would that have been a woman named Lily Kline, Detective?"

"Yes."

"Kline is a Jewish name, is it not?"

"In her case, I believe it is."

Rudy Blake rises slowly and objects. The trial finally seems to be wearing him down, straining his back and knees, making him appear even older than he is.

"This can't possibly be relevant, Your Honor," he says.

"Sustained. Get to the point, Mr. DeShields."

"Do you trust Sergeant Anderson?" DeShields asks Curry, who stares at the lawyer.

"Yes," Mel says finally. His forehead is wet, and he continues to sit a moment after DeShields says he may step down.

A few minutes after one, Arne Anderson faces DeShields again.

DeShields's questions to Mel about the absence of Jews in the MPD and his attitude toward Jews in general weren't surprising, but the queries regarding Lily and Janine definitely were. What does DeShields know about him and Janine? That question, at least for the moment, nettles Arne more than the prospect of the lawyer's attack on the detectives' case against Rose.

As he did with Curry, DeShields asks Anderson to take a cursory (and redundant) run through his personal history. Then:

"You were raised a Lutheran, Sergeant. Is that correct?"

"Yes, I was," Arne replies. "Swedish Lutheran. Augustana Synod."

"Tell us, please, what a Swedish Lutheran boy learns about Jews in the course of his religious education?"

"That Jesus was a Jew."

"Okay. But so were the Pharisees and the other officials who hated Jesus and eventually put him to death. Isn't that correct?"

This time it's Scofield who's on his feet.

"Objection, Your Honor. That question is irrelevant."

"Sustained," Nordahl says. "To the point, please, Counsel."

"Did you grow up believing that the Jews killed Jesus Christ?"

Anderson stares at DeShields. There's no mystery what the defense is attempting to establish. Arne is more worried about what might be coming.

"I was brought up believing what the Bible said was correct—that the Jews were responsible for Jesus's death."

"Did any Jews live in your neighborhood when you were a boy, Sergeant?"

"Not that I was aware of. On our block there were only Lutherans, Catholics, and a large house full of Baptists." Arne manages a slight smile. He has mainly fond memories of Twenty-first Avenue South.

"Did you know any Jews in the Army?"

"A few. Good guys, mostly. Good soldiers."

"Good *friends*, Sergeant?"

"One or two, maybe."

"How about now? Any Jewish friends among your colleagues, friends, and neighbors?"

Okay, Arne thinks. Here it comes.

"I lived with a Jewish woman for a couple of years, until earlier this summer."

"Lily Kline."

"Yes."

"You're not together now?"

"No."

"Who initiated the breakup?"

"Objection!" Scofield cries.

But before Nordahl sustains, Arne says, "She did."

During a brief recess, Arne, told by the judge to remain on the stand, decides that DeShields knows about his affair with Janine Curry. The lawyer's investigator has done his dirty work and provided the attorney with a list of dates and places and maybe photographs as well. Arne also decides that DeShields won't use the information because it is irrelevant and Nordahl won't allow it. DeShields's intent, Arne figures, is to shake him up, take a bite out of his confidence, make him look wobbly and unreliable on the stand. He wonders how exactly Mel reacted—Mel didn't mention the reference to his wife when they briefly spoke during the lunch break—and, more to the point, what inferences Mel might have drawn from that line of questioning, or what Mel might have been told about DeShields's snooping.

When Arne's testimony resumes, DeShields says, "You have more than once been accused of using excessive force—of brutality, in plain language—when dealing with suspects, have you not?"

"Yes, I have," Arne replies. "Twice."

That much is on the record. And, like the references to the women, not relevant to this case.

"You had occasion to question Henry Montgomery—Bud Montgomery, as he's called—about Teresa Hickman's murder, is that correct?"

"Yes."

"More than once."

"Yes."

"Do you recall a particular interaction with Mr. Montgomery one evening a week or so after Mrs. Hickman's death, in the alley behind the Montgomerys' apartment building?"

"Yes."

"That was the evening you and Detective Riemenschneider beat Mr. Montgomery so severely he required medical attention. Burst an eardrum, cracked a rib, knocked out some teeth, and opened several wounds requiring stitches. Do you recall those details, Sergeant?"

"Yes."

"You and Detective Riemenschneider beat up Mr. Montgomery that evening because you believed Mr. Montgomery murdered Mrs. Hickman. Isn't that correct?"

"That's correct. We thought we could persuade him to confess to killing her."

"Why did you think he murdered Mrs. Hickman?"

"Because he repeatedly beat up Mrs. Hickman's sister and raped Mrs. Hickman. He's a violent man, and Mrs. Hickman was living in his apartment. His alibi for the night of her murder was weak, and the man who supplied it, an alcoholic coworker, had disappeared."

"Thank you, Sergeant. That will be all."

Homer Scofield cross-examines Anderson. It may be Arne's imagination, but the county attorney seems to be exhibiting a confidence he didn't have a few days earlier, wearing it like a handsome new suit.

"Do you still believe that Bud Montgomery murdered Teresa Hickman, Sergeant Anderson?"

"No, I don't," Arne says.

"Isn't it a fact, Sergeant, that several persons who you at one time or another considered suspects in Mrs. Hickman's murder have been investigated and, for one reason or another, been eliminated as suspects? I'm talking about, besides Bud Montgomery, Anthony Zevos,

Michael Ybarra, and Kenneth Landa—all of whom have credible alibis and are no longer suspects. Is that correct, Sergeant?"

"Yes. But, like I said, Bud Montgomery's alibi was and still is questionable."

"Is Julius Casserly a suspect, Sergeant?"

"No."

When Scofield is finished, DeShields quickly rises to redirect.

"Why isn't Julius Casserly a suspect, Sergeant?" he asks.

"He never was," Arne says. "He's not even a credible witness. There's no reason to believe what he said about Teresa Hickman riding away that night with two strange men. I believe it's possible, given his familiarity with that part of town and his predilection to hang around lovers' lanes after dark, that Casserly happened upon Mrs. Hickman and Dr. Rose in Rose's parked car that night. But Rose already told us that she was in his car with him that night, at least until she wasn't. Rose told us they'd been parked at Lake of the Isles and then drove off together."

"Have you or your colleagues questioned Mr. Casserly since his testimony?"

"No."

"Have you or your colleagues questioned Robert Gardner since his testimony?"

"No."

"Why not?"

"Because we don't believe that either man had anything to do with Teresa Hickman's murder. We believe that Dr. Rose murdered Mrs. Hickman."

"Do you believe that Dr. Rose blacked out with Mrs. Hickman in his car the night of her murder?"

"I think it's possible, but—"

"Thank you, Sergeant. That will be all."

Stepping down, Arne looks around the room on the chance that Mel might be there, but his partner is nowhere in sight.

CHAPTER 14

A clear majority of the reporters present this afternoon believe the detectives' testimony to be a victory for the defense.

DeShields has used his putatively hostile witnesses to shine a bright light on both the city's historic anti-Semitism *and* a universal loathing of dentists to explain why an upright citizen has been arrested and prosecuted for a crime he did not commit. The canny lawyer had already trotted out another half-dozen individuals whose possible involvement in the Hickman murder could summon reasonable doubt about Rose's guilt, while establishing beyond doubt that the victim was a promiscuous woman who made herself available to dangerous men.

No one, not even Oscar Rystrom of the *Star*, will say the following in so many words, but the journalists' personal admiration for Dante DeShields is obvious. If readers were able to eavesdrop on the scribes over their whiskey and short ribs at Smokey's, the latter's hero worship would be embarrassingly clear.

"Intellectually, the guy is head and shoulders above everyone else in the room, maybe in the building," says George Appel, hoisting his lowball glass, and no one disagrees.

Adds a *Tribune* copy editor named Jimmy Hilliker, "Damn me if I don't just love to say the guy's name: *Don-tay Duh-Sheee-ulds.*" Heads nod, people laugh. No one calls Hilliker a fairy.

By contrast, the press has little good to say about the prosecution, whether in Smokey's boozy din or on the clotted pages of their publications.

After this week's proceedings, Appel writes, "It is the consensus of the courthouse cognoscenti that the prosecution has lost its way."

Rystrom writes, "Court-watchers agree that Scofield is overmatched and Blake has seen better days. They've let the defense inject the names of too many suspicious characters, making the idea that someone other than David Rose killed Teresa Hickman seem plausible. It may be that DeShields believes Rose's 'blackout' defense isn't going to be enough, so he's putting his chips behind the suggestion that there's another killer.

"Wisely, he will keep Rose off the stand."

In a dispatch filed for the outstate Sunday papers, Miles Mckenzie argues that "Teresa Hickman's devil-may-care social life made her susceptible to several horrible possibilities. It's not out of the question, given the woman's proclivities as enumerated by defense witnesses, that she jumped from one man's car to another that fateful April night, had intimate relations in one or both, and died in the last one—which may *not* have been Rose's Packard."

Robert Gardner's testimony is mentioned in all of the weekend accounts, though only in passing. Of all the "alternative possibilities," writes the AP's Martin Rice, "tall, skinny, and myopic as he is, Gardner must surely be the least likely. And, even given our profession's lowly status a mere peg or two above used-car dealers and dentists, the young reporter would fit nobody's image of a back-alley killer."

On the Saturday following his testimony Robert plods up the narrow stairs to the bureau the way his younger self would have approached a dental appointment. Once upstairs, he slips into the bureau and as unobtrusively as possible makes his way to an empty desk. (He still doesn't have one of his own.) "All hands are on deck," as Miles likes to say—even Meghan, whom Robert hasn't seen in weeks—but no one gives him more than a passing glance. Miles has not asked him to be part of the case coverage since his subpoena.

"*You're* the news today, buddy," the chief said when it became clear that Robert was going to testify. The chief didn't tell him what his job might be when the trial is over. In fact, in the office this late Saturday morning, Robert isn't sure he still works here. He can't be the first Unipresser compelled to testify in a criminal case, but he might be the first to do so in such an ambiguous role—witness, possible suspect—in such a high-profile trial. He wonders if Mckenzie, when the weekly staff meeting adjourns, is going to let him go.

In fact, now that he's here, he's more curious about Meghan's presence and her role in the Rose trial coverage than his own. Robert can see her long, shiny hair, the bones of her skinny shoulders, the delicious swerve of her ass and graceful taper of her left leg as she stands, hip cocked, in the group surrounding her father-in-law's desk. As usual, Miles is doing most of the talking, but Robert can hear her voice, when she joins the discussion, and her sunny laughter at something Tommy says. Not invited to take part, Robert pretends to find the past week's entries in *St. Peter's Log* interesting.

When the meeting breaks up, Meghan is the first one out of the chief's cubicle. She grabs her bag and heads for the stairs. She gives Robert a fluttery wave and a little smile over her shoulder, gestures he'd expect more from a colleague than a lover, or ex-lover. She is in a hurry. Probably on her way home to make a baby with one-eyed Howie, Robert muses darkly.

Pullman and Hickok—Milt is back at work but inconvenienced by a cast and crutches—stop by the desk, where Robert tries to look engaged. Both men clap him on the shoulder.

"You survived DeShields, kid," says Hickok with a rare grin. "Not everyone can say that."

"Certainly not the chuckleheads who were on the stand before you—that smut peddler and that crazy cabbie," Tommy adds. "I'm not sure I believe your story about why you were running around in the dark back there, but I don't think you killed the girl."

"Me neither," Milt says, swinging past him on his crutches. "You're not the type."

Robert forces a smile.

"Kind of you to say so," he replies.

When Mckenzie calls him, Robert is feeling slightly more relaxed about his situation. Amid the pervasive reek of tobacco and perspiration in the boss's cubicle, he picks up a whiff of Meghan's perfume, which almost makes him giddy. He is desperate for a woman, yet doesn't have the vaguest idea who that woman might be now. He surprises himself by asking Miles if he still has a job.

Mckenzie, who's pawing through a pile of teletype dispatches, looks up.

"You didn't kill the girl, did you?" he says.

Robert laughs.

"No, I didn't."

"Well, then you still work here. You just can't cover the trial, is all. Until the proceedings wrap up, you'll cover everything but."

An idea Robert has been toying with since the moment he took the stand bubbles to the surface.

"Would you be interested in a sidebar?" he asks. "What it's like to be a witness in a high-profile murder trial? 'The View from the Witness Stand,' we could call it." And, like a hyperventilating tyro in one of those goofball movies about newspapers, he forms the headline with his hands.

Mckenzie shakes his head and growls. "Aw, Jesus, Bob, you know I hate that first-person shit. We're reporters here, not fucking diarists."

Robert reddens and hopes Hickok and Pullman didn't hear his suggestion.

"Just a thought," he says.

Mckenzie lights a Viceroy and goes back to his reading.

"A bad one," he says. "Now go pick up the damn phone and see if our new coroner, Dr. Alice Whatsisname, has the names from last night's pile-up on the Belt Line."

Since his testimony and the county attorney's subsequent threat of a perjury charge, the driver has been sleeping on a cot in the supply room at Canary Cab's cinderblock headquarters and, come morning, cleaning himself up in the employees' bathroom.

"You're lucky you got a roof over your head," O'Shaughnessy has told him a half-dozen times in the past three days. "I hear you bitchin' about the accommodations, you're out on your ass."

If the driver didn't have documentation that his brother-in-law has been skimming serious money from the firm and therefore from its downtown owners—reputedly associates of Bunny Augustine—he wouldn't be here at all. He also knows, for the same reason, that his brother-in-law will never throw him out and will continue to assure Margaret Casserly, Fat Jack's kid sister, that the driver has committed no crime against God or the state and that all everybody needs is a little time for "the whole goddamn thing to blow over." Besides, O'Shaughnessy is down three drivers this summer, not counting vacation days, and can't afford to lose another one right now.

Watching the driver struggle to take a sponge bath in one of the men's room's cruddy wash basins, the big man says, "Maggie don't sound like she wants you back anytime soon, Juice. Maybe what you gotta do is leave town for a while. Don't you have a cousin in Alaska or someplace? Just do me a favor and wait until Crum and Knutsen are back here for good."

The driver knows what Margaret said—to her brother, to the neighbors, to the busybodies at Holy Name—after his testimony was quoted (and misquoted) in the *Star* and run alongside an eyes-closed photo that made him look like a mental patient. The headline read:

CITY CABBIE—WITNESS OR SUSPECT?
Lurid Testimony Raises Questions in Court

He hasn't spoken to Margaret directly, but has it on good authority—O'Shaughnessy and the driver's own son, Benedict, the oldest of the Casserlys' six kids—that he's no longer welcome at home.

"Mom had a guy from the hardware store change the locks," Benedict told him on the phone. "Then she had some guys from Holy Name clean out the garage. They burned a lot of your stuff in the alley." The boy hung up before the driver could say a word. Not that he knew what to say. After the police raid, he merely wonders what was left of his stash.

A couple of the other drivers have asked how well he "really" knew Teresa Hickman, not sure if he should be treated as a local celebrity or the grouchy misanthrope they've always known. Because three-fourths of the Canary drivers have sketchy histories, no one is likely to give him much guff. If anything, his status among the other Canaries may have risen a notch with the "lurid testimony" headline. He hasn't pulled a shift on the street yet, so who knows how fares will react when they realize who's behind the wheel? The driver suspects that a typical fare —a typical *male* fare anyway—will have the same questions the other drivers have had, if more delicately phrased.

In the closing arguments scheduled for next week, DeShields will no doubt tar him as a possible suspect, along with Bud Montgomery, the Zevos punk, that weasel Ybarra, and the skinny mystery man with the goggles. But two of them for sure and, who knows, maybe all four had sexual relations with Terry Hickman while all *he* did was lie. If the cops have anything more than his own foolish words, he'd be bunking in a jail cell right now instead of in the supply closet at the Canary Motel.

The driver actually feels an unexpected sense of liberation. The wife and the kids, not to mention the house and yard, had gotten to be too much. He'll be better off with a rented room where he can have his privacy and come and go as he pleases. Most of the time he spends in the car anyway, even when he's not working, and, come dinnertime, he can sure as hell improve on the franks-and-beans, caterwauling kids, and his wife on his back for one damn thing or another. For his meals—he's never been a big eater—he'll find a spot like the Palace where some cute little number with a sweet ass and the top couple of buttons on her uniform undone serves him blueberry pie and tops off his coffee.

He doesn't worry about the possible perjury charge. They have to prove he was lying, don't they? So how are they going to do that? And like the man says, *he's* not on trial, the Jew dentist is.

It will be a whole new experience to be noticed out in public. The picture in the paper didn't do him any favors, but he imagines the likeness to be sufficient enough to spark some recognition. People will spot him reading the paper at a lunch counter and whisper, "That's the guy that was friends with the Hickman broad. You can bet your ass he knows more than he's let on."

He's always believed, given his interests and habits, the old anonymity suited him, but maybe a little notoriety will be a plus. If their marriage is annulled, the wife is going to want money, of course—for raising the kids and cash for the mortgage and utilities—but he figures that O'Shaughnessy will be willing to share a little of his unearned Canary take, lest word of his skimming reaches Bunny Augustine's pals. If worse comes to worst, the driver can take some of the extra shifts he's been dodging to help make ends meet.

The driver rinses his mouth, pulls on his undershirt, and squints at himself in the flyspecked mirror above the sink.

"I'm free!" he says—but not so loud that the guy who just stepped out of the stall behind him would notice.

On August 22, Fred MacMurray is laid to rest in Lakewood Cemetery, on a shady rise overlooking Lake Calhoun, surrounded by his wife of twenty-eight years, eleven children, relatives from back East (Dr. Fred grew up outside of Pittsburgh), and dozens of county and municipal employees who "did business" with the genial medical examiner over the past several years. Arne Anderson and Mel Curry are among the several police officers present, standing shoulder to shoulder in their dress blue uniforms, though Arne and Mel drove separately to the cemetery.

Closing arguments in Rose's trial begin when proceedings resume on the twenty-fourth.

Scofield, apparently having used the break to polish his delivery, seems confident and fit—"bright-eyed and bushy-tailed," George Appel will describe the young prosecutor in the next morning's *Tribune*.

"Your responsibility," Scofield tells the jurors, who seem neither bright-eyed nor bushy-tailed after the better part of a month's worth of testimony, argument, and delay, "is to right a terrible wrong. No, *two* terrible wrongs. Not only was Teresa Hickman murdered by the defendant, she has been defamed by the defendant's counsel, who desperately wants you to believe that she practically begged for her own defilement and death.

"The truth is, Mrs. Hickman was a well-mannered, well-liked, albeit rather naive child of rural America who, having decided to raise her family in the big city, was seduced and victimized by a series of brutal men, the last of whom, Herschel David Rose, strangled her when she threatened to raise her voice on her own behalf, and then dumped her lifeless body in the weeds beside a desolate trolley track. Compounding the outrage is the fact that Mrs. Hickman was raped and murdered by the very man she had turned to to relieve her physical pain. Imagine that, ladies and gentlemen. This poor young wife and mother believes she is in the hands of a healer, only to discover—too late—that the healer is a killer!"

Scofield recounts Teresa Hickman's arrival in the Twin Cities, her lodging arrangements with the Montgomerys, and her employment at the Palace Luncheonette. He describes her social life as "typical for a farm girl trying to make sense of the big city and not without an occasional error of judgment." He moves on to her "trusted sister's referral" of Dr. Rose, her "unfortunate interaction" with the dentist, and her "fatal, final appointment" on the night of April 8. He paints a graphic picture of the two of them arguing in his car about "their baby," the dentist's explosive rage, and his murderous attack—"wrapping those large, powerful hands around her slender, pale throat, then squeezing the last breath of life out of her helpless body!"

Then Scofield startles everyone, including his tablemates, and sits down. His hands shake. He is sweating profusely and looks unnaturally pale. The prosecution will have the opportunity to rebut the defense's close, but even DeShields seems taken aback by Scofield's abrupt conclusion.

Rose remains still as a statue. He hasn't shown any emotion, hardly any physical movement at all, this morning. Miles Mckenzie will later write, "While his wife and brothers grimaced, exchanged horrified glances, and shook their heads during the prosecutor's dramatic close, it's not certain whether the defendant batted an eye."

This will change when, after a brief recess, DeShields rises and begins to speak. "Bright-eyed" would now be an understatement—the defense attorney's eyes burn like hot coals. He rises slowly on his short legs as though he's preparing to bound across the attorneys' table and attack the prosecutors with his bare hands. The jurors, the audience in the gallery, and even the judge sit still in anticipation.

"Ladies and gentlemen," he begins, facing the jurors, "there is only one wrong you are duty-bound to make right today, and that is the state's vicious attempt to rip an innocent man from the embrace of his wife and family, to remove him from the profession for which he trained and constantly improved himself, and send him to prison for the rest of his life.

"The state has not proved its case. It has resorted instead to the most outlandish attempt at character assassination that I have ever witnessed in a courtroom. Here's the truth, ladies and gentlemen— Dr. H. David Rose is a good and honorable man. He is also a Jew, and a dentist, and because the detectives who investigated Mrs. Hickman's murder are lazy and incompetent bigots, he became a convenient scapegoat in their shameless rush to condemn."

DeShields will continue, without so much as a sip of water or a glance at the papers in front of him, for nearly three hours.

He paints a detailed portrait of his client, also a product of small-town America, a doctor's son who earned college money selling magazine subscriptions door-to-door, a graduate of the University

of Minnesota's highly regarded dental college, a loved and honored
family man and accomplished professional, with a loyal patient base
and a long career untarnished by formal complaints. He has embraced
innovative protocols and techniques to reduce his patients' pain and
fear, and, unusual among his colleagues in this part of the country,
offered evening and weekend hours to better serve working men and
women. He has even, when necessary after dark or during inclement
weather, escorted his patients home following a procedure.

"Did he have a sexual relationship with Teresa Hickman?

"Mrs. Hickman said he did, that the baby she was carrying was
his. But *he* says he didn't have sexual relations with the woman, and
there's not a scintilla of evidence that he did. One thing for certain:
that unborn baby was not her husband's. Private Hickman was thousands of miles away in Europe and she was desperate to find a way to
solve her predicament. She asked Dr. Rose—no doubt one of the few
upright, honorable men, maybe the *only* upright, honorable man, she
knew in Minneapolis—to help her. While Dr. Rose is a kindly man,
ever willing to assist his patients when they need help, he is neither a
fool nor a pushover."

Then DeShields recreates the "short, unhappy life of Teresa
Kubicek Hickman," who "was tired of the boring life and callow farm
boys she grew up with and, like uncounted other young people seeking
work and excitement, moved to the big city, where any number of men
were only too glad to show her a good time. Terry Hickman was a very
attractive young woman. By all accounts, she hungered for male attention and had a difficult time saying 'no.' Terry Hickman, sad to say,
was a classic example of the textbook nymphomaniac, who, in her best
friend's words, drew men like flies.

"Consider, for instance, the cab driver who was fixated on Terry,
who made up stories about her, who lied on the stand about their relationship.

"And what about the sinister figure seen lurking in the darkness
where and when Terry was murdered—the tall, thin man with glasses?
Who was that man, and what was he doing skulking about down there

at that hour? If he was an innocent passerby, on his way home from work or an evening out with friends, why hasn't he come forward? Why, whoever he is, haven't the police been able to identify him and find out what he knows about the murder?"

Yes, DeShields continues, for a while on the evening of April 8, Mrs. Hickman and Dr. Rose were together in his car, driving around the west side of town, discussing her predicament.

"She made an unreasonable demand, and Dr. Rose reasonably turned her down. They argued, and maybe said things that each would want to take back if given the opportunity, and in this highly stressful situation Dr. Rose—weakened by lack of proper nutrition and a good night's sleep—blacked out. What happened after that no living person—with the exception of Teresa Hickman's killer—knows for sure."

After a brief pause, DeShields continues.

"So here we are—eight o'clock the following morning. It's gray and chilly, and the MPD's detectives, members of the department's crack Homicide Squad, are roused out of bed or taken away from their breakfast tables, and sent to investigate a young woman's body found in the weeds alongside a trolley track. They glance around the crime scene with their blurry, uninterested eyes. But besides the young woman's body, which is fully clothed and bearing no obvious marks of trauma, there is nothing to see. No blood, no evidence of a struggle, no murder weapon, no witnesses. The investigators take another cursory look around the site, chat briefly with the citizen who happened upon the body, and call it a day.

"Detective Hessburg agreed that the police made, and I quote, 'quick work' of the crime scene. It was the weekend, after all, and the detectives had lawns to rake and snow tires to replace, just like the rest of us. Whatever their priorities that dreary April morning, it wasn't determining the murderer of this twenty-one-year-old wife and mother."

As it happened, the lawyer goes on, the "cursory investigation" required after news of Mrs. Hickman's murder hit the papers quickly turned up a number of possible suspects—"men who preyed on young, naive, attractive women, who beat their wives, who offered employment in exchange for sex, who took compromising photographs of gullible girls, who leered and stalked and harassed and, in this case, quite possibly raped and murdered one such girl when the opportunity presented itself."

But, he says, shaking his large head sadly, "instead of investigating and pursuing those men, our sleepy gumshoes concentrate their limited energy on a middle-aged family man with no criminal record or history of bad behavior. A man who, if anything, showed Teresa Hickman no small measure of kindness since her arrival in town. But the police found Dr. Rose an irresistible target. He was a Jew, a member of that most despised of human races, *and* a dentist, a member of the most detested profession in America. Here was a *Jewish dentist*! Here was their man!"

DeShields takes a deep breath and stares into the jury box, whose occupants now sit so still they might have been in a trance.

"And who led the vendetta against Dr. Rose?" he says at last. "MPD Sergeant Arne Anderson.

"We've learned a lot about Sergeant Anderson over the past several weeks. High school football player, war vet, married man, divorced man, longtime cop and investigator. But what we've also learned—from his own mouth as well as from his partner, who presumably knows him as well as anybody—is that he's a lifelong anti-Semite, raised to think of Jews as Christ-killers, that he's disreputable and dishonest, and quick to inflict bodily harm on a helpless suspect if he thinks that suspect deserves a beating. He has no Jewish colleagues, and his professional experience with Jews has to all intents and purposes been confined to a small group of North Minneapolis hoodlums.

"And think about this, ladies and gentlemen. Sergeant Anderson had been living with a woman named Lily Kline. But at the time of Teresa Hickman's murder, their relationship was on the rocks, and shortly afterward Miss Kline, a Jewess, booted Anderson out of their apartment in what must have been an ugly scene. It's not difficult to imagine what this no doubt painful and embarrassing rejection might have added to the sergeant's already negative feeling about Jewish people.

"Sergeant Anderson is an angry, bitter, violent man—in police vernacular a thumper—who, our research has determined, is not only feared by private citizens but unpopular among his colleagues as well. You heard, just last week, his partner of the past several years, Detective Melvin Curry, when asked if he trusted Sergeant Anderson, give something less than a ringing endorsement. If his partner doesn't trust Sergeant Anderson, why should we? Why should *you*, ladies and gentlemen of the jury, when an innocent man's life hangs in the balance?

"The fact is, Sergeant Anderson, on behalf of the state of Minnesota, had only this sad, stooped, Jewish dentist, with not a single piece of forensic evidence to connect him to Teresa Hickman's murder. Surely a healthy, young woman, if she were being strangled, would fight back—would bite, scratch, and strike out with her fists—yet when Dr. Rose was examined by the police a day after Mrs. Hickman's murder he bore no signs of a struggle. What we have instead of evidence—of cold, hard, irrefutable proof—is bigotry, ignorance, superstition, sloth, incompetence, and a half-dozen men far likelier to commit rape and murder than this defendant.

"If all that doesn't add up to reasonable doubt, ladies and gentlemen, then I don't know what does. You must do the only right thing and vote to acquit."

The courtroom is silent for several moments. DeShields's glowing eyes move from one juror to the next, ending with the second of the two young women seated at the end of the first row. One of them raises her hands to her mouth and begins to sob. Three other women in the box are dabbing at their eyes with tissues. Several of the men, after briefly making eye contact with DeShields, stare at their hands in their laps.

Asked by Judge Nordahl if he wished to rebut the defense's close, Homer Scofield says nothing. Rudy Blake glances at Scofield, leans toward him, and whispers something that no one, apparently including Scofield, can hear.

Finally, Scofield shakes his head and says something so softly that no one will hear this either, forcing the judge to ask him again. Then Scofield says, in an only slightly louder voice, "I have nothing more, Your Honor."

It is 4:10 p.m. when bailiffs lead the seven men and five women of the jury out of Courtroom No. 1, down the hallway fifty-odd steps, and into the monastic confines of Jury Room No. 3.

They had a few moments to compose themselves and listen to Dante DeShields ask the judge, first, to dismiss the murder charge against Rose and then, after the judge denied the motion, to require the jury to reach one of only two possible verdicts—guilty of murder in the first degree or acquittal—also denied. Instead, in his instructions, Nordahl told the jury that they must choose among first- and second-degree murder, first- and second-degree manslaughter, not guilty, and not guilty by reason of insanity.

The packed gallery buzzes like a shaken beehive as the jury begins its somber shuffle to the jury room. The reporters flee the press tables, those up against a deadline throwing elbows en route to one of the half-dozen pay phones in the corridor, the others expressing befuddlement at the turn of events. Even Mckenzie, Appel, and Rystrom, with sixty years of reporting experience among them, say they can't recall a trial closing like this one, with the defense's virulent ad hominem attack on a police officer and the prosecution's astonishing unwillingness to rebut.

Pushing toward the exits, the journalists mentally compose their headlines:

ROSE DEFENSE CALLS COPS INCOMPETENT, BIGOTS;
PROSECUTION MUM

LAWYER'S ASSAULT ON STATE'S CASE LEAVES
ROSE PROSECUTORS SPEECHLESS

Rose remains seated. So do Ruth and his siblings and siblings-in-law. Only Sam's wife, Noreen, stands and, hands on her hips, stares at the vacated jury box. The Roses look like members of the audience of a long and dizzyingly complex theatrical drama whose sudden ending has left everybody drained and confused.

Ronnie Oshinsky mumbles something about the judge's instructions being favorable to the defense, but no one seems to be listening.

DeShields, mopping his face with an enormous checkered handkerchief that might seem comical in other circumstance, tells the Roses they can repair to the room set aside for the defendant and his family or try to enjoy an early dinner at a nearby restaurant, though he says he senses a speedy verdict and advises they stay close by. He gives them no feeling one way or the other as to what he believes the verdict will be.

The defendant says, "I'd prefer to stay pat for a few more minutes."

He is holding Ruth's hand, but otherwise reveals no more emotion than he has throughout the trial. His brothers decide they need a drink and excuse themselves, with wife and girlfriend trailing behind them.

Rose looks around for Arne Anderson, whom he hasn't seen since the detective's testimony two days ago. He knew that DeShields was going to challenge the investigation, but the personal nature of the attack surprised him. He feels no ill will toward the police, despite the obvious bias of some of the detectives, and thought Sergeant Anderson was a diligent, honest, and likable man.

If Anderson were in the room, Rose would be inclined to walk over and offer an apology for his lawyer—maybe even try to lighten the mood by saying, "Nothing personal, you understand." But Anderson is nowhere to be seen, and, in any event, Rose is pretty sure there are rules about a defendant speaking to a witness during a trial.

Moments later, Ronnie tells him that Homer Scofield collapsed in the lavatory and was on his way to Hiawatha General Hospital.

To the surprise of nearly everybody, with the possible exception of Dante DeShields, the jury sends word to Judge Nordahl at 5:35, slightly less than an hour and a half after beginning deliberations, that they have reached a verdict.

In another fifteen minutes, everybody who departed the big room has hustled back inside. The more astute observers notice that Private Hickman and Walter Kubicek, who were not present during the closing arguments, are not in the courtroom for the verdict, either. Nor are the victim's friends, Connie Bannister and Kenny Landa, as though the North Dakotans have finally abandoned Terry to the big city.

When the room is more or less settled, Nordahl asks the foreman if the jury has in fact come to a verdict. The foreman, a sepulchral Northern States Power Company supervisor named Lawrence Hammer, says it has. A bailiff takes the envelope from Hammer and hands it to the judge, who silently reads its contents. The judge then hands it to the clerk of court, who reads the verdict aloud:

"We, the jury in the above entitled action, find the defendant guilty of manslaughter in the first degree."

Rose blinks, swallows, and purses his lips. Ruth squeezes his arm, closes her eyes, tips back her head, and lets a couple of large tears roll down her lightly rouged cheeks. DeShields immediately begins squaring the papers in front of him as though he must pack up and rush to another trial. Across the table, Rudy Blake stands and nods his head toward the jury. He no doubt wonders if Scofield, whom he last saw flat on his back in a county ambulance, would be available for a congratulatory phone call. Maybe Homer will learn about his first district court victory on the radio.

When the judge gavels the court to order for a final time, he asks the defendant if there is anything he wishes to say.

After a moment of apparent indecision, Rose says he does. The room falls silent. It will be the first time most of the people in the gallery hear his voice since his "Not guilty" declaration a month ago.

"I have always thought of myself as a decent human being who has dedicated himself to reducing or eliminating pain. I still think of myself that way because I have never knowingly harmed another person in my life."

He glances around the room as though he might have forgotten something, and then concludes that he has nothing more he wants to say.

"Thank you, Your Honor," he adds and sits down.

Judge Nordahl sentences Rose to five to twenty years in the state prison at Stillwater, the standard punishment for first-degree manslaughter in Minnesota.

Then, while family and lawyers gather around the convicted man, the jurors, most of the reporters, and the gallery exit the courtroom like water draining out of a bathtub. A sense of exhaustion, mingled with the stink of perspiration and the dregs of abandoned tuna salad sandwiches, hangs over the chamber. The buzz is subdued. It is not one of anticipation or excitement anymore, but not one of disappointment or outrage, either. The likely truth is that while the brevity of the jurors' deliberation was surprising, few people are shocked by the verdict. Most are relieved that the drama is finally over.

The jurors have collectively decided not to speak to the press.

Milt Hickok will later quote an anonymous source, likely an outlying member of the panel, saying that a "significant majority" went into the deliberations primed to vote first-degree murder and its automatic life sentence without parole, but that a few "moderates" argued persuasively for the lesser determination of manslaughter. No one seemed to believe Rose's "blackout story," Hickok will report, but no one was convinced that he'd planned to murder Mrs. Hickman.

A few moments after a sheriff's deputy leads Rose away, in the grand atrium on the courthouse's first floor, under the blind marble gaze of *The Father of Waters*, Dante DeShields, with Rose's family behind him, says that he will appeal his client's conviction, alleging, though not enumerating, "at least two-dozen reversible errors." He finally looks as though the process has tired him, if only for the moment.

"Meantime," he says, with a few degrees less heat than he radiated during the closing, "an innocent man will spend tonight in a jail cell, the victim of religious hatred and official ineptitude, while Teresa Hickman's killer prowls the streets, seeking his next victim."

* * *

It's Augie Fuller's idea to celebrate Rose's conviction at Smokey's. He has managed, with cash from the squad's slush fund, to secure one of the bar's back rooms for a cops-only party. Arne comes because he has nowhere better to go and because Mel will probably bring Janine and because the "refreshments" will be on the department's dime.

After fulsome toasts by Augie and Ed Evangelist, the officers and a few wives, girlfriends, and "dates" spread out among the wobbly tables to eat Smokey's spaghetti and meatballs and wash it down with pitchers of Gluek's. Whiskey, club soda, and ginger ale bottles stand open on several tables.

Leaning close to Anderson, Charlie Riemenschneider says, "On the level, Sarge, you think we'd have won this one if Rose wasn't a Jew?"

Only Charlie, a widower, has chosen to join Arne at his table. The others on the squad are wary of Arne's disposition in the wake of DeShields's bruising close and sense something off-kilter about him this evening. Arne, for his part, is trying, unsuccessfully, not to stare at Janine Curry, who is sitting with Mel and the Wrenshalls in the opposite corner of the room. Someone has fed a handful of dimes into the jukebox next to the door; it's playing "Stranger in Paradise," and Arne fights off the fantasy of dancing with Janine, who's exceptionally beautiful tonight in a sleeveless, form-fitting yellow dress.

"Probably not," Arne says, absently. "And we might not have won if DeShields had found out earlier about the shoe that turned up on Euclid Place."

Riemenschneider squints through his smudged spectacles at nothing in particular.

"That fuckin' shoe," he mutters, draining his lowball glass of the last finger of Canadian Club. "What happened to that shoe anyways?"

Across the room, Janine makes eye contact with Arne, and then turns away when Mel leans close and whispers something to her. Looking over her shoulder, Mel catches Arne's gaze.

"Damned if I know," Arne says.

A few minutes later, Rudy Blake joins the party and asks for the group's attention. His eyes are already rheumy, and he's unsteady on his feet. Someone pulls the plug on the jukebox, and Blake announces that Homer Scofield has been admitted to Hiawatha General, suffering from dehydration and nervous fatigue. "The good news is he's expected to return to work after Labor Day." Three or four people clap halfheartedly.

Rudy smiles weakly, congratulates the detectives on "our shared victory," and shuffles toward the door. Someone plugs the jukebox back into the wall, and Sid Hessburg, his jacket off and tie undone, starts dancing to "Rock Around the Clock" with an attractive young woman none of the assembled has seen until this evening. Across the room, Mel Curry gets to his feet and walks toward the door.

"Jesus," Riemenschneider says, "I can't tell you how much I hate that nigger music."

Frenchy LeBlanc, in a natty houndstooth sport coat, has grabbed a chair at their table.

"That's Bill Haley and the Comets, Charlie," he says. "He's as white as your ass."

Riemenschneider raises his empty glass and waves at one of the waitresses.

"Well, fuck 'im," he says. "He *sounds* like a nigger."

Anderson is on his feet now and makes his way toward the door. After a moment of indecision, he's decided to follow Curry instead of wandering across the room, sitting down beside Janine, and draping an arm around her naked shoulders. In the hallway outside the party room, he sees Rudy Blake sitting on the linoleum floor with his back against the wall, his head lolling on his chest, the silver hairpiece sliding over his right eye. A tiny white-haired woman Anderson assumes is Rudy's wife stands beside him, apparently waiting for him to get up.

"Need help, ma'am?" Arne asks.

The woman shakes her head as though her husband slumped semiconscious in the hallway of a saloon is nothing to be concerned about. She smiles at Arne.

"He's only resting," she says. "It's been a long day."

Arne, bumping against the wall, walks down the hall, pushes open the screen door, and steps into the alley, where he knows Curry is waiting.

Mel is leaning against the building's brick wall, on the other side of a half-dozen garbage cans, smoking a filter-tipped cigarette. Unusual for this time of night, they have this stretch of alleyway to themselves.

Arne lights a Camel. His hands shake, but he tells himself it's the booze and the stress of the trial. Like the lady said, it's been a long day.

"I'm sorry," he says.

Curry looks at him without replying for a moment.

"She says she's sorry, too," Mel says at last. He flicks his glowing cigarette butt into the alley.

He is quiet again for a moment, and then says softly, "What kind of man fucks his partner's wife? What kind of woman fucks her husband's best friend? She says it's over, but she calls your name in her sleep."

Arne takes a deep breath and says, "Mel"—but even after weeks of rehearsing his exit line the words aren't there when he wants them.

That doesn't matter because Curry has drawn a short-barreled Smith & Wesson revolver from the holster inside his jacket and thrusts it out toward Anderson like an accusation. He fires three shots that form a tight scalene triangle in the center of Arne's chest, and then watches his partner—wide-eyed and mouth open—sit down in the alley and die.

WINTER 1956

CHAPTER 15

P ity the city editor who had to deal with the events of August 24, 1955.

If his responsibility was one of the morning papers, the *Minneapolis Tribune* or St. Paul's *Pioneer Press*, he had just approved the front page with its Second Coming type along the banner—*QUICK DECISION: ROSE GUILTY!* in the *Tribune*, *DENTIST DRAWS MANSLAUGHTER SENTENCE* in the *Pioneer Press*—accompanied by photos of the Roses, pale and pokerfaced, leaving the courtroom, one of the young jurors weeping in the arms of an older woman, Rudy Blake and Dante DeShields in separate conversations with reporters on the courthouse steps, and the familiar yearbook photo of Teresa Kubicek Hickman.

In both papers the trial coverage and jury verdict filled two-thirds of the next day's front page, plus most of three pages inside.

Then, less than an hour before the late edition went to press, the city room phones began ringing off the hook and the first breathless word arrived of the murder of MPD Detective Sergeant Arne

Anderson and the attempted murder of the wife of Detective Melvin Curry at Smokey's Bar on South Fourth Street. Several of the journalists who weren't back at their desks banging out trial coverage were within feet of the carnage when all hell broke loose at the bar.

Meghan Mckenzie was the lone representative of the local United Press bureau on the premises. Still only a UP stringer, with no specific assignment, she and her husband were celebrating their five-year wedding anniversary with lawyer friends in Smokey's main room. She was on her way to the toilet when, after nearly stumbling over Rudy Blake outside the men's john, she was pushed aside by Mel Curry, who strode in purposefully from the alley. She saw a pistol in Curry's hand and figured the detective was rushing toward trouble inside.

She turned and followed Curry the few steps into the party room where the murder squad had been celebrating and watched him walk toward his wife, who was dancing with one of the younger detectives—Reynard LeBlanc, she learned his name was—and without a word fired three shots in the woman's direction. The cop she was dancing with flinched and staggered backward, tipping over a table covered with half-finished food and drinks. As the woman, in a gorgeous sleeveless dress, screamed and fainted, several cops lurched to their feet, a few of them shouting at Curry while most of the rest of them sat back down again, too drunk to do anything but fumble for their holstered weapons.

Then a burly, bespectacled detective Meghan recognized as Charlie Riemenschneider slammed a folding chair across Curry's shoulders, and Curry pitched forward on his face, his snub-nosed revolver skidding across the greasy linoleum. Riemenschneider, LeBlanc, and two or three others piled on, cursing and pummeling the shooter with their fists. The air, heavy with cigarette smoke, now stunk of gunpowder and sweat.

Curry, usually a steady shot and firing at point-blank range, had missed his wife. Amazingly, the bullets hit no one, only savaged the photo gallery on the wall behind the tables, defacing the portraits of Ferdinand Twyman and three or four bewhiskered Hiawatha County jurists from the late 1800s whose names nobody in the room would know.

In the five seconds that followed, one of Smokey's back-sink men rushed into the room waving his arms, his high-pitched shriek shredding the stunned silence.

"Hey!" he screamed. "Dere's a guy shot up bad inna alley!"

Even from the perspective of the following February, the overlapping events of that August afternoon and evening seem no less preposterous than they did in the days and weeks immediately following the mayhem.

After a week of intense, sensational, some would say hysterical news coverage, there didn't seem to be much more to say.

Meghan Mckenzie got her first United Press byline, writing, per her father-in-law's instruction, an on-the-scene account of the shootings in the conventional third-person voice. ("No first-person drivel out of this shop, sweetheart.") Miles, Hickok, and Pullman filled dozens of column inches with features on both the trial verdict and the shootings. Hickok's respectful sidebar reprising Arne Anderson's life, wartime heroics, and police career, and Tommy's tear-jerker detailing the cruel irony of the fashion model whose "million-dollar looks and bearing" were nearly destroyed by three "twenty-cent bullets" were widely read and discussed. Janine Curry's injuries, sustained not by gunshots but during her fall and the ensuing chaos, were significant. Doctors said that, owing to a broken hip and dislocated knee, she would probably have difficulty walking for the rest of her life. Her smile, disfigured by several broken teeth and a fractured jaw, would never be the same.

Pending Rose's appeal and Curry's trial there wasn't any more relevant news.

Robert Gardner, whatever his status as a suspect in the aftermath of Rose's conviction, remained on the bureau's masthead, though he was no longer the junior-most staffer since the hiring, a week before Christmas, of a pretty St. Ansgar College grad named Jennifer

Hendricks. Miles made it clear, however, that Robert would not be assigned anything having to do with the Rose-Hickman case. Snowstorms, multiple traffic fatalities, four-alarm fires, and visiting celebrities—so long as they're not *too* celebrated, in which case Miles himself would shoulder the task—will be the young man's topics in the foreseeable future.

On his own, without a word to anyone, Robert made several attempts to write the "definitive portrait" of the small-town girl and her ill-fated adventures in the big city that he envisioned after Teresa Hickman's murder. But the right words wouldn't come, or wouldn't come quickly enough for an impatient young writer, and he gave up a couple of months after the trial's conclusion. Maybe he would try again later, when he knew more about the world and the craft required to describe it. He would dream about Teresa Hickman's body in the weeds along the tracks for two or three months after that, and then not at all.

It's early February when Robert asks Jenny Hendricks to go see *East of Eden* at the RKO Orpheum. They both worked that night so they caught the late show. Then, recalling a secluded spot where they can make out, he drives west on Highway 12 in a light snowfall and they end up, not exactly by chance, just down the road from the Starlight Motor Hotel. However the night plays out, Robert is thrilled to be in the company of an attractive young woman again. He considers the fact that she's not married a positive development.

Not long after the Rose trial ended, Robert, at wit's end, had "staked out"—there was no other way to describe it—Pam Brantley's apartment on West Forty-fourth Street. Her name, never mind the memory of her voice and body, was enough to arouse him, and he told himself, with a desperate man's logic, that he had nothing to lose. Robert's sister, brother-in-law, and infant nephew had moved to a little pastel-colored rambler in the fast-growing suburb of Bloomington, so, aside from Pam or Karl, nobody was likely to notice his Ford coupe parked at odd hours near the apartment buildings overlooking the abandoned streetcar tracks.

After three days without spotting either one of the Brantleys—or for that matter a skinny guy with glasses coming or going outside their building—he called the couple's apartment only to be told by an operator that the number had been disconnected.

The next day, when he wouldn't start his bureau shift until four-thirty in the afternoon and Karl was likely to be at the hospital, he entered the building for the first time since the previous April and noticed that *Brantley, K & P* was no longer Scotch-taped to the mailbox in the entry. With his heart throbbing in his chest and his cock stirring between his legs, he climbed the stairs and knocked on the familiar door, certain now she wouldn't be there. And she wasn't. A gray-haired woman in a nurse's uniform answered the door. He mumbled an apology and realized that it would be only by another happy accident if he ever saw Pam again.

Robert has seen Meghan often enough at the bureau to take the spark off whatever electricity he imagined might still exist between them. Every once in a while he saw her with her husband—yet another tall, skinny guy with glasses, although this one had streaks of premature silver in his gleaming dark hair and seemed to hold his head at an odd angle when speaking, a tic that Robert attributed to his having only one functioning eye. Meghan always smiles when she sees Robert, and they often chat when they run into each other coming or going. But the small talk is never about anything very personal, and there's never so much as a wink or allusion to their summer affair.

At the bureau's Christmas party—Smokey's was abandoned by the regulars after the shootings, most of the cops, lawyers, and reporters redirecting their business to Gino Rinaldi's red-sauce trattoria down the block—Robert learns, during one of Miles's boozy toasts, that Meghan is pregnant. "The baby—with any luck a boy—is due in June," Miles announced.

Jenny Hendricks, who grew up on a Blue Earth County dairy farm, is smart, funny, and athletic. She "adores" horses and loves to sing. In February, after their third date—*Oklahoma!* at the Riverview, a couple of blocks from her Thirty-eighth Street apartment—they have sex on her living-room rug, and Robert tells himself that this is a woman he could marry even if he'll never burn for her body the way he did—still does—for Pam's. Jenny seems to like him a lot, too.

Miles taps Jenny to help out with the Rose appeal later in the month. Dante DeShields releases a statement in which he again cites "numerous" procedural errors and, for the first time, mentions the shoe recovered by police near Lake of the Isles the day after the murder. According to DeShields's statement, "The prosecution hid the existence of the missing shoe from the defense in a blatant violation of the Rules of Discovery. The existence of that shoe gives credence to the account of witness Julius Casserly, who testified at trial about a car parked on Euclid Place, and the apparent abduction of Teresa Hickman by two men in that car, on the night she was murdered."

Responding to reporters, Rudy Blake says the second shoe had not been hidden—it had been "inadvertently misplaced by investigators." In any event, the shoe would only reinforce the fact that Rose and Mrs. Hickman were in the vicinity of Lake of the Isles and Euclid Place when they were driving around after her dental appointment. "They argued and struggled in his car," Blake said. "Then she tried to escape and the shoe fell off, this before he killed her and drove her body over to the streetcar tracks near Forty-fourth Street."

Those are Blake's last words on the subject. The following day, he announces his retirement.

The Minnesota Supreme Court declines to hear DeShields's appeal of Rose's conviction. Rose, who has been free on a $100,000 bond, is ordered to report to Stillwater Prison on February 27.

Mel Curry's trial would likely have been eventful, but on February 29 (1956 is a leap year), Curry, through his lawyer, a down-at-the-heels public defender named Clement Bonsell, pleads guilty to first-degree murder and attempted second-degree murder. Hiawatha County Attorney Homer Scofield asks for a life sentence with no chance of parole, and District Court Judge Roy Winkler grants the request.

* * *

The night before his lawyers drive him to Stillwater, David Rose sits by himself in his living room, staring out the bay window at Zenith Avenue. There are several inches of fresh snow on the lawn, shrubs, and outstretched limbs of the boulevard elms, and the snow muffles what few sounds rise above the late evening quiet of the neighborhood.

The words of the Christian carol "Silent Night"—"all is calm, all is bright"—come to mind, though the music in his ears at the moment is "Clair de Lune," from the Debussy recording slowly turning on the Magnavox.

Before Ruth went upstairs to iron the white shirt he will wear tomorrow morning, she turned off, at his request, the lamp beside his chair, so he sees little of his reflection in the window. He feels the warmth of the meerschaum bowl in his hand and is aware of the piano playing softly on the phonograph.

Rose has said his goodbyes to Margot and Lael, who are spending the night at a cousin's house, and to his brothers, in-laws (except Ronnie Oshinsky, who will be part of his escort to the prison gates), and the handful of Linden Hills neighbors who remained cordial during the past ten months. He has signed the papers relinquishing the lease on his office space and authorizing the sale of his tools, equipment, and furniture to the pair of young dentists—the Negro brothers Walker and Emlen Johnston—who will open their first practice in Rose's space before the end of next month. Ruth, Ronnie, and Sam, God bless their good hearts, took care of the negotiations. (Rose's license was promptly revoked after the high court denied his appeal.)

The family's financial situation has been extensively discussed and more or less settled. Despite several public assertions and widespread perception, Rose was not a wealthy man. His practice income covered the office expenses, utilities, taxes, upkeep of the Linden Hills home, and the cost of driving a late-model Packard, but left little for a more luxurious lifestyle. (The car was sold after Ruth decided she wanted something "less conspicuous." The house will go on the market in April.) His brothers have paid the legal bills, and Ruth's family will make sure that she and the girls can relocate to an acceptable location in St. Louis Park. The Roses' daughters will continue to attend public school, regardless of where the family resettles, and spend several weeks at camp in the summer. Believing it is "important to stay busy," Ruth intends to work at least part-time for one of the Oshinsky enterprises.

Tonight the couple shared a simple supper at the dining-room table that, not long ago, had been piled high with legal documents and law books. There seemed little left to talk about—no more decisions to discuss, no more contingency plans to evaluate. Ruth has never suggested that an apology was in order. On several occasions, including this evening, Rose has expressed his regret about the developments of the past year, but neither he nor his wife believes a regret is the same as an apology. Privately, she has spoken to Ronnie about the possibility of a divorce, but that's all it will be—a possibility—for the time being.

Now, alone in front of the window, the words of the Christmas carol fade and Rose is left to his fate.

What a fool I was to succumb to that urge and opportunity, he muses.

True, it wasn't the first time and, if it hadn't been discovered, wouldn't have been the last. But he was not a sex fiend. He did not ogle women on the street and had no interest in filthy pictures. He enjoyed watching the show at the Whoop-Tee-Doo Club after a long day upstairs, but that was all he ever did—*watch* and maybe chat a moment if one of the girls stopped by his table. The truth is, those women, with their coarse language and clownish makeup, frightened him—they were not his type, to say the least. He never cheated with one of Ruth's friends or cousins, either, even after zoftig Myra Oshinsky tried to push him into the upstairs bathroom one New Year's Eve a dozen years ago.

In his office at night he was his own man—not a husband or father, but the master of his private domain. Most nights, he had the second floor to himself, and on the rare evenings he didn't, the racket from the club downstairs would drown out the noise behind his doors.

The sedation, when he felt it necessary, was a tool that presented itself quite by chance, not something he incorporated into his practice with any purpose other than relaxing a nervous patient and reducing her pain. The fact that it relaxed the occasional attractive and amenable woman was a wholly unintended development. Nobody was ever completely unconscious. The women he made love to always knew, more or less, what was going on and submitted without objection or struggle. He knew what he was doing.

There were seven women in all—mostly ordinary, working women, closer to Ruth's age than to Terry's, but each appealing in her way. Grace Montgomery and a couple of the others were married, and all were unhappy for one reason or another. He liked to think they appreciated his kindnesses.

Teresa Hickman was unique. She was several years younger than the others and very sensual, very seductive. She showed herself off that first night, not in the vulgar fashion of the women at the club, but more subtly, coquettishly, slipping off her coat, for instance, and turning to reveal her backside while she hung the coat on the rack, then catching his eye while he watched her, and smiling in a way that he doubted most men, not only a dentist, could resist. She didn't object that January night when he stepped around her, brushed his hand against the small of her back, and locked the outer door.

A few minutes later, she sat back in the big chair and laughed at his line about a better way to remove her lipstick, knowing exactly what he meant. She was so composed and compliant, he thought he might skip the capsule and simply administer a little novocaine to block the dental pain. But then he thought he'd best not take anything for granted and gave her the sedative.

After he repaired her tooth, he let her doze in the chair for another half hour. Then he caressed her cheek with the back of his hand and, when she opened her eyes, helped her out of the chair and led her, his arm around her narrow waist, into the outer room and onto the settee. She let him kiss her and slide his hand between her legs.

What a fool I was to succumb to the urge and opportunity! Then again, how many healthy men, given that opportunity, would have declined it?

Ultimately, his mistake was not the sex, but not being willing to pay for it. The cost of an abortion. Or cash for her own apartment. Even if it was more than he could afford, he could have borrowed the money from his brothers, telling them that it was to cover a hike in the office rent or to replace a piece of worn-out equipment. His brothers rarely asked questions and never refused him.

Of course, he couldn't be sure when she made her demand that April evening that she was in fact pregnant, let alone by him. As the trial witnesses made abundantly clear, Terry was a wanton young woman and any one of a number of men could have been the baby's father. She was calculating, too, waiting that last night until he'd finished the dental work and they'd had sex before making her accusation. She knew what she was doing, too, even under the influence of his pill.

Later that night, in fact—it might have been when they were in the car—she told him that the baby's father "might be" the Landa boy. She said that he had driven down to Minneapolis in early January and the two of them had spent the night at his hotel. The problem was, Kenny wouldn't have the cash for an abortion and would be terrified of what his family—not to mention his cousin's family—would do if they found out. There were already rumors that Landa, not her husband, was the father of her first child. So Terry brought her problem to him, to Dr. Rose. She obviously believed that he would be willing and able to help her, especially if he believed that she would go public if he didn't. It was blackmail pure and simple.

Even worse was her ingratitude. He'd eliminated the cause of her physical pain and provided her with friendship and advice. And he would have done a great deal more if and when she needed it. He sometimes imagined Terry as his mistress, like the paramours of well-to-do European businessmen and politicians, with their own apartments and "allowances." After all that, for her to threaten him—well, who could be surprised if he was angry?

But did he kill her?

Despite the jury's verdict, the state Supreme Court's de facto affirmation, and the opinion of eighty-two percent of the Minnesota public, according to a *Tribune* poll conducted after the trial's end, Rose can't decide. He will concede, given his own account of that April night, that there's no other *plausible* explanation for Teresa Hickman's death. But tonight that explanation seems as flimsy as a dream.

He doesn't *know* what happened that night. He doesn't know or can't remember.

Which, granted, doesn't mean that he's not a murderer.

The driver stares at the photo on the day-old *Star*'s front page: Dr. Rose sitting on a bench in the admissions area at Stillwater Prison, "awaiting processing." To the driver's eye, Rose looks the same as he did in the courtroom, in a starched white shirt and striped tie. The driver is sure the guy would wear the same dead-eyed expression whether someone was sucking his dick or lighting his feet on fire.

The driver wonders if Rose and ex-detective Curry, the other hometown killer of recent notoriety, will bump into each other in the pen. Considering the amount of time they'll be there, a meeting would seem inevitable. When they do, he wonders, what will they say to each other? Maybe Rose will work on Curry's teeth if he's willing to treat one of the cops who sent him to prison and if Curry doesn't mind the Jew poking a drill in his mouth.

Two days later, the driver spots one of the pretty jurors—the one who was crying in the newspaper photograph the day after the Rose verdict—on a street corner downtown. The papers identified her as Miss Melinda Wakeley, twenty-five, with a Fourteenth Avenue South address. The several times he's cruised past the house, however, he's never caught sight of her, in the yard or coming and going, the window shades on the house always pulled down, so he more or less gave up. Now, spotting her waiting for the light to change at Sixth and Marquette, he can't believe his eyes. *What are the odds?* But he's almost positive it's her.

He pulls into the first open space he sees and jumps out of the yellow car. He loses sight of the girl, and then spots her again on the other side of Marquette, a few steps from the Rand Tower entrance. Darting into traffic, he is knocked off his feet, run over, and dragged fifty feet by the southbound No. 4 bus. He is rushed to Hiawatha General Hospital, where he lingers for eight hours before succumbing to a fractured skull and multiple internal injuries.

"I never saw the guy," bus driver G.V. Higgins tells the *Star.*

Higgins is not charged.

ACKNOWLEDGMENTS

When I was a kid, I was fascinated by the crime stories published in the Minneapolis papers. One of the most memorable involved the murder of a young rural Minnesota woman and the eventual arrest, trial, and conviction of a middle-aged Minneapolis family man—her dentist, of all people. I found the case shocking, tragic, sordid, and at times incomprehensible. But with the limited experience and nascent vocabulary of a ten-year-old, I pored over the lurid particulars the way my buddies studied the box scores on the sports pages.

It would be a mistake, however, to say that *The Secret Lives of Dentists* is based on the actual Mary Moonen–A.A. Axilrod homicide case. The book you've just read is fiction; it was only *inspired* by the infamous events of the spring and summer of 1955. With my novelist's hat on, I have invented the characters, places, institutions, scenarios, timelines, and conversations that occasionally echo the real thing, but exist on these pages solely for my storytelling purposes. Well, Minneapolis circa 1955 is pretty much the way I remember it.

I need to credit—by no means for the first time—the invaluable work of Twin Cities journalist and author Larry Millett, whose vivid review of the Moonen–Axilrod case in a wonderful compilation of true-crime features entitled *Murder Has a Public Face* (Borealis Books, Minnesota Historical Society Press, 2008) refreshed my memory and fired me up to tell my fictional story.

My thanks also to Dan Mayer and his crew at Seventh Street Books for their confidence, encouragement, and attention to detail. And to my wife, Libby Swanson, for everything else.

ABOUT THE AUTHOR

W.A. WINTER is the pen name of William Swanson, a Minneapolis journalist. Swanson is the author of three true-crime books—*Dial M: The Murder of Carol Thompson*; *Black White Blue: The Assassination of Patrolman Sackett*; and *Stolen from the Garden: The Kidnapping of Virginia Piper*—published by Borealis Books, an imprint of the Minnesota Historical Society Press. Writing as W.A. Winter, he has published, besides *The Secret Lives of Dentists*, three suspense novels available online from Kindle Books and Smashwords.com: *Handyman*, *See You / See Me*, and *Wolfie's Game*.

Author photo by Libby Swanson